Don't Listen To Chubster MaGee

A NOVEL

BY

GREG TARLIN

ISBN: 978-0-578-84860-0 (paperback)

MAX LISTENS

Chubster MaGee wasn't chubby. Far as Max could tell, he didn't even have a weight problem. Maybe he'd been a little porky as a kid, maybe even fat, but now, though certainly no Adonis, Chubster appeared as fit as any other regular sitting on one of the stools at 'Sully's Brew & Chew' and, in fact, was probably in better shape than a lot of the other patrons occupying those stools. And why wouldn't he be? The man was always on the go, heading somewhere, meeting someone, planning something. Somehow, he appeared energetic even seated with the boys at the bar. It was, Max thought, just one of those nicknames that seem to stick. It's a guy thing, he figured. You could bump into a six foot guy named 'Shorty' or a three hundred pounder dubbed 'Tiny'. No one gave it a second thought. He'd known a 'Tex' who wasn't from Texas, a pot-bellied 'Slim' and a bald-headed barber named 'Red'. Sometimes nicknames were self-explanatory and actually made sense. Max remembered his High School friend, 'Stats', who knew every sports statistic and came in pretty handy settling lunch room arguments.

Different for girls though, he felt. You weren't going to meet a flat-chested woman who answered to 'Busty' or a model named 'Butch' or a short girl called 'Stretch'. Nicknames didn't seem as important to the female sex, nor did they find ironic monikers quite as amusing as did their male counterparts. In fact, most of the nicknames that they did use seemed to involve food. 'Peaches', 'Cherry', 'Muffin'. He'd noticed the correlation but had not yet developed a theory to explain it.

Max himself had never really had a nickname; none were ever applied so nothing could take hold. He had mixed feelings about this lack of familiarity. Often nick-names were given because you were well-liked or very good at something or because you were unique. On the other hand, they could be derogatory or sarcastic, unwanted labels, sometimes earned, sometimes not, that could follow an individual for years. Mostly, Max felt that never having been tabbed with anything significant or perma-nent merely meant that he was a solid guy, a regular Joe, and he was fine with that.

Besides, you certainly couldn't give yourself a nickname. That just was not done. Oh, occasionally some half-assed hipster would try but his friends, if he had any, would simply ignore his feeble protests and continue to call him by his given name or something worse.

Plus, Max was older now and not all nicknames age well. Once you rounded forty, going by 'Sparky' or 'Rooster' or 'Skip' was not going to fly. Not for a CEO, not for a doctor and not for any guy trying to get a mature woman into the sack.

Chubster's name wouldn't have gone over too well in the night-clubs but ap-parently that didn't matter since he was supposedly married. Supposedly because neither Max nor anyone else that knew Chubster had ever met a Mrs. MaGee. Rumor had it that she, unlike her mysterious husband, actually had a job and made a decent wage whilst her ner'do'well spouse maintained no discernible form of income. Oh, he had plans all right, and he had ambition he said but he could never be a nine to five guy. No, he claimed to be an entrepreneur, an idea man, and once in a while he would pull a roll of bills from his pocket, ill-gotten or otherwise, and buy a round or two for his cronies. If asked, which he seldom was, Chub would say he had done some odd jobs. To which Sully, Max's boss and the proprietor of the aforementioned 'Brew & Chew' would inevitably opine that doing odd jobs was not a job, just odd.

Whether Chubster MaGee's occasional windfalls were, indeed, less than legitimate was often a topic of conversation among the regulars and it seemed not to matter if Chubster was privy to the discussion or not. He'd never disappeared for more than a couple weeks, no one had ever been called to bail him out and no parole officer had ever stopped by to check on him, so any conjecture as to criminal behavior was just that, conjecture.

For his part, Chubster MaGee felt that his biggest obstacle to success was a serious lack of financial backing. He was confident that his ideas were sound, if only people would get behind them. And, of course, there would be plenty of wealth to spread around for all those who'd had the foresight to believe. And it wasn't as though all the ideas were that bad. Max himself had been tempted to invest once or twice and was almost always willing to listen, if only to break up the monotony of bar-room banter centered on sports and politics. Take, for instance, the electric suit. This particular notion came to Chubster during the oil crisis some years ago. Fuel costs had skyrocketed and during the cold winter months people were spending much more than normal just to stay warm.

"So," Chubster explained to Max one slow evening at the bar, "say you live alone, or maybe with one other person in a condo or an apartment or maybe a small house, and you're paying the heating bill, you, not the landlord. So you don't really need to heat the whole place but you kind of do because what else are you going to do, wear a bunch of sweaters or pile blankets on, but if you do blankets you can't really walk around to make dinner and clean and stuff so you give in and turn up the thermostat and you pay a bunch of dough to keep warm. But...," and here's where Chubster would smile slyly and do his long pause, because Chubster was the master of the long pause, "what if you had an electric suit?"

Max was intrigued. "I'll bite. What's an electric suit?"

"Same concept as an electric blanket but without the cord."

Max was reluctant to show too much interest since Chubster was tough to stop once he started rolling. But business was slow and moreover this idea didn't seem as impractical as some of MaGee's previous schemes.

"OK," Max said, "I'm listening."

"All right," Chubster continued, "so you head home from working all day at your crappy job..."

"That's assuming your job is crappy."

"All jobs are crappy."

"Well, that's debatable."

The idea man was undeterred. "It's cold out and your car's cold or the bus is cold or you're walking in the cold and you're freezing your butt off..."

"I get it. It's cold out."

"...and all you want is to be warm. So you get home and the place is like an igloo because heat is so frigging expensive, and you had lowered the thermostat when you left that morning. But instead of turning up the heat as soon as you walk in the door, you go over to your electric suit and you unplug it."

"I thought you said it had no cord."

"It doesn't. It has a power pack attached. You plug it in in the morning and it charges all day while you're at work at your shitty job..."

"I thought it was a crappy job." Max couldn't help himself.

Chubster ignored him. "So it's all charged up, has the same warmth as an electric blanket, has a knob to control the temperature but it looks like those head to toe pajama things you wore when you were little..."

"Maybe you wore."

"It's got a hood, footies, a pouch and a long zipper."

"Sounds sexy."

"You get out of your work duds, slip into the suit, zip up and bingo, you're snug as a bug in a rug and toasty warm. You can walk around or hang on the couch. Either way, you don't have to turn on the heat and you, my friend, are saving a boatload of money. If there's two of you living there, you could have two suits. More suits than that and it probably defeats the purpose, big electrical bill and all that. But for singles or couples with no kids, it's perfect." Chubster took a breath, satisfied with his pitch. "Whataya' think?"

Max hesitated. Surely there had to be the usual assortment of flaws that most of Chubster's ideas contained. Surprisingly, he could think of none.

"You know," he said, "I have to admit this does not sound like a terrible idea."

Chubster smiled. "Wow. High praise."

Max stared at the ceiling. "I'll need some time to figure out the drawbacks."

"That's fine," said Chub, "take your time. But for now, sign this." He pushed a sheet of paper across the bar to Max and placed a pen on top.

"What's this?" asked Max.

"It's a non-disclosure agreement. It's so you won't steal my idea."

Max could have been offended. He could have argued. He could have reminded Chubster how long they had known each other and how many beers on the house he had proffered the idea man over the years. But all that would have taken time and he was, after all, supposed to be working. He signed the paper.

Max actually did take time to think it over. Most of Chubster's get-rich-quick schemes could be easily dismissed, discarded as so many crackpot concepts and transparent scams. But, on occasion, like the proverbial blind squirrel who manages to find a nut, Chub would stumble across something that might, just maybe, somehow make sense. There was the lemon twist cutter shaped like an ice cream scoop which, he claimed could make sixteen cuts at once and would soon be owned by every bartender in America. The latex pop-up punching bag, anchored by a layer of sand at its bottom, whose blank countenance stood ready for the superimposition of the photographic face of your most hated enemy, be it your ex, your boss, your mother-in-law, whoever you truly wanted to give a symbolic beating.

The great majority of Chubster's ideas ranged from the slightly flawed to the completely illegal to the down-right ridiculous. But this one, this electric cloak, seemed different.

"I'll give you one thousand dollars to fund the suit," said Max, "if you can get nine other suckers in this joint to put in the same. That is ten grand, should be enough to produce a prototype."

Chubster looked hurt. "Suckers?"

"Excuse me. Investors."

Chubster considered. "And I can use your name while convincing these investors of the viability of my invention?"

"Yes," said Max seriously, "don't know how much good it will do you. I'm not exactly managing a hedge fund but yes, you can use my name."

Chubster appeared momentarily startled. He was more accustomed to Max pointing out the myriad defects in his plans. But Chubster MaGee was, if nothing else, confident. His surprise was brief.

"Deal," he said. "I'll draw up the contract."

"Contract?"

"Agreement, pledge, whatever. Just something in writing I can show the boys."

"Sure, I'll have my attorney look it over."

"Max. Come on"

"I'm kidding, Chub. Jeez. Just make sure you don't add any extra zeroes to the amount."

"Humn, I hadn't thought of that," said Chubster. He winked and walked away.

The electric suit never came to be. The money was never collected, the prototype was never made. Bobby Deets, the union electrician who drank nothing but 'salty dogs' and seemed to have no other clothes than his blue denim work-shirts derailed that train. He brought up the possibility of electrocution, the financial liability should something go wrong with the wiring or power pack. Chubster argued that, to his knowledge, no one had ever been fried by an electric blanket. But the seeds of doubt had been sown. Naturally, Chubster was depressed for a day or two but he was a resilient fellow and soon even he seemed to have moved on. The bar chatter returned to free agents, economic complaints and admiration for the aesthetically pleasing derriere of the newest bar-maid.

All of this was swirling through Max's mind as he prepared for whatever MaGee's latest pitch might be. Chubster had again approached him but this was unusual. Chub requested a formal sit-down, a meeting whenever Max could take a break, something to be discussed not across the oak bar top but rather in a booth, the farther away from the bar-flies and eaves-droppers the better.

"I'm not doing anything illegal," said Max.

"This is barely even illegal."

"Well, that's reassuring."

"Max, you've known me a long time. Just give me a couple minutes of your time when you can. This could be a big pay-day. I know you make a decent wage working here but you're not exactly getting rich and I know, whether you admit it or not, you don't want to be serving suds to these boozers and cheapskates for the rest of your life. For God's sake, Max, how many times can you talk to the same loser on the same stool about the same goddamn weather?"

"Present company excepted, of course."

"Very funny."

For one of the first times since he'd been behind that bar, Max was speechless. Did Chubster really know him that well? Sure, he wanted more money, but who didn't? And yes, his job was pretty mundane but compared to some other forms of employment it was pretty sweet. No heavy lifting, no soul-draining monotony with no two days exactly the same. Attractive women to flirt with, a few laughs, sports on the TVs. Then again, in other ways it wasn't so great. Working weekends and holidays, at least in his first years, not so much now. No sick leave, no paid vacations and not much hope for advancement. Why couldn't he have been an athlete, a businessman, maybe an artist or a musician?

"Max, hey Max, you still with me?" His mind must have wandered.

"All right," said Max. "When things slow down we'll get a booth. You can explain your cockamamie idea, I'll tell you what's wrong with it, politely of course, we'll shake hands and forget about the whole thing. Fair enough?"

"You, my friend," said Chubster, "have a poor attitude."

*

The next few hours at the bar were just busy enough to delay Max's pow wow with Chubster but slow enough to leave plenty of moments for reflection. It wasn't as though the big talker had said anything profound; Max had told himself the same things a hundred times before. But that was in his mind, quietly, maintaining an appearance of inscrutability, not allowing the patrons to be wise to his momentary ruminations. Somehow, hearing it said out loud had struck a nerve. Though fairly content with his job, his apartment, his quality of life, Max knew there was more. He was often envious of those people who'd done more, who'd seen more, who had more. Maybe Chubster was making sense.

'Sully's Brew & Chew' was far more brew than chew. Max had tended bar there for a few years now and his comfort behind the taps was at least partially to blame for his personal stagnation. It was easy to drift into complacency in the business of food and drink. In what other field of employment could you watch the big game on TV, listen to music, down the occasional complimentary cocktail and walk out the door with a wad of cash in your pocket and maybe even a telephone number or two?

Max surveyed the tavern's interior as the restaurant slowly emptied. Three big screen television sets hanging behind him, dangling above the shiny shelves of libations, top-shelf to not so much. A few high-tops, half dozen black vinyl booths, some wooden tables with aged wicker chairs, walls plastered with the usual assortment of sports logos and Irish wisdom, a pool table and dart-board toward the back next to a hallway leading to the restrooms. 'Cheers' it ain't, thought Max. The only scrap of originality in the entire place was the vintage jukebox stocked with nothing but late sixties, early seventies soul platters – Motown, Atlantic, Stax, all the great labels. This was, as Max had been vehemently and frequently informed by his owner, the only music that mattered. Those entering the joint expecting Celtic fiddles emitting from the speakers scattered through-out would find no such tunes. Surprisingly, almost no one complained about this lack of musical diversity. Once in a while a group of college kids from the nearby univer-sity would wander in, having decided to be adventurous and skip the usual undergrad haunts – 'McNasty's', 'The Quad', the 'All Nighter' (which, curiously, was not open all night) and all the other trendy dives that lined College Ave, choosing instead to have a pop at this old-fashioned drinking man's saloon. They'd listen to the classic R & B, these songs sung with love, sorrow and passion long before they were born. Soon enough a couple would make their way to the jukebox in the corner, slowly peruse the selections, then return to their group and shrug, the search for something more current obviously unsuccessful. They were at least polite enough and smart enough not to complain. To do so would have proven fruitless. Max would have referred them to Sully who, de-pending on the tone of their voices and the shape of his mood, may have ordered them to vacate his establishment post-haste or kindly explained the obvious merits of the sweet soul music playing overhead as opposed to the utter rubbish, the rap crap and hip-slop that passed for music today. Either way, he'd have gotten his point across and the undergrads seldom offered a rebuttal. Whether this was due to the eloquence of his argument or the size of his rather imposing frame really didn't matter.

Sully was a big man. His father, 'Big Sully', was of formidable size as well and his grandfather, 'Old Sully', had required an extra large coffin before entering the pearly gates. Sully's son, 'Little Sully', though only a lad of sixteen, appeared well on his way to becoming the biggest Sully of them all. The boy's high school football coaches tried mightily to recruit him for the gridiron but his father would have none of it, insisting his progeny continue playing the sport of his ancestors – soc-cer. Sully's better half, Mrs. Sullivan, a petite woman born and raised in the States and, unsullied if you will, tried her best to convince her husband that perhaps 'Little Sully' was better suited to the American game, his body type not exactly lending itself to sprinting up and down a half acre of God's green earth. Her rea-soning fell on deaf ears and so it seemed the youngest Sully was headed in the direction of tavern owner rather than National Football League lineman.

Sully had inherited the 'Brew & Chew' from 'Big Sully' who had learned the business from 'Old Sully' back in County Cork. They still served an excellent beef stew and though it wasn't nearly as popular as it had once been, no one could claim it wasn't authentic. Sully had been know to dabble in the kitchen from time to time but for the most part spent his days in his cubbyhole of an office or roaming the front of the house, greeting regulars, solving problems, coping with crises and basically maintaining as much order as one could hope for in a busy, boisterous Irish pub.

There was a general consensus among the staff, Max included, that as far as owners went, Sully wasn't bad and most everyone at the 'Chew' agreed they'd seen worse. He had, to no one's surprise, inherited the traditional Irishman's fondness for ale but he chose not to imbibe while working; only at closing would he deign to down a few pints. He would yell and curse a bit, but only if you deserved it, and when it was done it was done; he never held a grudge. Max was quite fond of Sully and fairly sure the feeling was mutual.

*

Chubster MaGee was waiting patiently in a corner booth and when Max determined business was slow enough to to take a break, he asked Dolly, one of the older waitresses, to keep an eye on the bar, then carried two drafts over, set one down in front of his friend with the plans, slid in opposite and waited. Chubster took a long swig and wiped his chin.

"This is a pre-meeting," he said. "The meeting before the meeting. Did I already mention that?"

"Must have slipped your mind. Don't think I've ever been to a pre-meeting before. This is pretty exciting." Max sipped his beer.

"The real meeting will be with King."

"King?"

"Yeah. He's the boss, the money man, the big cheese."

"King?" Max again.

"No last names, so for now and forever, he's just King."

"I know your last name."

"Henceforth. Going forward. No more last names."

Max smiled. "Did you just say henceforth in 'Sully's Brew & Chew'?"

"I'm an educated man, Max, and so are you." Chubster surveyed the room, appraising the other patrons. "That's why we're the two people sitting in this booth. Now shall I go on?"

Max leaned back. "I'm sorry. Sometimes I can't help myself. Please continue."

"OK," said Chubster, "first let me alleviate any apprehension you may have. You will not be involved in the actual event..."

"Event?...Sorry."

"You'll be heading up what I'll call pre-production. You'll be more of a casting agent, a recruiter of sorts.."

"Like in 'Ocean's Eleven' or 'The Magnificent Seven?'" Another voice. Neither Max nor Chubster had noticed 'Biz' emerge from the restroom and pause near their booth.

"Jesus, Biz," said Chubster, "where did you come from?"

Biz had attained his nickname by comparing every conversation or situation to something cinematic or televised. He was a walking, talking entertainment ency-clopedia. His job must have allowed him more than enough time for viewing mov-ies on his tablet or reading about them on the internet. He was rather nondescript in appearance, harmless enough, probably a nerd in high school but he was part of the gang and though not exactly a catch or the life of the party, he was well received by the small beer drinking community who Max considered regulars. Biz didn't hit on the waitresses, he didn't get drunk and he didn't cause problems. He was, as far as the other stool squatters were concerned, a good egg.

Biz shrugged, motioned to the mens' room behind him. "Just taking a leak, Chub. Why, what's the matter? Why aren't you guys at the bar anyway? What are you doing over here?"

"This is supposed to be a private conversation. That's why we're over here."

"Oh," said Biz, "OK, I'm sorry. Don't see too many private conversations in 'Sully's...Hey, Max."

"Hey, Biz," said Max.

Biz smiled. "Hey, maybe we should get you guys a 'Cone of Silence'"

Chubster glanced at Max. "'Get Smart'" said Max.

Chubster stared at Biz. "How old are you anyway?"

"What?" Now Chubster was glaring. Biz hesitated, raised his hands. "Okay, okay, I'm going."

"Now," said Chub, watching Biz walk away, "where was I?"

"I'm a recruiter."

"You won't be there, you won't have a weapon, no one you recruit will have a weapon and the only crimes they commit will be misdemeanors."

"Crimes?" said Max.

"Maybe. Maybe something minor. Nothing involving you." Chubster leaned back, sipped his beer.

"Since this is a pre-meeting, I'm guessing you're not going to tell me what we're doing."

"That would be a good guess," said Chubster. "This is just to see if you'll agree to the next meeting, the one with King."

"And if I don't agree to the next meeting?"

"Then," said Chub, we drink our beers, shake hands and walk away. No hard feelings. But Max, I think this is the one. I know I've said that before, I'm like the boy who cried wolf. But I swear, I truly believe this is it."

"OK," said Max, "just one more..."

Chubster interrupted. "I know what you're gonna' ask. Why me? A perfectly legitimate question."

"I thought so."

"Because, Max, you're honest. You keep your word. You've got a good eye for people, you've got the gift of gab and everybody likes you."

"My ex might take issue with that."

"And you're a wise-ass," said Chubster, smiling. "But you're funny, so it's okay."

"I will not hold a gun. I will not hurt anyone. I will not steal anything. I will not be anyone's alibi..."

"Max, relax, you don't have to do any of that shit. Plus you haven't had the real meeting yet or heard the plan. You're getting way ahead of yourself. You might not even want to participate."

"What's the pay-off?" asked Max.

"For you?"

"No, Chub, for my uncle. Whataya' think?"

"One hundred, fifty thousand dollars. That's a lot of tips, my friend."

There are certain moments in life, important moments, memorable moments, moments that might change everything. They don't happen often and sometimes when they do, they go without notice. But once in a while and this, Max thought, this could be one of those occasions, once in a while one of those moments is staring you right in the face. Might be an interview, might be on the playing field, might be with a girl. And now here was Chubster MaGee, a person whom Max never would have imagined having a profound effect on his life. Yet there it was. One hundred and fifty thousand dollars. It would take him ten years serving brews to save that much money. He leaned back in the booth. "Set it up," he said.

*

The next day found Max racked with doubt. This was not unusual. He'd never been one to jump right in, take risks, throw caution to the wind. He'd considered opening his own place a dozen times but always failed to pull the trigger. Shaky partners, economic recessions, employee theft, just too many things could go wrong. Didn't they say that three out of four restaurants went belly up in the first three years?

Chubster wasn't the only bar hustler he'd been approached by with a get-rich-quick scheme. Max had turned down plenty of them, too. Like his father, and a million other fathers had said, if it sounds too good to be true, then it probably is. Besides, whatever plan Chubster and his associates had cooked up was bound to be shady if not downright criminal. That was way too much money to be legitimate. Max hadn't been in trouble in a long time. Sure, he'd spent a night or two in a jail cell but those were youthful transgressions, long ago and mostly forgotten. There was no way he was doing time at this juncture in his admittedly mundane existence. One hundred, fifty thousand dollars would definitely change his life but it wasn't a million. One flaw in the plan, he told himself, and he was out.

At home, Max tried to distract himself, pass the time until the meeting which Chubster had arranged. He thought about phoning the idea man and backing out but that just wasn't who he was. One thing Max prided himself on was keeping his word. Max had never broken a promise, never not done what he'd said he was going to do. Often, whatever he intended had taken longer than planned, procrastination being one of his many flaws, but in the end he would always come through. He'd told Chubster he would attend the meeting and so, attend he would.

Max's apartment was small, a one bedroom walk-up about a half mile from the bar. Not much room for pacing but that didn't stop him. The cat, Rufus, followed, probably hoping his owner was headed for the refrigerator. Max would stop in the kitchen, turn around and head back to the living room, once again empty-handed, the cat staring up at him, confused but not deterred. "What?" Max would ask his furry roommate. "What?"

How had he ended up with a cat anyway? In no way was he a cat guy. Rufus had just shown up one day, like a pal who's been tossed out by the wife for a night or two and just wants to crash on your couch. But, Max soon realized, Rufus had no feline home or cat wife to return to, no decorative collar, no name tag identifying his owner, and soon he was that guest who won't leave, who drinks your milk and leaves crumbs on the counter and hair in the sink. Actually, Max figured, he really didn't eat that much, he was surprisingly good company and on those nights when Max was entertaining a female visitor, Rufus seemed to earn him a few extra points on the desirable bachelor scale. Hey, he thought, if a cute, furry animal could help him in the romance department, he'd bunk with a panda bear, a sloth, whatever you have.

*

Ginny O'Riley, Sully always claimed, was not hired at his Irish American establishment simply because of her name. Nor, would he declare, had he put a great deal of emphasis on her pretty red hair, green eyes, freckles and fine figure, as his friends rolled their collective eyes. No, it was because of Ginny's extensive experience in the service industry and the positive references she received from former employers that led to her spending the last few years waiting tables at 'Sully's Brew & Chew'. Sully would, of course, follow this questionable explanation by declaring that Ginny's looks and name certainly hadn't hurt her case.

Ginny, for her part, wouldn't give Sully's remarks a second thought, even when they were repeated while she stood close by. She would simply shake her head and go about her business, killing the customers with kindness just as she'd done for the last eighteen years. She'd had a lot of managers in that time, beginning when she became a 'Hooters' girl not long after high school, continuing through all manner of restaurants and lounges varying in class and capacity, and as managers went, Sully wasn't bad. If you didn't want to be sexually harassed, she thought, don't work in bars. And that went for the men as well. There was something about the familiar feel of the staff that seemed to encourage all kinds of flirtation and innuendo. Of course, the uniforms likely didn't help. Whether it was short shorts or tight tops, it was evidently difficult for the horn-balls in the booths to keep their minds on their meals or the bartenders from patting bums. And the language, well, anyone who'd been in a kitchen on a busy Friday night when the entire crew was 'in the weeds' would hear curses old and new, some of them made up right on the spot and frequently spouted by a bespectacled, pony-tailed young server who, when hired six months prior, would never have dreamed of calling a cheap tipper a cocksucker. But hey, they lived on those tips so this was serious business.

Ginny tried hard not to think of herself as a walking, talking cliché. A single mom who'd made a single mistake, one parent raising a teenage daughter as best she could, working steadily, sometimes two jobs to make ends meet. No college degree, no mini-van, no house in the suburbs and no handsome, successful husband to get bored with. But, she would tell herself, she didn't end up on the street and she didn't end up on the pole. She was no gold-digger and with her looks, everyone said, she could have been. She had loved the wrong men for the right reasons and it was never about money. Some days, when she was feeling down, she wished it had been. But only for a moment.

Ginny was the first to notice Max had been acting a little strange. Not strange exactly, but not himself. Not as sarcastic as usual, not hurling insults at the regulars which, to her surprise, they always loved. No jokes, no flirting, no nothing. She wanted to ask him if anything was wrong, why no smiles, no laughs. But she knew how much she hated it when someone asked her that question, simply because she hadn't been her normal, perky self, a few less giggles, a few less winks, a few more nods. "Why the long face?" they'd ask. "Where's that smile?" they'd say. No harm intended, of course, but that didn't lessen her desire to take the corkscrew from her apron and jam it forcefully into their skull, the punishment obviously not fitting the crime. Couldn't she have a bad day, she thought. Couldn't she be in a mood? Couldn't they just leave her alone? And so she left Max alone. At least for a while.

"How's it hanging?" she asked him during an early evening lull.

"Girls don't ask that question," said Max with a slight smile. But it wasn't his usual smile, Ginny thought.

"Well, that's pretty sexist," she said.

"Life is unfair."

"Tell me about it. My sixteen year old daughter just unfriended me on Face-Book."

Max knew Ginny had a teenage daughter, though he'd forgotten her name and since he'd heard it on numerous occasions he wasn't about to ask again. It was odd, he could serve someone once or twice and remember their name for life. But he had a terrible time with the names of his friends' children. Perhaps some kind of passive / aggressive bitter bachelor attitude he theorized. He'd even seen Ginny's kid a couple times when the youngster had stopped in 'Sully's to wait for her mom to get off work. A pretty girl, at least from a distance, though she'd not been gifted with her mother's flaming tresses. Instead, her hair was dark, Black Irish Max thought they called it. She had, however, begun to develop a figure like Ginny's which was surely going to be a problem during her awkward adolescence if adolescent boys were still the same brain-dead horn-dogs they were in Max's high school days.

Ginny had often described the daughter as a handful and a drama queen but wasn't that true of every teenage girl? On her few visits to Sully's she'd seemed quiet and studious if one can be considered studious while staring at a cell-phone. At any rate, Max had more important things to consider than Ginny O'Riley's offspring.

"I thought," said Max, "Face-Book was for old people now."

"Yah, I guess it is but she wants to stay in touch with her aunts because they're cool."

Max smiled. "I think you're cool."

"Oh, Max, you're such a sweet-talker."

"So I've been told."

They noticed Sully approaching "Ginny, darlin', have you asked Max why he's been shuffling around here the last couple nights like his dog died?"

"I have a cat," said Max.

Ginny ignored him. "I asked him how it's hanging."

Sully: "You can't ask him that, dear."

"Is there a rule-book I'm unaware of?"

"It's unwritten," said the owner.

Ginny tried to sound offended. "You piglets have asked me if I shaved my privates."

"Well," said Sully, "that's a legitimate question." Max shrugged in agreement. Sully turned his attention to Max. "Now then, Maxi-pad, everything okay with you?"

"Everything's aces," said Max.

"Okay, good enough for me." Ginny shook her head as Sully continued. "Now, Max, why don't you change the Killians keg and we can all get back to the business of making a living."

Max glanced at Ginny and headed for the cooler. Sully winked at her, then walked away. Ginny went to check on her only table but Max wasn't surprised when, a few moments later, the cooler door opened and she poked her head in. "Anyone home," she said.

Max continued moving kegs so he could tap the Killians. "You're a riot," he said.

Ginny walked in, shivered. "Man, it's freezing in here."

"I know," said Max, "please don't ask me how it's hanging now."

Ginny laughed. "Listen, Max, you've heard all my crap a hundred times so if you've got a problem or need someone to talk to or whatever, you know I owe you."

"Yeah, you probably do." He finished changing the keg. "Come on," he said, carrying the empty barrel, "let's get out of here." They paused outside the cooler door. "There's no big problem. Just doin' a lot of thinking. Probably one of those mid-life crises you read about. You know, what am I doin', how'd I get here, where am I going?"

"Wow. Deep stuff," said Ginny.

Max smiled. "I know. Plus mulling over a business opportunity. So...I'll try to lighten up a bit."

Ginny gave him an unexpected hug and put her hands on his shoulders. "Well," she said, "you know what they say. When opportunity knocks..." She turned to go, took a few steps, then paused. "Unless it's got anything to do with Chubster McGee. I know you're smarter than that."

Max watched her walk away, put his head down and made his way back to the bar. You haven't committed to anything, he told himself, you're just gonna' go to a meeting and listen, that's all. A voice shook him from his thoughts.

"McFly...Hello, McFly."

It was Biz. Max looked around, saw the regulars staring at him. "Sorry, Biz, daydreaming I guess." He took a can of PBR from the chiller, slid it down the bar to the entertainment expert who caught and cracked it open.

"Sam Malone could curve it," said Biz.

"I'm sure he could," said Max, "I'm sure he could."

*

The meeting was to be held at 'The Freemont'. The old hotel had a pub on the first floor, dark and quiet. Leather booths and red table lamps. Servers in white shirts and black pants, ties tucked in between buttons as though trying to hide. A few tiers above the 'Brew & Chew', Max decided. He'd often wondered about tending bar when he got older. Bartending was, for the most part, a young person's game. Nobody was going to hire him at an 'Applebee's or a 'T.G.I.F'. They wanted a certain look and though Max was by no means unattractive, his weathered features wouldn't quite fit the bill.

When the 'Chew' got busy on a Thursday or Friday night, you had to hustle. But there was no hustle at 'The Freemont'. The wait-staff seemed to glide between tables and no loud voices or raucous laughter emanated from within. Well-dressed gentlemen sat at the smooth mahogany bar sipping their martinis and well-kept women indulged in complicated cocktails that were likely better to look at than to drink. They spoke softly, perhaps business, politics, philosophy. They made plans for the remainder of the evening with nary a mention of the Super Bowl or the Kardashians. Maybe, Max thought, it would be interesting to have a conversation that didn't involve the weather or the comparative figures of the Fox news women.

Working in an establishment like 'The Freemont' would be a nice way to end his career, that is if you could call bartending a career. Something to consider, should Chubster's alleged road to riches not pan out.

Chubster MaGee seemed to emerge like a phantom from the shadows. "Punctual as ever," he said, patting Max's back. "Another admirable quality."

"Stop it," said Max, "you'll make me blush."

"Come on, wise guy. King's in his booth."

"His booth?"

"You know what I mean. Come on."

Chubster led Max to a corner booth, a crescent shaped cushion lining the bench seat of a large, round table. King, or at least the man Max assumed to be King, sat in the very center of the booth, his back to the wall. He appeared, Max felt, appropriately regal, not quite enormous but certainly corpulent, impeccably dressed and carefully groomed. He sported a pencil mustache and jet-black goatee giving him a rather devilish countenance. Seated to his left was a stern faced man in a dark suit, a muscular fellow with close-cropped hair and an air of suspicion. Either, Max thought, a bodyguard or an accountant in terrific shape. Directly across the table was an under dressed mook in a shiny, silk electric blue athletic jacket and scally cap. He was red-faced and pot-bellied and if ever a call went out from central casting for a typical Irishman, this was their man.

King spoke first. "Good evening, gentlemen."

"King," said Chubster, "this is Max, the guy I was telling you about."

"Of course. Nice to meet you, Max. Chubster speaks very highly of you."

"He's just trying to get in my pants."

"He's kidding," said Chubster, quickly elbowing Max.

King smiled. "Of course. Very good. "This," he said, motioning to his left, "is my associate, Mr. Doe. You'll find he is a man of few words. Across the table, wearing his Sunday best, is Duffy, obviously a charmer and all-around man of the people." Duffy smiled, stuck out his hand while Doe nodded slightly and never moved.

"Now," said King, "before we begin our little conference I need Mr. Doe to properly greet our new friend. You don't mind, do you, Max?"

"Not at all," said Max.

Mr. Doe slid his stocky frame from the booth, stood and motioned for Max to raise his arms. The bodyguard carefully patted him down, kneeling to frisk the interior of Max's pant legs.

Max looked down. "You could at least buy me a drink first." Duffy laughed but Doe was not amused. He finished with Max, slipped back into his seat.

"Gentlemen," said King, "please sit."

Duffy made room for them, sliding toward King, his mug never leaving his hand. King sipped from a tea cup and an untouched glass of water rested on a coaster in front of Mr. Doe. Max and Chubster joined the table.

"Now, Max," began King, "I can see you have a unique sense of humor and I do appreciate a good laugh as much as the next fellow. However, I feel I must inform you that this is a serious meeting to discuss a serious plan for a serious endeavor which, hopefully, will lead to some serious monetary gains."

"Sounds serious," said Max, regretting it instantly. "Sorry," he said. "It's the bartender in me. Being a wise-ass is basically part of the job. I'll try to behave."

"No need to apologize, Max. We're just getting to know one another."

"Speaking of which, King is not a name I've encountered too often and, being in the service industry, I meet a lot of people. Is it a nickname?" Here he went again with the nicknames. Why, he thought, couldn't he just keep his mouth shut?

"As a matter of fact, yes it is, but there is certainly no reason to get into names right now, or even later on for that matter. I'm sure you're more curious as to why you're here."

"How'd you guess? Oh, sorry, sorry. It's like a gag reflex. Can't help myself. No more remarks, I promise." Max folded his hands on the table like a proper school-boy at his desk. He glanced at Chubster, then looked seriously at King.

"Very good. Before we start, would either of you care for a beverage?"

"I'm good," said Max. "Alcohol makes me even more mouthy. Conversation lubrication, you know."

"Ah, yes," said King, "and you, Chubster?"

"If you're offering."

King motioned with his hand and an attractive, middle-aged server strode over. "Tracey, my dear, I believe we require your service. Chubster?"

"Tallest, coldest draft you got. Domestic's fine." Chub glanced at King, then back at Tracey. "Please and thank you."

"And perhaps," King said, "an ice tea for our new friend." Max nodded politely. Tracey smiled, nodded, turned to go. Everyone except Doe watched her walk away.

"All right, Max, just what has Chubster informed you thus far?"

"Not much. Basically that you need a recruiter of sorts."

"Yes," said King, "a recruiter. I like that. It sounds very corporate and this is, after all, a business venture. We need someone totally unknown and unaffiliated with my organization...That would be you, Max...To enlist a variety of other unknown and unrelated individuals to supply a large and lengthy diversion."

Max leaned forward. "A diversion?"

"Yes. Now, there is no need for these individuals to know why they are creating a diversion. They will be handsomely paid in cash. It's possible some of them will be arrested but if so they will be bailed out and their fines paid by an anonymous benefactor, also unknown and unrelated to you. They may be questioned about events that took place concurrently during the diversion but will have no information to give since they were never made aware of such events."

"But," said Max, "they'd be questioned about me."

"Indeed they will," said King. "But you'll be gone. With one hundred, fifty thousand dollars you should be able to take a nice, long vacation. And those being questioned won't know your real name, they won't know where you live or where you work."

"Chubster didn't mention anything about disappearing."

"Max," said Chubster, "you've got nothing holding you here. No wife, no kids, no mortgage, no big-time career."

"Is this," said Max, turning to Chub, "another reason you thought of me for the job?"

"Well, yeah, sure."

"It's not forever, Max," said King. "You can come back in a year or so, after things die down. Resume your life. The events of November 7th will be long forgotten."

"Yeah," said Max, "speaking of which, what are these mysterious events of November 7th"

Tracey returned carrying drinks and cocktail napkins on a small wooden tray. The conversation paused as she set down Chubster's beer and Max's ice tea. She addressed King. "Will that be all?"

"Yes, thank you, Tracey. That's fine for now." Tracey departed and King continued. "Now then, where were we? Oh, yes, the mysterious events. You may want them to remain a mystery. The less you know, the more difficult it will be for the authorities to connect you in any way."

Max turned to Chubster. "Do you know?" His friend nodded. Max looked past him at Duffy. "What about you?"

"It was my idea," said Duffy.

Max stared at Mr. Doe. "I'm sure Mr. Chatterbox here knows." Doe showed no expression. "Well, gentlemen, as much as I enjoy playing "Jimmy the Dunce', I feel I must be clued in. You guys could be killing the president for all I know."

"No, no," said King. "Nothing that spectacular, I'm afraid. We're robbing the stadium."

"During the big game," added Duffy, "at the end of the third quarter."

Well, thought Max, there it was, cards on the table. They were going to rob the stadium. He took a long drink, set the glass down, wished Tracey would come back to check on them, give him time to think. Holy mackerel, rob the stadium. That was huge. What happened to all Chubster's crazy little plans? This was big time. He should have known. Big rewards entail big risks. And questions, boy did he have questions.

"And my recruits?" asked Max.

"Are going to swarm the field in such number and diversity as to require every security guard and police officer in the building to clear them out."

"And more of your associates will be visiting whoever is left in the counting rooms," said Max.

"How'd you know?" asked Duffy.

"I sold peanuts there when I was a kid."

Everyone paused and Max was grateful for it. King sipped from his tea cup, his pinkie finger extended like the lord of the manor. Duffy and Chubster pounded their beers, Max drank his cool refreshment and Doe stared at the three of them as though he could telepathically cause their heads to explode. Max managed to keep his thoughts to himself, resist proclaiming how much fun the burly minion must be at a party. There was a time and place and this definitely was not it.

"Duffy here," said King, "has worked at the stadium for fifteen years. He knows every nook and cranny. He knows the pick-ups, the times, locations and who's doing what, when and where. The men in the counting rooms know him and more importantly, they trust him."

"Look it," said Duffy, "I been thinking about this for years. Two counting rooms, each with two retired detectives keepin' an eye on things. The walkie-talkies will be goin' bananas."

King held up his hand. "Duffy, I'm sure Max gets the idea."

"Seems like," said Max, "including me, you'll have a pretty high payroll for this operation. Is it worth it?"

Duffy smiled. "A hundred thousand crazy fans spending money like drunken sailors. Eight dollar beers, pizza, dogs, programs, souvenirs..." The Irishman paused. "Believe me, it'll be worth it."

Duffy took a swig of beer, satisfied. Max thought it over. It was a pretty good plan but lots of plans sound pretty good at the beginning until things start to go wrong. Every heist movie he'd ever seen seemed to be moving like clockwork until someone double crosses someone or something unexpected happens. 'Biz' would tell you that and probably cite examples, too. And what about the leaving town part? It was true he didn't have much tying him down but at least he was safe and sound, secure in his job and comfortable in his apartment. And what about Rufus?

Max looked at Duffy. "Even if you get in the counting room, how you gonna' get all that money out of there? You're talkin' bales of cash."

Duffy was tempted to answer, glanced at King, thought better of it.

"These details," said the big boss, "don't concern you, Max. As I've previously stated, the less each of us knows about the doings of the others, the better. You do your job, Duffy will take care of his and Chubster the same."

That reminded Max. Just what was Chubster's part in this, anyway? He tabled that thought for the time being. "What happens," he asked, "if I decline the offer?"

"Then Chubster here," said King, "finds another recruiter. You go your way, we go ours and we never met. No harm, no foul."

"How do you know I won't tell?"

"Oh, I'm afraid that would be unwise."

Unwise? Max looked at the others. No one spoke, no one blinked. Who the heck said "unwise"? People said something was stupid or dumb or something was dangerous. Nobody said "unwise". It sounded menacing. Max sipped his ice tea, addressed King.

"What's the payment schedule?"

"You get fifty thousand to start. You'll receive one hundred more when the job is done."

"How do I know I can trust you?"

King smiled. "How do I know I can trust you? Actually, Chubster has vouched for you and I'm sure he'll vouch for me. Max, have you ever heard the phrase, 'honor amongst thieves'? I've not always been on the right side of the law and I must say I've done some things that I'm not proud of but anyone who has ever had any dealings with me will tell you one thing, I always keep my word. A

21

man's word is very important, would you agree?" Max nodded. "I am a man of honor and I expect those around me to follow suit". King seriously surveyed the table.

Duffy lifted his mug. "I'll drink to that."

Chubster lifted his as well. "To honor," he said. They tapped mugs and drank, wiping the foam from their lips.

"I think," said Max, "we're forgetting one thing. What do I use to bankroll my recruits? You don't expect me to use my fifty because..."

"Ah, yes," said King, "you are, of course, referring to the seed money for our venture."

"Exactly."

"Fear not. No need to use your own funds. Chubster and I have formulated a preliminary plan that should supply you with an adequate amount to entice thoseyou find the most willing and able to create the greatest chaos."

"What a surprise," he said, staring at Chubster who meekly shrugged.

"Now, Max," said King, "surely you didn't expect me to simply hand you fifty thousand dollars without first demonstrating some sort of competence in casting and execution."

"Excuse me," said Max. Things were getting complicated. Should he just put an end to this right now, get up from the table, thank them for their time and walk away, give up on the cash and return to his comfortable existence? Ambition was a wonderful quality but it could be dangerous. "I am not going to jail for a hundred, fifty thousand dollars."

"No one expects you to, Max."

"I will not be present when you do the stadium. I will not be present when Chubster executes the preliminary. I will recruit, I will facilitate and then I will disappear. Is that acceptable?"

"But Max," said Chubster.

"No buts, Chub. Is that acceptable?"

King smiled. "That's fine, Max. Chubster will do what he does, you do what you do and we'll do what we do. I don't need to know the details concerning the preliminary, just that's it been done. I don't want to know how you talk the recruits into storming the field. I just want to see it happen. And I'm sure you don't want to know how we carry out our plans nor how we secure the money, only that you acquire your share. Difficult to squeal or confess when nobody knows nothing, pardon the vernacular. Fair enough?"

Sure, it was fair, he thought, but was it possible? How many people would he have to recruit? It was true that he'd been at a game once when a fat, naked guy had run on the field and it had taken a dozen guards to subdue him and escort him out of the building. But there would probably be hundreds of security personnel at the big game. This was not going to be easy.

And never mind all that, what about the principle of the thing, the ethics, the morality? He would be a thief. He'd never been a thief before. You couldn't go back from that. But, and it was a big but, a hundred, fifty thousand dollars was a lot of money. A person could be tempted to bend a principle or two. Max contemplated all this as the others relaxed. Tracey returned to the table, asked if anyone needed anything.

"Well, Tracey," said Max, "I believe I've changed my mind and need a drink. Glenlivet, neat, with a water back, please."

"Anyone else," she asked. Duffy and Chubster raised their empty mugs and King nodded. Tracey took the empty glasses and departed.

King leaned back, smiled. "You know, Max, Oscar Wilde once said the best way to rid oneself of temptation is to yield to it. So...do we have a deal?"

*

When the meeting was over and Max had emerged from the darkened recesses of 'The Fremont', he knew he had much to consider. He'd never been big on life changing decisions and his idea of risk was betting a hundred on the over in the Super Bowl. Ambition was all well and fine but he spent a great deal of his shifts waiting on ambitious guys with nothing to show for it. Guys whose ventures failed, who invested in the wrong start-up, guys who handed their hardearned money to the wrong financial advisor. You didn't read about 'Sully's regulars in 'The Wall Street Journal'. Their IPO's didn't boom, their apps didn't take off, their prospects didn't pan out. They went back to work for other guys, guys who were smarter, guys who were luckier, guys who paid them enough to support their nice, normal lives. A roof over their heads, a car in the drive-way, two weeks vacation and enough left over for a burger and a beer at 'Sully's. They sat on their stools and swapped stories of close calls, near-misses and coulda'beens. Sometimes, after a few too many, someone would admit to an awful idea, a "what was I thinking", an abject failure. They'd all laugh and toast and order another round, comforted by the thought that at least they'd tried. At least they had that.

Max declined Chubster's offer to share a cab, said he needed the night air to clear his mind and it was, after all, a nice evening for a walk. Chubster, naturally, thought walking was for chumps and told Max he'd see him the next day at the bar, then sped off in a taxi to wherever Chubster always sped off to. Which reminded Max, just how well did he actually know Chubster MaGee? Sure, he'd been serving him beers for a number of years and they were sort of friends, certainly more than acquaintances. He knew Chub had a wife, well, allegedly anyway, but he'd never met the woman. Biz said she was like Vera, the much-maligned but never seen spouse of Norm's on 'Cheers'. Mike Babcock, an insurance adjuster for one of the big companies downtown theorized she was under concrete in Chub's garage, just another false claim casualty. Tommy Cynovich wanted to see a picture and even demanded to be put on the phone with the mystery missus. Chubster merely chuckled, declared he would never bring the little woman into a dive like 'Sully's, nor would he allow her to mingle with the miscreants and degenerates who congregated there, present company excepted of course.

There was no mention of little MaGees so the lack of pictures in Chubster's wallet or on his phone was never challenged. Even the denizens of 'Sully's knew better than to pry into a couples' lack of children. More often than not, the reason would be either sad or tragic and the big flat-screens behind the bar had enough sad and tragic to go around.

As far as Max could tell, Chubster had not spent significant time in jail, at least not in the years Max had been slinging suds at the 'Chew'. If Chub had some sort of ongoing relationship with King it would explain the quick exits, week long absences and sudden windfalls he infrequently showed up with. The fact that he never did seem to disappear for any significant length of time was actually encouraging. Maybe these guys really did know what they were doing.

Max walked slowly down the unfamiliar streets. This was not his milieu, he thought, though he couldn't for the life of him remember how he knew that word. Must have read it and looked it up. It certainly wasn't tossed around at 'Sully's when they were discussing neighborhoods and ballparks. No, these streets were different. The shops were more upscale, the restaurants more elegant, the bars more reserved. No one was asking him for spare change, no one was yelling or swearing and the only cops he saw looked bored. It was, he decided, nice. A hundred, fifty grand would not put him there but it would be a taste.

So okay, he didn't really know Chubster that well but, when you really thought about it, who in the bar did he really know that well? Most everything he knew about the regulars, they had told him themselves. There were no background checks, he wasn't vetting anybody. If they said they had a wife and kids, who was he to doubt it? If they claimed to be a veteran he took them by their word. Tony Corelli said he was a plumber and he certainly had the requisite dirty clothes and blackened fingernails to attest to such a vocation. In fact, Tony said his first wife had left him because of those fingernails. Even though his bride had held those hands on the alter, the nails well-scrubbed but still dark around the edges, knowing full well that they would be dark forever more, she'd not let go and run for the door but instead had stated her intentions to love and obey. Not too many years later, those same dirty fingernails had apparently driven her mad, like 'Lady MacBeth' and the imaginary spots. Not long after the divorce Tony found a chubby-chaser who loved him dearly, dirty digits and all, and the rotund plumber seemed to be living happily ever after, or at least as happily as someone who spends his days knee deep in sewage can be. But maybe Tony wasn't a plumber. Maybe he was a serial killer, constantly digging shallow graves, sometimes by hand. Serial killers, thought Max, probably needed a cold beer after a hard day's work just like anybody else.

And what about Joey Shostak? Word was, he'd been a great high school ballplayer who'd hurt his arm pitching for a Cubs Single A farm team. Now he wore a tie and sold cars. He still looked like an athlete and even came into 'Sully's in sweats some nights after playing in an over forty basketball league. There was no absolute proof of any schooldays glory. Joey wasn't the kind of asshole who'd bring in a yearbook or old newspaper clippings. He never bragged and only mentioned a sporting exploit if the conversation called for it.

Frannie Francis, known to her middle school students as Miss Francis, preferred drinking beers with the boys rather than chardonnay with her teaching colleagues and, after proving that she gave as good as she got, was accepted as just one of the guys. Justifiably jaded after two decades dealing with teens in the public school system, she was probably the most deserving of the regulars when it came to an after work refreshment. Max had never had a teacher like Frannie and could not recall waiting on one either. The woman could out-drink, outlast and out-wit any of the boys and was fond of letting them know. She had no concern for standard propriety, no regard for political correctness and no respect for personal boundaries. Everyone loved her.

And then there was Miss Peabody, the bar's dowager mascot and local eccentric. Peabody, was that even her real name? It was just too fitting. And why did she insist on living across the street in a second floor apartment instead of on the Hill with the other rich folks.

Rumors swirled around her and her money, much of it started by the old biddy herself. Tales of royal relations and missing husbands could never be confirmed but they certainly regaled the occasional visitors who found themselves seated beside her. Max never questioned anything she said. She was, after all, his best tipper and free entertainment to boot. So, he decided, to sum up, he didn't truly know jack about anyone. Sure, some of his customers would hand him a business card from time to time, proclaiming their professional skills but what did that really prove? He remembered his old buddy, Terry, printing up fancy cards that announced in raised gold leaf, 'Talent Agent', and Terry worked at Sears. Little did the female recipients of this token of introduction realize exactly what particular talents Terry was seeking. And, to the amazement of Max and Terry's other pals, it worked. Soon, Terry, no Brad Pitt, as his friends would frequently describe him when informing others of this simple but remarkable con, was awash in young ladies with wide eyes and short skirts. It's true that plenty of girls laughed at Terry and his preposterous card, dismissing him as just another Walmart Romeo with no look and no game. Didn't bother Terry though. As he always said, even the best ballplayers only get one hit every three at bats.

Usually when Max was lost in thought and finally reached some kind of conclusion, he felt satisfied, like he had given it his best shot and maybe even solved a problem or settled on an opinion. Not this time. So, he either took Chubster MaGee at his word or he didn't. He walked home, flipping that coin in his mind, over and over and over.

*

MONDAY

The conversation at the bar the next day was heated and Ginny came late to it. She'd overheard bits and pieces while waiting for her drinks at the service station but hadn't really caught the gist. When she finally found herself with a few minutes to spare, she wedged herself between Tony and Biz and leaned on the bar. The boys didn't appear to mind.

"What's the topic, fellas?" she asked.

"Max thinks I'm a serial killer," said Tony, smiling.

Max shook his head. "That's not what I said."

Ginny looked at Tony. "Well," she said, "I don't know if he's a serial killer or not but I do know he's a damn good tipper and isn't that what's important?"

Tony smiled. "Thanks, Ginny...I think."

"Your barman here," said an unfamiliar voice, "is merely pointing out the illusory nature of being, positing the theory that we really can't know anyone else, what they're thinking or, for that matter, what they do with their time."

Ginny stared at the new patron, the elderly gentlemen in an old suit, seated next to Joey, his overcoat draped over the empty seat beside. He sat upright, his silver hair parted perfectly, his matching mustache trimmed to just the right length. What was this guy doing in Sully's, she thought. "When did Frasier get here?" she asked.

Biz laughed out loud, almost spitting his beer. "No," he said, wiping his chin, "Max was just making conversation and he said it had occurred to him lately that he didn't really know his regulars, what they were actually like, you know, like inside thoughts, feelings, desires..."

"I believe that's what I just stated," said the old timer.

"I was just putting it in layman's terms."

"Thanks, Biz," said Ginny, "but I understood Mr...ah..."

"Vanderbilt. J.P. Vanderbilt."

"You're kidding," said Joey.

"I beg your pardon."

"Okay, Mr. J.P. Vanderbilt, I'm Ginny O'Riley and these are the boys." Vanderbilt lifted his martini. "A pleasure."

Tony emptied his mug. "Look, Max, if you don't believe I'm a plumber, you can come with me tomorrow and snake some toilets."

Max set a fresh beer in front of Tony. "I never said you weren't a plumber. I was only saying you never really know anybody. Jeez, just read the newspaper when they're asking the neighbors about some guy who beat up his wife. Oh, he was a nice guy, they say, always willing to help out."

"Now I'm a wife beater."

"No, no, no. That's not the point."

"Tony put in my dishwasher," said Joey.

"Yeah, and Joey sold me a car," said Biz.

"How come you're not curious about Frannie?" asked Tony. "Maybe she's a serial killer."

"That's an idea," said Frannie.

Max gave Tony a look. "We all know she's a teacher. She couldn't make those stories up."

"She had my buddy's kids in class," said Joey, "and they're frigging monsters."

"They're all frigging monsters," said Frannie. "But I'm curious, Tony, what else did you think I might be?"

"I don't know. I just didn't want you to feel left out."

"Aw, such a sweetie. Maybe I'll give you a reach-around later."

Tony blushed. "See, that's the thing. I never knew a teacher talked the way you do."

Frannie grinned. "I'm unique."

"Okay, everybody," said Max, "I get it. Sorry I brought it up. Let's talk about the weather for a few more hours."

Ginny was enjoying this and hoped she wouldn't get sat for a few more minutes. "Oh, Max, don't pout. I think it's a great subject. For instance, all you bozos think I'm just a waitress and a single mom. But you don't know what I do when I'm not here. You don't know what I'm up to on my days' off. Maybe," she said, winking at Max, "I'm the serial killer."

"Ginny," said Tony, "if I ever have to get done in by a serial killer, I hope it's you."

"Frannie's right," said Ginny, giving him a hug, "you are a sweetie." She backed off, made a face. "Oh, boy, sure smells like a plumber."

"Hey!" said Tony.

Ginny spotted new customers. "Gotta' go. Carry on, gentlemen."

Max watched her hurry off to greet the newcomers. Ginny was always smiling at work, always pleasant, always nice. She seemed, as far as he could tell, content. Why wasn't he?

"Hey, Max," said Tony, "you're daydreaming again. You started this conversation."

"Yeah, one of the great regrets of my life."

"No, no," said Joey, "this is good. For instance, none of us really know what Biz does."

"We don't even know his real name, do we?" asked Frannie.

"What do you guys think I do?" asked Biz, obviously enjoying the chit-chat even if it wasn't about movies or TV.

Joey leaned back, looked Biz up and down. "You live at home with your mother in the house you grew up in. You're downstairs now, in the partially finished basement. You work from home designing video-games for a small company in California and you have every season of 'Saved by the Bell' on disc."

Biz looked appalled, Tony amazed, Max amused. "Wow, Joey," said Max, "that was impressive. Tony, your turn."

"All right," said Tony, "give me a second...Okay, you were a wiz in high school, got accepted to college at sixteen, couldn't handle it, had a nervous breakdown, dropped out and now live on the meager earnings from your job as a parking garage attendant and a small trust fund set up by your grandfather."

"Jesus," said Biz, "I'm getting depressed."

"Hold on," said Max, "Frannie?"

Biz put his head in his hands, stared at the bar. "Oh, no."

"You did go to college but spent most of your time playing 'Dungeons and Dragons' and not getting laid. You graduated but ended up working for the 'Geek Squad' at 'Best Buy' until you started your own little computer repair company and have grown it to three employees. You spend your free time perusing Eastern European mail-order brides on the internet when you're not watching television."

Biz shook his head. "Oh, my God."

"Hold on," said Max, "my turn."

Vanderbilt set his martini down on one of 'Sully's wrinkled coasters. "I must say," he said, "this is far more interesting than the typical lounge conversation."

Max ignored him. "Okay, okay," said Max, "Biz is not your real name." He paused as everyone looked at him expectantly. "Your real name is Sheldon..."

Biz couldn't believe it. "Sheldon."

"You're a low level IRS agent who works in a small office setting up clandestine rendezvous and money laundering stings for the more senior agents. On Friday nights you're part of the all male dance revue at 'Eggs & Sausage' on Second Ave. How'd I do?" Max looked around at the astounded, speechless faces of his small clientele. He was pleased with himself, satisfied that he had steered the discussion back from its precipitous dip into deep thought to a more comfortable air of fatuous, ball busting banter.

Finally, Biz lifted his head, spoke up. "What the Hell, people? I thought we were friends. Although, Max, I do give you props for creativity. But man...Anyway, my real is Howard, I'm an IT guy for Symtac over on the East side. I own a condo, have a number of long distance relationships with girls I met on 'Plenty O' Fish' and I'm writing a spec script for 'Law and Order'. Happy?"

"What's a spec script?" asked Tony.

"Take it easy, Biz," said Max. "Don't get mad. We're just giving you the business...The business, get it?"

Everyone but Biz laughed, even Vanderbilt.

"You're a riot," said Biz, trying not to laugh.

Two heavy set men in suits sat down at the end of the bar. Max glanced at the boys, muttered "long distance runners", then went down to serve them. He needed to concentrate on his job, he thought. He was starting to drive himself crazy. He was bringing too much attention to himself, raising eyebrows. Either do the deed for King or don't, but make a damn decision. It wasn't that complicated. He'd said yes but it wasn't too late to say no. He took care of the newcomers and walked back to the crew, hoping the conversation had moved on.

"Hey, Max," said Joey, "guess what Rockefeller here used to do for a living."

"That's Vanderbilt," said the older man.

"Yuh, right, whatever. Guess what he did for work."

Max had his back to the gang as he rang in drinks at the computer terminal. "I was kind of hoping we'd moved on to a new subject by now."

"It was your idea."

"Don't remind me."

Max turned around, looked at the anxious faces awaiting his less than educated guess. Apparently no new topics were on the table so he may as well make the best of it, not turn it into anything bigger than the pointless exercise he'd created and the others were enjoying. He appraised the well dressed gentleman in front of him. "Okay, he's a retired astronaut."

"Wrong," said Biz.

"I give up," said Max.

"He was a friggin' gigolo," said Joey. "Can you believe that? Women paid him for dates."

Max, like every other long time bartender, barber and hair stylist, thought he had heard it all but, he had to admit, this was a new one. Vanderbilt was smiling, pleased that he had impressed 'Sully's motley crew of patrons. "First of all," he said, "thanks, Joey, for that concise definition of the word gigolo, though I must say I was already familiar with the term. And secondly, why in God's name, Mr...ah..."

"Vanderbilt."

"Mr. Vanderbilt, why would you admit that rather personal information to this group of knuckleheads?"

"Hey," said Tony.

"No offense, boys," said Max.

"None taken," said Joey.

"First of all," began Vanderbilt, "I was under the impression that the main point of this chat was honesty. And secondly, I was no common street gigolo. I was a gentleman escort. I accompanied refined ladies who occasionally required a discreet paramour. Gigolos are merely male prostitutes, providing physical service to women in need. I offered my clients far more than that."

"Are you saying you didn't bang 'em," said Frannie.

Vanderbilt looked appalled. "These were sophisticated women, professional women, widows, divorcees, busy women without time to seek proper companionship but sometimes in need of physical or emotional comfort. I supplied whatever was required."

Frannie looked at Max. "Sounds like he banged 'em to me."

"Goodness," said Mr. Vanderbilt.

"Okay, okay, Mr. V. Take it easy. Don't get all huffy. She meant it as a compliment."

"Oh, yes, of course. I tend to get a bit defensive about my career."

"Are you kidding," said Tony. "I'd be bragging, telling everyone, writing my memoirs even."

"Thank you," said Vanderbilt. "You're too kind." He turned to Max. "Uh, excuse me, uh, Max, I believe it was."

"Yes, sir."

"Please, if you don't mind, I'd like to buy these fine fellows and the lady a drink."

"You bet. But let me just check." Max addressed the others. "Would you fine fellows care for another? You too, Frannie."

"Is this a rhetorical question?" asked Tony.

"Thanks," said Joey, "now you're being too kind."

"Remember," said Frannie, "just 'cause you buy me a drink doesn't mean I'm gonna' do you."

"My word," said the old buck, but quickly noticed the others were laughing and relaxed.

"Thanks," said Biz, "very nice of you."

Max mixed up another martini for Vanderbilt, then let it sit in the metal shaker to chill while he fetched beers for the boys and a Dewars on the rocks for Fran. He was happy that the subject he'd foolishly proffered earlier had run its course. And he was more than a little bit intrigued by the older man. Odd that he'd shown up at the bar soon after Max's meeting with King. Max recalled skimming a book once that proposed as one of its main suppositions that there were no coincidences. He strained the martini, put the ice in a rocks glass and set them both in front of the new guest. He was roused from his thoughts by a familiar voice.

"Hey, Max," Ginny called, "a little help."

She was standing at the service end of the bar, though Max hadn't heard the sound of the drink ticket dispenser. "One sec," he said, ringing up the cocktails on Vanderbilt's tab. He set it on the bar, headed down to Ginny. "What's up," said Max. "I don't see a ticket."

"I figured it out," she said.

"Figured what out?"

"You." She was grinning now. "I figured you out. The reason you're acting so weird. Business opportunity, lots to think about, what do we really know about people. This is all about Chubster. You're involved with one of his lame-brained ideas. I warned you and now you're having doubts." She folded her arms across her chest, smug, satisfied, waiting for his response.

Max knew Ginny was smart and that there was no good reason to bullshit her. "I've known Chubster a lot longer than you have," he said.

"And?"

"And once in awhile he does have a good idea."

"Really?"

"Yes, really."

"Are you going to tell me this great idea?"

"I can't."

"Max, we tell each other all sorts of stuff."

"I know. You're right. Usually we do. But this time I just can't. Maybe later if I decide to go along with it. But right now...I'm sorry." He glanced over his shoulder, saw a couple seating themselves, turned to go. "We'll talk later, okay?" Ginny said nothing. "Okay?"

"Okay," she said.

*

Max was right, Ginny thought. She hadn't known Chubster as long as he had. But she felt she'd known him well enough. She'd always fancied herself a good judge of character except, of course, when it came to boyfriend material. And Chubster was not boyfriend material. He was a customer and customers were her field of expertise. She prided herself on her ability to size up belly-achers and cheapskates within minutes of they're being seated. She could tell pretty quickly if the guys flirting with her were being jerks or just having fun. She could look over a couple and quickly decide whether to chat or leave them alone. Above all, she was well aware that some customers, not many but some, were impossible to please. You could kill them with kindness, you could get them new meals, take items off the check, field their complaints, all the while keeping your composure and never once losing that smile and still, still they were unhappy. Maybe they were in a mood, maybe they had a bad day, maybe, just maybe, they were a plain old asshole.

Ginny was working on a theory in regard to assholes. She and everyone else in the world seemed to agree on one thing, that yes, indeed, some people were simply assholes. And yet, not one person, not a single one, actually considered themselves an asshole. How could that be, she wondered. Self-perception was one thing, acknowledging ones' flaws another, but admitting to assholery was apparently an impossibility. Her theory, as she was quick to admit when it came up in conversation, which it often did, was obviously a work in progress.

Ginny could generally get a read on her fellow employees as well after only a few shifts. She determined which line-cooks wouldn't last the year and which busboys would rifle an unattended purse if given the chance. Managers were easy. Come in on time, do your job, bring no drama and they'd leave you alone. Screw up and they wouldn't. Hostesses were tricky. They came in all ages and attitudes. It took Ginny a bit longer to figure out whether they could be more easily swayed by psychology, bribery or flattery. Inevitably, she knew she'd become their favorite server and soon she would be accumulating tables with wit and wiles. But with warmth and kindness, too, she felt. She needed to reassure herself that she was a good person and not some manipulative tip whore.

Chubster was, of course, a customer and he fell into one of Ginny's least favorite categories, the big talkers. All the big guys with big lines and big tales and big plans. They wanted you and everyone in the vicinity to know who they've met, where they've been, what they've done and where they're going. And if you were lucky, maybe they'd let you in on their next adventure, meet their famous friend, accompany them to the exclusive party. Oh, please, thought Ginny. Who fell for such nonsense?

Almost as bad were the sweet talkers. Their voices were lower, their intentions romantic. The compliments flowed out like water from a fountain, how pretty you were, how smart, how funny. They'd never met anyone quite like you, with the same sass, the same charm. They looked you in the eye and whispered in your ear, made no mention of your ample bosom or shapely derriere for wasn't that what all the 'how to' books on picking up chicks told them to avoid? Flatter her eyes, not her boobs. Admire her shoes and notice her perfume. What a big, heaping pile of crap, Ginny thought.

She had to admit that Chubster was not a sweet talker. He'd never hit on her and supposedly had a wife at home. And as far as big talkers went, he wasn't bad. He wasn't as loud or as cocky as most. But still. He did have some con man in him, offering up his ideas like so much snake oil, using his huckster's rapid line of patter to convince you that investing your hard earned cash would be a most wise and logical decision.

The notion that Max had finally fallen for one of Chubster's misbegotten endeavors perplexed her no end. One of the things she found most endearing about Max was his utter lack of pretension. He was real. He wasn't a struggling actor or musician or writer. He wasn't simply biding time until the perfect opportunity to open his own place presented itself. He was simply a bartender, a good guy, a good listener and a good friend. When she'd let him know during her first week at Sully's that she didn't date fellow employees nor did she, as the kids said, hook up, he hadn't seemed fazed in the least. He didn't laugh, he didn't argue, didn't cajole. He treated her like a buddy and, at the end of the day, you did not bullshit your buddy. And so, she felt, if and when they did speak later about his involvement with Mr. Chubster MaGee, the last thing he'd do was lie.

"Excuse me, miss." Ginny was deep in thought but she did hear the voice the second time. "Excuse me. I say, excuse me."

Ginny glanced to her right and saw it was the old man, Vanderbilt, trying to get her attention. She hoped he hadn't decided to come out of retirement and was looking for new clients. "Can I help you?" she asked.

35

"Perhaps. I was wondering if you were familiar with a Miss Peabody who, I've been told, does sometimes frequent this establishment?"

"Well yes," said Ginny, "I do know a Miss Peabody who frequents this establishment. And I have to say, it's a bit more frequent than sometimes."

"I'm afraid," said Vanderbilt, "you're making light of the way I speak."

"No, not at all." Ginny sidled over to the old timer, put her hand on his shoulder. "I'm just having fun with you. That's what we do here at Sully's. We have fun. Right, boys?"

"Like chimps at a buffet," said Joey.

"I'm giddy," said Tony.

Frannie raised her glass. "To fun."

Biz looked at Vanderbilt but had nothing. He glanced at Ginny. "That's okay, Biz," she said, "take your time." She turned back to Vanderbilt. "Now then, Mr. V., what is it you want with Miss Peabody? She an old customer?"

"Oh no, no, not at all. Miss Peabody is a dear old friend. We've known each other for a very long time."

"Well then," said Ginny, "maybe you could enlighten us. Just what is Miss Peabody's story. We've been trying to figure that lady out for a long time."

"Yeah," offered Joey, "she's obviously got manners and money but she comes in here and hangs out with us."

"What are you trying to say?" asked Tony, straining to keep a straight face.

Joey wasn't sure Tony was kidding. "You know, she should be over at 'The Ritz' or 'The Four Seasons'"

Ginny ignored them and addressed Vanderbilt. "So anyways..."

"Oh, I couldn't possibly speak behind Margaret's back. I can only tell you that she is a singularly warm and caring woman who always lived life to the fullest. But you probably know that already."

"Well," said Biz, "at least now we know her first name.."

As much as Ginny was enjoying this new subject and the way it had alleviated her wandering mind from Max's questionable adventures with Chubster MaGee, she knew she had to get back to work. She could sense Sully giving her the stink eye from the kitchen doorway. "Okay, boys," she said, "keep grilling Mr. V. here and I'll be back." She hurried off, all four men watching her walk away and Frannie watching them watching.

"See anything you like?" asked Max, returning from the other end of the bar.

"As a matter of fact," said Tony, grinning.

Mr. Vanderbilt got up from his stool, pulled a money clip from his pocket and surveyed the surroundings. "Well, gentlemen, as much as I've enjoyed our conversation, I'm afraid I must be off. Max, my tab please, if it's not too much trouble."

Max pointed to the small piece of paper tucked neatly into a shot glass at Vanderbilt's seat.

The older man removed it, glanced at the small print, turned to Joey. "Excuse me, Joseph, I'm afraid I've forgotten my reading glasses. Could you tell me the total, please."

Joey looked at the slip. "Thirty nine, fifty."

Vanderbilt set the tab on the bar and placed a hundred dollar bill on top of it. He turned to Max. "I believe there's enough there for another round and a modest gratuity for yourself. It's been a pleasure and I shall be back." He extended his hand.

Max shook it. "Thank you. Nice to meet you and we hope to see you soon. Should we tell Miss Peabody you were hoping to see her?"

"That would be most kind."

Mr. Vanderbilt took his jacket, placed it over his arm and shook hands with Joey, Tony and Biz, grasped Frannie's hand with both of his. They thanked him for the drinks, told him not to be a stranger and that they'd see him again. They watched him exit 'Sully's and by the time they turned back to Max, he was already pouring their beers.

"Well," said Tony, "that was interesting."

Max stared at the taps as he topped off another mug. "Every day is different."

★

TUESDAY

Max spent the next day wrestling with his conscience but in the end, the lure of the money, the chance to break out of the monotony, the opportunity for excitement and risk all won out. He found himself walking down an unfamiliar sidewalk with Chubster MaGee. Chub had come in the day before, somewhat agitated, and insisted that Max accompany him on this mission. They were in the East End now, a particularly shabby section of the city, pawn shops, barber shops and chop shops. Chubster said they were going to see 'Cranky Sam' and his crew to set up the seed money venture. Max had his usual reservations but the idea man proclaimed that this was all just part of the gig, that it was a preliminary introduction, an errand of sorts. Max really had no desire at this point to meet anyone else but Chub had sat on a stool for hours, slowly chipping away at the bartender's resolve and Chubster was, if nothing else, persistent. Besides, he said, Cranky Sam ran a legitimate business and Max might want his car serviced there some day.

Cranky Sam, thought Max, as they strode by small Hispanic grocerias and second hand clothing stores, here we go with the nicknames again. Was this another ironic one? Was Cranky Sam actually going to be a jovial fellow, warm and good-natured? Chubster took his mind off that speculation.

"Look," he said," you should probably know that Cranky Sam is a little person."

"A little person?"

"Yeah, you know, a midget, or maybe a dwarf. I don't know. I'm pretty sure a midget. But they prefer little people anyway."

"They?"

"Yeah, all his employees are little people, too. Dwarfs, midgets, whatever. Just don't want you to be surprised and stare at them. Sam doesn't like that."

"He might get Cranky." Max smiled.

Chubster did not. "Yes, he might get cranky. He gets pissed off pretty easily. Ergo the nickname."

"Ergo?" asked Max.

"I may have used that improperly. But you get the point."

"I was kind of hoping the nickname was ironic."

"Not this time. But no worries. We treat him with courtesy and respect, politely explain things and be on our way. It's all part of the plan."

"Oh good," said Max, "as long as it's part of the plan."

Chubster ignored the sarcasm and ceased walking. They were standing in front of a large corrugated steel door. Above the sign was a faded sign, "Cranky Sam's Body Shop."

"I guess he likes the nickname."

Chubster gave Max a look and pressed a button at the side of the door. "Remember what I said, be polite, show respect and don't stare."

They heard the mechanical door's motor turn on and watched as it slowly opened. Max had entered plenty of car garages over the years but this one was different. It was clean and neat, almost immaculate, not a single scattered tool or engine part. Nothing lay on the freshly swept floor. The walls were covered with instruments of the trade, all carefully arranged without a cobweb in sight. Five big, shiny red toolboxes dominated the space and any extra tires and rims were stacked in the corners. The tattered fold-outs and girlie calendars that Max had encountered in every other auto shop he'd had the misfortune to visit were nowhere to be seen. The only calendar he spotted was a 'World Wildlife' and even featured the correct month. Four extremely short men occupied themselves with vehicles in various states of disrepair, three of them standing under hydraulic lifts, the fourth laying on a low rolling sled made for under carriage work. None of them, at least from a distance, appeared remotely dirty. The door slid down behind them and a fifth man, apparently Cranky Sam himself stood facing them as they entered, his arms folded, a scowl on his face. He was the smallest of the bunch. His blue mechanic's shirt and pants were spotless; he smelled of cologne. He was bald-headed and his pate glistened as though polished rather than shaved.

"Hey, Sam," said Chubster.

"That's Cranky Sam to you."

"Right, sorry. Good afternoon, Cranky Sam." Chubster smiled but Sam seemed to have last smiled during the Reagan administration. He looked at Max like he'd spotted a huge stain on his spotless floor.

"Who's this asshole?"

"This is Max. He's a friend of King's."

"Nice to meet you," said Max.

"No it isn't. It definitely is not nice to meet me. And I doubt this is a social call."

Apparently, thought Max, Chubster wasn't kidding about the non-ironic nickname. His nickname theory obviously needed work. The other little people were finishing up whatever repairs they'd been working on and beginning to wander over. Max tried hard not to think about 'The Wizard of Oz' but couldn't help wondering what kind of cinematic comparisons Biz would be making to these miniature mechanics.

"You know why we're here," said Chubster. "King wanted us to have a little chat."

"King." Cranky Sam virtually spat the name. "That fat, pompous, arrogant bastard!"

"That's the one," said Chubster, grinning again.

"That motherfucking son-of-a-bitch," said Sam. "That two-faced cocksucker!"

Chubster reached in his coat pocket and all four of Cranky Sam's associates started toward him. Chub put up one hand and extracted a gold poker chip with the other. He held it out to Sam. "King says you owe him a favor. A big favor."

"That no good, lying piece of shit says I owe him a favor."

"Is he mistaken?" asked Max, as sincerely as possible.

"Oh," said Sam, staring at Max, "now you're asking questions?"

Max held up both hands. "Sorry."

"Well," said Chubster, "is he?"

"Is he what?"

"Is he mistaken?"

Cranky Sam walked slowly toward Chubster who was trying unsuccessfully not to look nervous. Sam held out his hand, palm up. Chubster glanced at Max who pointed at the chip. Chubster placed it carefully into Cranky Sam's tiny hand and took a step back. "No," said Sam, staring at the chip, "he's not mistaken."

Chubster did his best not to audibly sigh. He waited as long as his rapidly spinning brain cells would allow before speaking. "Should we go over the plan?"

Cranky Sam looked at him as though he'd come across a pinhead at the circus. "No, you fucking idiot," he said, placing the chip in his shirt pocket, "why don't me and the boys just beat you to death with a tire iron and then we'll all try to guess what the plan was."

Max had never seen his friend at such a loss for words. All Chub could get out was a feeble "what?"

"I'm kidding," Sam assured him with only the slightest hint of a smile. He glanced back at his minions who appeared amused but uneasy. "Jesus, this guy's got no sense of humor." Now his employees laughed out loud. Sam turned back to Max and Chubster. "Why the Hell would we kill you before we heard the plan?"

Chubster seemed to regain his composure somewhat. "Well," he said, smiling weakly, "we were kind of hoping for no killing at all."

"Were you? Okay, we'll table that idea for now. You tell me the plan and it'd better be fucking brilliant."

"Well, ah, it's more King's plan than mime and..."

"Don't mention that fat fucks name again or there will be killing. Come on, let's go in the back." Sam headed for a door at the rear of the garage. Chubster and Max followed but the pint-sized shop boss stopped midway, turned and addressed Max. "Not you, just Chubster. You stay here." He continued to the door as Chub shrugged like a man resigned to his fate.

Max stood still, watched the pair exit through the door. The little motorheads in overalls stared at him like vultures eyeing roadkill. Once again Max wished he'd listened to Ginny. But, he had to admit, this was a lot more interesting than his typical day at the bar. He was frightened and he was nervous, but he was alive. He could feel the adrenaline pumping as one of the crew, a powerfully built midget whose name-tag identified him as Jim, came closer, stopping a foot or so away and looking him up and down. "How tall are you?" the undersized employee asked.

Max glanced at the other mechanics awaiting his reply. "Five foot, ten," he said. A long, uncomfortable pause followed as Max awaited a second question. There appeared to be none coming. Maybe, he figured, they were having a conversation. "How tall are you?" he asked his inquisitor.

"Why the Hell would you ask that?"

Max couldn't help himself, never could. "Who are you," he said, "Cranky Jim?"

"Funny. That's funny," said Jim without a trace of a smile. "We got a comedian. I think I saw him on 'HBO'. Did you have a special on 'HBO'?"

Max had never possessed much of a filter. He was well liked and witty so it had never been a problem with friends and family and came in rather handy at the bar where abusing and ridiculing the customers in a fraternal tone seemed to somehow make them feel more comfortable. But now, when he was greatly outnumbered by a band of ominous small folks, all of whom appeared to have spent considerable time at the gym, now was probably not the best time to go that route. Still, he stared at Jim. "'NetFlix,'" he said.

Jim looked confused. "What?"

"NetFlix," said Max. "The special was on 'NetFlix.'" The other diminutive car jockeys seemed to be advancing toward him slowly though it was difficult to tell with the slight movements of their tiny feet. "I'm kidding," said Max, smiling broadly.

"We don't kid," said Jim, serious as a hurricane.

"Sorry, I didn't see the sign."

"You don't quit, do you? You got a problem with little people?"

Max knew he had to show restraint, to quit while he was behind; no more funny stuff. He could probably handle two of the mechanics but all four at once was a beating waiting to happen. "No, no problem," said Max. "I'm sorry. I guess I'm a little nervous."

"Nervous," said Jim, spitting on the concrete floor. He walked by Max, shaking his head in disgust. Max wanted to ask him if he had a problem with big people but for once in his life kept his mouth shut and instead watched the miserable little grouch reach the steel plated mens' room door and disappear behind it. The others now seemed disinterested and made their way to the tool room lockers like middle school students disappointed by the cancellation of a scheduled courtyard fight.

Max decided the best course of action at that time would be to just stay put and do or say nothing until Chubster emerged from his sit down with the appropriately named Cranky Sam. Unfortunately, those unoccupied moments enabled him to reflect on his current situation. Though he hadn't yet done anything morally wrong or officially illegal, it certainly appeared he was headed down that slippery slope. Backing out now was possibly still an option but not for much longer. Max's train of indecisive thought was interrupted by the reappearance of Chubster and Sam from the back of the garage. Neither looked particularly happy but Chub was in one piece, so apparently Sam had kept his temper in check. Chubster was a man on a mission as he quickly strode toward Max, took him by the elbow and maneuvered him to the door from which they'd originally entered.

Max spoke quietly. "How'd it go?"

Chubster shushed him with one finger and the two men stood in front of the large steel door, waiting patiently. Chub turned back and looked at Cranky Sam. "I'll see you on Halloween." Sam made no reply but pressed the buzzer to raise the door.

Max glanced back and smiled. "Have a nice day!" he shouted.

Chubster pushed him outside as the door closed behind them, looked at Max sternly. "He doesn't like wiseguys."

"I don't think he likes anybody."

"Come on, let's go." They began walking back the way they'd come.

"Well?"

"Well what?"

"How did your little meeting go?"

"Fine."

"Fine? That's it?"

"Look, Max, you're better off knowing as little as possible."

"So why did I have to come along?"

"Moral support."

"You put my life in danger for moral support?"

"Your life was never in danger."

"Really. Could have fooled me."

"They're just a grumpy bunch, that's all. You'd probably be grumpy too if you were three feet tall. Besides, King would have been really pissed if they killed us." Max didn't even bother with a reply to that pitiful reassurance. "Just be cool, okay," continued Chubster. "In this situation, ignorance for you really is bliss."

"All right," said Max, "if you say so."

They retraced their steps in silence, past the rundown storefronts and over-flowing garbage cans, walls of inner city graffiti, some of it profane, some quite beautiful, past the unemployed hustlers with plans even more outlandish than Chubster's, past the old Hispanic ladies, not much taller than Cranky Sam and twice as wide, lugging bags from the grocerias, determined to make their way home without distraction.

Plenty of time to think, mixed emotions and all. On the one hand, Chubster was undoubtedly correct; best to be left out of this shady loop and the less he knew the better. On the other hand, his curiosity overwhelming him, Max felt he could at least have a peripheral conversation. "You know," he said, "not every little person is grumpy."

"Really. I didn't know you were friends with many little people. Haven't seen too many at the bar either."

"The munchkins were pleasant," said Max.

"The munchkins were fictional."

"Good point."

They walked another block in silence. "You know," said Chub, "interesting thing is Cranky Sam has a beautiful wife. I am not kidding. Smoking hot."

"No way."

"Yes way. At least that's what I heard. And listen to this. She's regular sized."

"Come on."

"I kid you not. It's the craziest thing. Maybe we'll meet her some day, get to check her out." Chubster paused. "Probably best if we don't though. You think he's cranky now. I hear he's super jealous."

"And she puts up with it?"

"I guess. It's unbelievable. They say she adores that little asshole."

They walked on, silent again, both men contemplating the injustice of the universe. It was bad enough, Max thought, that the pool of available women was already lessened by gold diggers, cougars, sugar babies and rock n'roll groupies. Now he had to add midget lovers to the list. Sure, there were girls who didn't mind dating bartenders and there were even some who thought the job was cool. But there certainly wasn't a category for mixology mollies or websites and chat rooms for same. Max had to work hard for some TLC. He wasn't a man in uniform and he didn't play pro ball. He wasn't powerful and he wasn't connected. He was in the same group as insurance salesmen, accountants and lab technicians. He had to earn it. Before he could become more aggravated, Chubster broke the silence.

"Have you ever dated a midget?"

"What?"

"You know, have you ever slept with a little person? I'm just wondering if maybe it goes the same way sometimes. You know, maybe there's some pint size cuties who are attracted to guys our size."

"No, Chubster, I've never slept with a little person."

"Yeah, me neither. Does kind of fuel the imagination though. World of possibilities and all that, if you catch my drift."

Max gave him a look. "I suppose so."

"I mean think of the positions."

"Okay, I get it. Let's move on. What was that about Halloween back there?"

"I thought we decided you were on a need to know basis."

"Just trying to change the subject," said Max.

"The seed money venture will take place on Halloween. That's all you need to know right now. We talked about this. You're better off staying out of the loop."

"No, no, you're right. It's just, I don't know, I'm so curious. I don't know what exactly is going on, I'm still not sure why you chose me and for the life of me, I can't believe I signed up for all this."

"You signed up for this because it's exciting and chances are you're going to make a pile of dough."

"What do you mean chances are?"

"Well, my friend, nothing in life is guaranteed."

Right again, thought Max. There are no sure things. He knew that. Everyone knew that.

Things happen. Things go wrong. Like the song said, that's life. He watched the other pedestrians passing by. People headed home, people headed to work, people running errands, everyone bound for somewhere, resigned, bored, exhausted. No one looked excited. No one looked happy. Max thought of the old body snatcher movies he'd seen as a kid, with their visions of humans possessed by aliens and turned into pods, robotic, emotionless shells of their formerly animated selves. Had he missed the news? Was there an invasion while they were in the garage? He glanced at Chubster who seemed as empty as everyone else. Max pictured Ginny and hoped they hadn't gotten to her shell; that would be a shame.

A few blocks later and Max was through trying to amuse himself. His thoughts had again turned serious as he prepared to part ways with Chubster. One thing was certain, it had been an interesting day. Chub stopped at a corner, turned and extended his hand. "Well, that was interesting, huh?"

Max smiled. "Yuh, I guess you could say that."

"You guess?"

"Chubster, every day with you is interesting."

"Aw, shucks."

"So," said Max, "now what?"

"Well, we've got a few days til Halloween. You'll see me at the bar and I'll give you the necessary updates."

Another look from Max. "You're going to give the necessary updates. After that are you going to debrief me with some intel?"

"Now, you see, Max, you keep asking why I chose you for this mission and there it is. It's because you're funny. You're a funny guy. I didn't want to pick a boring guy with no sense of humor."

Max played along. "So all that stuff you said about being honest and dependable was just bullshit?"

Chubster didn't hesitate. "Absolute bullshit."

"Okay," said Max, smiling, "just checking."

Chubster grinned. "I'll see you at 'Sully's."

"You bet."

Max watched Chubster go, then walked off in the opposite direction. You bet? When did he start saying 'you bet' he asked himself. What was he, an old cowpoke? Jesus.

*

WEDNESDAY

Max arrived at 'Sully's the next afternoon precisely at four forty five for his five o'clock shift just as he always did. He was nothing if not consistent. He had decided a long time ago that being a man of routine made life easier. Less decisions. If you knew what you were going to eat every Monday morning, then that left more time for deep thinking. That was the theory anyways. Not that he'd filled up all his spare time with deductive reasoning or philosophical epiphanies. On the contrary, he seemed to have simply supplied himself with more space for useless mind wandering and random observations. Pieces of forgotten dreams, snippets of pop songs and past sporting events cruised the empty chambers of his brain. But maybe routine wasn't so great after all. Maybe he should be more spontaneous. The decision to join in Chubster's latest get rich quick scheme was pretty damn spontaneous so his new theory would be tested soon enough.

Miss Peabody was already seated on her regular stool and Ginny was standing beside her. Sully was nowhere in sight, probably in his office at the computer watching English soccer or Japanese porn. Millie, the only bartender older than Max, was behind the taps, waiting on the blue collar types who got off work at three or four. No sign of Chubster or 'Sully's newest patron, Mr. Vanderbilt. Max clocked in, then stood behind Millie and rested his hands on her shoulders.

"How's my girl," he said.

Ginny looked his way. "Hey, I thought I was your girl."

"Get in line, Toots," said Millie, as Max rubbed her shoulders.

"Well," said Miss Peabody, "I gave Max an extremely generous tip the other day and he said I was his girl."

"Geez," said Biz, seeming to appear, as ever, out of nowhere. "I wish somebody was my girl."

"Listen, hon," said Millie, extracting her self from Max's gentle hands and walking toward Biz, "you tip like Miss Peabody here and I'll be whatever you want." She winked at the grinning regulars as she cashed out her last few checks. Millie was a great winker. Max had always admired her optical dexterity. She'd obviously been winking for years, developing an astonishing arsenal of winks. She could do the quick side wink, letting others know she was conning whomever she seemed to be sincerely addressing. Or the straight forward 'just kidding' wink.

She had a marvelously slow, sexy wink, rarely displayed but quite dramatic when employed. Max had even witnessed her wink through tears, a confusing demonstration but potent nonetheless. He himself had never been able to wink. Though it hadn't been a great hindrance in life, he'd always envied those who could. When, in his youth, he had attempted a wink, it appeared as though he had something in his eye or was merely trying to blink. Naturally, he soon desisted in even trying and resolved to simply carry on, winkless. He did, however, become a fairly adept whistler and felt that skill somewhat compensated for the lack of the other.

Everyone, including Max, loved Millie. She was old school, tough but fair. She could banter with the best, flirt with the lonely, comfort the distressed. In her time, she'd shut off cops and priests and everyone in between. She made every man who sat at her bar feel like they'd known her for years or soon would. To the female customers, she was like an old sorority sister, someone you could trust with a secret or ask for advice. She still had a decent figure and, most agreed, was quite attractive for a woman of her age. Though she wore no wedding ring, better for tips she said, Max knew there was a husband at home and three grown kids. Her history was a bit cloudy and while she professed to have tended bar forever, a few tattoos and acquaintances indicated otherwise.

Millie grabbed her pocketbook and turned to the regulars. "All right, folks, time to get out on the street and make some real money." She gave a 'thumbs up' sign, winked and smiled broadly. "Good night and God bless."

Max watched her go with great affection. He appreciated people with a sense of humor and distrusted those without. Thank goodness for people like Millie and Ginny. Max felt laughter was one of life's great pleasures, right up there with good food and good sex and besides, if you didn't have a sense of humor in the restaurant business, you'd probably end up stabbing someone with a steak knife.

Max ambled over to the familiar faces around the bar, nodding as he went. "Biz...Ginny...Miss Peabody..."

"Good afternoon, Max," said Miss P., formal as ever, at least until her third cocktail kicked in.

Biz nodded. "Hey, Max."

Ginny grinned. "Hey, Maximillian."

"It's Maximus," said Max.

Miss Peabody said, "I've always been fond of the name Maximillian."

"What about Maximus?" asked Max.

"It's rather brutish, don't you think?"

Ginny laughed. "I concur."

Biz looked confused. "I thought it was just plain Max."

Max shook his head. "That's me, just plain Max." He looked at Ginny. "See what you started." He turned and hurried off to greet two new businessmen at the far end of the bar. Ginny watched him go, smiling. She stopped when she noticed Miss Peabody was staring at her.

"When, my dear" asked the elderly patron, "are you going to admit to yourself that you have a crush on that man?"

"A crush?" Ginny looked shocked. "What. I don't have a crush on Max. He's just a nice guy and a good friend. Besides, I don't go out with co-workers."

"Or customers," Biz chimed in.

"Well then, I'm afraid one of you is going to have to quit."

Ginny tried to laugh it off. "Oh, please," she said, "Max and I don't feel that way. We're friends." She paused, glanced at Biz. "Without benefits."

Max returned. "So, what's the topic?"

Biz said, "Ginny's dating policy."

"What about it?"

"How she won't go out with customers."

Max looked at Ginny. "Or co-workers."

"If Tom Cruise was a customer," said Biz, "bet she'd go out with him."

Ginny had had enough. "Exception to every rule, Biz. Look," she said, "the real topic is how to get more dirt out of Miss Peabody here concerning our recent visitor, Mr. Vanderbilt."

"Oh, yeah," said Max. "The old man whore who came in yesterday." He glanced at Miss Peabody and regretted the description immediately. The elderly barfly was appalled.

"What?" she croaked.

Ginny put her hand on Miss Peabody's shoulder. "He's kidding. It's a joke. He calls all the single male customers that." Ginny stared at Max, who needed no further prodding.

"That's right, Miss P. You know me, always goofing around. I'll try to clean up my act a little."

"Yes, please do. I don't believe I've ever heard such a term before. Goodness."

"Well," said Max, "he certainly seemed like a very nice gentleman."

"And generous," Biz chimed in.

"Yes," said Miss Peabody, apparently recovered from the previous shock. "He's a lovely man. We go back quite a way, though I must admit we lost touch and haven't seen each other in over twenty years. Is he still handsome?"

"I'd do him," said Ginny. Now it was her turn to apologize. "Oh, sorry. Just kidding. We've really got to get more serious around here. Anyway, he still looks good, very distinguished, and well dressed, too."

"Yes, that sounds like Jonathan. Always dressed to the nines. Do you know there was a time when some in our group thought he may be a homosexual."

"I don't think you have to worry about that," offered Max.

"No, quite right. He's actually most fond of the ladies."

"Including you?" asked Ginny.

"Including me. And what, may I ask, did he have to say about me?"

"Well," said Max, "he was pretty tight-lipped about you. Very gentlemanly."

"He said you were warm and caring," added Biz.

Miss Peabody appeared to blush. "Really?"

"Oh, yeah," said Ginny, "and he seemed mighty anxious to find you and get reacquainted. Maybe he's been carrying a torch for you all these years."

"I highly doubt that, dear. Jonathan always had his pick of the girls and even now I'm sure he would make a wonderful sugar daddy for some young chippie."

"He said he'd be back," said Max. "If you're not here the next time he shows up I'll try to nail him down to a time or get a number."

"Thank you, Max. I just hope he won't be disappointed when we do reconnect. I'm not the young woman he may recall."

"Well," said Ginny, "he's not exactly the young stud that you remember. So you're even. Besides, you're still hot. Right, boys?"

"Oh, yeah," said Biz.

"Absolutely," said Max, "I'd..." Ginny shook her head. "Agree."

Max looked at Ginny, thankful once again that she knew him so well, that she was aware of his occasional lack of filter and was willing and able to suppress his remarks when necessary. If only he'd known her years ago, maybe he would have avoided a few altercations and insults.

He smiled in gratitude and shuffled down the bar to wait on a middle aged couple who seemed genuinely pleased to be in each other's company. They were well dressed, attractive and so involved in conversation that Max had to interrupt to take their order. Though both wore wedding rings, he knew instantly they weren't married to each other. They sat diagonally, their knees almost touching, their attention to one another complete. They listened and laughed, their gaze never wandering to Max or the other customers or the big flat screen bolted to the wall above the bottles. Truly married couples, Max knew, did not sit diagonally. They sat facing the bar, looking around, checking their phones, watching the TV, hoping the bartender or someone might say or do something entertaining. They would speak to each other without turning their heads, and when they did, true interest or laughter was rare.

That was, of course, Max knew, quite the generalization. He'd seen happily married couples at the bar, chatting, listening, rubbing a shoulder or holding a hand. Just not too often. His observations in that area hadn't totally jaded his opinion of marriage as an institution but they certainly hadn't helped.

Ginny watched Max watching the couple. She had heard his theories on married couples at bars before, and though she fancied herself an optimist, a glass half full kind of gal, she knew he was usually right. After all, she'd been through it herself. She was well aware that marriage was tough, that love fades, interest wanes, passion dwindles. She wouldn't be a hard working single mom if that wasn't the case. Everyone says you have to work at marriage, she thought, but why? Why did you have to work at marriage? Who made that rule? Shouldn't you just be happy and content with your one true love? What the Hell happens?

She watched Max set up the enraptured lovebirds with tequila shots, limes and salt. They slammed down the booze, licked the salt and sucked on the limes, paused to kiss the brine from their lips, then laughed as if they'd done something truly exciting. Okay, she decided, that's enough. She put a gentle hand on Biz's back. "Oh, well," she said, "back to the grind."

"Oh, Ginny," said Miss P., "before you go, I've been meaning to ask, have you seen Mr. MaGee lately?"

"Chubster?"

"Yes, Chubster, though I can't imagine why he goes by that nomenclature. My goodness, the man's not even heavy."

"Actually," said Ginny, "I haven't seen him in a few days." She glanced down the bar. "I know Max has run into him. Why, what's up?"

"Oh, nothing, dear. It's just that sometimes he's quite entertaining with his outlandish ideas and plans."

"Entertaining, huh," said Ginny. "I guess you could say that. I'll keep an eye out."

"Oh, don't bother, Ginny. And please don't tell him that I was inquiring. I wouldn't want him to get the wrong idea, you know, thinking that I may want to invest. His schemes are most amusing but I must say I'm quite fond of my money."

"No problem, Miss P. I hear you."

Max watched out of the corner of his eye as Ginny headed back to her tables. He backed up the preoccupied couple with drinks, then thought it best to leave them be. Let them have their moment of happiness, their flash of passion. Who was he to judge? You grab joy when you can. Right or wrong is subjective, he figured, especially lately.

He made his way down the bar, checking with each patron to make sure they had everything they needed, that they were content. Biz pointed to the TV. "Max," he said, "watch this play."

Max turned and looked up, his back to the customers, and watched as a team in blue performed a perfectly executed fast break ending with an astounding alley-oop slam dunk. "Whoa," said Max, watching the replay.

"Hello, boys." The voice was deep, almost comically so, and very manly, like someone making fun of late night television announcers. Max recognized it instantly. Louis Papasian, aka 'Nuggets'.

"Hello, Lou," said Max.

Biz turned in his stool. "Nuggets! What the..." Biz and Nuggets shook hands. "Wow, long time," said Biz.

"True that," said Nuggets, plunking himself down on the stool between Biz and Miss Peabody.

"The lovely woman to your left," said Biz, "is Miss Peabody. Miss Peabody, this is 'Nuggets', or, ah, Louis if you prefer."

"Well," she said, "what does he prefer?"

"Nuggets is fine," said the deep toned newcomer, smiling and extending his hand.

"How do you do," said Miss Peabody, gently touching his fingers.

"Pleasure to meet you."

"Interesting nickname," she offered.

"Yeah, long story I'm afraid."

"And not exactly appropriate for a family establishment," said Max.

Nuggets looked at him curiously. "Family establishment?"

"So," said Biz, "what's happening? How's it going, or maybe I should say, how they hangin'?" He started to laugh but noticed that Max was not amused.

"Yeah, Louis," said Max. He was, of course, usually a fan of nicknames but in this case, not so much. "What's new? What brings you back to town?"

"Oh, you know, just rolling along, trying to make a living and stay out of trouble."

"We saw you on TV a couple times," said Biz.

"Yeah," said Nuggets, "I guess I had my fifteen minutes of fame."

Well, thought Max, that was true. He'd heard the story many times, second hand, third hand and straight from the horse's mouth. Whether embellished, exaggerated or ridiculed the basics always stayed the same. Nuggets had been a regular patron at 'Sully's, another idea man searching for the big score. A few years back, while watching a Discovery Channel segment on testicular cancer, he'd had what he felt was his epiphany. Men who survived that particular type of cancer, after having the diseased testicle removed, often chose to replace the missing member with a fake. The urologist would implant a small sack of silicone or saline, similar to those used in breast augmentation surgery, allowing the patient to once again possess a perfectly natural looking scrotum.

Nuggets' idea was simple. Though he had no testicular cancer or signs thereof, he would have his average size balls replaced by giant fakes and then set off on a career as an internet porn sensation. Most of 'Sully's denizens agreed this was the most absurd plan they'd ever heard but were grateful for the amusement and chance to brainstorm porno names and toss off one-liners. They were also quite willing to point out that Nuggets, inflated balls or not, was not exactly a handsome devil. Rather, they concurred, he was an average looking guy at best, a four or five if truth be told. Instead of defending his appearance, Nuggets chose to explain that he was not chasing a Hollywood dream where good looks played such a large part in one's success. No, his aim was the adult film industry, a business in which the men need not possess a manly jaw line or ripped physique as long as they had other attributes and abilities. And, as for the doubters who focused on his lack of experience performing in front of the camera and the problems that may or may not arise, Nuggets was not swayed, claiming there were pills for just such difficulties. He was, in fact, fairly confident that once on set he would come shining through. Since no one was actually taking Nuggets who, of course, was still Louis at the time, seriously, neither was anyone actually trying to talk him out of this ridiculous venture. Indeed, it could be said, that some were virtually daring him to do it.

Nuggets was not to be dissuaded. Hundreds of girls, he argued, had obtained giant fake mammaries to increase their odds of becoming porn starlets or earning feature stripper money. And porn was a billion dollar industry, filled with average guys blessed with enormous shlongs. But where were the big balled actors? He, Louis Papasian, would fill a niche.

Though it took some time, Nuggets eventually located a surgeon willing to perform the operation, the only stipulation being that the he would not remove the existing testicles but would instead surround them with the large round fakes. This, according to Dr. Mentkiwicz, would insure that Nuggets continued to receive a normal amount of testosterone from his nether regions, a necessity for his chosen profession which neither he nor his barstool cronies had thought to address.

The surgery was, as they say, a success, and following the requisite recovery period, Louis was off to Los Angeles, his grapefruit sized testicles dangling loosely in his relaxed fit jeans. Upon arrival, he proceeded directly to the largest adult modeling agency in town and, much to the surprise of the permanently bored owner, revealed his newfound singularity. Whilst most male talent applying at this well established supplier of adult performers were asked to drop their trousers and awkwardly demonstrate their ability to obtain and maintain a quality erection, no such request was made of Nuggets. He was immediately signed to a contract and, following the usual 'polaroids', was congratulated on his imagination and initiative, then sent home to await the calls that the manager assured would soon be coming.

So far, so good, thought Nuggets, though he did resist the urge to ring up 'Sully's and inform the boys of his impending pornographic glory. Besides, he wasn't a mean person and was not intent on making his friends jealous. He simply wanted to demonstrate to them, and even more so to himself, that he had finally done something right.

And for quite a while it appeared that he had done just that. The calls did come, and thanks to a generous supply of 'Viagra' and the hard working girls of porn valley, so did Nuggets.

He showed up on time, performed capably and maintained a pleasant demeanor. The women and producers found his extraordinary enlargement interesting at first and one company went so far as to build a franchise around him, garbing him in superhero wear and casting him as 'SackMan'. Nuggets was thrilled with his newfound notoriety and willing to share his story with anyone inquiring.

Soon, the internet gossip sites were doing short pieces on him and these items were picked up by network television on programs such as 'TMZ' and 'Inside Edition'. He was even mentioned in jokes on late night talk shows, a sure sign that in these short attention span times, he had made it.

But, as with any novelty or one trick pony, Nuggets fame was short lived. The girls grew bored, perhaps finally noticing that he was neither handsome nor well endowed. 'SackMan' sales were plunging, indicating a lack of interest in the perv public. Nuggets held on, doing scenes with Bridget the Midget and Chesty Morgan, possessor of an eighty-six inch bust-line. But it was no use. He was yesterday's news, his finances dwindling, his prospects vanishing. Resigned to his fate, he gave up his over priced condo, sold his convertible and headed home. And now there he was, back at 'Sully's, just like old times.

"So," said Max, "what's going on, what's the plan?"

"Oh, no plan," said Nuggets. "I got a call from Chubster. Said he might have some work for me."

"Really," said Max.

Biz looked surprised. "The kind of work you were doing in California?"

"No, I don't think so. But whatever it is, I could use the money."

"And what, young man," asked Miss Peabody, "kind of work is it you do?"

Max looked at Nuggets sternly. Biz was smiling.

"Oh, well," stammered Nuggets, "you know, odd jobs, consulting, sales, ah, anything to pay the bills...Hey, Max, how about a cold one."

"I see," said Miss Peabody, as Max poured a draft, though she clearly did not. Max placed the mug in front of Nuggets who quickly took a long swig.

"I got that," said Biz, pointing to the beer.

"Thanks, Biz. It's nice to be back."

Biz smiled. "So, you still got 'em?"

Miss Peabody looked flustered. "I'm terribly confused."

"Anyways," said Nuggets, ignoring the question, "about Chubster. Has he been in lately?"

"That's odd," said Miss Peabody. "I was just asking Ginny about him."

"Ginny's still here?"

Max nodded, pointed to the red headed waitress delivering drinks to a nearby table.

"Wow," said Nuggets, "she still looks good."

"After all the girls you've seen," said Biz.

Nuggets shook his head. "Those girls are plastic. Ginny's real."

"What girls are plastic," asked Miss P.

"Anyway," said Max, paying no attention to the perplexed matron, "he still comes and goes. Did he say what the job was?"

"No. You know Chub. Got to be all mysterious and secretive like he's on to something big. And normally I wouldn't get involved with one of his crazy ideas. God knows I've had enough of my own. But this time he sounded different. Less crazy, you know. And I haven't exactly been raking it in since I got back. So, I don't know, I just figured what the heck."

"Did he give you his number?"

"Yeah, but he said we couldn't talk on the phone. Said he'd see me here."

"That sounds like our Chubster."

"Yeah, right." Nuggets stared at his beer. "Man, I must be getting desperate."

"Hey," said Max, "maybe he's finally on to something."

"You're just saying that to make me feel better, Max. Which I do appreciate. But maybe I should just go, forget about it."

"Hey," said Biz, "at least finish your beer. He might show up and you may as well talk to him, see what he has to say."

Nuggets nodded and sipped his brew as Max went to serve the lovebirds another round.

"Is that Louis Papasian?" The voice was Ginny's and she seemed genuinely excited to see her old friend.

"Hey, Ginny," said Nuggets, standing to receive a big welcome back hug.

"How's our 'B' list celebrity?" she asked, grinning.

"More like 'Z' list you mean," said Nuggets.

"Come on, you were on TV."

"Were being the important word there."

"I watched one of your movies," said Ginny.

Nuggets was shocked. "No, you didn't."

"You're right, I didn't." She smiled. "Are you blushing/"

"You were in the movies?" asked Miss Peabody.

Now Nuggets was flustered. "Ah, just some small roles."

"Small?" said Biz.

"Anything I may have seen?"

"Oh," said Max, returning, "I highly doubt it."

Nuggets looked at Ginny. "I'll say this, Ginny. You still look great."

"I doubt as great as all those California girls," she said.

"Those girls were fake," said Nuggets. "You're the real deal."

"Are those the plastic girls from before?" asked Miss P., by now almost to herself since no one else was listening.

"Speaking of fake," said Biz.

"Ooops," said Ginny, glancing at her tables, "gotta' go." She looked at Nuggets. "Don't leave yet."

Not only was Max surprised by Nuggets' reappearance but by Ginny's warm welcome for the old regular as well. Had she actually been attracted to Nuggets when he was a frequent guest at 'Sully's' or was he just one of the boys she was fond of, innocent flirtations and occasional hugs notwithstanding? He did recall her being the only female in the joint who, upon hearing Nuggets' plan, did not label him a pervert and his venture utter lunacy. It was, she had said, more valid than most of the hair brained scams and schemes she'd heard over the years. And, as far as Max knew, Nuggets had never hit on Ginny, apparently respecting her dating policy. So why shouldn't she be happy to see an old friend? What was of more concern was just what kind of work did Chubster have to offer the big balled ex porn star? Max was under the impression that all the grand heist roles had been filled. Had Chubster talked to Nuggets about the gig before speaking to Max? That would be rather disconcerting, he felt. Chubster had been virtually begging him to participate. And now this. Chubster, Max decided, had a lot of explaining to do.

*

Later, when Chubster entered 'Sully's and quickly seated himself at the bar, Max was thankful for Nuggets' absence. The ensuing conversation would be awkward enough without the presence of the other idea man. Though Max was obviously busy slinging drinks and serving plates, Chubster was, as always, anxious.

"Hey, Max, big news." To his credit, Chubster kept his voice low. The secretive nature of their endeavor had at least provided a modicum of decorum.

"Hold on," said Max, as he placed a pair of 'Sully's 'big boy burgers' in front of two UPS drivers. He glanced at Chub. "You want a beer?"

Chubster could barely sit still. "Yuh, yuh, sure." He watched Max hustling and tried to remain calm. "When you have a minute." Max nodded, drew a pint and swiftly set it down in front of Chub. "Tomorrow's the day," Chubster said quietly.

"Whataya' mean? What day?"

"The pre-lim. The beginning."

"Just a minute." Max made a martini in a mixing glass and set it to chill while he took an order, then poured the drink and placed it in front of a businessman perusing the newspaper. He looked at Chubster. "Did you call Louis Papasian?"

"Nuggets?"

"Yes, Nuggets. Did you call him about a job?"

"Did you see Nuggets?"

"He was here yesterday. He said you called him."

"Yuh, I called him. You seem upset."

"Should I be?"

"What do you mean?"

Max leaned close, almost whispering. "Did you offer him the job first? Before me?"

"No, no, God no. He was a backup plan."

Max stepped back, stared at Chubster. He glanced down the bar, noticed a large patron with an empty mug. He held up one finger, then hurried down to the tap, looking back at Chubster as if suspecting the idea man might bolt the premises at any moment. It was weird, he thought, that he was getting upset about possibly being the second choice for a criminal enterprise. He'd always been competitive but he shouldn't be jumping to conclusions. Besides, Chubster had been known as a big talker, not a liar. He placed a beer in front of the big fellow, received a nod in return, then went back to resume his conversation. Again, he leaned toward Chubster. "Okay, speak."

"Look, Max, you were never a sure thing. You've always been skeptical of my ideas and this is a time sensitive event. So if you had said no, which you have to admit was a strong possibility, I would have needed a substitute. Nuggets is a decent guy. And he's like you, no wife, no kids, no mortgage, nothing holding him down."

"So, now I'm in a group with a guy who disfigured his scrotum to get laid and make some cash. Is that what you're telling me?"

"Hey, that was a good idea. Wish I'd thought of it."

"Oh, I'll bet you do."

"Listen, Max, you were always my first choice, swear to God."

Max stood up straight. "Well, now what are you gonna' tell Louis? He came all the way back from California."

"I'll tell him," said Chubster, "that the position's been filled. I never guaranteed him anything on the phone. Plus he was done out there anyway. He was already planning on coming back."

"He's not gonna' be happy. He already seems pretty depressed."

"I know, I know. I'll think of something."

"Well, think fast, 'cause he could walk in that door any minute."

Chubster looked glum, but only for a moment. "So," he said, "do you want to hear the news or not?"

Max watched two attractive nurses in colorful scrubs seat themselves at the far end of the bar. He addressed Chubster. "Yes. I want to hear the news. Just hold on." Chub looked like a disappointed toddler but managed to refrain from protesting the delay. Max approached the ladies as casually as ever. They were pretty, they were smiling and they were in his domain. He would not allow Chubster the satisfaction of appearing anxious. He smiled, placed one hand on the bar. "Hello, girls. Care for a cocktail?"

"Humn," said the blonde. "What a good idea."

"What," said the brunette, leaning forward, "would you suggest?"

Chubster fiddled with the coaster that rested beneath his beer, trying unsuccessfully to relax, his attention roaming from the front door to Max's flirtations with the nurses. After what seemed to Chub an inordinately long time for such a busy bartender, Max finally returned and stood, arms folded. He glanced back at the girls who he'd left giggling and smiled, then looked seriously at Chubster.

"Well?"

"All right," said Chub, keeping his voice low. "Tomorrow we begin. We're gonna' get your seed money to recruit with. You're not part of it but I thought you might want to watch." He panned the bar to make sure no one was listening, motioned for Max to come closer. "Listen, you know the section of Main Street where the commercial district is kind of ending and the residential is beginning, down where the last 'Starbucks' is?"

"Yeah, I guess so."

"There's a convenience store, I think a dry cleaners and a couple cafes. Then the houses start."

"Yeah. Okay."

"Those cafes have some outdoor seating and it's supposed to be nice tomorrow, so if you want, and you don't have to, but if you want, sit at one of those tables around four o'clock."

"You know," said Max, "tomorrow is Halloween."

Chubster leaned back on his stool and smiled. "Precisely."

Max stared at him. "Precisely?"

"Yes, precisely. I think you'll find it pretty interesting. But like I said..."

"I know, I know. I don't have to go."

"And I'm not telling you to go. But, you know, you said you were curious. You're off tomorrow anyway, right?"

"Yeah," said Max, "we'll see."

"All right," said Chubster, getting up and placing a bill on the bar. "Just figured you'd like to know." He smiled, tipped an imaginary hat and turned to go.

"Hey, Chubster." Chub turned back. "Don't forget about Nuggets."

Chubster nodded. "I won't." Max watched him go, then returned to the nurses.

*

THURSDAY

The following day was unseasonably warm for the end of October. It would be nice for the trick-or-treaters and their parents, Max thought. They wouldn't have to put their costumes on over long underwear or hooded sweatshirts. Sitting outdoors at one of the cafes downtown as Chubster had suggested would be quite pleasant on such a day. One more temptation as Max grappled with the decision at hand. To go, or not to go, to observe whatever felonious stew King and Chubster had cooked up.

Try as he might, Max could not keep the anticipation from his mind. He'd always prided himself on the relaxed contentment with which he passed his days off, but Chubster had planted a seed of anxiety he could not escape. Though not obligated to keep the late afternoon rendezvous, he nonetheless felt compelled to do so, and had given up his night shift just in case. He knew if he didn't, he'd regret it later on. If he stayed home, and in a day or two Chubster handed him a sack of cash with no explanation, he felt his head might explode from curiosity overload. Chubster, he was sure, would never reveal the source of the ill-gotten gains, no matter how often he was badgered or how harshly interrogated. No, Chubster would just wear that Chubster smirk and remind Max that he should have been there, that he was told ahead of time, that he had no one to blame for his own lack of information but himself. You snooze, you lose, Chub had always been fond of saying, though normally in reference to his own shenanigans and why they needed to be done post haste. And yet, what possible good could come of it. More than likely, something illegal was going to go down and, while Max would simply be an innocent bystander, he'd still be in the vicinity, likely a witness. So why take the risk?

Why indeed? That was the question Max pondered as he went about his day. He'd always treasured days off, considered them the ultimate reward. Free time. That was, he believed, what it was all about. Time to do what you wanted to do when you wanted to do it. He didn't work so he could buy a nice car or stylish clothes or fancy dinners. He worked to buy time. We are, he theorized, indentured serfs, struggling to earn our freedom. Heck, wasn't that why he'd signed up for this crazy caper in the first place? One hundred, fifty thousand dollars would buy a lot of days off.

Someone had given Max a t-shirt that said 'Stay calm and carry on'. That seemed appropriate. He ate his meals in a leisurely fashion, did a load of laundry while watching 'Sports Center', walked to the corner bank to deposit his tip money, even tried to read a book.

Nothing was working. He found himself watching the clock, something he'd always avoided. There was time enough for clock watching at work. Max was not a religious man. Though he wished he believed in an afterlife, that he had faith, he just couldn't buy into the whole Heaven and Hell thing. This existence was it, he felt, so you damn well better make the best of it. And if you weren't at work, you should never encourage time to pass quickly, no matter how excited you may be about the future. Moreover, there was no excuse to ever be bored. There was always plenty to do, or watch, or read, or listen to. Half the reason he had settled into bartending was the whole Monday to Friday, nine to five, living for the weekend thing did not match up well with his philosophy.

Like most people, Max had fooled himself a thousand times over the years, but this day, this thirty-first of October, he could not do so. He had to go, had to see for himself whatever mischief Chubster had arranged to take place on that particular patch of Main Street. He watched the clock strike three, grabbed a light jacket and headed out the door.

*

Ginny O'Riley cherished her days off as well. Of course, there were chores to do, tasks to attend to and errands to run. But there was no clock, there was no schedule. She could do basically what she wanted when she wanted. She could dress down, she could eat crap, she could go the whole day without smiling or even conversing with another human being if she was so inclined. Her daughter, Emily, certainly wouldn't care or even notice, hypnotized by her cell phone like any good teenager, relentlessly checking her social media. And if Ginny spent the day watching old movies or taking a three hour nap, she refused to feel guilty. She'd earned it. That day's freedom was bought and paid for.

So it was with that mindset that Ginny decided on that lovely Autumn afternoon, she would do one of her favorite things in the world. She would take a book and a sweater and walk down to the 'Cozy Cafe' where she would purchase an iced coffee and maybe a snack, sit outside in the sun, read a chapter or two and watch the world go by.

When she'd rounded a corner and glimpsed the patio in front of the cafe, she saw a familiar face. Max was seated at a small round table, drinking coffee and reading a newspaper. This was, she thought, certainly a surprise. She'd been coming to that same cafe for a couple of years and not once had she seen her bartending buddy here. In fact, she had no recollection of mentioning the cafe to Max so the chances of him researching her activities and showing up to find her and perhaps profess his undying love were less than likely. This, she figured, was just one of those coincidences life occasionally throws at you. She approached the table. "Well," she said, "this is a coincidence."

Max glanced up from his newspaper and did an old-fashioned double-take. "Oh, hey, Ginny."

"What's a' matter? You didn't recognize me?"

Max was momentarily flustered. This was something he hadn't counted on. Ginny would be watching him watching...what? She'd be a witness, too. There might be questions. And that other voice in his head, the one he tried mightily to ignore, was scolding him. He should have never come, he should have stayed home, what was he thinking?

Ginny put her hands on her hips, pivoted slightly each way and smiled. "You don't like my outfit?" She was wearing yoga pants, a faded Bob Marley t-shirt, an ancient sweater and her hair pinned up in a messy bun.

Max grinned. "No, it's hot."

Ginny set her book on the table as Max put his newspaper down. She looked around, making sure she was at the right cafe, that she hadn't somehow ended up on Max's side of town. Satisfied she was, indeed, at the 'Cozy Cafe', she placed a hand on one of the white wicker chairs she'd grown so fond of those last few months. "I've never seen you here before."

"I've never seen you here before."

"Very funny. I come here all the time. Do you?"

"Ah, no, actually. First time here."

Ginny had an assortment of questions but hesitated. "I'm gonna' grab something inside. Okay if I sit with you? Were you meeting someone?"

"Well, the Queen of England was supposed to be by but I think she's standing me up."

Ginny laughed. "Save my seat."

She went inside to order as Max's mind raced. Did Ginny really hang out here? Did she know something? Had Chubster enlisted her, too? Or was this, as she'd said, just a coincidence? Max had seen a load of coincidences in his time but this one seemed much more significant.

Ginny emerged carrying an iced coffee and some kind of pastry, sat down, took a sip and a bite and looked at Max. "So. What are you doing here?"

One thing Max had learned during his bartending career was how not to panic. It could be St. Patty's night at 'Sully's, loud drunken Irishmen three deep at the bar, spilled Guiness and plates of half eaten corned beef dinners covering every surface, Max pouring pints and clearing dishes like a one man army; even then he stayed calm, cracking wise and bantering with the boys, flirting shamelessly with whatever women were able to squeeze their way through the throng to reach the taps. So the sudden appearance of Ginny at the site of whatever transgression Chubster had planned was not going to throw him. He looked at Ginny. "What am I doing here?"

"Yuh. That's right."

"Isn't it obvious?"

"No."

"I'm enjoying this lovely day, drinking a mighty fine cup a' joe and catching up on current events."

"Come on, Max. You live on the other side of town. No cafes over there?" Ginny glanced at her book, a mystery by one of her favorite authors. But for now, the mystery of Max's presence was more fascinating.

"I decided to go for a long walk. Thought I might see some early trick-or-treaters. And there's really no regular houses near my street. Just stores and apartments. You've got everything over here."

Ginny gave his answer some thought. It actually sounded somewhat convincing. It was true the 'Cozy Cafe' was in sight of some old Victorians and a few triple-deckers. She'd even passed some early Halloween revelers on the way over. And yet, something still seemed off. "I thought," she said, "you hated Halloween."

Max took a sip from his mug. "I never said that. Said I hate to work on Halloween. I'm way too old to stand behind that bar in a costume. It's awkward, it's uncomfortable and it's embarrassing. I thought we agreed on that. But I don't hate the holiday. It's great when you're a kid."

Ginny tried to recall prior years and earlier conversations. She, too, had grown weary of dressing up for work, especially since the neanderthals who populated 'Sully's expected females with figures like Ginny's to don the skimpiest outfits possible, which was all well and fine for the giggly young servers and hostesses but had grown pretty stale for the more mature members of the staff. Maybe Max was right, maybe they had talked about this before; she couldn't remember every conversation. And they both had the day off so there must have been some sort of similar mind set. She gazed down the street toward the houses Max had referenced. "Okay, well" she said, "have any trick-or-treaters come by yet?"

"Only a couple. But it's still early."

"I know," said Ginny. "I'm still amazed they make 'em come out before dusk now. We would have never come out before dark when I was a kid."

"I know. Tough to soap windows and smash pumpkins in the light of day."

"I didn't realize you were once a juvenile delinquent."

"Hey, that's good clean fun."

"Soaping windows is good clean fun. I get it."

"No, I didn't even realize..." Ginny was laughing and under different circumstances he knew he'd be having a wonderful time. She was a great girl with a great sense of humor, old enough to know better and young enough not to care. But he couldn't really enjoy himself, not while he scanned the neighborhood looking for some kind of sign or clue, something happening or about to that was interesting or unusual. Trying to pay attention to Ginny, while usually effortless, was today proving to be a bit problematic. She must have noticed.

"Looking for anything in particular?" she asked.

"Oh, you know, just checking things out, observing, people-watching."

"Really? Not that many people to watch."

"Oh, there's a few."

Ginny followed Max's gaze, then glanced at him. He was still the same flirtatious wise-ass she'd grown used to, but there was something different, something off. She couldn't put her finger on it but that was all right. She was having a nice time; she had the day off, she had her iced coffee, she had her book, and now she even had her own personal mystery to solve.

"Like that guy," said Max. "Who's he?"

Ginny followed the trajectory of Max's finger and saw a dirty, hairy, disheveled street person across the road and about a half block down. The man was slowly pushing a shopping cart bulging with blankets and trash bags.

"I don't know who he is. What, do you think he's a friend of mine?"

"Thought he might be in your book club." Ginny laughed. "No," said Max, "I'm kidding. Just figured you might have seen him around the neighborhood."

"Why?"

"You know. Every neighborhood has a guy like him, sometimes even a her. Usually pushing a cart like this guy, or riding an old bicycle or just walking around looking for cans."

Ginny was intrigued. "You sound like an expert."

Max looked at her. "I'm surprised you don't know this stuff. The guy's name is usually Rusty or Duke or Smitty and everybody knows it. And there's stories, always stories. You know, like he used to be a regular guy who got hit in the head, or he was in Vietnam or maybe he was a college professor who lost his mind, his wife and all his money. And if you're from the neighborhood, you're supposed to have a story of some kind of encounter, like you had a short but strange conversation or you saw him wearing his clothes inside out or perhaps you'd offered a small kindness or, even better, he'd offered a small kindness to you." Max leaned back, satisfied.

"Wow, Max," said Ginny. "I'm impressed. What, did you do your thesis on these guys?...Anyway, I hate to disappoint you but I've never seen that man before in my life, in this neighborhood or anywhere else."

Max shook his head. "Really."

They both watched as the cart pusher turned down a side street and disappeared from view. Max was starting to wish he'd stayed home and watched television. Things were getting, well, he wasn't sure of the appropriate word but they were getting something. First Ginny shows up and now this guy, who was as stereotypical a neighborhood bum as he'd ever seen, appears at almost the precise time and place Chubster said to be. What was next? Was Mr. Vanderbilt going to wander by?

Ginny was even more fascinated than before. Max arrived and suddenly her part of town had its very own hobo, a hobo who Max seemed overly interested in. In fact, Max seemed quite interested in all the surroundings. Sure, he was his same old amusing self but it was like in the movies when the crooks are casing the joint. A lot of looking around, a lot of questions. And, Ginny recalled, there was a bank less than a block away.

"Hey, look," she said, "there's your trick-or-treaters."

Max followed the direction of Ginny's finger and saw five young revelers come around a corner and turn down Main Street. "Yup. See. Told ya'"

Max and Ginny squinted into the distance, trying to determine the costumes as the youths climbed the stairs to the front door of an old Victorian. They pressed the doorbell and held out their orange bags and buckets.

"Well, let's see," said Max. "There's definitely a devil. And the one all in white has to be a ghost."

"I think one's a zombie but it could be a Frankenstein. We'll know better in a minute."

An elderly woman had answered the door. It was hard to tell if the kids actually yelled 'trick or treat' but they were presented with candy bars nonetheless, then retreated back down the stairs on their way to the next house, a rundown ranch with an unkempt front yard. They were closer now, their costumes easier to discern.

"Yup," said Ginny, "that's a zombie, all right. And a Batman, too."

"I think they're all boys. Girls don't like their whole faces covered. That last ones got a full head mask, some kind of goon, I think."

"Don't tell me. You're an expert on goons, too."

"As a matter of fact..."

No one had answered the door at the ranch house so the gang moved on to the next residence, a two story structure whose first floor contained a convenience store. Ginny seemed surprised when the group approached its entrance. "Are they gonna' trick-or-treat the convenience store?"

Max watched as the zombie held the door for the others. "Sure looks like it."

"I don't think they're going to get anything for free in there. I don't think the owners even know what Halloween is. They're from some country I've never even heard of."

"Not India?" asked Max.

"No, some place more exotic. They're super nice people but I'm sure they have different holidays."

"Look at that. They're coming out already."

The trick-or-treaters emerged from the store, turned in the direction of the small bank branch next door. Max spotted the bum with the shopping cart reappearing from the side street he'd earlier gone down. "Hey," said Max, "your boyfriend's back."

"Ex boyfriend," said Ginny, and they both laughed, then watched as he pushed his cart past the youngsters. Max thought he noticed a quick nod but wasn't sure; they were almost a block away. He wished he had binoculars but that would be ridiculously suspicious.

"Did you see that?" asked Ginny.

"Did I see what?"

"The hobo. I think he just looked at his watch."

"What?"

"The homeless guy. I think he's wearing a watch."

Max considered this as the trick-or-treaters entered the bank. The bum kept moving and soon turned down the next side street. It did seem odd for a homeless person to wear a watch but what did Max know; contrary to his previous expounding on the subject, he was no expert on the destitute and the displaced. Maybe they needed to know the time, closing hours for shelters, meal times at food pantries. It wasn't exactly a UFO sighting.

"Maybe," said Max, "he's got an appointment. What's more curious to me is why those kids are going in that bank."

"Well," said Ginny, "I don't know if they have candy, but they always have lollipops. I guess they're just going in every door they can. You know what's funny though, two more doors down and they'll be at 'Hancock's Funeral Home.'"

"Well, that should be interesting."

They sipped their beverages and waited for the youths to exit the bank. Just what was happening around here, Max wondered, and where the heck was Chubster? A hobo with a watch, trick-or-treaters going in a bank, Ginny showing up at this place at this time. And why was it so quiet? Those kids were making no noise. No laughter, no shouting, no giving each other the business. Just a determined bunch going about their task as though on a mission. They acted more like short census takers than Halloween revelers.

Ginny, too, was lost in thought. What was taking the kids so long in the bank? Were they waiting in line to yell 'trick-or-treat'? How long does it take to grab a couple lollipops anyway? And didn't it appear as though Max was waiting for something to happen? Not to mention the hobo on a schedule. She peered down the block and saw him once again steering his cart onto Main Street and rolling it toward the bank.

"Hey," she said, "here comes your brother again."

Max looked to his right and smiled. "Beauragard!"

Ginny looked at him. "Beauragard?"

"I honestly don't know where that came from...What do you think is taking the kids so long?"

"I don't know," said Ginny. "Maybe they're robbing it." Max looked serious but Ginny smiled. "You know, taking the whole basket of lollipops."

Max relaxed. "Yuh, right. But they'll probably give 'em the pops with the blue dye so when they exit the bank, kaboom. Blue trick-or-treaters...Oh, speak of the devil..." Max grinned and elbowed Ginny. "Get it? Get it?" The little devil and his cohorts emerged from the bank, moving more quickly now. They hustled down the sidewalk and reversed direction, heading back from where they had come.

"What the heck," said Ginny. Now she knew something was up, something had happened, something that Max may have been anticipating. Her bartending buddy was silent, watching seriously as the kids and bum approached each other from opposite directions. As they passed the homeless man, each costumed youth dropped his candy bag into the shopping cart and then kept moving. The bum behaved as if he hadn't even noticed. There was no hesitation or recognition from either party.

"Did you see that?" asked Ginny.

"Yuh, of course I saw it."

"Well?"

"Well, what?"

"What's going on?"

"I haven't the slightest idea what's going on."

Both the trick-or-treaters and the bum simultaneously turned down side streets and were soon out of sight.

"Come on, Max, you seriously have no idea what just happened?"

"I swear...Look."

A middle-aged man in suit and tie pushed open the bank door and looked around frantically, then began quickly placing a call on his cell phone.

"Must be the bank manager," said Max.

Two well-dressed young women, most likely tellers, stuck their heads out the door but the manager motioned for them to get back inside.

"Max," said Ginny, "I think those kids just robbed that bank."

Though it had taken longer than it should have, Max had finally put two and two together.

He could hear the sirens in the distance. "I don't think those were kids."

*

That night, safely back in the confines of his apartment, Max sat on the couch with Rufus and watched the news, paying far more attention than usual as the afternoon's events near the 'Cozy Cafe' were prominently highlighted. Even the cat seemed interested as one of the anchors teased the story at the beginning of the broadcast: "And later, one of the strangest robberies committed in this area in quite some time, a crime that was definitely no Halloween treat for the bank's employees. We'll have that report and others straight ahead."

"Great," said Max, looking at his pet. "Just great." Rufus eyed him curiously. This was a different tone of voice than he was used to. "Well, not your fault. Guess you deserve some dinner." Max got up and went to the kitchen. He could hear the national news as he opened a can of cat food, spooned some into a bowl and placed it on the floor. Rufus padded over and, after a quick sniff and examination, began eating. Max grabbed a beer and went back to his spot on the couch as the newscast returned from commercial. This time the camera focused on the female anchor, a curvaceous blonde who wore black rimmed glasses in an unsuccessful attempt to tone down her allure. Normally Max concentrated on her cleavage but not this time. It seemed, he thought, that this time he should pay attention to the story. Even Rufus appeared to sense that something important was happening, not bothering to finish his chow before rejoining Max for the news.

The attractive newscaster was excited. "And, by far, the most interesting local story we're following tonight," she began, "is a holdup at the North Main Street branch of the Liberty Bank late this afternoon, apparently pulled off by a group of early trick-or-treaters."

"That's right," said the male co-anchor, a silver haired dandy who quite often appeared to be stifling a smirk. "This Halloween robbery was no holiday for the bank employees victimized by the pint sized thieves who made a clean getaway. Thankfully, no one was hurt. We go now to Eva Lopez at the scene. Eva."

Max didn't appreciate the way the creepy anchor said Eva's name. It was too familiar. What was that newsman's name anyway? Kent or Brent or Brad? Whatever. Max wondered whether the older man was boffing Eva, a petite but shapely brunette, but only for a moment. He had far more important things to consider right now.

Eva was doing her remote from just outside the Liberty Bank. Police cars, their lights flashing, idled nearby as various officers briskly walked in and out of the building. Eva began her report.

"Thanks, Brock..." That's it, thought Max, Brock. What a tool. Who names their kid Brock. Rufus stared at him quixotically. Max refocused as Eva continued. "I'm standing just yards away from the bank branch at which today's brazen robbery took place. All we know so far is that the five perpetrators were short, they were outfitted in Halloween costumes, masks included and they apparently knew exactly what they were doing. The odds that this was an elaborate prank by some mischievous trick-or-treaters has pretty much been ruled out because of the professional manner in which the bank was robbed. The heist went down like clockwork and the only evidence remaining are five Halloween costumes found discarded in some bushes on a nearby street. The police are hoping that someone, perhaps a neighbor from one of the residences in the area, saw something and they will be setting up a tip hot-line later this evening."

The pretty blonde co-anchor popped up superimposed in a corner of the TV screen. "Eva," she said, "it's Jesse here. Have you heard anything from the bank's employees, and why specifically they neither pressed the alarm button nor gave out the money stacks containing those blue dye packs we always see in the movies?"

"Well," said Eva, "nothing has been officially confirmed yet, but my sources tell me that the young teller who dealt with the apparent ringleader of the gang was so traumatized after reading the note she was handed that she was unwilling to risk the alarm button or the dye packs. And though the authorities are not releasing the contents of that note for obvious reasons, one officer on the scene was allegedly heard to say that it was the most vile, disgusting thing he'd read in all his years on the force."

Max looked up. "Cranky Sam," he said aloud. Rufus gazed at his owner, may have nodded in agreement. Now, thought Max, it was all starting to come together, the midgets, the bum, the seed money. But why the heck did he have to be there? Why did he have to know where the seed money came from? Damn Chubster.

Jesse, the blonde anchor, reappeared. "Eva, have they any idea yet on the ages of the criminals?"

"Well," said Eva, "that note seems to indicate that at least the leader of the crew, in this case the person wearing the devil costume who is assumed to have written the note, at least he was an adult. Even in this, the age of the internet, the note seems too vulgar and threatening to have been written by a young person."

"And," said Brock, showing up on screen, "what about the others. Any word on their ages?"

"We're told that they did not speak so any conjecture at this point would be simply a guess. As it now stands, we don't know if they are youths or little people, and I'm surmising that it will be some time before we do. This is Eva Lopez reporting live from the Liberty Bank on Main Street. Now back to Jesse and Brock."

The two well groomed anchors again filled the screen. "Well," said Brock, "this proves once again that truth is, indeed, stranger than fiction."

"That's right," said Jesse. "And obviously we will be following this story very closely and let you know of any new developments the moment they happen. We'll also be giving out that tip line number as soon as it's in place."

Yeah, thought Max, I'll be following it pretty closely, too.

"That's right," said Brock, "I'm afraid the police are going to need all the help they can get on this one. And now here's Bruce with the weather."

Max flicked off the television before they could cut away to Bruce and his colorful clothes and charts. He stood up and went to a kitchen cupboard, selected a bottle and poured a strong one. He looked down at Rufus who had followed and was eyeing him curiously. Max addressed the cat. "You want one, too?"

*

FRIDAY

Max's hasty departure from the 'Cozy Cafe' had not sat well with Ginny as he knew it would not. But he'd had to act quickly, the expiration of his admittedly enjoyable flirtations with her over for the time being. He was sure the police would interview and take names of anyone in the area, witnesses and suspects alike, and there was no way he wanted his name attached; it could come back to haunt him later on. Again he wondered, why had Chubster enticed him to the scene in the first place? And more importantly, why had he decided to go? He had one, and only one, part to play in this enterprise and from then on that's what he would do. Enlist enough crazy people to properly storm the field and that's it. No more meetings, no more conversations, no more observations and no more visits to grumpy midgets who may or may not have just robbed a bank.

Ginny had been surprised, then irritated when Max stood up from the table they were sharing at the cafe and announced he was leaving. He'd not had time to make up some lame excuse for his departure, just said that he'd rather not get involved, that he didn't have time to speak at length with police officers when he had no information to give, that he didn't need to see his face or hear his voice on the evening news, and that she should probably scram, too. Ginny knew he was full of crap, told him so and that he should stay; it was the right thing to do. Max had said he was sorry, grabbed his newspaper and fled. He knew, without turning to look, she was glaring at him as he swiftly walked away. It wasn't his fault, he had told himself; it was Chubster's.

And there they were the next night, back at 'Sully's with news of the heist still emanating from the flat screens hanging behind the bar. Friday night and the place was busy. In fact, Joey was standing behind Tony, waiting for a seat. The patrons were finally more interested in something other than their cell phones, all eyes on the TV sets hung above the bottles and, after numerous requests, Max had removed the closed captioning and turned up the volume. This was against Sully's policy except for playoff games but when the owner had emerged from his office to see what all the hub bub was about he had voiced no complaint and, instead, stood transfixed like the rest of the crowd.

"Jesus," said Joey, looking around. "Where'd all these people come from? I haven't see some of 'em in months."

Max wasn't as busy as the scene would indicate since the customers appeared more intrigued by the news than their drinks. "Apparently," he said, "this robbery makes for great entertainment."

Tony glanced over his shoulder at Joey, then back at Max. "They're here to see Ginny. She's gonna' be on the news."

"What," said Max.

"Yeah, I guess she was an eyewitness."

Joey was excited. "Ginny's gonna' be on the news?"

"Shush," said Tony.

Joey was amazed. "Did he just shush me?"

"Look, there's Ginny."

Max turned to the set to see his red headed co-worker standing next to Eva at the 'Cozy Cafe'. Must have turned off the TV too soon last night, he thought. Great.

Eva began. "I'm here at the 'Cozy Cafe' approximately one hundred yards from the 'Liberty Bank' with a clear view of the front entrance. With me is Ginny O'Riley, a regular patron of the cafe and neighborhood resident who witnessed the coming and going of the bank robbers. Ginny, can you describe for us what you saw."

Sully's Irish tenor boomed out. "Look, everyone, it's Ginny! Hey, Ginny, you're on the telly!" Ginny hustled over to the bar and Sully put his big arm around her shoulder, pointed at the newscast. "Nice outfit, darlin'"

"Says the fashion-plate." Sully glanced down at his stained sweater and well worn black slacks but only for a moment.

Eva placed the microphone in front of Ginny. "Well," she said, "I was just having my iced coffee like usual and then we saw these trick-or-treaters."

Eva yanked the microphone away to momentarily interrupt. "We?"

Damn, thought Max, here it comes.

"You know," said Ginny, looking around nervously, "the other cafe customers." Eva nodded. "So it seemed a little odd that the Halloween kids would go in a bank but they had just gone in the convenience store so...But then they were in the bank for a long time and we were joking about how long does it take to get some lollipops..."

Eva again. "Joking with the other customers?"

"Yeah, right. And then they came out but instead of continuing down Main Street they turned back the same way they came. They turned down that side street there," Ginny said, pointing, "and that was it. They were gone."

Max felt a momentary sense of relief. Was Ginny going to do the whole interview without mentioning him? And what about when the cops questioned her? It would look strange him leaving so quickly.

"And then?" asked Eva.

"And then nothing. It was a few minutes 'til someone came out the bank. I think it was the manager. He was on his phone. He looked pretty frazzled."

"But," said Eva, "you still didn't know the bank had been robbed?"

"No, no way. It was just a bunch of kids, least that's what we thought 'til all the cruisers started showing up. Then we knew something was going on."

"Did the police question you?"

"Yup. Just like you're doing. Same questions but not as perky." Ginny smiled and Eva blushed.

"Nice one," said Tony.

"Okay then," said Eva, apparently ready to wrap up.

Ginny tilted her head toward the microphone. "Ah, no one got hurt, did they?"

"No, thankfully no one was hurt, just pretty frightened. So that's it for now. I'm Eva Lopez and..."

Ginny grabbed the microphone and grinned. "And I'm Ginny O'Riley and you can find me working downtown at 'Sully's Brew and Chew', featuring the best pub grub in town." The bar erupted in shouts and applause at the mention, drowning out Ginny's halfhearted apology to the flabbergasted reporter as Sully hugged her closer..

"That's my girl," he boomed. "A round for the house!"

Ginny handed the mike back to Eva who seemed more amazed by the waitress's unsolicited advertisement than by the Halloween robbery itself. Professional journalist that she was, Eva quickly regained her composure as the customers roared their approval at Sully's largess, an occasion Max knew to be as rare as a four leaf clover. Eva finished up. "Back to you, Jesse."

The remote of Eva and Ginny at the scene dissolved and was replaced by Jesse and Brock back at the studio. "Well," said Brock, "that was certainly a first."

"Smart girl," said Jesse. "Naturally we will be following this story closely and bring you all the latest developments as they happen. Back after this."

Max muted the television volume, switched back to the sound system and set about filling Sully's unusual command as fast as he could. He watched Ginny politely extricate herself from the owner's embrace and head back to her tables, his immense feeling of gratitude overwhelming. He hadn't actually asked that she not mention his being at the cafe and yet she'd been kind enough not to. What a great girl, he thought. He looked up from the taps and noticed her standing at the service mat. She wasn't smiling. Max scurried down the bar, grabbing empties as he went. "Ginny," he began, but she interrupted.

"I need these drinks, Max."

He'd never heard her sound so serious. He poured the cocktails and kept his mouth shut.

She placed them on her tray, nodded, handed him a folded cocktail napkin and walked away. Max unfolded the napkin and stared at it. Written in bold print were three words. 'You owe me'. Well, he figured, that's true.

He tossed the napkin and went back to work but it was tough to concentrate. He surely did owe Ginny, but just what did he owe? Had he misjudged her and was now about to be a blackmail victim. He'd certainly misjudged people over the years so it wouldn't be the first time. No, he was just being paranoid. He'd been watching too much ID channel where someone was always double-crossing their best friend or murdering their spouse. Ginny wasn't a blackmailer. Ginny was a sweetie. She was merely reminding him that she'd done him a favor and maybe she'd ask him to do her a solid. He pulled more tickets from the dispenser, poured drafts and set them on the mat. Ginny returned, grabbed the beers without a word and dropped another folded napkin before walking away. Max hesitated, then picked it up. Only two words this time. 'Big Time'. Oh boy, he thought.

*

Ginny, too, had a hard time concentrating. It wasn't fair of Max to put her in that situation. She hadn't actually lied to the police but some might say she had withheld information. True, Max hadn't requested she not mention his presence at the scene but it was pretty damn obvious that's what he wanted. And why? She didn't know but she was certainly going to find out and he was going to tell her. He at least owed her that much.

Later, towards the end of the night, when Max was loading cases of beer onto the two-wheeler in the walk-in while Sully minded the bar, she confronted him. Ginny moved the milk crate that had propped open the walk-in's door and waited for it to close. Max didn't seem too surprised to see her.

"Oh, hey," he said. "I was kind of expecting you." He knew better than to smile.

"Max, what the fuck?"

Max couldn't recall Ginny ever cursing like that in front of him before nor was the harshness of her voice something he was familiar with. He searched for words. "You sound upset." That, he realized was probably not the best opener.

"I sound upset? Duh. You don't think I have a right to be upset?"

"I didn't say that."

"Yes, Max, I'm upset. I'm actually pretty pissed. Out of the blue, you show up in my neighborhood and we end up watching a bank get robbed and then you hightail it out of there like you're driving the getaway car and I'm stuck talking to the cops and going on TV."

"I thought you did great on the news." Ooops, another bad choice. Ginny grabbed a box of butter pads and hurled it at him.

"Are you kidding me! I don't care about the news. I care about what the Hell is going on. And you better tell me. You owe me that much."

Max picked up the box and returned it to its shelf, hoping the few seconds it took might calm things down. He looked at her seriously. "Ginny, I can't tell you."

This was not the answer Ginny expected. She scanned the walk-in, searching for some kind of blunt instrument she could pummel him with.

"I want to tell you," he continued. "I really do. But it would be dangerous. You're better off not knowing."

"Bullshit."

"No, seriously. I was stupid and got myself into a bad situation and I'm not bringing you into it."

"This is unbelievable."

"But," Max pleaded, "I will tell you when this is all over. I swear. I will tell you everything. I promise."

Ginny shook her head. "Great. Bet you money this has something to do with Chubster. I warned you."

Max said nothing. What, he thought, could he say? Ginny gave him a look that was almost more sad than angry, a look of profound disappointment. "Fuck you, Max." She turned and left the walk-in, Max watching her go, dejected, speechless.

★

SATURDAY

Millie was tending bar the next afternoon when Chubster and Nuggets started arguing. She wasn't all that familiar with Nuggets but she'd heard Chubster argue a hundred times before. Usually it was an amiable debate concerning the relative merits of Chubster's latest get-rich-quick scheme or the numerical attractiveness quotient of whatever newswoman was currently appearing on the TV or perhaps a dispute regarding the decision to pinch-hit in the previous night's ballgame. Chubster was known to have an opinion on every subject and would stick to his guns even if that subject happened to be an area of expertise for the opposing debater.

Whether shower heads with Tony, diesel engines with Joey or sit-coms with Biz, it mattered not. Chubster would explain, as pleasantly as possible, why you were wrong. But this particular argument was different. It was louder and neither man was smiling.

"I came all the way back from California."

"I didn't tell you to come back just for me, Nuggets. You said you were planning to come back anyway. Said there was no more work out there for you."

"Right," said Nuggets. "So I came back for this work, your work."

"I never promised any work. Said I might have a job for you."

"Well, what happened to that job?"

Chubster hesitated, drank from his mug. "It went to somebody else."

"It went?" Nuggets was getting louder. "What do you mean it went? It didn't went. You gave it to someone else."

"Okay, yes, you're right. I gave it to someone else. Calm down."

Millie walked over. "You two need to chill. I'm way too old to be breaking up bar fights."

Chubster looked hurt. "Millie, you know us. We're not gonna' fight. Just havin' a lively discussion. Speaking of chilling, why don't you grab us a couple of frosties, please and thank you."

"All right," said Millie. "Just keep it down."

Nuggets waited until she'd delivered their beers and moved on. "So, who got the job?"

"I can't tell you that."

"You can't tell me that? What are you now, a spy, a secret agent?"

Chubster paused, took a sip. "You know, at least I thought of you when an opportunity to make some dough came up. I don't remember you calling me up when you were out in Hollywood boning porn stars and getting paid to do it. There must have been some work for crew or extras or even a pinch-hitter but I doubt old Chubster Magee ever crossed your mind."

Nuggets was flabbergasted. He surveyed the room as if finding himself suddenly inserted into a 'Twilight Zone' episode. "You're kidding, right? You must be kidding me. I risked my life for that work. I put chemicals into my body, important parts of my body. Everybody thought I was out of my mind."

"Not me."

"Besides that, you're married. At least you're supposedly married. Don't think anybody has ever actually met the wife. Anyway, why would I think of a married guy for porn?"

"My moral or ethical principles concerning my marital situation should not have entered into it. There was work and money out there and you never thought of me."

"I can't believe you're trying to turn this around on me. You are some piece of work, I'll tell you. Some friend."

"I am your friend, Nuggets, and there still might be something for you down the line. This enterprise is just getting started."

They sat in silence for a minute, nursing their beers. "Well," said Nuggets, rising from his stool, "I hope there is. Because I've got a lot of free time on my hands and I'm gonna' find out what you're up to and I'm gonna' find out who you gave the job to." Nuggets turned to go, hesitated, looked back at Chubster. "You've got my number."

Chubster nodded, watched his old friend go, then turned back to the bar. "Hey, Millie, what time does Max get in?"

"Five o'clock. He's working a Saturday 'cause he took off Halloween."

"Oh, yeah, yeah, that's right. Halloween. You don't usually work Saturdays either."

"Yeah, I'm filling in, too."

Chubster looked at his watch, glanced at the TV, heard Ginny's voice. She must have come in the back entrance and was emerging through the bar. "Hey, Millie."

Millie, like everyone else, was always glad to see Ginny. "Hey, sweetie. You're early."

"You know how much I enjoy coming to work."

"Don't we all."

Ginny bent down, tucked her coat and pocketbook under the bar, stood and spotted Chubster. "Hey, Ginny," said the idea man.

Ginny spoke seriously. "I need to talk to you."

Chubster looked chagrined. Now what? This was supposed to be a private matter. There weren't supposed to be complications or extraneous characters. He'd done his job and so had Cranky Sam. His thoughts were interrupted by a firm hand on his shoulder. Ginny spoke softly. "Come on. Just take a minute."

"Well, uh, I was waiting for Max."

"Oh, I'll bet you were."

"What do you mean?"

Ginny ignored the question. "Let's go."

They stood by the entrance to the hallway which led to the restrooms. Biz always said it looked like the one on 'Cheers'. It was one of the only spots in 'Sully's where you could have a fairly private conversation. Chubster looked at Ginny. She still hadn't smiled. "What's up, Ginny?"

"Why don't you tell me? What kind of crackpot scheme have you got Max mixed up in?"

Chubster smiled. "Crackpot? That's a pretty old-fashioned word for such a young girl."

"Okay, I'm old school. Now talk."

"I don't know what you want me to say."

"Listen, Chub, I've never given you crap about your ideas before. Sometimes they're pretty funny and once in a while they even make a little sense."

"Gee, thanks." Chubster smiled again. Ginny did not.

"Shut up and listen. Max is my friend and he hasn't been himself ever since you enlisted him in whatever cockamamie scam you're currently running and I've got a feeling that this one is not even legal."

"Ginny, you're getting all carried away. What did Max tell you anyway?"

"Max wouldn't tell me anything. That's why I'm asking you."

Chubster was relieved. Maybe he could still lie his way out of this. "Look, Ginny, Max is a big boy. Occasionally I find a way to make some extra cash and sometimes I ask a friend to help out. But I would never do anything illegal. You know that. I've got principles, and my reputation and besides, a wonderful wife at home."

"Supposedly."

"What do you mean supposedly?"

"No one's ever seen her."

"That's a nice thing to say. I thought we were friends."

"We are friends but I'm telling you right now if you've gotten Max mixed up in anything that's gonna' cost him, well, we'll be a lot worse than ex-friends."

"Don't worry. Jesus, you act like you're his girl or something. Nothing bad is gonna' happen to Max. I promise." He looked at Ginny as sincerely as a bullshit artist like himself could. He felt it was a good effort. "Can I go back to my beer now?"

Ginny nodded slightly and he took a step but stopped when she spoke. "Hey, Chubster."

"Yuh."

"How long have you had that watch?"

"What?"

"Your watch. I don't recall you wearing a watch."

Chubster looked down at his wrist. "I don't know. Somebody owed me money and gave it to me. I don't remember how long ago.

Ginny smirked. "Really?"

"Yuh, really. My god, who are you, Columbo?" He headed back to his seat at the bar.

Ginny watched him go. That had been the least reassuring reassurance she'd ever heard. But maybe Chubster had a point. Max was a big boy. He didn't need her or anyone else to take care of him. And she wasn't his girlfriend so...She was about to check on her tables when she noticed Max and Miss Peabody enter Sully's. They'd come in the front door, which employees were not supposed to do. Most likely, Max had encountered Miss Peabody on the sidewalk and decided to accompany the old girl; help her reach her seat at the bar, gentleman that he was. They passed Ginny on the way and Miss P. lit up when she saw her.

"Hello, dear. How's my favorite redhead today?"

"Great, Miss Peabody. How are you?"

"Still breathing, right Max?"

"That's right. Better than the alternative." Max looked at Ginny like a puppy dog hoping for a bone. "Hi, Ginny."

Ginny hesitated, then nodded. "Hey, Max." Then back to Miss P. "I'll visit you at the bar."

"That's fine, dear. You take your time. I know you're a busy girl."

Ginny hurried off as Max guided Miss Peabody to her stool which he helped her mount.

He assumed his post at the taps, relieving Millie and mixing Miss P. her usual

Jim Beam Old Fashioned. Amazingly, Chubster had managed to keep quiet for five minutes with only a nod to acknowledge Max's arrival. Max was back in his domain, the place he felt most comfortable, and if not for Ginny's vexation and Chubster's impatience, it would have been another nice, easy lucrative shift. Why had he been so easily tempted? Life as a bartender wasn't so bad. He approached Chubster, leaned in, looked him in the eye. They spoke simultaneously. "We need to talk." It was almost comical but neither man laughed. Max was about to continue but Chubster's attention had been diverted by the television hanging behind Max's shoulder. He turned to see the game being held up by the 'Special Report' scroll.

Miss Peabody was watching, too. "Max, dear, could we please have the volume?"

Max grabbed the remote as Jesse, the anchorwoman appeared on screen. He turned down the music and turned up the TV.

"We're interrupting today's game to bring you breaking news concerning yesterday's heist at the Liberty Bank on Main Street. In an effort to help with the investigation, local law enforcement have chosen to release footage from the bank's security cameras in hope that a viewer may recognize one or more of the costumed perpetrators. We go live now to Eva Lopez standing by with that tape."

Max glanced back at Chubster who shrugged but dared not smile. The bar patrons had grown quiet and Max caught a glimpse of Ginny making her way over. Great, he thought, returning his attention to the television set as Eva came into view, standing once again next to the bank branch from the previous day.

"That's right," said the pretty reporter. "There's been a lot of discussion as just what exactly went on in that bank yesterday and how five pint size bandits were so easily able to get away with so much money. Now we can see for ourselves and, obviously, public curiosity is not the main justification for the release of this film, but rather the optimistic belief that someone watching might recognize these tiny crooks. So let's take a look."

Everyone sat in silence as the grainy security camera footage filled the screen. Max glanced at Ginny but wished he hadn't. She looked at him like a mother would look at a very naughty boy, a boy who had done something very, very bad. Ginny had her hands on her hips, an expression of disgust and disappointment on her face. Max knew that look. Years ago, during his misspent youth he'd seen it on his own mom's face many times. And he knew then, as he did now, that he'd rather receive a beating from his pissed off pop, may he rest in peace, then ever see that look again. He turned back to the screen as Eva continued.

"Of course," she said, "there is no audio on these tapes so we'll have to pay close attention. We see the trick-or-treaters enter the bank and at first nothing seems amiss. The other customers do not appear shocked or surprised and, in fact, seem somewhat amused."

On screen, the bandits mill about, grabbing a few lollipops from baskets, apparently waiting for the other customers to leave. When the last of these exits, the zombie stations himself at the door as the devil approaches the first teller.

"Now," said Eva, sounding a bit excited, "here's where things really get interesting. Keep your eye on the devil." The teller smiles as the little demon takes a piece of paper from his pocket and hands it to her. She unfolds the note, reads and her expression changes dramatically. She clutches her hand to her heart and drops out of sight behind the counter.

Max regarded the shocked looks on 'Sully's regulars.

"Holy shit!" said one.

"What the..." exclaimed another.

"Oh, my," said Miss Peabody. "I believe that girl has fainted."

"Let's watch that again," said Eva, as the tape rewound. "At first it seems the teller has ducked down to press the alarm button but when we slow down the tape we see an absolute look of horror on the young woman's face and it becomes clear that, after grabbing at her chest, she faints. Whatever vile, vicious threat was written on that note has shaken the bank teller to the core. The authorities are keeping the contents of the note to themselves for obvious reasons so it may be some time before we learn what it said. Now keep watching. The other teller goes to assist her fallen co-worker as the devil scales the counter. Here things really speed up."

Max shifted to survey the rapt audience seated at his bar, everyone transfixed, their glasses and mugs ignored on the counter, their small talk paused, their mouths agape. He took note of Chubster's empty stool. The flimflam man was nowhere to be seen, his half finished draft sitting forlornly like a recently departed cartoon character's cloud of smoke. Max was about to check with Ginny, see if she'd observed Chubster's hasty exit but thought better of it and shifted his gaze back to Eva.

"We see the second teller look at the devil and listen to his instructions as the ghost and goon arrive at the counter and hold out their candy bags. Now, watch over in the corner of the screen. We'll slow it down for you."

Max could hardly believe what he was watching. If this was, indeed, Cranky Sam and his boys, then this was not their first rodeo.

"Here comes the manager," said Eva. A middle-aged gentleman in coat and tie emerges from a small office but does not notice the miniature Batman lurking just outside his door and now Max is certain these are no youngsters as that Batman has stepped behind the manager and placed something at the small of his back and ushered him to a nearby chair. The manager protests but the Batman says something to him and the manager shuts his mouth and quickly sits down.

"So," said Eva, "everything is becoming clear now. The first teller has fainted, the manager is under guard and the second teller is afraid for her life. Though we haven't yet seen any weapons, any guns or knives, it is easy to see why no alarm button was pushed nor blue dye packets handed out." The second teller fills the bags with cash and the miniature crew are quickly out the door. "Once the other customers had vacated the bank," Eva continued, "the entire operation took less than three minutes, a very professional job. If these trick-or-treaters are kids, than they're criminal prodigies." The robbery footage ended and the telecast shifted back to Eva outside the bank. She wrapped up the remote. "I'm told we'll be replaying this tape on the evening news and probably a couple more times tomorrow. If you see anything at all that might be of help with the investigation, please contact the police department tip line. I'm Eva Lopez for Channel Four News. Now, back to Jesse."

Jesse appeared, still at the news desk, the tip line phone number scrolling on the screen below. "Quite a story and we'll be bringing you any developments as they happen. We now return you to your regular programming."

Max turned off the volume, replacing it with Sully's soul mix emanating from the speakers scattered throughout. The game returned, the clientele resumed their conversations and Ginny departed to check on her tables as Max surveyed the bar, determining who needed service.

"My word," said Miss Peabody. "Those poor girls."

Lennie Goodman had sat next to the older woman. Lennie was a cubicle guy; he had one of those middle management positions which consisted mostly of going to meetings and whose actual work, if there was any, proved undetectable to any of the blue collar regulars such as Tony or Joey who actually did something. Nonetheless, Lennie was harmless and likable, willing to buy a round or contribute to the small talk that coursed through 'Sully's. "Tell you what," he said. "I would love to read that note."

Miss Peabody shook her head. "I'm sure it was quite beyond the pale."

Lennie looked at her. "Beyond the pale. What does that mean, beyond the pale?"

Paul Bishop, a tall, silver-haired insurance adjuster whose friends called him Bish spoke up. "It means outrageous, over the edge, beyond the limits of human decency."

"Exactly," said Lennie. "That's why I want to read it."

"Oh, my," said Miss Peabody, as Biz arrived at the bar.

"Hey, Max, hey, Miss P.," he said. "What'd I miss?"

*

Later, as he mindlessly cleaned the now mostly deserted bar, Max was again lost in thought. When he'd earlier lifted Chubster's unfinished beer from its coaster, he'd discovered a small envelope folded underneath. The note inside instructed him to meet MaGee outside 'Dandy Don's Diner' Monday morning at ten. Max noted that the note included a few exclamation marks for emphasis so obviously Chubster felt this was to be an important meeting and, at this point, who was Max to argue. He bent down to extract one of the final racks from the glass washer and when he stood up Ginny was standing at the bar with her daughter.

"Max," said Ginny, "you know how you're in my doghouse right now and how I'm really mad at you and how you really owe me?"

Max realized this was a rhetorical question. "Ah, yah," he said. "Yes I do."

"Well, you remember Emily." That was it, he thought, that was her name, Emily. Ginny continued. "Can she just sit at the bar and you keep an eye on her while I finish up? I've got some booth dwellers that are about to pay. I know she's too young to be at the bar but Sully's not here and I'll just be a few minutes."

Max smiled at Emily, looked at Ginny. "Course. Sure."

Ginny motioned for Emily to grab a stool, then hurried back to her customers. Max nodded to Emily and grabbed another rack of glasses. Emily was a pretty young girl but was doing her best to hide it. Torn jeans, a baggy sweatshirt, no thought to any kind of hairdo and a minimum of makeup. Apparently, no style was the current style.

"You're in the doghouse," she said. "What does that mean?"

"It means," said Max, "that right now I am not your mom's favorite bartender."

"Usually you are."

Max smiled. "I'm glad to hear that."

"So what'd you do?"

"Oh, you know, nothing big."

"She was pretty mad last night, like super agitated."

"I'll bet."

"So you must have done something really shitty."

Max gave her a look. "Are you allowed to say that?"

"Say what?"

"You know."

"Shitty?"

"Yes, that."

Now Emily looked at him. "Don't change the subject."

Max began hanging the clean glasses from the brass fixtures above his head so they could dry properly. Emily was momentarily distracted by the alert from her cell phone. She was, Max thought, not your average teenager, but then again, he was certainly no expert on average teenagers. He observed her texting, her delicate fingers flying across the tiny keyboard. How do they do that? It took him forever to write a text. Did he have giant thumbs? Giant gorilla thumbs?

"My mom," said Emily, "says she's gonna' find out what you did. Says she's gonna' get to the bottom of it, whatever that means."

Max paused. "Really? She said that?"

"Yup. And she said I can help."

"Who are you, Nancy Drew?"

Emily was confused. "What? Who?"

Max went back to work. "Never mind."

Emily sent another hasty text, then set the phone down on the bar. "So," she said, "do you think my mom's pretty?"

Max shook his head. "What am I supposed to say to that?"

Emily smiled slightly. "The truth."

"Your mom," said Max, "is a very attractive woman."

"Do you think I'm pretty?"

Jesus, thought Max. Where the heck was Ginny? "You don't expect me to answer that, do you?"

"Why not?"

"Because I'm a grown man and you're sixteen years old."

"I can't be sixteen years old and be pretty?"

"That's not the point."

"Jeez," said Emily, picking her phone back up. "I didn't ask you to bone me or anything. Man, you need to chill."

Max almost dropped a glass. "What the..."

Ginny arrived in the nick of time. "Hey, guys, everything good?"

Emily answered without looking up from the phone. "Yuh, super."

"You have," said Max, "a very interesting daughter."

"Interesting," said Ginny, "is kind of an interesting choice of adjectives."

Emily looked up. "I asked him if he thought I was pretty and he got all freaked out."

Max shook his head. "I did not get all freaked out."

Ginny looked at her daughter. "Em, you can't go fishing for compliments. If someone wants to tell you you're pretty, they'll tell you you're pretty. You shouldn't ask."

Emily was texting again. "Yah, whatever. He had no problem saying you were pretty."

Ginny stared straight at Max. "That's only because he's on my shit list."

Max was about to speak but thought better of it. So far, absolutely nothing had gone well since hooking up with Chubster. And now Ginny and her typical teen were both mad at him. This was not part of the deal. He'd worked with Ginny for three years now and not once, not on good days or bad, in the weeds or out, wrong pours or lost tickets, not once did she snap at him, complain or give him the stink eye. Never. And then, just days after getting involved with Chubster MaGee, he was on her shit list.

Ginny placed her hand on Emily's shoulder. "Come on, honey, it's late. Time to go." Then to Max. "Thanks for watching her."

"No problem. Any time."

"Oh," said Ginny, finally a slight smile. "You don't want to say that."

Max nodded. "You're probably right."

Mother and daughter headed for the door but Ginny glanced back. "We're going out the front door. Don't tell Sully. See you tomorrow."

"Okay, see you tomorrow."

Max stood motionless, watching them go. He would talk to Chubster in the morning, maybe tell him that he wanted out, that he quit. Just finish cleaning, lock up and sleep on it. Tomorrow was, as everyone said, another day.

*

Ginny's ride home with her daughter wasn't exactly pleasant but at least it wasn't as silent as usual. Competing with Emily's cell phone was generally a losing proposition and the teen's monosyllabic grunts of acknowledgment were quite often the only indication that they were even conversing. However, this trip was different. Max had, for better or worse, apparently made an impression.

"So," said Ginny, "did you find anything out?"

Emily shook her head. "Nope."

Ginny figured that was the end of it and was about to fiddle with the radio dial when her daughter surprised her. "Why," she asked, "do you like that guy so much?"

"What do you mean? I don't like him that much."

"Yes you do. You're always talking about him."

Ginny was flustered but happy to be having an actual conversation. "Well," she offered, "he's nice, and he's interesting and he's funny..."

"Are we talking about the same guy?"

"Em."

"Well, he didn't show any interest in me."

"And if he had," said Ginny, glancing at her daughter, "you'd be telling me how creepy he was. It's not easy for single guys without kids, you know. Not many teenage girls sit down at that bar."

"He seemed all nervous and jumpy."

"Listen, Max is usually the king of that bar. He tells stories, cracks jokes, insults the regulars..."

"Insults the regulars?"

Ginny continued. "They love it. And he's nice to the waitresses and he works hard and," she added, smiling, "he flirts with women of an appropriate age."

"I knew you liked him."

"Hey, you asked me a question, I gave you an answer."

"Why don't you just hook up with him if he's so great?"

"Well," said Ginny, staring at the road straight ahead, "for one thing I'm mad at him. And for another, you know I don't go out with co-workers."

"Yeah, you might want to adjust that rule. Your selection process hasn't exactly been getting you a lot of winners."

Ginny glanced at Emily. "So now my sixteen year old daughter is giving me dating advice."

The teen shrugged and went back to texting. Ginny's first inclination was to argue the point but, unfortunately, Emily was right. Her recent dating history was fraught with losers, liars, miscreants and social defectives. She'd tried the dating sites with little success unless one considered being matched up with narcissists, whiners, under-achievers and mama's boys a success. She and her bitter single girl-friends had even renamed the matchmaking companies, 'OK Stupid' and 'Plenty O' Fakes'. And on those rare occasions when 'Match.com' actually found her a reasonable candidate, he'd soon be apologizing profusely and crawling back to the same ex he'd claimed to hate. Blind dates proved even worse; what were her friends thinking? The whole process was exhausting.

Maybe Emily was right. Maybe she should change her rules. She couldn't count the number of pleasant, attractive diners who'd asked for her number, though she, like her fellow servers, had always believed these men to be lazy, hitting on women who, by nature of the business, couldn't just brush them off and walk away but, in fact, had to stay put, smile and act somewhat attainable. But what if one of those men that she'd never given a chance was actually a decent guy?

And what about Max? Disregarding these recent shenanigans he was, from all indications a decent man, a good guy, no baggage and not bad looking either. He had respected her boundaries from day one, always been there when she needed a favor or just someone to listen. She knew damn well that he'd like nothing better than to take her in his arms but not once, even after a few post work cocktails, had he tried to force the issue.

But that was the Max she'd known days ago. This new Max was remote, myste-rious and undoubtedly up to no good. True, he was presumably being influenced by the shameless and shifty Chubster MaGee but that was no excuse. So maybe her dating philosophy had been prescient, helping her avoid hooking up with a prospective crook or con man. Much as she hoped this wasn't the case, only time would tell.

*

MONDAY

Max stared down at the knapsack which Chubster had placed on the floor next to their booth in 'Dandy Don's Diner'. Max had preferred to speak to him outside the establishment but Chubster insisted it be done inside, over eggs and bacon. It was mid morning so the diner, a refurbished dining car from some ancient rail line, complete with vinyl booths and vintage metal advertising signs hung throughout, was half empty. Nevertheless, the men kept their voices low.

"So," said Max, "this is it?"

Though Max had barely touched his breakfast, Chubster was hungrily polishing off his eggs and home fries, sopping up the leftover egg yolk with his white toast, pausing only long enough to sip his coffee and wipe his chin with a bundled up napkin.

"Yup," he said between bites, "that's it. That's the seed money. You take that and find thirty or forty speedy lunatics to run on the field at the end of the third quarter and you're home free, all done. The tickets are in there, too. Duffy called in a bunch of favors and the seats are all over the stadium."

Max finally lifted his head and looked seriously at the idea man. "Chubster, I'm nervous. Strange stuff is happening. Coincidences, new faces at the bar, people asking questions."

"Really," said Chubster, leaning back and patting his stomach. "Like who?"

"Ginny for one. She was near that bank job you told me to go watch..."

"Suggested. I said you might find it interesting."

"Well, she found it a little too interesting. And Nuggets is snooping around. And right after you enlisted me some old buck named Vanderbilt shows up looking for Miss Peabody and claims he's a retired gigolo."

"A gigolo?"

"Yeah, you know, a male escort."

"A man whore?"

"Yeah, I guess. Ex man whore."

Chubster found this quite amusing. "That's great. A retired gigolo. And you guys think I'm full of shit. Does he have a big unit?"

"What? How the Hell would I know? Look, we're getting off topic here. The point is I'm nervous."

"Listen," said Chub, pushing his empty plate toward the booth's edge, "I'm nervous, too. I've never done anything this big before or this illegal for that matter. But this is our chance. This is the risk I've been waiting for. And risks come with possible rewards and possible consequences. You know me, I'm mostly all talk and no action. Well, this is real action. And if no one gets hurt and we make a pile of dough, it's all good, right?"

"That's fine for you, Chub," said Max. "But I think it's too much action for me. And besides, someone could get hurt. I think I want out. I'm resigning. Give the job to Nuggets or somebody else. I promise you I won't say a thing. You have my word."

Chubster shook his head. "Are you serious? You can't quit. You met King. You heard the plan."

"You said I could go to the meeting and join up or not."

"Yuh, that night you could have decided to decline the offer. But not now. You can't say yes, then waffle for a couple days and then say oh, I changed my mind."

"Why not?"

"It's just not done. Max, you quit now and you will owe King a big favor. Big. You saw what Cranky Sam had to do to repay his favor."

"So that was Cranky at the bank."

"I didn't say that. But if you don't do this job now, you'll have to do a worse one down the line."

"Why?"

"Why. Are you kidding? Are you being naive? Max, this is serious business and these are serious guys. Besides, you quit now and that's on me, too. Not good." Chubster shook his head. "Not good."

Max paused, took a bite of toast and sipped his coffee. Was this the proverbial rock and a hard place he always heard about, a financial 'Sophie's Choice'? He was certain he did not want to go to jail but knew that a favor for King later on could entail ever greater risk than the one he was currently facing, perhaps a stint in the big house considerably longer than whatever sentence he'd currently receive for distributing stolen money. Of course, there was a third option. Quit and refuse to do whatever favor King had in mind in the future and, while that seemed the most ethically desirable, it was also likely the most physically threatening. Max looked at Chubster who emptied his mug and said nothing, always a bad sign when it came to the scheming chatterbox.

"How," said Max, glancing again at the knapsack, "do you know the bills can't be traced?"

Chubster appeared encouraged by the question. "I bought a couple things already. Besides, you're not actually buying anything anyways. You're giving the money away. Long as you use the cash correctly and don't start buying stuff, there's not even anything to trace."

"And when do I get my money?"

"Just as agreed. Fifty thousand when you're done recruiting. Another hundred after the game. Assuming everything goes well."

"And if it doesn't?"

"Then we'll all be shit out of luck."

Max leaned forward. "You're sure King will keep his word?"

Chubster was expecting the question. "Max, you heard King at the meeting, honor amongst thieves and all that. And anytime I've worked for him before, and I'll admit they were much smaller jobs, but any time I've done stuff, he's come through, no problems."

Max nodded as the waitress appeared, coffee pot in hand, offering to refill their cups.

"No, thanks," said Chubster. "I think we're done here. Max, are we done here?"

"Yup," said Max, smiling at the waitress. "We're good. Thanks."

The waitress, a thin middle-aged woman with faded tattoos and over bleached hair, flashed her best robotic smile and ripped a small check from her pad. "Okay," she said, "I'll take this when you're ready."

Chubster quickly grabbed the bill. Well, thought Max, picking up the heavier than expected knapsack, at least this version of Chubster was generous. They paused outside the diner and shook hands. Chubster looked at Max seriously, their hands still clasped. "You have," he said, "five days. Good luck."

*

Max was home counting the cash and separating the tickets when Ginny called. Considering the last few days' events, getting a call from her was surprise enough but the nature of the conversation even more so.

"Hey, Ginny," said Max into the phone. "What's up? Thought you were still mad at me."

"I am."

"Oh." Max wasn't sure of the proper response. An awkward pause seemed appropriate.

"Listen, Max," said Ginny. "Do you want to get some dinner tonight? Or maybe grab some drinks?"

Max lowered the phone, stared at the device as though it was possessed., then placed it back to his ear. "Are you asking me out on a date?"

"Yes, Max," said Ginny as though speaking to a five year old. "I'm asking you out on a date."

"Oh, uh, yah, sounds great. But I thought you didn't date co-workers."

"You gotta' cut back on all this thinking."

"You have no idea," said Max, staring at the piles of money on his coffee table.

"So," said Ginny, "I was thinking maybe the 'Bistro' over on Broadway."

"Sure, that's fine. But I'm paying."

"Damn right you are."

Max smiled. "When were you thinking?"

"How about eight. I'll meet you at the bar."

"You don't want me to pick you up in my Rolls?"

"Max, if you had a Rolls, I would have broken my rule long ago."

"Okay, but I'm a little nervous. This isn't a trick, is it?"

"I guess," said Ginny, "you'll just have to wait and find out."

She hung up without saying goodbye. Max stood motionless for a few moments, doing some more dangerous thinking. What just happened? The same woman who, a day before, was furious with him, the same woman whose rule about not dating co-workers or customers had always seemed rock solid, so much so that he'd never even attempted to convince her to break it, that same woman had just asked him out. So, now that he'd embarked on his new career as a criminal, beautiful Ginny O'Riley, wonderful Ginny O'Riley, kind, caring, funny Ginny O'Riley had decided to go out with him. Maybe it was true that women were attracted to bad boys. No matter. He couldn't cope with those thoughts right now. He forced himself back to the task at hand.

He told himself to go slow, think things through, proceed with caution. Obviously he couldn't bring all the money with him on his candidate search. But he did have to bring enough. Should he get a gun, he wondered. His ex had hated guns, wouldn't allow one in the apartment and even after the divorce, he'd hardly given his lack of firearms a second thought. But now he'd be propositioning complete strangers with an unusual offer, strangers who could be unfriendly, suspicious, possibly large and angry. A little self defense didn't sound too bad. But there was no time for an application and background check and no way was he going to the black market; the last thing he needed in this stressful endeavor was to break another law. No, what he needed was an opening line, an approach which would intrigue prospective participants, something that would encourage interest rather than suspicion, a proposal that would amuse rather than anger.

Max did have one idea. He'd been mulling it over the last few days, pros and cons, flaws and advantages. After much reflection and a serious lack of alternatives, he'd made his decision. He searched the hall closet and found an old leather briefcase with a combination lock that his parents had given him years ago, apparently believing, or at least hoping that he'd pursue a career requiring just such an accessory. Bartending, being a profession without much need for the transport of important contracts and documents, the briefcase had sat in the closet gathering dust for as long as he could remember. Now, as Max cleaned its exterior and checked the still functioning lock, he was glad he'd never trashed or re-gifted it. He placed a few small, banded bundles of cash and a handful of tickets inside, locked the combination, grabbed his jacket and headed out the door.

He'd walked by the local copy shop hundreds of times before but had never had reason to stop in. Now he sat on one of the uncomfortable plastic chairs, the unflattering lighting beaming from the florescent bulbs overhead, revealing every pore and skimpy whisker hair of the university students who were obviously the store's main clientele, and waited patiently for the business cards he had ordered. He'd been informed by the milk white goth girl behind the counter that it would take about an hour to print them but he'd decided to wait. The magazines available to pass the time – 'Wired', 'Mother Jones', 'Spin' – were not his favorites but they'd do. It was not a 'Sports Illustrated' kind of place.

Max must have dozed off when he heard his name, or at least the name he'd chosen for this enterprise being called. He wiped his lips, hoped the young customers hadn't noticed the old-timer drooling in the corner. The pale girl who'd taken his order was waiting behind the counter, a small rectangular package resting in front of her. Max rotated the box so he could read the sample business card taped on top:

LAST NICKEL PRODUCTIONS
Jim Johnson
Casting Agent

Max smiled at the salesgirl, noticed her name tag for the first time – Tulip. "Looks good," he said, reaching for his wallet. "What do I owe you?"

"Twenty four, ninety five," she replied. Max used his own pocket money to pay and smiled again as Tulip eyed him curiously. "So," she said, handing him his change, "are you casting anything right now?"

The question caught Max off guard. He'd thought he'd had a good idea but hadn't considered it paying off quite this quickly. "Well, ah, Tulip," he said, addressing her seriously, "as a matter of fact we are but I've got to be honest with you. We're a very small independent film company. Some people might call what we do guerrilla film-making. Are you familiar with the term?"

Tulip popped a stick of gum between her ruby red lips. "I think so. Low budget, right?"

"Oh, yeah. Super low budget. And very secretive. Under the radar."

"Yuh, I noticed you didn't include a phone number."

"Oh, no. We'd get way too many calls. There's a lot of people out there want to be in a movie, no matter how low budget."

"Yuh," said Tulip. "True that. I've thought about it."

"Really," said Max. Maybe this was going to work out after all. "Any experience?"

"Couple student films I was in." Tulip paused. "Is nudity required?" Max hadn't really thought about that but before he could reply Tulip continued. "Cause I don't have a problem with nudity."

"Well," said Max, "it's certainly not necessary at this point in the process but you've definitely given me some food for thought on a number of different levels."

"I have?"

"Oh, yes. Now let me ask you an unusual question. Are you fast?"

Tulip was confused. "Am I fast?"

"Yes. You know, can you run fast? Are you speedy?" The young coed seemed struck dumb by the question. Max was unfazed. "You do have a runner's figure..." He leaned over the counter. "And you are wearing sneakers."

"Everyone wears sneakers."

"Yeah, that's true." Max felt the breath of a tall grad student on his shoulder, realized he was holding up service. "Why don't you take care of this man and then I'll try to explain myself." He stepped aside, waited as Tulip took care of the large bearded scholar. Maybe, Max thought, this was going to be easier than he'd figured. Some people wouldn't even care about the money. Just put them on screen, make them famous. Max almost laughed out loud as Tulip finished up.

"So," she asked, "why do I have to be speedy to be in your movie?"

By the time Max finished describing the huge climactic scene to be filmed at

98

the University stadium and how his people couldn't possibly afford to rent out such an edifice or pay the hundreds of extras that would be required for background shots and how the volunteers he cast would receive a complimentary ticket to the big game, a small stipend up front and a large one after they had run onto the field, said stipend increasing exponentially by the number of minutes that volunteer spent on the field before either re-entering the stands or being captured by security, and lastly being reimbursed for any legal costs or fines that may be accrued, well, by then Tulip was entranced. The production had everything she adored – art, risk, fun, anarchy, possibly even beauty. She wanted in.

Now Max was feeling confident, almost pushy. "Tulip," he said, "you mentioned earlier some student films you were in. And I assume you're still a student at the university." She nodded. "I wonder, do you think you could get access to some of the equipment they check out to the students in the film department? We could save some money that way, maybe pass it on to the cast." Max smiled broadly. Tulip assured him that not only could she acquire a camera and other equipment, but she could easily enlist one of the audio visual nerds to help out if Max needed.

For the first time, instead of feeling nervous and scared, Max was excited. He opened the briefcase, peeled off five one hundred dollar bills from one of the money rolls, handed them to the astonished copy shop clerk and, after making note of her phone number, school and work schedule, told Tulip he'd be in touch very soon. He deposited a few of the freshly printed business cards in his shirt pocket and placed the box containing the rest in the briefcase, closed and locked it and, with a smile and a nod, took leave of his first volunteer.

What a day, thought Max, as he navigated the familiar streets of his neighborhood. Turning the heist into an independent film may well turn out to be a brilliant idea. He'd easily secured his first runner and that night he had a date with Ginny. Things were going far too well. For a cynical optimist like himself, this was cause for worry. But Max was a big believer in streaks so he figured he'd just ride this one out, enjoy it and instead of imagining worst case scenarios, just concentrate on the positive. With that in mind he decided to pay more attention to his surroundings. He'd walked those streets before but was usually either daydreaming in the sunshine or head down and determined in the cold. He took his time, looked around, observing, taking it all in, noticing things for the first time.

Schools, ball fields, churches that he'd paid no mind to previously were now points of interest. People he wouldn't have looked at twice were now candidates. He decided to cross the fields behind the High School, paused at a concrete basketball court populated almost entirely by tall, thin African-American athletes involved in a ferocious hoops battle, racing back and forth, their muscled bodies glistening with sweat, their quickness and agility impressive, their bursts of speed majestic. This group, thought Max, would be a virtual bonanza. But his current state of elation had not completely clouded his mind. He was not about to be the white dude offering money to young black men so they'd help commit a felony. No, he'd come back with a camera person, maybe a sound guy, too. The more professional his independent film cover seemed, the better his chances of recruiting, not to mention decreasing the risk of being beat up and simply relieved of his money. He moved on.

Abutting the basketball court was a Middle School and a number of athletic fields – baseball, football, soccer, as well as a large, oval track. Max strolled through the youngsters playing and practicing their various sports as well as the older jocks strenuously circling the track, some making good time, others huffing and puffing, wondering how this had all seemed much easier not that long ago. Max had been a decent athlete himself back in the day and his memories of sporting glory were competing with angles and ideas concerning the recruitment process. He truly wanted to stop and chuck the old pigskin around or take a few swings at home plate but knew better, realized that he was no longer eighteen, or thirty for that matter, that he was just another middle-aged dreamer reliving his youth and carrying a briefcase.

He stopped to rest on a bench beside the track, eventually noticed faster runners joining the older folks doing laps. Apparently the young yuppie joggers slept a bit later than the old bucks. The newcomers were certainly fast enough for the job but Max worried they might not need money, especially ill-gotten gains. Not that they'd be morally opposed, just afraid of jail. He'd find out next time. He had more stops to make.

*

Ginny was having doubts. Since when did she take advice from her teenage daughter? She was about to break one of her longest standing rules, one that had worked well for as long as she could remember. Don't date customers or co-workers. Simple. Some people would say 'don't shit where you work' but she'd always hated that phrase. She could flirt with the patrons, hang with the boys, even bust balls on occasion, but she was not vulgar. In fact, that was one of the things she liked about Max; he seldom cursed. Whereas the guys in the kitchen would throw f-bombs around like bread crumbs and some of the stool squatters at the bar couldn't describe their day without a liberal sprinkling of blue language. Their boss was a bastard or their wife was a bitch or, even worse, their landlady was the 'c' word. Even Sully used a number of unfamiliar Irish swears that may or may not have been the filthiest adjectives and nouns in the lounge.

But not Max. He seemed to like everyone and when he didn't, he'd call them a dumb ass or a nitwit. Instead of fuck, he'd say fudge ripple. Instead of shit, he'd say sugar beans. She found it cute, endearing. But, she reminded herself, he was not being very cute or endearing right now. And now was when she'd decided to break her rule and go out with him. What the fuck, she thought, before catching herself and almost laughing out loud.

And what about the timing? Her favorite co-worker, her bar buddy who'd always been honest and forthcoming was suddenly a man of mystery, a man who knew that she was dying of curiosity. And she decides to ask him out? Obviously, he would think she wanted to pump him for information, seduce the truth out of him. Why wouldn't he think that? She would.

Then again, she remembered, he was still a man. And as her mother, sisters, friends and complete strangers had always told her, all men are dogs. They'll do anything to get in your pants, so surely Max would drop a few hints regarding his clandestine activities if he thought the evening might end in his favor. That wasn't the point though. She hadn't asked him out to solve a mystery. She'd asked him because, thanks to Emily, she'd realized that's what she wanted to do. And now, well now it seemed more complicated. See what happens when you break one of your golden rules, she told herself. Maybe she should back out, call him and say something had come up. She did have a teenager after all. They were always good for an excuse or an alibi.

She took a deep breath, calmed down. She was overthinking things. It was just a date. Simply go out, have a good time and don't ask questions. If he wants to bring things up, fine. But she would not press the issue. She recalled the Jets from 'West Side Story'. Play it cool. She smiled, opened her closet, placed her hands on her hips and stared at her clothes. Decisions.

*

For the first time in days, Max felt good. His idea to turn the stadium heist into a movie appeared to have a decent chance of working out. He'd secured his first volunteer, Tulip, and there was a possibility she could procure some free film equipment. Ginny had kept quiet about his presence at the Halloween hold-up and she'd even asked him out on a date. So what if it was her attempt to find out what he was up to. It was still a foot in the door. Besides, she was breaking her rule and she was breaking it for him. He'd spent most of his life being a nice guy and finishing last. Maybe his luck was changing. The thought made him grin but only for a moment. You couldn't walk alone with a big smile on your face. Sad as it may be, people would assume you were deranged.

He felt confident and wanted to do more recruiting but thought better of it. Instead he made his way to a nearby pawn shop. Tulip had seemed enthusiastic and sincere but what if, for whatever reason, she couldn't obtain a camera. Best to have a backup plan.

Max wasn't very familiar with pawn shops but, from what he'd seen in movies and on TV, 'Crazy Ed's Second Chance' appeared pretty typical. Walls hung with all manner of musical instruments, glass cases filled with watches and jewelry. An entire section devoted to electric guitars. Apparently there were a lot of guitar slingers out there whose services weren't exactly in demand.

The man sitting behind the counter reading a newspaper, who Max assumed was Crazy Ed, was currently demonstrating no signs of insanity but Max had no interest in ironic nicknames right then. Ed was big, bald and probably bad. He wore a fuzzy beard and muttonchops, sported a jean vest and appeared to have spent a great deal of his shop's profits on tattoos and silver rings. He looked up from his paper and addressed Max.

"Help you find something?"

"Ah, yah, as a matter of fact, yes, a camera, a film camera."

Crazy Ed pointed to a corner littered with electronics – cameras, tripods, camcorders, klieg lights, editing equipment. It wasn't well organized but most of the items seemed in good condition. Max took his time, lifting and examining cameras, wishing he'd done more research; there were numerous choices. Modern Sony camcorders, vintage Kodak sixteen millimeters, small hand-held devices couples had likely used to make memories with their toddlers, large units with attached microphones for the porno guys. Prices varied but Max knew he had to look professional so this was no time to be cheap. He selected one of the larger, newer units, then turned his attention to the tripods. He didn't actually need one but they didn't cost much and would probably assist in making it look like he knew what he was doing. They all appeared fairly similar so he grabbed the shiniest one and headed to the counter. Crazy Ed was doing the crossword when Max placed the equipment on the glass. The bulky proprietor put down his pen.

"All set?"

"I believe I am," said Max. "Are you Crazy Ed?"

Ed smiled slightly. "I believe I am."

"Nice shop."

"First time in?"

"Yup. First time in a pawn shop. Ever."

"You appear to be shooting a movie."

"Yuh," said Max. "I am...or rather we are."

"And you don't have your own equipment?"

"We're extremely low budget."

"I guess". Ed glanced toward the electronics. "Do you need any editing machines?"

Max hadn't considered editing. This film was never going to be made, never mind edited so obviously the answer was no. Besides, weren't people editing stuff on their laptops and 'Ipads' these days? "No," he said. "One of my associates is taking care of that. So just these, I guess."

As Crazy Ed began the paperwork, jotting down models and serial numbers, Max couldn't help but stare at the impressive fellow. He had to be at least three hundred pounds and it wasn't all fat. This guy, Max felt, would be tough to tackle on the football field. Ed swung the papers around for Max to sign.

"So, ah, Ed," said Max, picking up the pen, "you ever play any football back in the day?"

Ed looked at Max as if deciding whether to pummel him or answer the question.

"I only ask," said Max, now a bit nervous, "because we're shooting our big scene on the football field at the stadium."

"Before the game Saturday?"

"No, during."

"You don't own your own film equipment but you have enough money to rent out the stadium during the big game?"

Damn it, thought Max, this guy's asking good questions. Weren't big old pawn shop owners supposed to be dumb? "Uh, no, no, of course not. We're kind of underground filmmakers, you know, as I said, very low budget, everything sort of clandestine, you know, ah, a very seat of our pants operation."

"Oh," said Crazy Ed. He was hard to read.

"But," said Max, "it's our big scene, our finale, and we budgeted most of what we do have to pay our actors."

"Pay your actors to do what?"

"Um, to run on the field and avoid security."

"Is security in on the deal?"

I wish, thought Max. "No, I'm afraid not."

"So you're offering to pay people, um, your actors, to run on the field and try not to get tackled and beat up by security?"

"Well, when you put it that way."

"They'll get arrested."

"There is that chance but we bail 'em out and pay court costs, plus more money after we're done."

"Sounds pretty crazy."

Max was straining. "Well, you are Crazy Ed, right?"

Crazy Ed paused, apparently mulling over another question. He did not disappoint. "What's my motivation?"

"Your motivation? To make a few bucks I guess, and a free ticket to the game."

"No, no, my motivation in the film. The story."

Damn, thought Max, this was a lot easier with Tulip. "Ah, yes, your motivation in the film," he said, stalling for time. "These are very good questions."

Crazy Ed leaned back, folded his massive arms across his enormous chest. "Well," he said, "I did a lot of theater in college."

As usual, Max spoke too quickly. "College?"

Crazy Ed looked vexed. "Yuh, does that surprise you?"

"No, no, no, no, of course not. Why would it?"

"Just because I'm big does not mean I'm dumb."

"Obviously. You are obviously not dumb."

"I played Falstaff, Big Daddy Pollitt, I was the understudy for Tevyue in 'Fiddler on the Roof'"

"Wow, that is impressive. We are definitely going to consider you for our next project, I mean if you think you might like to try acting again."

"I'd consider it."

"But for now, let me just pay you what I owe..."

Max was about to peel off some bills from one of the rolls but remembered Chubster's warning about the stolen cash and proffered his credit card instead.

Crazy Ed rung him up on an ancient cash register. Max signed the receipt, rummaged in his pocket for one of his brand new business cards. "And why don't I leave my card so you can give this some thought. I'll come back in a couple days, give you time to think, and if you decide to sign up for the stadium scene you'll receive a thousand dollar advance. How's that sound?"

"Sounds good." Ed was looking around the shop as if he no longer trusted his own establishment. "Is this a hidden camera show?"

Max placed the camera bag's strap over his shoulder, picked up the briefcase and tripod and turned to go. "No, no, Ed, this is the real deal."

He headed for the door as Crazy Ed called out. "There's no phone number on this card!"

"No worries," shouted Max. "I'll be in touch!"

"And the name's different than the one on the credit card!"

"That's showbiz, my friend!" And, Max decided, as they say in the theater, exit stage left.

*

Millie was behind the bar when Mr. Vanderbilt finally reconnected with his old friend, Miss Peabody. Millie had no knowledge of their background stories but they certainly appeared pleased to get reacquainted. In the year or so that Miss Peabody had been frequenting 'Sully's Brew & Chew', not once had Millie witnessed the older woman sit anywhere but at the bar, quite often on the same stool. Various elderly gentlemen, some of obvious means, others of questionable pedigree, would request that she join them at one of the tavern's wooden tables or vinyl booths but Miss P. would graciously decline. She seemed quite content to banter with the bartenders, chitchat with the regulars and gossip with the waitresses while sipping her old-fashioned. Though it was quite evident she put a great deal of effort into her appearance, she nonetheless demonstrated no need for male companionship. Until now. On that day the old gal had departed her usual perch at the bar as soon as Mr. Vanderbilt suggested she do so. They proceeded to sit across from one another, smiling and giggling like two teens at the Junior Prom, frequently touching arms or hands.

Millie was not surprised to see Chubster MaGee come through the front door and head straight for the bar. Chubster was known to show up at all hours of the day, unlike most of the other regulars who, because of their jobs' consistency could be counted on to appear at the same time, more or less, every day. Chubster, lacking any evidence of steady employment, could come and go as he pleased, only periodically encumbered by whatever time constraints were required for his latest shenanigans. So Millie, presently slicing limes and lemons over a Jack Daniels cutting board with an extremely sharp knife barely looked up when Chubster sat down.

"Max here?" he asked, glancing from side to side.

Millie paused to stare at him before replying. "Hello, Chubster. How are you today?"

Chub looked sheepish. "I'm fine, thanks. Sorry, Millie. How are you?"

"Never better. What's going on?"

"I just need to talk to Max. No big deal."

"He called out. Asked me to cover so I'm doing a double."

"Oh, he say why?"

"I didn't ask. He's done me a lot of favors." Millie set the knife down, wiped her hands with a bar towel. "You got time for a cold one?"

"Is that a rhetorical question?'

Millie grinned, headed for the tap. "Pretty much."

She poured Chubster a frosty, placed it on a coaster in front of him, then strolled away to wait on two new customers. Chubster surveyed the establishment, sipping his suds, and noticed Miss Peabody seated across from a well-dressed, elderly gentleman in a corner booth. They were engaged in a rather animated conversation and Chubster was surprised, familiar as he was with the older woman's disinclination to abandon her familiar spot at the bar. He recalled that Max had mentioned unusual things occurring at 'Sully's. Was this one? He awaited Millie's return.

"You notice Miss Peabody's off her stool?" he asked when she was again standing in front of him.

"Yeah," said Millie. "What are the odds?"

"Who's the old buck?"

"I don't know. I heard somebody had been asking about her lately. Maybe he's an old friend. But they sure are happy to see each other. Look at 'em. They were definitely never married."

Chubster failed to laugh, instead staring seriously at Mr. Vanderbilt. "You think I should go talk to him?"

"What?"

"You know. Check him out. Make sure he's on the up and up."

Millie was baffled. "What are you, her father?"

"No, no. But, you know, you don't want anybody to take advantage of the old gal, do you?"

"She's a big girl, Chubster. I'm sure she'll be fine."

Millie returned to her fruit, Chub returned to his beer and Miss Peabody and Mr. Vanderbilt seemed to return to their youth, laughing, flirting and having a grand time. Chubster watched the old couple and Millie watched Chubster. She had not often seen him this serious. He appeared completely lost in thought.

*

Max, as always, had no idea how to dress for his date. Years of over dressing, under dressing, looking good, looking bad, but mostly just looking okay. Why did he even care? No one had ever called him out on it, at least not since his white tux at the Junior Prom and he was still sure that white tuxes were cool. Hadn't James Bond worn one? Besides, there really was no place to turn to for the common man's sartorial advice. Women had countless magazines and TV shows but what was available for guys? 'Queer Eye for the Straight Guy'? Come on. 'GQ' magazine? Yes, if you had three hundred dollars for a pair of shoes. Or you could ask your buddies, none of whom had any fashion sense but were perfectly willing to ridicule yours. He decided, as he quite often did, to go middle of the road – dark jeans, salmon colored dress shirt and brown suede blazer, no tie. And, because Max was a man of conviction, he tucked the shirt in. He'd determined a few years back, when grappling with the tuck or no tuck quandary, that he was not a follower of trends, not one of society's fashion lemmings. He would, as he had done since grade school, tuck in. If that made him appear old or un-hip or boring, so be it. A man had to have some principles.

Later, seated across from Ginny at 'Bella Bistro' in a small corner booth, Max felt secure in his clothes. Ginny, too, had apparently chosen the safe route – tight jeans, loose blouse, short black leather jacket, though it must be said, Max felt, that no matter what the curvaceous waitress had picked to wear, Ginny's appearance was in no danger of ever being considered average. Having long ago resigned himself to Ginny's dating protocol, Max had forced himself to not dwell on just how pretty she actually was. Easier to concentrate on his bar duties that way. But now, with no stained 'Sully' t-shirt, no soiled apron, no hair in a messy bun, there was no over-looking Ginny O'Riley.

Max was still curious. "So," he said, "what's going on? Why are you breaking your rule for me?"

Ginny sipped her wine. "Well, actually it was Emily's idea."

Max almost spilled his beer. "Emily? Your daughter, Emily?"

"That would be the one."

"She hates me."

Ginny smiled. "Emily's hates everyone. She's sixteen."

"Oh, that's reassuring, I guess."

"But she does think you're a step up from the men I've been dating recently."

"She does?"

"Yup, that's what she said."

"Well," said Max, smiling, "from the stories you've told me, the bar was set pretty low."

"That may be so. But why overthink it? Why don't we just, you know, relax and enjoy the evening."

Max considered the stress he'd been through lately, Ginny's lovely appearance and her brilliant suggestion. "That, my dear, is a capital idea." He grinned, raised his glass. "Here's to a relaxed, enjoyable evening." Ginny smiled and tapped his glass with hers as the waiter arrived.

*

Ginny had not intended to question Max's recent activities and peculiar behavior, nor did she plan on sleeping with her co-worker; one broken rule at a time, she thought. Likewise, Max had no intention of sharing his somewhat criminal escapades and their connection to one Chubster MaGee, and getting Ginny into the sack, pleasant as he assumed that would be, was not his goal this night, not on what he hoped would be the first of many spent together.

But alcohol has a way of altering the best of intentions and Max and Ginny found themselves walking through the cool October air towards Max's apartment where, they had agreed, a short nightcap, a hot cup of coffee and a cab ride home for Ginny would be the conclusion of a lovely evening. At least that was the plan, but when Ginny slipped her arm through Max's and huddled closer for warmth, other thoughts began to take place. Thoughts that were quickly put on hold when, hesitating at a curb before crossing the street, Ginny looked at Max with great affection.

"You know," she said, "it's nice to have the old Max back."

Max flinched. "Uh, oh, here we go."

"What do you mean here we go?"

Max caught himself, not wanting to upset things before they started. Maybe it was just an innocent remark, not the lead in to an interrogation. "Sorry," he said. "Sorry. I've been a little defensive lately. Come on, let's cross."

They hurried through the intersection. The chilly night and rapid pace seemed to be having a somewhat sobering affect. "I wasn't going to start asking questions," said Ginny. "I wasn't even going to mention the whole bank thing."

"You weren't?"

"No, I wasn't even going to mention Chubster MaGee."

"Okay, okay, I get it. I'm sorry. It's just, you know, you were really mad and then tonight you don't seem so mad and it's a little confusing..."

"Good. Women are supposed to be confusing. It's another one of our prerogatives."

"Well, I certainly didn't mean to ruin things but I've had a lot on my mind lately and I think we've had a great first date and..."

Ginny flashed a brief smile. "How do you know we're going to have a second?"

"I don't," said Max, taking her hand. "What I was about to say is that right now the only thing on my mind is you."

"Oh, what a sweet talker."

"That's me. I'm a regular Romeo. Anyway, here we are."

Max released Ginny's hand, fished in his pocket for the keys to his apartment, unlocked and opened the door. He ushered her past the entrance and trailed her up the stairs in what he felt was a gentlemanly fashion. The sight of Ginny's shapely bottom and the alcohol imbibed earlier obviously clouded Max's mind for those last few moments before reaching his door. For if they hadn't, perhaps he would have recalled how he'd left the apartment and the new purchases that he'd neglected to put away. He hadn't imagined that this beautiful redheaded object of desire would be coming back to his place, at least not on the first night. If he had considered such a possibility, surely he would have secured the camera and tripod and briefcase safely out of sight and the date may have proceeded as liquor influenced nights so often do. But he had not hidden the equipment and when Ginny entered the small bachelor pad and slowly looked around, she could not help but notice the aforementioned items laying on the kitchen table in plain sight. Max followed her gaze but it was all he could do not to slap his forehead like some straight man in an old comedy reel. Ginny hesitated, but only for a moment. Some things simply require comment.

"Okay, Max," she said, "I have tried very hard not to ask any questions but what the Hell?" She approached the table. "A movie camera, a tripod and a briefcase. What is going on? What are you up to? Or should I ask what are you and Chubster up to? If he's got you mixed up in a porno..."

"Jesus, what? No." Max was sobering up quickly now and any thoughts he'd had earlier of romantic cuddling or hot messy sex were departing like birds from a cage. He tried stalling. "How about that nightcap?" he asked, opening a cupboard.

Ginny placed her hands on her hips. "Max," she said.

He shut the cupboard. "Okay, okay, I can explain."

"I'll bet."

"Hey, it's not like I've done anything wrong."

"No."

"No. It's a movie camera. Not a gun."

"Then why are you acting so defensive?" Ginny almost seemed to be enjoying this, watching Max squirm.

"Cause you're making me."

"Okay," said Ginny, smiling slightly. "Sorry. Why don't you pour us those drinks, we'll sit down and you can tell me whatever you want. If it's none of my business, you can tell me that, too. But I'll bet you dollars to donuts this has something to do with Chubster MaGee, who, I think you'll remember, I warned you not to get involved with"

"How could I forget?"

"Very funny."

"Okay," said Max, relaxing just a bit. "Fair enough." He reopened the cupboard, pulled down a bottle, poured two glasses as Ginny made her way to the couch. She removed her jacket, made herself comfortable. Rufus strolled in, stared at Ginny for a moment and, apparently satisfied, scaled the couch and lowered himself onto her lap. Max walked over, handed Ginny a drink, paused momentarily, then chose to sit in the old easy chair diagonally across from the couch. "I see you've met my roommate."

Ginny petted Rufus who purred approvingly. "I forgot you had a cat. You don't really seem like a cat person. What's his name?"

"Rufus."

"Oh, hi, Rufus."

"You don't have anything about cats, do you, you know, allergies or anything?"

"No, but I have to say I pictured you as more of a dog guy."

"Yeah, you'd think, right. But he kind of picked me."

Ginny sipped her drink. "Anyway."

"Right." Max cupped his drink in both hands, leaned forward. "Okay," he said, "let's see."

"Jesus, Max, relax. If you don't want to tell me..."

"No, I do want to tell you. But I'm not supposed to tell you. I told Chubster I wouldn't tell anyone, including you."

"Then don't tell me."

"But then you'll think I'm up to no good."

"I already think you're up to no good. What's the difference?"

Max leaned back in his chair, stared at his glass. Now what, he thought. How much lying was he going to do? It was bad enough lying to strangers but now he was contemplating lying to someone he truly cared about. On the other hand, if he told Ginny the truth, he'd be getting her involved, possibly putting her in danger. Lying seemed the better way to go, lesser of two evils and all that. He took a deep breath.

"We're making a movie," he said.

"You and Chubster are making a movie?"

"Yes, that's right and no, it's not a porno."

"Okay, I'll bite. What kind of film is it?"

"An underground film. Very low budget. The whole thing's on the sly."

Ginny was, to put it mildly, surprised. "Let me get this straight. You two knuckleheads are actually making a real movie. A secret movie."

Max looked hurt. "Knuckleheads?"

"Come on."

"Well, actually we're helping to make it. There are, you know, backers, producers."

"Of course there are."

"We're really just working on one big scene, the finale."

Ginny took a long swig from her glass. "And the secret producers of this secret movie hired you two because of your extensive experience in the entertainment industry?"

"Hey, I entertain people behind the bar every day." Ginny didn't laugh and Max regretted trying to make her. An evening that had seemed so promising had lost its shine. Why hadn't he just told her a friend left the equipment? Why hadn't he thought quicker? What if he just sort of told the truth?

"Okay, look," he said. "We're not really making the movie. We're more like casting agents. They need a lot of extras for the big scene and the filming's gonna' be kind of illegal 'cause they can't afford the location fees and the permits and everything so I'm just recruiting people who need some money and I'm not tricking anybody, I'm telling them it's a little dangerous and they could possibly get arrested but if I get enough of 'em this could be a big payday for me." Max paused, took a breath, stared at Rufus who appeared quite content, nestled in Ginny's lap.

"Okay," she said. "Let's slow down. What location?"

"Oh, yeah. Um, the stadium."

"The stadium. The big finale is in the stadium?" Max nodded. "When?"

"Saturday."

"Saturday. When Saturday?"

"During the game."

"You're recruiting extras to do what Saturday during the game?"

Max felt trapped. He felt sad. Worst of all, he felt foolish. How could a plan that sounded so logical when proposed by King now seem so crazy? He looked at Ginny seriously. "Run on the field"

Ginny needed a moment. She shook her head. "Run on the field. Run on the field this Saturday during the biggest game of the year."

"I know it sounds insane but if we can pull it off, it'll be an unbelievable finale."

"I'll say. Are you running on the field? Is Chubster?"

"No, no. Like I said, I'm just a recruiter. That's it."

"Could you get arrested?" asked Ginny.

"I don't think so but, I don't know, I guess there's a chance."

"And Chubster?"

"Chub's like a middle man. He hired me, thought I'd be good at recruiting, you know, gift of gab and all that."

"Well," said Ginny, "this might be the craziest idea I've ever heard of but at least it explains why you've been acting so weird."

"I didn't want to tell you. I didn't want to tell anybody. Didn't want to get anyone else involved. And you can't tell anyone either. Promise me you won't."

"Promise you?"

"Please."

Ginny smiled for the first time in what seemed like forever. "Man, the boys at the bar would get a big kick out of this."

"Ginny, I'm serious. I'm asking you as a friend."

Ginny leaned back, emptied her glass and held it out towards Max. He got the hint, stood up and took it from her hand, then returned to the kitchen for refills. Ginny was glad for the break. Time to think. She was still fairly shocked. She knew Chubster would get involved with most anything if it meant making a buck. But a movie? Wait a minute, she thought. What about the bank and Max's hasty exit from the cafe?

"Hey, hold on," she called out. "Does all this have anything to do with that robbery the other day?"

Damn, thought Max, more lies. "No," he said. "No, but since I was already involved with something, ah, against the law, I didn't want to be connected to anything else. Just a precaution."

"Really?"

"Yes, really." Max was beginning to dislike himself. Lying was not a great way to start a relationship. He finished refreshing the ice in their drinks, emerged from the kitchen, handed Ginny her glass and sat down, again choosing the chair.

"Okay," she said.

Okay, he thought. That's it? Why didn't she pepper him with more questions, break him down, make him confess? But he knew why. Because she trusted him. "So," he said, "do I have your word?"

"That I won't reveal your crazy hijinks?"

"Hijinks? Who says that?"

"Excuse me. Your moronic enterprise."

"I think I preferred hijinks."

Ginny took a drink, looked directly at Max. "On one condition."

Uh, oh, he thought. Now what? He was trying to do the right thing, sort of. He wanted the money and he didn't want Ginny to hate him but this was hard, the proverbial thin line. "Okay," he said, "one condition. What is it?"

Ginny leaned forward, smiled. "I want in."

*

Max couldn't sleep. The date had not gone as planned. It wasn't that he expected Ginny to be curled up in the bed beside him. That was not his intention nor, for

113

that matter, a probability. Max was a gentleman and Ginny was a lady. Of course if she had thrown herself at him, well...But that, he thought, was not the point. Because now, instead of a possible girlfriend, he'd gained another partner in crime. Ginny, filled in on the details, the mass exodus from the stands at the end of the third quarter, the variety of runners Max intended to enlist, the comical vision of countless security guards chasing all manner of fools around the playing field as the players, thousands of fans and, indeed, millions of television viewers looked on sounded more and more interesting. In fact, Ginny said, it sounded like fun. She was excited by the risk and when Max reminded her of the disdain she had earlier demonstrated for anything having to do with Chubster MaGee, she remained undeterred, acknowledging her previous skepticism for all things Chubster related but avowing that this particular endeavor intrigued her and, with only the possibility of some minor misdemeanors, her enthusiasm was not dampened. Of course Max had failed to confess the true nature of that final scene in the stadium, pleading ignorance as to its relation to the script's entirety and the story within, all very hush hush, he said. As much as he was aware that such a revelation would have caused Ginny's immediate departure from the project, not to mention her possible exposing of the plan, he couldn't take the chance. He'd have to stall, let her help out with the initial casting, then fill her in before the actual robbery, give her enough time to quit and not take part but not enough time to ruin the project.

Rufus couldn't sleep either, what with all Max's tossing and turning, and Max took the opportunity to address the cat aloud as he often did. When you live alone, he felt, you can speak to your pets directly, with no one around to decide you're a kook. "What is it with the movies," Max asked his furry friend. "You mention making a film and everybody's eyes light up." Rufus seemed fascinated by the question but failed to respond. "They all want to be in show biz, no matter what the level." Max got out of bed, made his way to the kitchen for a glass of water, maybe a snack. Rufus followed, perhaps intrigued by Max's commentary, more likely hoping for a snack of his own. Max poured himself a glass, took a half empty can from the refrigerator and, bending down, scooped it into Rufus' bowl, then watched his pet eat. "You'd probably like to be in the movie, too, wouldn't you? Probably be tough to catch you in that stadium, I'll bet...Hadn't really thought about animals...No, can't risk it. I'm not running so you're not running." The cat looked up from its food. "And," said Max, "that's final."

*

114

Max and Rufus were not the only ones unable to sleep. Ginny hadn't even made it into bed. The cab ride home had been twelve minutes of anxiety and self-doubt. What was she thinking? One minute she'd been denigrating Chubster MaGee and his idiotic get-rich-quick schemes, the next she was enlisting in one. Judging by the driver's name printed on the prominently displayed hackney license – Ali Akbar Pasavati, and his obvious affinity for the Middle Eastern thrash metal blaring from the cab's tinny speakers, he probably wasn't the wisest choice from whom to seek advice. Or was she just being racist? So many questions. She spent the short ride picking at the cat hairs left by Rufus on her dark blouse and wrestling with her thoughts. Nothing was set in stone, she decided. She hadn't signed a contract. She could always change her mind. In fact, judging from Max's reaction to her desire to be included, he'd probably be relieved.

The taxi stopped in front of Ginny's small house, she over-tipped as always and soon was seated at the kitchen table, staring at her cup of tea and quietly analyzing her recent behavior.

Was her life so staid, so uneventful that she needed something, anything, no matter how foolish, to shake things up? Or was her attraction to Max coloring her motives, affecting her decisions? And what about that attraction? Emily, sound asleep in her bedroom, was the one who'd declared that Ginny was attracted to Max. She got up from the table, silently stepped over to Emily's door and stood listening to her daughter's peaceful breathing. Emily is right, she thought. I am attracted to Max.

She returned to the kitchen, set the cup down in the sink and peered out the bay window into the dark, watched the leaves on a large maple tree shimmer with the moon's reflection. Perhaps she was overthinking things. Making a movie, no matter how low of quality or minute of budget, still sounded like more fun than spin class or watching TV. She would simply show up, help Max recruit, be his film crew, whatever was needed. She started toward her bedroom, satisfied with her decision. After all, she thought, what did she have to lose?

*

TUESDAY

Max was up bright and early the next morning, at least bright and early for a guy used to bartending until one in the morning. He knew exactly where he was going, the athletic fields and basketball courts he'd visited the day before, and hoped to get there at the beginning of the day while the drunks and druggies were still asleep. He was hoping to speak with the serious athletes not only because they appeared to be strong and fast but just as important, they might very well be unemployed. They certainly had a great deal of leisure time on their hands. And if these folks had no money but had hope, if they had not yet given up, then making a movie and earning some quick cash could prove tempting.

When Max, while approaching the school fronting the fields, spotted Ginny seated on a green park bench, his emotions were mixed. Usually happy to see her, he realized that he must have been counting on his reliable no nonsense girl coming to her senses and abandoning this crazy project. No such luck. He now had, for better or for worse, the first member of what may or may not turn out to be a crew. Ginny gave him a little wave. Arriving at the bench and setting down his equipment and briefcase, Max noticed her clothes – sneakers, jogging pants and sweatshirt. She was there to work.

"Guess you were serious," he said.

"You seem surprised."

"I'm always surprised when anyone does what they say they're gonna' do. It's the cynic in me, I guess."

Ginny stood up. "Well, sorry to disappoint you but I'm an O'Riley and O'Rileys always do what they say they're gonna' do."

"Jesus," said Max. "That sounds annoying."

"Very funny. Are we doing this or not?"

"Take it easy, eager beaver. I never knew a waitress who was a morning person before."

"Well, now you have. Here, I brought you a coffee." Ginny reached into a small brown bag resting on the bench, extracted a cup, handed it to Max.

"You brought me a coffee?" He took a sip. "Ginny, I believe this is going to be the beginning of a beautiful friendship."

"We already have a beautiful friendship, dummy."

"Oh, yeah." Max stuck the briefcase under one arm and lifted the tripod with the other. "Okay, you grab the camera and let's do this."

Max had picked the basketball court for the first stop. These were the true athletes. The track, while surely used by some young speedsters, was more heavily populated by soccer moms and weekend warriors. Moreover, those huffing and puffing flatfooted runners were not ideal candidates. Most had money or jobs or both. Max could tell by their expensive exercise attire and the late model cars parked nearby. The tennis courts were generally deserted and the baseball fields featured mostly gangs of elementary and middle school students, still not quite jaded enough to abandon pickup games, laughing, talking and having fun in their jeans and hoodies.

So basketball it was, and though there were not nearly as many players vying for an opportunity to get on the court as the previous day, there were still an adequate amount for a spirited contest. Max placed the tripod on a metal bench set back a bit from the asphalt but kept a strong grasp on his briefcase. Ginny followed suit, holding the camera close. They watched the game, appreciated the speed and power, the grace and teamwork. Max decided to set up the tripod, guessing this might attract their attention between games. When Ginny motioned with the camera he shook her off. He was not unaware that most of the participants were African-American and he wanted their permission.

After a few more minutes of vigorous scrimmaging, one of the taller young men slammed down a dunk with authority. His teammates voiced their approval, high-fiving and heading for the sidelines for a drink while those who had sat out rushed onto the court to practice their jumpers. One of the players on the winning team grabbed a 'Gatorade' from a cooler and made his way over to Max and Ginny. He was over six feet, his t-shirt soaked with sweat, his arms and forehead glowing.

"Hey, man," he said.

"Hey," said Max. Ginny waved.

"What's going on?"

"Well," said Max, "it'd take a few minutes to explain but basically we're looking for a few quick athletes to appear in a movie we're making."

"No shit."

"No shit," said Max. "But it's very low budget. Kind of an underground film."

The ballplayer looked long and hard at Ginny who, despite her outfit, could not hide her curves, then turned his attention back to Max. "You making a porno?"

"No, no, we're not making a porno." Max glanced at Ginny. "She's the cameraman, ah, you know, camerawoman. She's shooting the film, she's not in it."

The man seemed disappointed but recovered quickly. He turned toward the court, shouted. "Hey, Spider! Hey, Rufus! Come over here!"

"Your friend's name is Rufus?" asked Max.

"Yeah." Two more tall hoopsters hustled over. Max determined that the skinnier one whose knees and elbows were tattooed with spider webs was probably Spider.

"My cat's name is Rufus," said Max.

"You name your cat after my homeboy?"

"No, I've never met your homeboy," said Max as the two players stood by.

"Well, that's a weird coincidence," said the original player.

"What's a weird coincidence?" asked the human Rufus.

"This dude got a cat named Rufus."

All three young men looked at Max. "Is it a black cat?" asked Spider.

Ginny stifled a giggle but Max was getting anxious. "Ah, no," he said. "Actually, it's a calico cat."

"Forget the cat. This guy says he's making a movie. Needs athletes."

"Hi," said Max, extending his hand. "I'm Jim Johnson. This is, ah Jeannie. We represent 'Last Nickel Productions'".

Ginny gave him a look. Jeannie? Why didn't she get to pick her fake name? This hadn't been discussed.

"I'm Charles," said the original player. "This here is Rufus and this here is Spider but you probably already figured that out."

Max did some awkward handshakes and fist bumps with all three. Ginny smiled, hid her annoyance with the name thing. "Nice to meet you," she said.

"What kind of movie you makin'?" asked Rufus.

Spider looked Ginny up and down. "Is it a porno movie?"

"No," said Charles. "Ain't no porno. She's the camera lady."

Spider, too, could not hide his disappointment. "Oh."

"Anyways," said Max, trying to bring things back around to the task at hand, "we've got a scene at the end of the picture that requires some speedy, elusive extras and if it's okay with you gentlemen we'd like to do some interviews, maybe shoot some film of you running, you know, kind of an audition."

"So," said Charles, "you figured that since us black folks are so good at running from the police and eluding arrest, that we'd be ideal candidates for your project, that right?"

"No," said Max, taken aback. He'd been accused of many things over the years, cynicism, sarcasm, even pessimism but never racism. "We don't care about color. We'll take those white boys over there if they're faster than you." This possibility appeared to amuse Spider and Rufus.

Ginny spoke up. "We just want some fast athletes who want to make some quick cash and see the big game for free."

"Saturday?" asked Spider.

"At the stadium?" asked Rufus.

"That's right," said Max. "Good seats, too."

"Hold up, Spielberg," said Charles. "What's this gig pay?"

Max noticed the other ballplayers trickling over, curious about the man speaking with Charles and the pretty lady holding a camera. One of them, the shortest member of the group, seemed irritated.

"Yo Charles," he said. "We playin' ball or not. You still got the court."

"Hold on, Pishwee," said Charles, his eyes never leaving Max and Ginny. "We talkin' business here."

Max was struggling to remain calm. He and Ginny were vastly outnumbered and there was a large stash of money in the briefcase. But it was daytime and no one had done anything the least bit threatening. Ginny actually remained pretty relaxed considering she was the only woman in sight. She smiled and nodded at each young man as they arrived, then went back to fiddling with the movie camera as though she knew what she was doing and was making some last minute adjustments.

"Whoever is picked," said Max, regaining his composure, "will get one thousand dollars today and two thousand more after the game. There's a bonus if you don't get caught."

"What do you mean don't get caught?"

"When you run on the field at the end of the third quarter."

"Say what?" said Charles.

"It's a comedy," said Ginny, "and that's the big scene at the end. The stars run on the field and we need a bunch of other runners to join them."

"Yeah," said Max, "and it would be way expensive to rent the stadium and pay thousands of extras to fill it up. So we have to do it on the sly."

"You can't just CGI that shit?" asked Spider, apparently a film buff.

Max was unfazed. "Too complex. We'd spend more money in the lab than we would paying you guys."

"Hold on," said Rufus. "We get caught, we get arrested."

"True," said Max. "But we'll bail you out and pay your fine. It's a misdemeanor, not a felony. And you'll end up with three thousand dollars in your pocket."

"And," said Ginny, "you'll be in a movie."

Charles was unimpressed. "So you come down here to pay a bunch of brothers to get their asses arrested so you jackoffs can make your stupid movie."

Max was undeterred. Somehow he'd regained his confidence. "It's not a stupid movie and we don't need a bunch of you. Just a few." He glanced at Ginny who encouraged him with a slight nod. "Look, we just thought you might want to make a few thousand dollars for a day's work. If you're not interested, no problem. There's fast people all over these fields. We'll just take our stuff and go over to the track."

"Wait a minute, man," said Charles. "We never said we were not interested. We just playin' with you, man. But let me ask you this, how we know you'll pay up after the game? We get contracts or something?"

Max paused. That was a legitimate question. He looked at Ginny, who shrugged. The crowd of players had grown quiet awaiting his response. Max figured, ironically, that the best way to deal with his giant lie was a shred of honesty.

"We can't do contracts," he said. "We can't leave a paper trail. This is truly guerrilla film-making. But if you can spend five minutes on that field, you will be paid, and if you can get back in the stands without getting arrested, you'll make even more. You have my word."

"I'm out," said Spider, turning away.

Rufus, Charles and the others watched him return to the court. A short, skinny, black player pushed his way forward. He wore Converse All-Stars, an oversized tank top and was younger than most of the others. You couldn't notice his thin peach fuzz mustache unless you stood close. "I'll do it," he said.

Max was relieved. "Excellent," he said. "What's your name, son?"

"Odell. Odell Jefferson."

Odell Malcolm Mahatma Martin Jefferson was a resolute young man and had always been so. Whether that had anything to do with his mother's choice of namesakes for her son's middle names was debatable as were the locations of Mrs. Jefferson's philosophical loyalties. But for whatever reason, Odell had chosen to take things more seriously than the majority of his schoolmates. He didn't skip, he didn't smoke, he didn't goof off. He seldom smiled. He'd been determined to graduate high school and had done so. Determined again to get into college, he'd succeeded at that as well. But his determination had clashed with his serious lack of funds to pay for his education, so for the time being he was between semesters, working the second shift at a car parts manufacturer, hustling to rustle up any other money when he could, and staying in shape by playing ball in the mornings.

Max extended his hand. "Nice to meet you, Odell Jefferson. I'm Jim Johnson and this is, ah, Jeannie Johnson, no relation."

"What are you thinking, Odell?" asked Charles. "We don't know this dude. He could even be a cop."

Odell eyed Max, serious as ever. "You a cop?"

Max shook his head. "No, no I'm not."

Charles was unconvinced. "What good is that. Cat might be lying."

Rufus disagreed. "No, man. You ask a cop he's a cop, they gotta' tell you the truth."

"Word," said another player.

Odell addressed Max. "It's a thousand dollars today, just to sign up, that right?"

"That's right," said Max. "If you pass the audition."

"You see that," said Charles. "He's gonna' film you running around like a dumb ass and then say you didn't pass the audition so no money. Come on, man, wise up."

By now Max was used to improvising. He reached in his coat pocket and took out a small roll of hundreds. "Okay," he said, peeling off one of the bills, "tell you what. I'll give you this hundred right now just to let us film the audition. If you pass, you get the other nine hundred. If you don't, you keep this hundred anyway. How's that for fair?" He held the bill out to Odell.

Rufus, for one, was impressed. "That does seem pretty fair, right, Charles?"

Charles appeared agitated by the equitable nature of the proposal. He was, like the lucky man carefully contemplating his three wishes before presenting them to the Genie, mulling over possible tricks, searching for catches and loopholes. Odell wasn't waiting for Charles' or anyone else's approval. He took the bill from Max, stuck it in his shorts pocket.

"Okay," he said, "let's do this."

"Great," said Max, grabbing the tripod. "We just have to pick a spot."

"What about the court?" Ginny asked.

"Oh, I don't want to interrupt the game. We can find another..."

Charles cut him off. "Hell, yeah, you can interrupt the game. We want to watch this shit. Right, boys?" The others nodded and murmured their support.

Max shrugged. "Hey, works for me." He and Ginny began setting up the camera court-side, Max affixing it to the top of the tripod like an experienced movie grip. At least this particular assembly had been foreseen by Max who'd practiced the day before.

"Okay," said Max, "Odell, why don't you go ahead out to center court. The young man took his spot as Max turned to his camera woman. "All set, Jeannie?" Ginny peered through the camera lens, gave Max a 'thumbs up'. "All right, Odell, why don't you start by showing us how quickly you can go from the center court to each corner, ah, you know, center to corner, corner to center, next corner, you get it, right?"

Odell got down in a sprinter's stance, looked at Max. "Say when."

∗

Nuggets wanted to bring his binoculars but knew he'd made the right decision by leaving them home. He was watching Max and Ginny and the ballplayers from a distance, a middle-aged white dude gazing at sweaty young black men, and though he realized he might cause curiosity among the other folks strolling the fields, he would have appeared far creepier had he been staring at those same athletes through binoculars. Unfortunately, as far away as he stood, it was difficult to determine just what exactly Max was up to. Whatever it was, Nuggets figured it was supposed to have been his gig, his money. Chubster never should have mentioned it if he was going to give the job to Max. Now, squinting through the bright morning sunshine, he could see it involved film equipment. And while Nuggets had spent the majority of his short-lived porn career in front of a camera, he was certain he knew more about making movies than Max the bartender.

Observing Max and Ginny seriously involved with filming the basketball players, one at a time, in some kind of speed and agility test, Nuggets felt confident in gaining a closer vantage point. He walked slowly forward, nodding to a few friendly joggers, then leaned against a light pole. He wished he'd brought a coffee or a snack, something to occupy his hands. It was hard to look casual when you were trying to look casual. He definitely did not want to be spotted by Max and Ginny but it wouldn't be the end of the world had it happened. The fields were a public place and he could characterize an accidental encounter as coincidental.

He contemplated his next move. Max and Ginny were friends; they'd always been kind to him, no matter how bizarre his plans and ideas might be. And though money seemed to be changing hands down at the court, Nuggets could spot no evidence of illegal activity, at least not from his distance. He'd certainly seen his share of drug deals during his stay in Hollywood but they usually occurred at night, were

123

transacted quickly and involved small envelopes and packages. Moreover, he remembered, they were never filmed.

*

Max and Ginny were completely absorbed in the task at hand, unaware that their old bar chum was curiously watching them from afar. Once the athletes had realized one hundred dollar bills were being handed out for audition tapes, there was no shortage of candidates. Even the few white ballplayers were trying out. For Max, it was an embarrassment of riches. These young men were fast, they were quick, they were agile and would most likely prove to be elusive. Max could probably pick half the necessary field jumpers from this group alone. He had to remind himself to be choosy. Who would be serious and reliable? Who could keep their mouth shut, both before and after the big game? Difficult questions to ascertain when simply going by a brief interview and a handful of sprints. Max glanced at Ginny who seemed to have miraculously become a professional camera woman overnight. He was pleased he'd chosen to go with video. Film stock was expensive and, unknown to Ginny, not necessary.

One of the few holdouts was Charles. He'd watched the auditions with great interest, rubbing his short goatee, perhaps hoping it might supply some answers. He walked over, stood on the grass behind Max. Max barely noticed. He'd been calling out instructions to a tall, bespectacled string bean who'd just taken a tumble on the concrete while trying to change direction too quickly.

"Oh," Max said, "you all right?"

The thin fellow scrambled to his feet, gave Max a thumb up. "I'm good," he said. "Let's go."

"Okay," said Max. "Why don't you show us a few more cuts."

"Let me ask you something," said Charles, now just over Max's shoulder. "How you know none of us are cops? You never even asked, just assumed cause we were young black guys, we couldn't possibly be on the force."

This, thought Max, glancing at a poker-faced Charles, was another good question. Why had he assumed none of them were cops? After all, that was incredibly careless and could have put the whole enterprise in jeopardy. Maybe he was a racist. He'd never considered himself one, at least not until this very moment. He turned to Charles.

"Are you a policeman, Charles?"

"No, but that's not the point. I coulda' been."

He was right. That should have been the first question asked, not only here and now but also of Tulip and Crazy Ed and everyone else from now on. Max needed to be more careful going forward. Being a criminal was not easy; lots to consider.

"You're right, Charles. Sometimes I forget that underground film-making can be an illegal activity. Of course I should have asked. But in my defense, I've neglected to ask that of any candidate so far, black or white. But I definitely will from now on. Thank you for that. I'm glad you asked that question."

Ginny came to Max's rescue, perhaps a bit too late. "He's not a racist, Charles. I can vouch for that. We work with lots of African-Americans and Hispanics."

Charles was unimpressed. "Just cause you work with 'em don't mean you like 'em."

Ginny shrugged, went back to the camera. Max realized continuing the discussion would prove fruitless and returned his attention to the court. "Anyone else," he yelled.

✳

Nuggets had just started to relax, enjoying the unusually warm Autumn weather, when he was startled by a deep voice.

"What's up, cousin?"

Nuggets turned quickly, saw a gigantic black man approaching, a smiling behemoth who could easily play nose tackle in the NFL. He was dressed for hoops though, enormous baggy shorts, an XXXL hoodie and over-sized Jordans. He held an old ABA ball with the letters 'Ribs' scrawled on it in black magic marker. Nuggets was not as concerned with nicknames as Max so took little notice of the name.

"Hey," he said.

"You watching my boys?" asked the big man.

Nuggets was trying to stay calm. The friendly giant didn't seem threatening, in fact quite the opposite. "Yeah," said Nuggets. "Some pretty good players."

"Damn straight, cousin. You play?"

"Oh, no. Used to but, you know, bad knees."

"Okay, cool. Well, you don't have to watch from way up here." The large ballplayer headed toward the court, paused and smiled. "We don't bite."

"Yeah, sure." Nuggets watched him go. "Thanks." The big guy had been pleasant enough and it was a tempting invitation but getting a closer view was not really an option. In fact, he wondered if he should beat a hasty retreat from his place at the pole in case the colossal ballplayer chose to point him out to Max and Ginny. He decided on a compromise position, stepping behind the trunk of a nearby tree so as not to be visible from the court. He felt stupid hiding from his friends but it was by no means the first time he'd felt stupid and, odds were, it wouldn't be the last.

*

Now it was Max's turn to be startled by the booming voice.

"What's up, cousins!"

He and Ginny turned quickly to see the smiling giant. Half the ballplayers called out "Ribs!", greeting him with enthusiasm. Max knew Biz would have pointed out the similarity to Norm's entrance on 'Cheers' but recognized that these youngsters would never understand the comparison. As for the nickname, a moniker he'd not heard before, there was no time right now to work on his theories. Ribs, not yet realizing things were different on the court today, grinned broadly and called out "I got winners!"

"Ain't no winners today, Ribs," said Charles. "Ain't no game."

Ribs smile disappeared. "No game?"

"These young bloods rather run around like monkeys. Think they're gonna' be movie stars."

"What? What for? What you talking about?" The big man looked perplexed.

Rufus held up his hundred. He hadn't done well in the speed and agility drills and might not make the cut but that didn't stop him from grinning. "For cash money, Ribs," he said. Look, check it out."

"Cash money for what. Whose cash money?"

Max saw his opening, walked over to Ribs and stuck out his hand. "Hi," he said. "Jim Johnson. Nice to meet you."

Ribs ignored the hand, eyed Max suspiciously. "Jim Johnson? Sounds like an alias to me."

Max had no reply for that so elected to let it slide. "And this is Jeannie Johnson, no relation. We are making an underground film and we're auditioning your friends, see if maybe they can be extras in the final scene."

Ribs looked around. A few other players held up their hundreds, smiled. "You're making a what?" asked Ribs. "An underground film?" He glanced at Ginny. "She in it?"

"No," said Max. "She's the cinematographer."

"She ain't in it and you're casting all men. You be tricking my boys into a gay porno movie, Johnson?"

The players lowered their bills, all eyes on Max. They hadn't considered this possibility. "No, no," said Max. "It's not a gay porno movie. It's not any kind of porno movie. Jesus." For the first time Max felt maybe he should be making a porno movie. Probably easier. Apparently everyone else was making one, judging by the responses he was getting when he mentioned the film. Plus then he would have had a part for Nuggets whose ire he was still somewhat concerned about. But the thought passed quickly, Max realizing that they weren't actually making a film at all so whether or not it was to be a porno was really academic.

"And you're payin' in advance?" asked Ribs.

"Hundred for the audition," said Rufus. "Nine hundred more if you get picked, more later on."

"Serious," said Ribs. "Then Ribs wants an audition. What I gotta' do?"

"Hold on, big man," said Charles. "You ain't heard the details yet."

"Well," said Max, before he was interrupted.

"Forget it, Ribs," said Odell. "You got to be quick, man. You got to be speedy. You got to have moves."

"Oh," said Ribs, staring at Ginny, "I got moves."

The others laughed but Odell was a serious young man. "Not those kind of moves, player. On the court, man, on the field."

"What field? What are you talking about, cousin?"

"The stadium. This Saturday. We gonna' interrupt the game, man. For the movie."

Ribs looked at Max. "Your finale is at the University football field?" Max nodded. "How we get in? That's a tough ticket."

"We've got tickets."

"Money and a ticket." Ribs paused. "What's the catch?"

"It ain't legal, fool," said Charles. "Probably get arrested."

"There is that possibility," said Max. "Did I mention the three thousand dollars?"

"Three thousand dollars," said the big man. "Whoa."

Max was staring at Ribs, his mind percolating again, notions brewing, scenarios being visualized. Damn, he thought, he was getting good at improvising. "Hey, Odell," he said. "How hard is it to move Ribs when he's on the low post, you know, under the basket." Max knew the game, he knew the lingo and he was pretty sure he knew the answer.

"Move Ribs off the post," said Charles. "Come on, man," he scoffed. "Look at him."

"That's what I thought," said Max.

Ginny walked over, smiled at Ribs, then spoke softly to Max. "What are you thinking,"

"I'm thinking," said Max, "that he doesn't necessarily have to elude security. He just has to be difficult to get off the field. In fact, I think I'd be more worried about getting him on the field." He addressed the jumbo candidate. "Ribs, ah, may I call you Ribs?"

"That's my name, cousin."

"Let me ask you a question. Ribs, could you resist getting physical with security guards and policemen if they were trying to arrest you on the field this Saturday, and keep in mind that it would be a misdemeanor and we would be paying your bail and court costs."

"So he says." This from Charles.

Max continued. "We don't want anyone getting hurt and we don't want anyone incarcerated."

"So," said Ribs, "you want to know if I can resist resisting arrest. That right?"

"Exactly."

"More money if I do?"

"Yes, more money if you do."

Ribs eyeballed Ginny again. "Hell, I could even resist her for enough money." He smiled broadly as the other players laughed. Max realized things were winding down, decisions had to be made, decisions that couldn't hurt anyone's feelings so badly that they would try and scuttle the operation. Some of the guys, obviously restless, were back on the court warming up, taking practice shots and stretching their legs.

"Okay," said Max, "we've made our first choices for now, but remember, we will need more of you as the week goes along. Ginny will take your numbers and give you your advance. You'll get more info as the game approaches." Max handed Ginny a list to look over. "What do you think?"

"Looks good," she said. "What about Ribs?"

"Oh, yeah," said Max, "he's in."

Ginny smiled, called out the first name. "Odell!"

*

Nuggets, who fancied himself a fairly intelligent man, a person with above average street smarts and a reasonable familiarity with the underground economy, was still perplexed. He watched as the players resumed their game, most of them pausing to exchange some kind of information with Ginny and collect what looked to be cash from Max. Even the black hulk who'd invited him for a closer look seemed to be in on the deal. Standing in the bright sunshine, shaded slightly by the tree, he was just as puzzled as he'd been upon his arrival in the park. He hung his head, stared down at his shadow resting on the grass that was beginning to turn brown, and realized the shadow probably knew as much as he did. There was, however, no time to dwell on his deductive failures. Ginny and Max were packing up their gear and about to come his way. He turned and quickly stepped off, looking like an over-dressed power walker. Tomorrow was another day and detective work was revealing itself to be as tedious as he'd suspected. Slow, methodical, boring. He wished he could convince himself to let it go, not hold a grudge, not even have an interest. To go and look for a normal job with normal hours and normal pay. But now, in addition to being angry and envious, he was curious. And that was probably the worst of all.

*

Later, back at 'Sully's for their evening shifts, Max and Ginny tried to act as ordinary as ever, to show no signs of the previous night's date nor the morning's recruiting. However, as Nuggets had earlier learned, acting ordinary when you're trying to act ordinary is easier said than done. It requires a certain calm and a peculiar focus on one's own self, a concentration on one's words and actions that, on any other day, would have been of little or no consequence. Thank goodness for the gossip concerning Miss Peabody and Mr. Vanderbilt. Whether it had been Millie or Chubster or Sully himself, someone had informed the regulars of the flirtatious reunion between the two senior citizens. And since neither party was present to either deny or confirm, the rumor that an ancient romance had been rekindled, that the two were now shacked up in an elegant hotel suite happily reliving their youth had been bandied about. Of course, as with most gossip, there was no real evidence that any such thing was actually taking place, but that seemed of little concern to 'Sully's patrons.

"Do you think," asked Biz, "that he expects Miss Peabody to pay for his services?"

"He said he was retired," said Tony. "Besides, Millie said he really seemed to like her. Laughing, holding hands, the whole deal."

"Oh," said Chubster, "he definitely likes her. Likes her a little too much, a little too fast if you ask me."

"What the Hell, Chubster?" said Frannie. "Who cares if he likes her too much or goes too fast? How many more years of romance you think they got left? They could be banging right over in the booth there and I'd be happy for 'em."

Ginny arrived at the bar, late to the conversation. "Who's banging in the booth?"

"Me and you," said Joey. "Later tonight." Joey sometimes surprised the others with an unexpected wisecrack, sexual or otherwise. Ginny, as usual, was not offended. It was, as mentioned earlier, par for the course.

"In your dreams," she said.

Joey leaned back, sighed. "That's probably true."

"They're talking about Miss Peabody and Mr. Vanderbilt," said Max. "And their scandalous behavior."

"Good," said Ginny. "We could use some scandalous behavior around here. Liven the place up."

Tony raised his mug. "I'll drink to that."

Chubster neither raised his glass or smiled. "I don't know what everybody's so happy about," he said. "Miss Peabody is our friend and this old buck could be taking advantage, maybe conning her out of her dough. We don't know anything about this guy."

Max looked at Chub, recalled their earlier conversation and his own misgivings. "Chubster does make a good point."

"Well," said Joey, "he's very polite, seems like a nice guy."

"And well spoken," said Biz.

"And," said Tony, addressing Chubster, "he's bought more rounds for us in a couple visits than you have in a year."

"Okay," said Chubster. "Very funny. Whatever. We'll see. I'm out of here."

And, with no smiles and no farewell, Chubster MaGee was out the door. Very un-Chubster-like behavior, Max thought. Maybe Chub, too, was getting a little paranoid, a bit stressed. They were, after all, involved in an illegal enterprise. Perhaps Max should be even more suspicious, not less. The recruiting was going so well, maybe he was becoming too relaxed. One thing was for sure; Mr. Vanderbilt was a stranger. He could be an undercover cop, he could be working for King, keeping an eye on things. Christ, he could be anything.

"Well," said Ginny, "Mr. Vanderbilt seems like a nice guy to me, a perfect gentleman. But before we discuss this further, Max honey, could you get my drinks?"

"Yes, of course, sorry."

Max met Ginny at the service bar and quickly mixed two Tanqueray and tonics. He appeared distracted, almost forgot the limes "You okay?" she asked.

"Yup, yup, just Chubster, you know. What was that all about? Now he's got me thinking."

"Relax. We're just making a movie, right. What does he think, Mr. Vanderbilt is the movie police?"

Max smiled. "You're right...As usual."

"Oh, I like that," said Ginny, traying the drinks and turning to go.

Max, as always, watched her walk away. Some things, he thought, just never get old. He returned to his customers, pouring drafts, mixing cocktails, fetching burgers and sandwiches and offering the occasional opinion or quip, a night at 'Sully's like any other. For a while at least. Bent over, grabbing a frosted mug from the chiller, he glanced at the front door and knew instantly that his typical night was about to become anything but. Entering 'Sully's was Cranky Sam, cleaned and dressed up for a night out, button shirt, suit jacket, perfectly creased trousers and well polished shoes. On his arm, a beautiful blonde, all curves and sparkling jewelry, normal sized, too. Apparently Chubster wasn't kidding. Mrs. Cranky was a stone cold fox. Much as Max enjoyed ogling attractive females entering his place of business for the first time, he was far more interested in Cranky Sam's motivation for visiting his establishment. No one involved in King's operation was supposed to know where he worked. Was this, hopefully, just an unfortunate coincidence. Maybe, thought Max, the unusual couple would sit at a table or a booth, not even notice him. He watched Sam say something to the waitress, then head straight for the bar, the missus by his side. Once again, Max had to stay calm though he felt his heartbeat increase. Why couldn't this have been one of those busy nights, every stool taken and customers crowding the bar? No such luck; two empty seats at the center awaited Cranky Sam's arrival. The ill-tempered midget reached up to remove the leather coat his gorgeous spouse was wiggling out of, placed it on the back of a stool, then held her hand as she situated herself. Cranky Sam climbed onto the adjoining seat. Judging from the speed and dexterity with which he attained his perch, this was not his first bar stool ascension. Max took a deep breath, ignored the rubberneckers staring at the diminutive newcomer and his beautiful babe, and greeted them like he would anyone else.

"Welcome to 'Sully's. What can I get you?"

Cranky surveyed the bar, not yet paying much attention to the bartender in front of him.

"A Kir Royale for the lady and a Heineken."

"Please," said his wife.

"Yeah, please." Now Cranky Sam turned to Max and a look of recognition, not necessarily a pleasant one, crossed his face. "Hey, I remember you."

Damn, thought Max. "You do?"

"Yeah. I remember. I don't like you."

His wife quickly scolded him. "Samuel!"

"I'm sorry to hear that," said Max. Jeez, did he really need this right now? He could just hear Biz, had he been in on the deal, quoting 'Casablanca'. Of all the gin joints in all the world, you had to walk into mine. Of course this wasn't quite so romantic as the movie and Sam was no Ingrid Bergman but the odds seemed similar. Max made the blonde her drink, popped open a Heineken, set them in front of the mismatched pair.

"No glass?" asked Sam.

Max retrieved a frosty from the chiller.

"Now, Sammy," said the doll, "you apologize to the bartender."

"What?" said Cranky Sam. "I'm just being honest. Sometimes you meet someone, you like him, sometimes you meet someone, you don't. It's human nature. I bet the bartender…" Sam paused. "What was your name again?"

"Max." He extended his hand to Sam's wife. "Nice to meet you."

"Candy." She smiled.

"So take Max here," Sam continued. "He probably doesn't like half the people at this bar. Maybe he doesn't like me."

"Don't be silly," said Max.

Candy giggled but a quick glance from Sam stifled that. "You see," said the little grouch. "That's why I don't like him. He's a wise-ass. Thinks he's funny."

Max noticed the rock on Candy's finger, a gem that was at least two sizes up from what the wife of an auto body man should be wearing. "Can I get you some menus?"

"Yes, please," said Candy.

Max handed them menus and tried to catch up with the rest of his stool squatters.

"You know them?" asked Tony.

"No, but he thinks he knows me."

"Maybe you served them before, maybe at a different bar."

"I think he'd remember that," said Joey.

"Good point."

"Are they married?"

Max glanced over. "Amazingly enough, yes."

Everyone groaned, quietly of course, or rolled their eyes or leaned back and swore at whatever god or divine entity they believed was above them. How does an uncouth, bald-headed midget get a knockout like that and, more importantly, why couldn't they get one? Another of life's great mysteries, one which was never likely to offer a satisfactory answer. But that wasn't the question on Max's mind. He'd been forewarned that Cranky Sam had married way out of his league so he wasn't quite as astonished as the rest of the crowd. No, what Max was still wondering was whether this visit was random bad luck or something else more devious. Thankfully, he had his regulars to keep things light.

"I don't think I can go home to my wife," said Tony, staring at Candy.

Joey nodded. "Yeah, I know what you mean."

"Well," said Max, "you can't sleep here."

"No worries," said Tony. "We're killing ourselves right after these beers."

"Yup," said Joey. "Can we borrow that serrated knife you cut the fruit with? That should work on a wrist, right?"

They all laughed and Max slid back down the bar to check on his newest patrons.

Cranky Sam looked as sour as ever. "What's so funny? They laughing at me?"

"Course not."

"Oh, Samuel," said Candy, rubbing her husband's back affectionately. "Let's just have a nice time. Enjoy the night out."

"Yeah," said Max. "What brings you to 'Sully's anyway?"

Candy smiled. "We heard the service was excellent."

"Well, don't believe everything you hear."

Cranky was, as usual, peeved. "Are you flirting with my wife?"

"Sam, you stop it right now! Or we're leaving."

"Okay, okay. Sorry."

Max was trying to understand the dynamics in this relationship.

"Actually," said Candy, "we heard the food was very good."

"Surprisingly, it is very good."

"What do you mean surprisingly?" asked Sam.

"Well," said Max, looking around, "we're not exactly a five star restaurant."

Cranky Sam, apparently satisfied with Max's explanation, went back to perusing the menu. Candy smiled at Max. "We're going to take our time if you don't mind."

"Oh, of course, absolutely. Take all the time you need." Max turned, saw Ginny standing at the service bar.

"Order up," she said, smiling.

Saved by the bell, Max thought, as he headed over and tore off the drink slip from the ticker.

"Unusual couple," said Ginny.

"You think?"

"Friends of yours?"

"No," said Max. "Why does everybody think that?"

"Well," said Ginny, staring at the blonde, "at least the boys can stare at her rack tonight instead of mine."

Max set her drinks down, glanced at Sam and Candy. "Come on, Ginny, you're much prettier than her."

"Yuh, right. I couldn't help but notice that he's a midget, or, you know, a little person."

"Very observant."

Ginny ceased smiling. "And the cops seem to think the bank robbers the other day might have been midgets. So, you know, just sayin'" Ginny strolled away but Max had no time to dwell on her inference. Two waitresses had drink orders up, some bar patrons were holding empty mugs and Sam and Candy had set down their menus. Here we go, thought Max, as he noticed the lounge filling up. You could go from twiddling your thumbs and making small talk with a couple stragglers to total weeds in a matter of minutes. Nature of the business. Normally Max would be pleased. More bank and the time flew. And, after all these years slinging drinks, he could handle anything. He didn't rush, he didn't sweat, he didn't make mistakes and he never panicked. But tonight was different. It was difficult to concentrate, too many things on his mind. Chubster's suspicions concerning Mr.

Vanderbilt, Nuggets recent return to town, Ginny's misguided assumption that she was involved in film production and, more importantly, her recent feelings toward Max. And now, to add to all that, he had a ticking time bomb of a little person seated at the center of his bar. Max needed to take care of some customers at the far end but he paused in front of Cranky Sam and Candy. "I'll be right back to take your order."

"That's okay, take your time."

The woman was not only hot, she was pleasant. What in the world was she doing with that foulmouthed dwarf? It was bad enough when average Joes like Max had to see ancient, rich guys with their seeing eye blondes who had obviously attached themselves like barnacles to the old-timers' wallets. There was, sadly, nothing new about marrying for money, but Cranky Sam did not appear to be wealthy. He still worked with his hands, owed favors to big shots and involved himself in low level crime. Even if you disregarded his height and surly nature, he wasn't exactly a catch.

Max finished with all the tasks at hand but paused to look up and down the bar, making sure he hadn't missed anyone. Satisfied that everyone was at least temporarily content, he returned to Cranky Sam and his lovely wife. Max felt compelled to walk a thin line, not too pesky but ready to serve.

"So," said Sam, "does your buddy, Chubster, work here, too?"

"Oh, no. But he does stop in from time to time." Max hoped the boys hadn't overheard that understatement.

"Who's Chubster?" asked Candy.

Sam never took his eyes off Max. "He's nobody."

Candy rolled her eyes. "You sure know a whole lot of nobodies."

Max laughed but Sam was not amused. Actually, far as Max could tell, Cranky Sam was never amused. Another strike against him, no sense of humor. Wasn't that what girls were always claiming was important in a man? A good sense of humor, someone who could make them laugh. Well, Max had made a lot of women laugh in his time but he hadn't amused that many into bed.

"Well, yeah," said Max, "actually that was kind of funny."

"See, honey," said Candy to her husband. "I told you I could be funny."

"Yeah, you're a regular Rodney Dangerfield."

Candy punched his shoulder. "You're mean."

For the first time, Sam seemed to pay some attention to his stunning wife. "You're right," he said. "Sorry." Was that a look of contrition, maybe even a smile that crossed Sam's face? Max wasn't sure. "So," asked the midget, "what's good here?"

Okay, decided Max, that's a nice normal question. Good. Maybe this visit was nothing to worry about. "Well," he began, "the pot roast is excellent. The chicken pot pie is a big seller. And 'Sully's makes a heck of a burger, best in the city two years running."

Candy had picked up the menu again. "How are the salads?" she asked.

"Good, good. Actually the spinach salad with salmon is one of my favorites." She put down the menu and smiled. "I'll have that."

"Very good." Max turned to Sam. "And for you, sir?"

Before he could take Cranky Sam's order, Max noticed Nuggets entering the restaurant and making his way quickly to the bar. He appeared agitated and when he soon found, as he surely would, that there were no unoccupied stools, he'd probably be even more so. Just don't crowd Sam, thought Max. Go hang with the boys. A seat will open up eventually. But once again, Max's inner plea went unheeded. Nuggets wedged himself next to Sam, so close he was leaning right over the little grump's shoulder.

"Max," said Nuggets, "we need to talk."

"Sure, Nuggets. Maybe later. But as you can see, right now I'm very busy."

Sam swiveled slightly, looked directly at Nuggets and, as usual, was not smiling.

Nuggets mumbled, "excuse me," but went right back to Max. "But this is very important, Max."

"I'm sure it is but..."

Cranky Sam interrupted. "Right now, pal, it's very important that you back the fuck up and stop crowding me before I crack open your skull and serve what small portion of brains you have to the other customers."

Oh, boy, thought Max. Because of the nature of the evening so far and because he was a big believer in streaks, he deemed it unlikely that Nuggets would go quietly into that good night. For his part, Nuggets, obviously not used to being spoken to so harshly, particularly by a midget, had an unusual look of bewildered perplexity combined with minor annoyance. All he could manage was "what?"

Sam's irritation seemed to be growing. "Are you deaf as well, you stupid prick. Back the Hell off!"

Candy turned to Nuggets, her hand on her husband's back. "He doesn't like to be crowded."

Nuggets looked at Max, perhaps for a sign, which Max was attempting to give, motioning with his hand in the direction of Tony and Joe and Frannie, a sign which Nuggets was apparently not discerning.

"Don't look at him, needle-dick!"

Needle-dick? Nuggets had never been called a needle-dick, not even on porn sets in the valley where the female talent were not exactly known for their kindness and understanding with any problems that might present themselves to the male co-stars. Nor had he ever been confronted by a little person. The situation called for a decision, one which he realized had no upside no matter which way he went. If he simply backed up and walked away, his tail between his legs, he'd never hear the end of it from the other regulars. If, on the other hand, he chose to stand his ground, argue and, Heaven forbid, fight, he'd be made fun of for picking on an undersized foe. Nuggets thought for a moment. He should have thought longer.

"Okay," he said, "chill out. I'm sorry I crowded you and I'll move along. But I think you should apologize to me for what you said."

Max had a feeling Cranky Sam wasn't big on apologies.

"That's fair," said Candy to Sam. "He said he was sorry."

The pint-sized hothead ignored her. "You think I should apologize to you?"

Nuggets stood his ground. "Well, you called me a lot of names."

"Oh, did I hurt your feelings?" Sam appeared ready to dismount his stool.

"That's not the point," said Nuggets, taking a step back.

By now the confrontation had become somewhat of a focal point for the bar-flies and waitstaff. Drink orders were piling up, patrons were pausing with their brew and their chew, even Sully could be seen peeking out the kitchen door. Like a schoolyard playground, everyone was waiting to see what would happen next.

"Now," said Sam, hopping off the bar stool, "are you gonna' run along or are you gonna' stay here and get your ass kicked?"

Please, thought Max, please, Nuggets, just leave. But Nuggets, whether astonished or scared, barely moved. Max had to try something. "Listen, Sam, he didn't mean..."

The midget turned quickly. "You shut the fuck up!"

Max looked to Candy for assistance but she shrugged helplessly.

"Well," said Sam to Nuggets.

"I'm not going to fight a dwarf."

"I'm a midget, you asshole!" shouted Cranky Sam as he swiftly booted Nuggets in his over-sized balls.

Max was well aware that every man, woman and child is afraid of something.

Fears, phobias, aversions; everyone has them. Some greater than others, some fairly universal like death or public speaking, others more unique like spiders or clowns. But there was one fear shared by every member of the male gender and that was harm or injury to the testicles. Every man he knew had been hit in the groin by a ball, or fallen on a fence, or been kicked in a fight and the pain was unlike any other and not soon forgotten. So for Nuggets, who'd undergone the aforementioned plastic surgery, that fear was multiplied exponentially, and justifiably so.

The former adult film star went down in a heap. Some in 'Sully's that night claim to have heard a popping sound, though this was unlikely due to the nature and volume of Nuggets' screams. Even Cranky Sam seemed surprised by the damage inflicted. One thing was evident; Nuggets was not about to get up and continue the fight. His screams were not ebbing and a small amount of fluid was puddling on the floor near his waist. Nonetheless, Sam stood over his prostrate victim, arms raised and cocked as he waited for Nuggets to rise, a look of consternation slowly crossing his face, the realization that the poor bastard would not be getting up at all and, in fact, appeared to have sprung a leak.

"What the fuck," said the midget.

Max arrived at his fallen friend's side. "Call an ambulance!" he shouted as he bent down and put a bar towel in Nuggets' hands. The flattened loser dabbed at his perforated groin and screamed even louder.

"I'm dying!" he yelled.

"You're not dying," said Max. "You're just losing fluid. Probably silicone or saline or something. Hold on. Ambulance coming."

Sully was on the scene now and whether Sam was intimidated by the owner's size or paralyzed by the sight and sound of his writhing foe, the little man offered no resistance when Sully escorted him from the restaurant. He did pause to look back and call to his wife, "let's go!"

Candy slid off her stool, shimmied into her coat and bent down to check on Nuggets. "Is he going to be okay?" she asked Max.

"They warned me this could happen," Nuggets managed to say.

Max looked at Candy. She appeared sincerely concerned. "Yes," he said. "It's a long story but this is not a serious injury."

"Like Hell it isn't," shrieked Nuggets.

Candy handed Max a folded bar napkin. "Here," she said. "Take this."

Max grasped the napkin as Candy stood up and hurried after her man. He stuck the paper in his pocket, got up and looked toward the door. Where the heck was that ambulance?

★

Later, after the EMTs had arrived to take Nuggets to the Emergency Room, after the small pool of Nuggets' leftover fluid had been mopped up, after the kitchen and waitstaff had returned to their duties and the chatter at the bar had reverted to review and conjecture concerning that evening's aborted fisticuffs, Max had found time to stroll over to the unoccupied service area and check out the napkin. Careful that no one was watching, he unfolded the note and stared at Candy's handwriting.

'Call me', it said in lovely script, followed by a phone number. Bad enough to get such a message from a miniature psychopath's wife but even worse was the illustration sketched below the number. Someone, presumably Candy, had rendered a skillful drawing of a woman's lips, open, inviting. Jesus, thought Max, as he quickly refolded the napkin and stuck it deep in his pocket. He had, over twenty years of bartending, received a few phone numbers on cocktail napkins, but not more than a handful of times had it happened and never had said phone number been accompanied by such an illustration. And the detail, the realism. Max was flabbergasted. Did Candy really draw this? How did she manage, with the insanely jealous Cranky Sam seated right beside her? How did she find time? Or had the napkin been pre-sketched? Did she bring these napkins to various establishments around the city, enticing unsuspecting bartenders into dangerously clandestine meetings? Or worse, was Sam in on the deal, secretly waiting for the adulterous rendezvous to begin, then angrily bursting on the scene to beat the poor bastard to a pulp while Candy giggled sadistically in the background?

Of course, many men, less cynical, less suspicious, would be delighted to be given such a note, especially from a woman as sexy as Candy. And many of those same men would not be dissuaded from following through on the offer, no matter that the overture originated from an extremely violent nut job's main squeeze. Circumstances being what they were, Max was likely in the minority and the reception of such a message from such a woman definitely did not make him happy. Quite the opposite. It was a distraction and a dangerous one. Max pulled the napkin from his pocket, crumpled it and tossed it in the trash. Tony's voice almost made him jump.

"Hey, barkeep! I'm parched."

Max hustled over to the plump plumber. "Sorry, Tony. It's been quite an evening."

"I'll say. How do you think Nuggets' doing?"

"No word yet."

"Don't think he'll be making any more movies," said Frannie.

"Wonder what kind of 'Get Well' card we send for this," said Biz.

Ginny appeared, put a hand on Tony and Joey's shoulders, leaned forward. "So, Max," she said, "what was it the bimbo gave you?" Son-of-a-bitch, thought Max.

"Whoa, Maxie," said Tony, obviously impressed. "You get that babe's number?"

"Hell," said Frannie, "that girl was so hot, I would have taken her number."

"I don't know," said Biz. "That's probably a pretty dangerous number. That little dude is crazy."

"She just wanted me to let her know how Nuggets was. That's all."

"Yeah, right," said Joey.

"So," said Ginny, "she did give you her number?"

"Yes," said Max, "but like I said, it's not what you're thinking."

Was Max becoming delusional or were the regulars participating in a group smirk? Man, that was unfair, he felt. He hadn't done anything to deserve that, had he? He hadn't asked for her number.

Ginny wasn't going to quit. This was too much fun. "Wouldn't it have made more sense to give her number to Sully? You know, like if she really cared or, more importantly, if there was a lawsuit or something."

"She makes a good point," said Joey.

"I always said she was a smart girl," said Tony.

Biz chimed in. "Not just a pretty face."

Damn, Max thought. When did these guys become Ginny's own personal 'yes men'?

Frannie was staring at her drink, deep in thought. "I've never been with a woman before but..."

"Maybe we should take a look at that napkin," said Ginny, as Max squirmed. "You know, just for verification." Her bar buddy lap dogs nodded in unison.

"I threw it away." The words were out of Max's mouth before he could stop himself.

"You threw her number away!" Tony acted like this was a personal affront.

"Really," said Ginny, smiling. "You got a number from a woman who looks like Miss July and you threw it away?"

Max needed to think fast. Enough was enough. "Listen," he said, "you guys are reading way too much into this. I wasn't gonna' call that woman no matter what the reason. Like Biz said, that little maniac is dangerous and the last thing I need is him checking her cellphone and finding my number on there. He doesn't seem like the real understanding type. Now, who needs a drink?" The gang was quiet for a moment. Maybe they'd bought his explanation. It was sort of true.

"I do," said Ginny, heading for the service area. Max, glad to get back to work, met her there. Ginny pulled the slip herself, handed it to Max. She grinned as he made her drinks.

"What?" said Max.

"Nothing."

"You don't believe me?"

"Course I do. None of my business anyway. Thanks for the drinks."

As Ginny took her tray and walked away, Max turned back to the crew at the bar. Was it his imagination or were they all staring at him? He was sure of one thing. The night could not end soon enough.

*

WEDNESDAY

The next morning, Max was up bright and early. He had far too much on his mind to sleep in. First order of business was breakfast with Chubster MaGee. Max related the previous night's encounter with Cranky Sam. The flirtatious wife, the assault on Nuggets, the raunchy note and everything in between. Chubster, on most days talkative and opinionated, paused for some time before speaking. Finally, after moving his scrambled eggs around without taking a bite, he made comment.

"This is not good."

"No kidding," said Max.

"No one is supposed to know where you work."

"I know that."

"But you think maybe it was a coincidence that he stopped in with his wife?"

"I hope so, but who knows?"

Chubster picked up a slice of toast, pointed it at Max. "Did they lock him up?"

"I honestly don't know," said Max. "Sully never came back to the bar. Don't even know if the little bastard got arrested or if anybody pressed charges or anything. Might be able to find out later today. I switched with Millie so I'm working the day shift."

"How come?"

"Want to do some night time recruiting. Think there should be some interesting characters out there."

"True that. What about the wife?"

"What about her?"

"You gonna' call her?"

"No. I told you, I threw her number away."

"That was probably smart.

"You think?"

"Okay, look," said Chubster. "I don't know why you're getting mad at me. I didn't tell Sam where you worked. And I didn't tell Nuggets to crowd him. And I didn't tell his bimbo wife to slip you an illustrated note."

"Sorry," said Max. "I'm obviously a little shook up. I don't mean to take it out on you."

"Forget it. It's fine. But I don't think there's anything we can do right now. Find out what you can from Sully. We'll go about our business. You keep recruiting. Maybe that was just a typical night out for the little fucker. Maybe he'll forget all about it."

Max was not convinced. "Yeah, maybe."

"Hey," said Chubster, taking a big bite of his eggs. "Look at the bright side. You're not the one who got kicked in the balls and an incredibly hot babe gave you her phone number."

"When did you become a glass half full guy?"

"Listen, if we can stay on course, we'll both be a couple of bank account full guys. Think about that and try not to worry."

Easy for him to say, thought Max. His part was over. He helped score the seed money. He didn't have to deal with a miniature maniac and a hazardous hussy. Max just stared at his omelet.

"Max," said Chubster, wiping his chin, "did you think making a hundred fifty large was going to be easy, no problems, piece of cake? Come on, man. You know better than that. There's always gonna' be hiccups. But if we're real smart and real careful and a little bit lucky, everything will be fine."

Chubster was right. Max had been starting to take the job for granted. Of course there would be issues to deal with. It was just that Cranky Sam was an extremely violent issue. "You're right," said Max. "You're absolutely right. But do you think you could at least ask King to muzzle Cranky Sam a little? I'm not gonna' be a good recruiter if I'm in the hospital."

"I wish I could, Max, I really do." Chubster stood up, took a last sip of coffee and pulled out his wallet. "But you only get to talk to King once. Even me. His attitude is, we get paid well so we deal with our own problems. Sorry." Chub put some bills on the table and was about to leave.

"Hold on," said Max. "When do I get paid?"

"You get fifty on Friday and the rest after the game, if everything goes well. If everything does not go well, you don't get the hundred and King's gonna' want the fifty back. He doesn't like to be disappointed."

"Wait, what? That's not how I understood the deal."

"Look at it this way. You're a private contractor, like a plumber. You get paid for completing the job, not just for trying. So complete the job. I'll see you Friday."

Chubster slapped Max on the shoulder and made his exit. Max pushed his plate away, stared at his coffee. A plumber? How the heck did he become a plumber?

*

Next stop was the corner convenient store on his way to work. It was still called 'Griffin's Easy Mart' even though it hadn't been owned by a Griffin in many years. Instead of 'old man' Griffin behind the counter, or maybe one of his daughters before they went off to college, now there was either an Abdul or a Mohamed or a Said. Perfectly pleasant immigrants who were probably afraid to rename the store because business might decline. Would just as many locals pop into 'Achmed's Easy Mart' for their beer and cigarettes, their newspapers and magazines, their over-priced bread and milk? Max had no idea. Over the years he'd served people from every corner of the globe and their country of origin and the color of their skin mattered far less than the type of tipper they were.

At 'Griffin's, Max purchased a dozen burner phones. He was beginning to think things through, trying to be more cautious. He'd realized that even though he was handing out business cards with no number, once he made a call on his cell, they'd have the number anyway. He was amazed he hadn't thought of that before. No wonder all those knuckleheads on the I.D. Channel got caught. And, of course, he paid with cash, his own. No more credit cards for anything, no paper trail.

His first call was to Tulip. Ginny was working a double so he needed a cameraman. Tulip sounded excited and said she was bringing her friend, Gooch, an amateur filmmaker. Gooch, she told Max, had his own equipment but wanted to be reimbursed if any of the gear got damaged. That was fine with Max. Now he wouldn't have to find time to return to his apartment and fetch the stuff he'd gotten from 'Crazy Ed's.

Max and Tulip agreed to meet downtown after they'd gotten out of work. Max had no idea what Gooch, the hopeful auteur, actually did for a living, not to mention whether Gooch was his first or last name, but Tulip assured him that Gooch could join them in time for the evening's casting call. Max felt sure there would be a larger selection of candidates in need of money once the sun went down.

He arrived at 'Sully's for his day shift a bit earlier than required, hoping for an audience with the big Irishman. The door to Sully's small, windowless office was open but Max knocked anyway.

"Hey, Max," said Sully, looking up from the mass of paperwork covering his desk. "You're here, like seven hours early."

"I switched with Millie. Needed the night off."

"Big date?"

"I wish." Max paused, glanced at the flat screen on the wall featuring eight separate camera angles of the restaurants interior, bar included. Sully had resisted installing cameras at first, not wanting his employees to feel untrustworthy, but the dependent decrease in his liability insurance forced his hand. The footage of Nuggets' testicular demise, Max thought, could likely be sold for more revenue than 'Sully's cleared in a week. Not that Sully would ever release it. He was old school; everything stayed in house.

"Well," said Max, "that was quite a night."

"No argument there."

"Any word on Nuggets?"

"He's in the hospital but at least he's out of the I.C.U. Could be he's there a while."

"What about the midget?"

"What about him?"

"Is he in jail?"

"No," said Sully. "Probably should be but I sent him home with his wife. Told her never to bring him back here. If Nuggets wants to press charges, that's up to him. Plenty of witnesses and the whole things on tape. Just not sure if the poor bastard wants it out in the world. He did get put down by a little person."

"But it was a sucker punch, er, kick."

"I know that and everybody'll be able to see that, but, you know, it'll end up on the internet and all those wankers will think it's comical as Hell and I'm not so sure Nuggets wants any more of that kind of fame. Plus, that little bastard gets out of jail, I got a strong feeling he holds a grudge. What happened anyway? Why was he so mad?"

"Said Nuggets was crowding him."

"Crowding him? That's it? Unbelievable. You know the guy, ever seen him before?"

"Yeah, he's my cousin."

"What!"

"I'm kidding," said Max. Sully could be so gullible. "I don't know him. Never seen him before in my life. And I hope I never see him again."

"Well, you won't see him in this joint, that's for damn sure. What about the wife?"

"What do you mean?"

Sully grinned. "Do you ever want to see her again?"

"I know you're not going to believe this," said Max, "but I seriously hope I never see her again either. That woman could be hazardous to your health."

Sully leaned back, looked up at the ceiling. "Oh, I don't know. She reminds me a bit of my dear departed mother, bless her soul."

Now it was Max's turn. "What!"

Sully slapped the desk. "I'm kidding. How do you like it?"

"Okay," said Max. "You got me, touche and all that. But listen, if you hear anything about Nuggets, how he's doing or whether he's pressing charges, will you please keep me posted?"

"Of course, Maxi Pad. Now go set up the bar like a good lad and make us some money. And no more fights."

Max saluted his boss and nodded, exited Sully's office and returned to the bar. Another reason, he figured, why he should have turned down Chubster's offer and just carried on in his routine, mundane job at this routine, mundane tavern. Where else was he going to find such a great boss?

*

Max met Tulip and Gooch down in the 'Square'. She'd picked the spot, sure that the area would present all manner of prospective participants. It was the most bohemian part of the city; even on a chilly Autumn evening the streets were filled with an eclectic mix of pedestrians. Ancient hippies, non-conformists and outlaws, suburban gawkers and neighborhood activists, a colorful tapestry of humanity that Max had seldom witnessed within the cozy confines of 'Sully's Brew and Chew'. These folks poured in and out of the bars, bistros and boutiques lining the narrow streets that comprised the 'Square', and Max, thoroughly unfamiliar with this part of town, was experiencing a sensory overload, an unexpected excitement.

Tulip, he noticed, fit right in. Dressed in bright red leggings, a jet black leather waistcoat with fringe, a floral scarf around her neck and bangle bracelets descending each forearm, she could have joined most any group walking by. Max, in his typical jeans and gray pullover, never felt so invisible in his life. Even Tulip's sidekick, Gooch, a large, pudgy fellow with red hair and beard dressed in rust colored khakis and a suede aviator's jacket, even Gooch had more style than Max.

Tulip suggested they walk around a bit, get the lay of the land, formulate a plan. None of the other denizens of the 'Square' paid much attention to the faux film crew, the hefty movie camera strapped to Gooch's back failing to draw interest.

There were more interesting things to observe. Some of the street performers hadn't headed South yet and had set up shop on various corners and sidewalks. Though Max couldn't imagine how the magician or acoustic musicians would come in handy on the ball field, he was intrigued by one act, four swarthy, dark-haired men who were entertaining a small crowd of onlookers with a series of flips, tumbles and acrobatics. Next to their tip bucket was a small placard reading 'The Flying Babushkas'.

"I've seen these guys before," said Gooch. "They're really good."

Max watched the smallest of the quartet leap over a human pyramid consisting of the other three, do a somersault in midair and hit a landing worthy of an Olympic gymnast. "Good," he said. "These guys are great. What the heck are they doing here? They should be on TV or at least in Vegas."

"Yeah," said Gooch, "but there's one problem. Keep watching."

The Flying Babushkas commenced a series of intricate tumbles, bounding back and forth over one another with immense skill until two of the agile acrobats bumped heads and fell groaning to the pavement. What then ensued was a heated argument among the foursome, spoken in some kind of Eastern European dialect and most likely centering on which Babushka had caused the mishap. As the debate continued, the impatient crowd dispersed and the tip bucket went unfilled.

"See," said Gooch.

"Yeah, I guess," said Max, but what he really saw was opportunity. "Do they speak English?"

"One way to find out," said Tulip. "Let me have some money."

Max reached in his pocket but the smallest bill he had was a twenty.

"That'll work," said Tulip. She took the money from Max and walked toward the Babushkas, smiling and clapping. "Great job, guys!" She dropped the cash in the bucket, making sure that they would notice the amount. "You speak English?"

Three of the four looked at the other, who stepped forward. "I speak the English," he said, sounding like a bad actor in an Indiana Jones movie. He glanced at the tip bucket, then back at Tulip. "Many thanks."

"You're welcome." Tulip motioned for Max and Gooch to join her. "We have a proposition for you. You understand 'proposition'?" The English speaking tumbler shook his head. Tulip tried again. "A job...For money."

"Oh, yes," said the spokesman, "job, performance."

"Yes," said Max. "A performance. For good money."

The other Babushkas approached, curious.

148

"How much this good money?"

Tulip turned to Max, who did some quick calculations. "Two hundred dollars today," he said. "For each. Five hundred dollars each after performance."

The English speaker addressed his fellows and spoke rapidly in as yet indeterminate language. His acrobatic cohorts appeared pleased with this financial information.

"Where this performance is?"

"This performance is at the football stadium. This Saturday."

"American football?"

"Yes, American football."

"This game not true football. This game for nancyboys." He grinned, again translated for his comrades who laughed heartily, clapping each other on the shoulder. "No matter," the Babushka continued. "What performance for?"

"For movie," said Tulip, pointing at the camera on Gooch's back.

The Babushka representative glanced at the camera, then back at Tulip.

"For porno movie?"

"Holy mackerel," said Max, as the Babushkas laughed.

"No, no porno movie," said Tulip. "You run on field, do your act, do not get caught by police. Understand?"

"Yes, police. We very good not get caught by police." The English speaking Babushka looked around the square. "No license. We do job for you. Money now?"

"No, no money now," said Tulip. "First film." Gooch unpacked the camera, set up his tripod.

"Performance Saturday. Why we film now?"

"Audition," said Tulip. The spokesman looked confused.

"Tryout," said Max. "Example. Demonstration. See how fast you move."

"Ah, yes. Demonstration. We very fast. Very quick."

"Good," said Tulip. "What's your name?"

"My name Bishku. He pointed at his comrades. "This Bishka, this Bishki, this George."

Tulip, Gooch and Max all looked at each other. "George?" asked Max.

"Yes, George," said Bishku. "Is problem?"

"No," said Max. "No problem. We ready, Gooch?" Gooch nodded, leaned down, peered into the camera lens. "Okay, let's go. See how fast you can move." Bishku shouted some unintelligible instructions to the other tumblers who swiftly formed a huddle and stood motionless. Max and Tulip waited patiently. Gooch glanced up at Max from his camera, shrugged. A few passersby had stopped by, their curiosity piqued by the tiny film crew.

"What's the matter?" asked Max. "What are you waiting for?"

"You director of movie?"

"Ah, yes," said Max, "I am the director."

"Then you say the 'action'!"

"Oh." Max couldn't help but smile. He took note of the small crowd forming around them, tried to sound professional. "All right. Quiet on the set. And... Action!"

The brothers burst into a flurry of activity, as though performing their show in overdrive. They hopped, skipped, jumped and tumbled, straddling and leapfrogging each other like a well oiled machine. They held Bishki, the lightest member, aloft, tossed him in the air and caught him effortlessly. They smiled, slapped hands and executed complicated dance steps, all with no accidents and no arguments. When they had finished, bowing to the assembled onlookers, they were rewarded with vigorous applause and generous tips. The brothers were pleased, grinning, sweat dripping from their faces.

"Is good?" asked Bishku.

"Oh, yes," said Max. "Is very good."

Tulip looked stunned. "Wow. I think I wanna' join."

"Money now," said Bishku.

"Yes," said Max, "money now." He held up a finger, asking for patience as the crowd dispersed, then extracted some bills from his shirt pocket and peeled off two hundreds for each happy Babushka. Max turned back to Bishku.

"I need phone number."

"Yes. Phone number. Of course." Bishku dictated his digits, took out his own cell. "Your number?"

"No," said Max, "I call you." Bishku appeared pained but did not argue. Max motioned for the others to come closer. "Important information," he said. "End of week, I give you tickets to game. You go to game. You watch game. At end of third quarter, you run on field, you perform five minutes. Understand? Five minutes. Then run back into stands."

Bishku translated quickly, then back to Max. "Escape from police?"

"Yes, escape from police."

"No problem. American police no good. They are soft, lazy. Not like home."

150

More back slapping and laughter from the Babushkas. Apparently their stay in the States had not brought with it a great deal of respect for the men of Max's country. He wondered what they thought of bartenders. He supposed that were you not matching them vodka shot for vodka shot or easily avoiding authority, then you, too, were lazy and soft, a nancyboy. Oh, well, he'd been called worse. The important thing was they were good and fast, he'd brought them in under budget and there was a decent chance they wouldn't have to be bailed out. He felt good, excited. The recruiting was going well. Was this what it was like to be a casting agent in Hollywood? Another career he may have an aptitude for.

*

Later that night, back at his apartment, Max was, understandably, wound up. He generally wasn't much for texting but was smart enough to make sure Ginny was up before calling her at midnight. After all, she'd just worked a double shift and that gave her every reason to decline a late night chat.

Ginny was, indeed, exhausted, but she was happy to see Max's text, told him to call, and when she heard his voice, so upbeat, so excited and pleased with the night's activities, she was happy for him. Of course that wasn't going to stop her from being a wise-ass. She interrupted Max before he could begin describing the evening's events.

"Are you alone?"

"Am I alone?" Max paused. "Well, Rufus is here. Does that count?"

"What about Tulip?"

"Tulip! Jesus, Ginny, I'm old enough to be her father."

"Yeah."

"Come on. Is that what you think of me? I'm trying to rob cradles?"

"I see you flirting with them."

"You know that's part of the job."

"I know. Sorry. Just busting balls. Force of habit."

"We should probably try to stay away from that phrase for the time being. Anyway, can I continue now? You want to hear about this night or not?"

"Oh, yes," said Ginny. "By all means, please continue."

Max recounted all that had happened in the square. Ginny asked questions, laughed at his descriptions of the Flying Babushkas' antics and laughed when Max related the arrival of Tania, Bishku's flame swallowing girlfriend. Ginny, impressed though she was, couldn't help but point out the difficulty in smuggling long metal skewers into the stadium, not to mention the possibility of a football field inferno, all of which Max had thought of earlier, regretfully ruling out the dark haired beauty.

The Babushkas were obviously the night's prize but Max said they hadn't stopped there. The mismatched trio, Max, Tulip and Gooch, had convinced a clown to be filmed but when the poor fellow, in full circus regalia and over-sized, floppy shoes tried to run, practicality outweighed comic relief and Max had to take a pass, though he did hand the sad entertainer a fifty for his trouble.

Most of the performers they'd encountered that evening, Max said, had evident flaws in their acts, as pertaining to that Saturday's goal. The jugglers, by the very nature of their chosen art, which required them to remain situated in a single spot, would have been far too easy to apprehend. The trio of teenagers executing tricks and jumps with their custom BMX bicycles could never have gotten those same bicycles into the stadium. The mime seemed promising but when Max auditioned him, he only pretended to run, raising one foot after another without ever moving forward.

Finally, Max told Ginny, after interviewing a couple dull-eyed hookers and a leather clad dominatrix whose five inch heels alone eliminated her from consideration, the faux film crew had called it a night. They retired to a small establishment called 'The Con Cave', a bar designed to resemble a depression era speakeasy with framed photos of that period's most notorious gangsters lining the walls. There, Max treated his cinematic sidekicks to rounds of 'Machine Gun Kellys', a mixture of bourbon and Bailey's Irish Creme that tasted far better than it sounded. He happily handed Tulip and Gooch two hundred dollar bonuses before parting ways. Max had been about to relate all he had learned about Gooch's rather unusual background when Ginny, amused though she'd been, confessed her fatigue and begged off the Gooch story until another day. Max, noting the late hour, understood completely and wished her pleasant dreams before hanging up.

Again, Max was feeling upbeat, at least for the short time before remembering that the entire enterprise, one which had helped bring him much closer to the lovely waitress, was based on a lie. And sooner than later, he'd have to tell her the truth. He looked at Rufus, the cat laying comfortably at the foot of his bed, shook his head. "Oh, boy," he said. Rufus eyed his owner curiously as Max switched off the light, flopped on his back and stared at the ceiling.

*

THURSDAY

Upon emerging from his apartment the next morning and exiting the hallway door onto the all too familiar sidewalk, Max was greeted by an unfamiliar voice.

"How you doin', Jim Johnson?"

Max was surprised to see Charles from the basketball courts leaning against his building's brick wall. No longer in shorts, sneakers and tank top, Charles looked sharp in black slacks and leather jacket, white dress shirt and dark, shiny loafers. He was smoking a cigarette. The player cleaned up well, thought Max, though this was certainly not his first thought. His first thought was 'now what?'

"Ah, Charles, right?" asked Max.

"That's right, brother. Good memory."

"Thanks. What brings you down here, Charles?" Once again, Max found himself rooting for a coincidence, but by now he wasn't sure there was such a thing.

"Looking for you, Johnson."

"Really? How'd you find me?"

"I work for the 'Buzzard,'" said Charles. "And the Buzzard is always looking for people. I find 'em. That's what I do."

"Someone named the Buzzard is looking for me?"

Charles smile. "No, brother. That was just a little background. I'm lookin' for you."

"Oh."

"We've got some business to discuss."

Max paused, watched the steady stream of pedestrians pass by, going to work, running errands, keeping appointments. Max and Charles were barely worthy of a glance. "Right here, right now?" asked Max.

Charles tossed his cigarette to the ground, stubbed it out with the heel of his shoe. He looked serious. "Right here, right now."

Great, thought Max, another complication. "Okay," he said, "what's on your mind?"

"You realize that you're bribing my friends to break the law?"

"Well, yes, technically I guess that's true."

"And that, if I wanted to be a good citizen, I could go to the police and give 'em a heads up on the whole thing?"

"I suppose you could," said Max. "But you'd be ruining the ending of a wonderful film. And your pals would all be pissed. No movie, no money."

"Or," said Charles, lighting another cigarette, "you could pay me to be quiet."

Damn, thought Max, now that he was a criminal he had to deal with other criminals. Part of the job, he supposed. "You're blackmailing me?"

Charles grinned. "Well, technically yes. You give me ten thousand. That is not a big blackmail amount. I figure you can afford that and still have enough to pay those idiots to run on the field Saturday and get arrested. It's a win, win."

Max definitely did not consider Charles' proposal a win, win. Far from it. For him, this was just one more bump in an extremely bumpy road, one which had commenced the moment he'd foolishly agreed to listen to Chubster's scheme, a road which was showing no signs of ending any time soon. Charles was obviously a wild card who couldn't be trusted, a common trait, Max figured, among blackmailers. Ten thousand, he reckoned, wasn't a deal breaker but it would put a sizable dent in his seed money. He wasn't sure how many scofflaws King expected on that field Saturday but Max felt, as in most cases, there was safety in numbers.

"How do I know," he asked Charles, "I can trust you? Maybe I give you the money and you still squeal on us or maybe you ask for more money. Who knows."

Charles looked genuinely hurt. "Jim, I thought we were friends. You come down the courts, make a bunch of promises we're supposed to believe, but I make one to you and you're all mistrustful. That cause I'm black, that it?"

"No, that's not it. I don't care what color you are. But look, here's the difference. I'm giving those guys money for doing something. You want money for doing nothing."

"Nope. I want money for not ruining your movie and I want money for not going to the cops. So my doing nothing is actually doing something. Which is to do nothing to stop your whole deal. You get it?"

Max was getting a headache. What was Charles, a lawyer? The novice blackmailer continued. "Look, it's simple. You give me the money, I give you my word."

"Your word?"

"That's right, brother."

Max needed time to think, time to stall. "Obviously," he said, "you've taken me by surprise."

"Obviously," said Charles.

"I want some time to think over your proposal. That's not big money for a blackmailer, true, but this is a very low budget film and that would be a major hit."

"Listen," said Charles, "I'm a reasonable man. And you can have some time to think. But realize this. You're gonna' spend way more money bailing these chumps out after the game. Not to mention court costs and fines and stuff."

"Well, we're hoping a lot of 'em make it back into the stands without getting caught. Besides that's our concern, not yours. Has nothing to do with your blackmail money."

Charles paused, distracted by a shapely blonde passing by, and in that moment Max had another idea, a long shot but Max was reaching. "Okay," he said, "here's a counter proposal."

"I'm listening."

"I pay you a legitimate fee to post bail and pay court costs for the players that get caught. You earn your money, the film gets made and no one is mad at you and you're not even a blackmailer. You're not a criminal, just a friend. Now that's a win, win."

"When do I get my money?"

"After the game, when the producers see it was a success. They have the money. How's that sound?"

Charles snuffed out another cigarette. "Sounds like you think I'm a fool. I make you a perfectly reasonable offer and you want me to get involved with your stupid fucking criminal enterprise?"

"But you are a criminal."

"That's not the point. I'm a professional. This half-assed plan of yours is doomed. You got twenty-four hours. Right here tomorrow morning. You feel me?"

"And if I don't feel you?"

"Then nobody makes any money. And everybody's pissed."

"Well, ah, you've got twenty-four hours to consider my offer, too."

"Shit," said Charles, spitting on the sidewalk. "I'll see you tomorrow."

Would it have been too much to ask, Max thought, to actually have two good days in a row? Maybe even a day and a half? The previous day had gone like clockwork; no problems at work, a productive night with his little film crew, the recruitment of the Babushkas, four extremely talented bumpkins willing to join the cause. Sure, he'd tossed and turned a bit in bed while contemplating his lie of omission to Ginny, but he'd felt good when he woke up, well rested, optimistic, confident, ready to go. He hadn't burnt the toast, the coffee was just right, he'd even had some nice, ripe honeydew melon, a healthy addition to what had rarely been a well rounded breakfast. Everything was perfect until he'd walked out his building's front door.

And now Charles had ruined it, though Max could hardly blame him. After all, wasn't Charley just another average guy trying to make a buck, morals and principles be damned? Wasn't that what Max was doing? He had no intention of hurting anyone but Charles hadn't threatened violence either. Still, no matter the method or motivation, Max had been presented with another problem, another worry and would have to find another solution.

✱

Ginny was already seated, mocha latte in hand, at 'Cup'a'Joe's, a small hipster cafe in the theater district when Max walked in, fifteen minutes late. "Hey, Spielberg," she said, "what's up."

Max nodded, smiled weakly and plopped down at her table like he'd just plowed the North forty, sighing, slumping, shaking his head. Ginny was surprised; he'd been so chipper not so many hours ago on the phone. Now he looked stressed, the proverbial weight of the world on his shoulders. "Jeez," she said, "nice poker face. I thought everything went great last night. What the Hell happened?"

"Fucking Charles."

Now she knew something was wrong, something that would make Max curse. "Charles?"

"Charles from the basketball court. The one who didn't try out."

"Oh, yeah," she said. "The talking guy. The skeptic."

"Yeah, well he talked to me this morning. He's blackmailing me."

"What?"

"Can you believe this shit?" asked Max.

Wow, thought Ginny. Two swears. Now she was sure things were serious.

Max surveyed the shop. These were not his type of coffee drinkers. He was used to hard drinking mooks who took theirs black and could care less how old the pot was, guys who weren't going for taste; they just wanted to wake up or sober up or maybe just get up. The clientele at 'Cup'a'Joe's was all artists and intellectuals, well mannered people waiting patiently for their iced lattes, their macchiatos, their cappuccinos with almond milk and cinnamon.

Ginny touched Max's arm. "Can I get you something?"

"Do they have actual coffee here?"

"Yes," said Ginny. "They have actual coffee here. I know you take it black. Hold on."

She stood up as Max leaned back in his wicker chair. Now she was having second thoughts about their questionable endeavor. Why hadn't she stuck to her guns concerning Chubster MaGee and his lousy ideas? It had seemed like fun and she did enjoy spending time with Max but the unexpected complications were obviously having a deleterious effect on the frazzled bartender. If things kept going like this, the poor man would have an ulcer by the end of the week, a condition you certainly didn't have to deal with while pouring drafts and serving burgers. That was one of the beautiful things about working in a restaurant. You came in, did your job and never took it home with you. There were no quarterly reports or deadlines to anguish over, no sales quotas to fill, no upper management butts to kiss.

Ginny returned to the table, set the cup in front of Max. "Okay," she said, "how exactly is he blackmailing you?"

"Says he'll tell the cops beforehand. Ruin the whole thing."

"Isn't that just gonna' piss off his friends?"

Max took a quick sip of his coffee. "That's exactly what I said."

"To who?"

"To Charles."

"How much does he want?"

"Ten thousand."

"Ten thousand," said Ginny. "That doesn't seem like a lot for a blackmailer."

"Well," said Max, "I have to say he does seem like a fairly reasonable blackmailer."

Ginny almost laughed. "Do you hear yourself? A week ago we were two typical restaurant workers. Now we're sitting here discussing the relative merits of our fellow criminals."

Max smiled slightly, shook his head. "I know, I know. But be that as it may, I think I'm headed over to the athletic fields. See how Ribs and his cronies feel about Charlie the blackmailer putting the kibosh on their easy money."

"I wouldn't exactly call it easy money. I wouldn't want to run on that field Saturday."

"Okay, good point. What are you gonna' do?"

"Well," said Ginny, "I was planning to recruit with you."

"You could come along. I'm sure they'd love to see you."

"No, this actually works out for me. I've got an appointment with Emily's Guidance Counselor in a little while..."

"Oh."

"Nothing bad. She's going to be a senior next year so just a little early college discussion."

"Wow," said Max. "Starts early, huh?"

"Oh, yeah, it's a whole thing and it happens fast. Grades, SATs, scholarships, financial aid, campus visits, extracurriculars and it's all a big competition."

"Well, I've met your daughter and she's a smart cookie. I'm sure she'll do fine."

"Yeah, probably. Long as they don't do interviews. Girl's got no filter."

"Like her mom."

"Hey." Ginny smiled. "Anyway, I'll walk to the High School, maybe scope out some candidates along the way."

"Sounds good," said Max. "I've got an idea for later if we get out of work at a decent time. Not sure you'll like it but I'll surprise you."

"Oh, sounds intriguing. Good luck with your basketball powwow."

"Yeah, thanks," said Max, rising from the table. And thanks for the fresh coffee. Think you spoiled me."

Ginny stood up and hugged Max warmly, looked him in the eye. "Be careful," she said.

"You, too." Max hesitated, then kissed her on the lips. For a moment at least, he forgot all about Charles and Chubster and everything else.

✱

Ginny felt good about the kiss and pleased that Max appeared to be his old self, complications notwithstanding, but something was still bothering her. She knew making movies, especially low budget pictures, was a difficult process. She did, after all, subscribe to 'Entertainment Weekly', but this film seemed to have more than its share of unforeseen dilemmas. True, it involved criminal activity but it wasn't as though they were robbing Fort Knox. They were simply hiring a bunch of cash strapped individuals to run on a football field. It was at the end of the third quarter and would hardly even delay the game once the field was cleared. Sure, some would get arrested and have to be bailed out but, hopefully, no one would get hurt and you had to admit it could end up being a pretty funny scene.

And yet there were questions, and not just the moral kind. The illegality of the venture hadn't stopped her; she'd jumped right in when she'd seen the film equipment in Max's apartment. No, these mysteries were more of the practical variety. Why couldn't Max tell her more about the nature of the film and who, in fact, was producing it? If it was so low budget then where was all the money in the briefcase coming from? And speaking of money, what about her? She'd signed on for kicks and they'd never discussed financial remuneration but if everyone else was getting paid, well...Not to mention Chubster's role in all this. Wasn't like him to hand the job over and step away. She resolved to confront Max at the end of the night, whether they embarked on his surprise mission or not. For now, she'd keep her eyes open for appropriate candidates. She'd committed to the enterprise and she always kept her word.

Ginny slowed her gait, looked around. The streets approaching the High School were lined with trees – majestic elms, weeping willows and the occasional ancient oak, all perfectly spaced as though their growth had been symmetrically planned. Some of the larger Colonials and Tudors along the way were fronted by well-trimmed hedges. And, unlike Ginny's more modest neighborhood, there was a streetlight on every corner. She'd passed an inordinate number of churches as well but doubted any of the priests or ministers would be inclined to invade the football field no matter how much money she promised to tithe. She smiled though, amused by the thought of old men in ecclesiastical robes fleeing burly security guards as the fans cheered them on.

A small squad of soccer moms went by, power walking in their designer spandex, chatting amiably as they went, modern day yentas who'd chosen physical fitness over mah-jongg. Ginny gave them a nod as they passed. She knew the outlaw nature of the assignment would have intrigued some of the women but they obviously did not lack for money and one or two would have pointed out the negative affect a well-publicized misdemeanor might have on their standing with the PTA.

She had just about resigned herself to arriving early at the school without signing up a single runner when she noticed a landscaping crew taking a morning coffee break. They were on a lawn bordering the opposite sidewalk, resting in front of a three story McMansion. Their lawn mowers sat silently nearby and piles of leaves were scattered strategically around the property awaiting their trash-bagged fate. The five men, a couple college boys and the others, older and Hispanic, looked up from their thermoses as Ginny crossed the street. The shapely redhead stopped at the curb and smiled.

"Hello, boys," she said.

The quintet of sweaty, dirt-stained lawn jockeys were obviously not used to being addressed by women who looked like Ginny. Maybe the two young men wearing their college sweatshirts, scrubbed and groomed and safely ensconced in their frat house would be visited by such a girl. Perhaps the older Latinos, cleaned up and stylishly attired at the neighborhood nightclub, could chat up a similar senorita. But now they just looked suspicious, confused, glancing at one another, trying to determine what this beauty was up to. One or two managed a mumbled greeting and the others a weak wave.

Ginny looked up at the blazing sun in a cloudless sky. "Warm for October, huh?" she said.

"Si, Senorita," said the oldest worker, a short, burly man, dabbing his forehead with a well-worn handkerchief.

The more handsome of the college boys flashed a wide smile, one that had probably benefited him on more than one occasion. "He agrees," he said.

"Well," said Ginny, "this looks like hard work. I hope they're paying you the big bucks."

"Yeah, right," said the second boy, shaking his head. The Hispanic gentlemen looked confused.

The first boy tried to translate. "La muchacha preguntale que, ah, trabajamos por mucho dinero."

Now all the Latino men smiled and laughed, the notion of large paychecks as foreign to them as pot roast.

"I assume that's a no," said Ginny.

"That's correct," said the first boy, again demonstrating his dimpled chin. "But of course there's the great benefits."

"Really?"

"No, not really," said his friend. "We're lucky to get this break, never mind a decent wage."

"I'm sorry to hear that," said Ginny. "But I might be able to help."

"Come on, lady," said the second boy. "What's going on? Why are you talking to us? Is this some shitty reality show where we all get pranked and everybody makes fun of us?"

"I don't see a camera," said the first boy.

"Que pasa?" asked the burly man.

The first boy held up a finger to the others. "Un momento."

"I swear to you this is not for reality TV," said Ginny. "No pranks, no scams. But I do have a business proposition for you. It involves big bucks but it also involves breaking the law slightly."

"Breaking the law slightly. Right," said the second college kid. "That's like being slightly pregnant."

"Funny," said Ginny. "But listen, you get to see the game on Saturday, or at least most of it."

The burly immigrant perked up. "Game?"

The first boy turned to him momentarily. "Football. American football."

"Oh." He seemed disappointed.

"Break the law slightly. See most of the game," said the skeptical boy. "Come on. What the Hell?"

The first boy whacked him on the shoulder, then turned to Ginny, smiled again. "You have to admit it sounds kind of fishy."

It sure does, thought Ginny. This was a lot easier with Max. Why should these guys believe her. She wasn't even carrying the briefcase with all the cash. "Okay, look," she said, "we're shooting a very low budget film..." She paused, waiting for the usual porno accusation but it was not forthcoming. "And the finale involves a bunch of people running on the field at the end of the third quarter. We can't afford to rent the stadium so we have to do it underground style."

"Even if you were telling the truth," said the second boy, "if this thing is so low budget, where do the big bucks come in?" The handsome boy nodded his head, as though his co-worker had finally asked a reasonable question.

"Each of you will receive two thousand dollars. One thousand before the game and the other after. Bonus money if you can stay on the field for five minutes and get back in the stands without getting arrested."

"And if we do get arrested?"

"One of the film's producers will bail you out and pay any court costs. You pocket the two grand."

The first collegian looked at the older workers who appeared to be waiting for some kind of explanation, curious as to what this muchacha bonita was proposing. The second student turned to the first. "Good luck translating that."

"Cinematico," said the first boy to his puzzled landscape associates. "Como se dice, uh, movie, por dinero."

The men seemed interested, especially the fattest, sweatiest member of the crew. "Con la muchacha?" he asked, almost drooling.

Here we go, thought Ginny, shaking her head. "Look," she said, "talk it over. Give it some thought. Are you back here tomorrow?"

"Yeah, one more day."

"I'll be back tomorrow morning with the money. Same time. You trust me, I'll trust you. Fair enough?"

The boys nodded and Ginny turned to go.

"Hey," said the handsome boy, "what's the movie about?

Ginny glanced back and smiled. "It's a mystery."

∗

Max was in a foul mood as he neared the athletic fields. Instead of a recruiter, which he'd actually begun to enjoy, now he had to be a negotiator. Charles had truly succeeded in putting a damper on a day which had begun with such promise. Gazing at the basketball court from a distance, Max was relieved to find no sign of the low level blackmailer. He arrived court-side, sat patiently on the wooden bench and nodded to the young men awaiting the game's winners. Ribs' imposing frame was taking up a large portion of the key and when the big man spotted Max, he winked and called for the ball. Rufus hit him with a bounce pass and Ribs backed his helpless defender toward the hoop and hit a baby hook to clinch the victory. His teammates bumped fists and went for water but Ribs went for Max, grinning like the bear that got the honey.

"What's up, man? You bring more money?"

Max looked at him seriously. "We got a problem."

The grin disappeared. "Shit, man. I knew it was too good to be true. What'd you do, man? Cancel the movie?"

"No, man," said Max. "I didn't do anything. It's Charles."

"Charles?"

"Yeah. He came and saw me this morning. Says he's gonna' tell the police, stop the whole thing if I don't pay him off. He's blackmailing me and ruining it for you and your boys."

Ribs sat down as the other players began to wander over, water bottles in hand. "Motherfucker. How much he ask for?"

"Ten grand."

"Motherfucker. Seems kind of low."

"That's what I thought," said Max.

"What's going on?" asked Rufus.

"Charles is screwing up our payday Saturday," said Ribs. "Gonna' go to the cops unless he gets ten large. He's blackmailing our man here."

"Motherfucker," said Rufus.

Max was ready to concur. Charles was a motherfucker. The group of athletes were talking among themselves now and they seemed none too happy. Charles was their friend, but this was business and in matters financial business often trumped friendship.

Max sensed the ballplayers were going to back him in this dispute but his senses weren't always correct. "So," he said, "what are we going to do about it?"

"We," said Ribs. "What are we gonna' do about it? Man, what are you going to do about it?"

"He's your friend."

"That don't mean he listens to us. Charles is a stubborn motherfucker."

"I understand," said Max, surprised that he was even having such a conversation, "that Charles is a motherfucker. I think we've established that. But won't he listen to reason? Won't he listen to his homeboys?"

"Homeboys?" Ribs looked annoyed.

"You know," said Max. "Friends."

"Man, you been watching too much TV."

"Charles is connected," said Rufus.

"What do you mean connected?" asked Max.

"He means," said Ribs, "that Charles don't have to listen to us or listen to you or anyone else, 'cept maybe the guys he's connected to."

This was not going the way Max had hoped. He could only imagine explaining to King why they had to call the whole thing off. "Well," he said, "either we cancel the scene and you guys get no money, or I pay Charles and everyone's cash gets cut in half." The hoopsters mulled this information over, talking it out, obviously not pleased with either choice. Max wondered what outcome he'd been expecting. Did he suppose they'd beat some sense into Charles, that maybe they would hold him, duct-taped and imprisoned in some dank, dark basement until after the game, or perhaps that they would actually kill him? Maybe he had been watching too much TV.

"This here," said Ribs, "is one of those conundrums. How much time you got?"

"Said he'd see me tomorrow morning. Pretty sure he's expecting the money."

"Oh, I'm sure he is." Ribs looked around. "Marvin! Where you at?" A short pencil thin point guard stepped forward. "Marvin, Charles your cousin, right?"

"No," said the young man. "He's my uncle."

"Okay, uncle. You get along?"

"Pretty good. I just stay out of his business. Don't ask no questions."

"Smart," said Ribs. "You know where he is right now?"

"Probably at the club."

"He's drinking this early?"

"They play dominoes in the morning," said Marvin. "If he's not here playin' ball and he's not locating somebody, then he likes to play dominoes. I don't know if they drink, too. Game's pretty serious. They play for real money so I don't think he's getting wasted over there."

"You think you could talk some sense to your uncle?"

"No thank you," said Marvin. "I'll tell him you're looking for him though, if you want."

Max was trying to recall if Marvin had made the cut the other day, if it was in the young man's interest to help solve this problem. Ginny had the list but Max decided to take a chance, go with his first inclination. "Marvin, you were hoping to make some money Saturday, right?"

"Yes, sir," said Marvin.

Good, thought Max, he's on the list. Maybe he could help, even a little bit. "Look," said Max, "you guys need money and we need this scene. Every film needs a big finale. You've seen 'Ghostbusters, right?" Heads shaking negatively. "Uh, all right, 'Rush Hour'?...No, okay, okay, 'Scarface'?" Now their smiles lit up, everyone nodding in approval. "And, uh..." Now he was thinking fast. "Maybe I can get you points."

"Points?" asked Ribs.

"That's part of the profits," said Spider.

"That's right," said Max.

"Profits," scoffed Ribs. "On your shitty little film. What kind of profits?"

"Maybe a tenth of a point."

"A tenth of a point. What the Hell is that?"

Odell stepped forward. "That's one tenth of one percent of the net profits. Not the gross." Odell glanced at Max who appeared slightly shocked at the young man's entertainment knowledge and motioned for him to continue. "So, say the movie makes ten million profit, one percent of that is one hundred thousand. And one percent of that is ten thousand."

"That don't seem like much for all of us," said Ribs.

"It's not," said Odell. "But you never know. If the film is super low budget, like this one, and it becomes a big hit, you know, like 'Blair Witch Project', could be a lotta' profits."

"That movie sucked," said Rufus.

"That's right," said Max. "And it didn't even have a big finale."

"It's finale sucked," said Rufus, apparently not a fan.

"And," Odell continued, "it made over two hundred million dollars. One percent of two hundred million is two million and one tenth of that is two hundred thousand."

Ribs mulled this over. He was impressed but not convinced. "Net?" he asked.

"Probably gross. Hollywood reports gross. Net's more secretive. But that thing cost like thirty thousand to make. Net had to be huge."

"How you know all this shit?"

"I read, man."

Max wondered why he hadn't suggested a full point. What difference would it have made? There weren't going to be any points because there weren't going to be any profits because there wasn't going to be any film. This caper was getting so convoluted it was starting to cloud Max's mind. Being a criminal was more mentally taxing than he had expected.

Ribs looked at Max. "This thing gonna' be any good?"

Maybe there was hope after all. "It's a good script, and if we can pull it off, this finale could be awesome. No guarantees of course, but it could be a big hit."

Ribs still had doubts. "That's something I been hearing all my life. No guarantees."

Max glanced at Rufus. "Well, I'll guarantee you one thing. It'll be better than 'Blair Witch Project.'"

Long pause. Ribs stared at Max. Odell seemed pleased with himself and Rufus still appeared to be angry at the makers of 'Blair Witch'. Max felt like he was waiting for the jury to be led in to render a verdict. The other players were silent, patient. Ribs surveyed his friends. "Okay," he said. "Marvin, you go get your Uncle Charles. You tell him we need to have a sit down. Tell him it's important."

"Yes, sir," said Marvin, turning to go.

Max looked at Ribs. "Thank you."

"Don't thank me yet," said Ribs. "That Charles is a disagreeable motherfucker."

*

Catholic Memorial Hospital wasn't far from the athletic fields. Around a corner and up a gentle hill, it had rested in the same spot for over a hundred years. Neither one of the country's finest medical facilities nor a dilapidated dump in need of demolishing, the institution was just as nondescript as most of the patients within, Louis 'Nuggets' Papasian being one of its most recent admissions.

Max had waffled furiously while deciding on the pros and cons involved in paying his big balled friend a visit. Certainly it was the right thing to do, but these days the right thing to do wasn't always the right thing to do. Nuggets might be angry that Max hadn't interceded earlier in his confrontation with the irate midget, thus saving both his dignity and any chance he may have had in making a comeback in the adult entertainment industry. He could still be irked that Max had been given the job that he, Nuggets, thought was his, though Max felt any grudge in that regard should be directed toward Chubster and not himself. Moreover, Nuggets may simply be in no mood for visitors; pain and depression didn't exactly make one yearn for social encounters.

Nevertheless, Max, having had what he hoped was a successful meeting with Ribs and the boys and his guilty conscience currently being chock full, was resolute in his determination to properly console his seriously injured regular. He would make an appearance, offer whatever sympathy and encouragement he could muster, then be on his way, but not before promising a return visit, one which both he and the patient knew would probably never occur.

After receiving directions from the ancient volunteers at the front desk, Max tried to keep his mind on the reason for coming to the hospital and not to notice the attractive nurses he was passing in the corridors. He did, however, hope that Nuggets had been given a hatched-faced matron for a care-giver and not some pretty young nursing student, feeling sure that any arousal in Nuggets' current condition could prove devastatingly painful.

Nuggets seemed neither surprised nor enthused to see Max. The hospital room was a standard one, generic in every sense, but at least it was a single. Nuggets was likely in no mood to explain his unusual injury to some old timer moaning and groaning about a bad case of shingles or his worsening emphysema. The room, sadly, contained few cards and flowers, evidence that Nuggets' chosen career path had resulted in hardly any friends, the attempt at porn stardom apparently not conducive to meeting your soulmate or pleasing your family. Nuggets, noticing Max, barely shifted his gaze from the hilarious shenanigans ensuing from the 'Let's Make A Deal' program showing on the small television which hung from the ceiling at the foot of his bed.

"Hey, Nuggets," said Max, suddenly regretting that in his hands he held nothing, not flowers, not candy, not a stuffed animal or balloon purchased from the tiny gift shop that greeted visitors upon entering the hospital, no, not even a card signed by the regulars at 'Sully's.

"Hey, Max," said Nuggets. He looked and sounded like a man resigned to his fate, no matter how unfulfilling and purgatorial that life might be. One has a great deal of time to reflect on one's past when confined to a hospital bed and that may be perfectly fine for a returning war hero or a fireman who has risked life and limb to rescue his fellow citizens from a burning building or perhaps even teachers, social workers and philanthropists. But for men like Nuggets, ne'er -do wells, slackers and underachievers, that same period of time may serve only as a reminder of a life pervaded by regret and remorse.

"How you feeling?" Max asked, wishing immediately that he'd opened with a more original question.

"How do you think I'm feeling?"

"Pretty lousy I guess."

"That's a good guess."

Max walked slowly to the side of the bed, paused next to the chair situated there. "Can I sit?"

"Suit yourself. The guy in the monkey mask is just about to find out what's behind the door."

"Sounds exciting." Max smiled but only for a moment. The prize behind the door was revealed to be a trio of goats and while the audience howled as though they had witnessed an act of comic genius, neither patient nor visitor followed suit. "Anybody else been in, you know, from the bar?"

"Biz stopped by, watched a little TV with me, and Sully came in. It was nice of him but I think he was basically trying to figure out if I was going to sue him."

"Are you?"

"Hell, no. It wasn't his fault. Besides, he offered to help pay my medical bills. I would like to sue that little bastard though but I can't even do that."

Max was actually glad to hear that news, but was curious. "Why not?"

Nuggets finally looked at Max. "How would that look in the courtroom? I get beat up by a midget and now I'm suing him."

"You didn't get beat up. You got sucker punched, um, you know, sucker kicked. I'm sure there's video tape."

"That's the other problem. That tape gets out there, it'll go viral. Deranged dwarf kicks big balled porn star in the groin. People eat that shit up. They'll think it's a riot. Probably end up on 'America' Funniest Home Videos.'"

"I think you have to submit those yourself."

"Whatever, man. The point is this is a no win situation. My family already thinks I'm a low level pervert. Now they'll just think I'm a loser."

Wow, Max thought. The visit was not going well. Cheering up Nuggets was, as he suspected it would be, a difficult task. They both watched the television. A woman in a nun's habit frantically searched her pocketbook for a paperclip. Max wondered if she was in costume or would a woman of faith actually spend her day groveling for money on a daytime game show? "So, um," he said, "what's the prognosis?"

"Well," said Nuggets, "the good news is I no longer have to buy pants with extra room in the crotch. The bad news is that my hopes for a comeback are pretty well dashed."

"Sorry to hear that. So that stuff they were cleaning off Sully's floor wasn't blood?"

"Saline."

Max nodded. The game show host was deciding who to select as the next contestant and the audience, dressed in their outlandish costumes, some homemade and impressive, others uninspired, clamored as if the M.C. was their pope and this was their chance at salvation. "So, what was it you wanted to talk to me about that night? You know, before the, ah, incident."

Nuggets stared at the TV. "Doesn't matter." And truly, in his mind it didn't. What good would it do now? He'd be laid up in that bed while Max and Chubster completed whatever shady and possibly lucrative endeavor they had embarked upon and to what point would questioning it serve?

"Seemed to matter a lot that night."

"That was before my, ah, incident."

"Sorry."

"No," said Nuggets. "I'm sorry. I'm obviously not in a good place right now, and I shouldn't take it out on you. I just hope you and Chubster know what you're doing and I wish you good luck. And as far as I'm concerned, that's the end of it. Time to move on."

"You sure you don't want to talk about it?"

"I'm sure."

Max was relieved though not totally convinced by Nuggets' declaration of disinterest, especially if the testicularly damaged patient managed to get himself discharged from the hospital before Saturday's game. Still, Max hoped that Nuggets might now be one less impediment in the litany of complications that had arisen since he'd enlisted in the misbegotten venture.

"So," Max asked, "you have any plans for when they let you out of here?"

Nuggets, judging by his expression, deemed the question foolish. "A plan?" He paused. "Plans are for normal people. People with normal jobs and careers and houses and families and friends and people who love them."

"Jeez, Nuggets," said Max, "you've got friends. You probably have a family that loves you and will forgive you for, you know, your questionable past. And you've had way more girls than me or any of those stool squatters at the bar will ever have."

For the first time, a slight smile crossed Nuggets' countenance as he glimpsed the pleasant but sordid memories from his days filming in the valley. "You're right," he said. "I've got no excuse to feel sorry for myself. My ideas, my actions, no one else to blame for the way my life has turned out."

"Except for the midget," said Max.

"Except for the midget," agreed Nuggets, and for the first time both men laughed right along with the easily amused game show audience.

*

Max went home. He had intended to do a little more recruiting before work but all he wanted was a nap. Which was not like him; he was not a napper, never had been. On those infrequent occasions when he did lay back and close his eyes for a well deserved rest, perhaps an hour, rarely two, he inevitably awoke with an overwhelming sense of guilt, a feeling that he had wasted a precious period of life which could have otherwise been used in a hundred different ways. He knew this self-criticism was silly. After all, was there really that much difference between a short timeout from the day's activities as opposed to reading the paper or watching TV? Did he regret the naps because of his Catholic upbringing? The church loved guilt; it thrived on it. He remembered his friend, Danny, from Scotland telling him that guilt was a useless emotion. But was it? Sometimes guilt came in handy. It could motivate you to do the right thing or at least not do the wrong thing. A guilty conscience might help you make amends, patch things up, get things done. And if he was going to feel guilty about a nap, how was he supposed to cope with helping to rob a stadium? That would be one heck of a story in the confessional.

But at that moment, guilt or no guilt, Max needed to turn off his brain. It had been overworked those last few days and needed a rest. He and Ginny could recruit after work but at that moment a nap seemed like a fine idea. Rufus, his cat, never felt guilty about napping. Why should he?

*

Ginny probably could have used a nap as well. Surely it would have been preferable to another meeting with Emily's guidance counselor, meetings she had come to abhor as much for their banality as for their critical analysis of her only child. Perhaps these conferences would have proven more interesting had Emily actually done something noteworthy, something overt. Backtalk a teacher, sneak a cigarette, get in a cat-fight with the class gossip, some act of academic impropriety that at least made sense to Ginny and her recollections of her own high school mischief. But no, Ms. Bodega wanted only to discuss Emily's attitude, her lack of school spirit and failure to participate in any and all extracurricular activities; moreover her apparent disgust with anyone and everyone associated in any way with Edison High, whether they be teachers, students, principal or custodian, it mattered not. True, Ms. Bodega would admit Emily's grades were fine, in fact exemplary and that she caused no drama or distraction in class or assembly but, and wasn't there always a but, she was capable of so much more. Ginny wondered why, after being summoned to the school on prior occasions to hear this same criticism, she would have to revisit the same subject once again. She had spoken to Emily about Ms. Bodega's remarks but her daughter was a brilliant and precocious debater who swatted away these simplistic arguments like so many houseflies, convincing her mother that high school was, indeed, a colossal waste of time for anyone with even a modicum of independence and creativity, a fascist environment filled with rigid conformity and rote memorization. Ginny, like Ms. Bodega before her, would point out that high school is whatever you make it, that there is ample opportunity to learn what you like and be who you want. To which Emily would invariably reply that this was exactly what she was doing, learning what she liked and being who she wanted to be. Ginny, usually exhausted from another long shift at the bar, and equally tired of these conversations, would end the discussion with a simple declaration. "I need a drink."

But there she was, once again, seated in Ms. Bodega's cramped office, across from the all too familiar guidance counselor, a petite woman of thirty some years, dark-haired and olive-skinned. Ginny noticed, likely for the first time, that Ms. Bodega appeared to be in excellent physical condition, her frame slender, her arms well-muscled. Perhaps she was a runner, Ginny thought, picturing the little lady racing across the football field and wondering what sort of salary a high school guidance counselor makes.

"Miss O'Riley," said Ms. Bodega, "does Emily share with you the work she's doing at school?"

"I'm not sure what you mean. I see her grades."

"No, I mean does she ever bring home tests, projects, papers she's written? Do you ever see what she's actually doing in class?"

The question seemed somewhat accusatory but Ginny kept calm and paused to think.

"I've seen a couple drawings I guess but I mostly just go by the grades which, as you know, are really good."

"So you don't read her essays?"

"No. Do most parents?"

"Probably not." Ms. Bodega reached in a folder and pulled out a few printed pages stapled together. She handed them to Ginny. "So you haven't read this?"

Ginny took the papers, stared at the title page: 'Sneaky G and the Secret Flick', by Emily O'Riley. Ginny's mind was racing. She had mentioned the low budget film to her daughter and her conversation with Max, but was certain she'd revealed few details. Heck, she didn't know many details to reveal anyway. She took a breath. "No, I haven't. Is there a problem?"

Ms. Bodega leaned back. "Well, Miss O'Riley, your first name is Ginny, is that right?"

"Yes."

"Is that Ginny with a G?"

"Ah, yup." Ginny was quickly getting the picture.

"Well, I think this 'Sneaky G' person is you."

Ginny tried to act casual, and why shouldn't she? She hadn't actually broken any laws...yet. "Well, no one has ever called me 'Sneaky G' before, at least not that I'm aware of. Maybe it's a coincidence." She glanced at the papers again, read a few lines.

Ms. Bodega held out her hand. "May I?" Ginny handed her the essay. The Guidance Counselor took the papers, adjusted the stack and read aloud. "Her mother was acting differently than she'd done before. True, she'd had all manner of phases in her personal life since E's birth and the subsequent divorce from T. She'd dated unusual, sometimes suspect men, she'd changed jobs and apartments and had taken up various hobbies and pursuits, most of them short lived..." Ms. Bodega paused, looked at Ginny. "Is this sounding familiar?" Ginny nodded and the Counselor continued. "...But she'd never acted secretive before, never engaged in any clandestine activity, never dated anyone from work before and, at least as far as E knew, never done anything even remotely illegal."

Ginny couldn't stop herself. "She told me to date Max!"

Ms. Bodega put down the papers. "So this is about you?"

Ginny was not easy to fluster but everyone has their limits. "Look, I don't know. Maybe.

What was the assignment?"

"It was Mrs. Perry's AP English class. They were told to write a short fiction and as the old axiom goes, to write what you know."

"So it's fiction?"

"Is it?"

"What does that mean?"

"Well, the piece is quite detailed and I think we've established that the main character, this 'Sneaky G,' is modeled on you. Are you making an underground film, Miss O'Riley?"

Ginny looked around the office, the framed diplomas hanging on the wall, the bookcase lined with volumes concerning child development and adolescent environments, the small photo of Ms. Bodega's handsome fiancee prominently displayed on her desk. "Am I making an underground film? No, I am not making an underground film."

"Now," said Ms. Bodega, looking, for the first time, anxious, "forgive me, but I must ask the next question. Are you, in any way, involved in the production of pornography?"

Ginny prided herself on her cool and calm temperament. It took a lot to rile the veteran waitress. Arrogant managers, sexist customers, hot-tempered cooks, all had tried and failed. But this, this was something else. "Are you fucking kidding me! You called me in here to see if I was making a porno movie because of a story my daughter wrote, a fictional story!"

"I'm sorry, Miss O'Riley but..."

"And even if I was making a porno, what business is that of yours or this school's or anyone else?"

"Well, it is illegal in this state to make adult films."

"It is?"

Now it was Ms. Bodega's turn to be flustered. "Yes, and you are an attractive woman and though the story doesn't actually detail the content of the movie, it does mention the possible illegality involved and we're concerned about all our students and their parents and I'm sorry if I offended you but I do very much care about Emily and all my students and..."

Ms. Bodega's unease with the conversation seemed to settle Ginny's nerves. "Okay, okay, I get it. I'm sorry I yelled and I'm sorry I swore. But if you look at it from my side, you know, I'm just trying to do the best I can. Emily is, as you know, very creative and has quite an imagination. Ginny took the papers from Ms. Bodega's desk, perused them again. "Look, I'm sure there's some stuff in here that's based on me, but I can assure you there's no need to worry. You won't see me on the Playboy Channel and I'm not doing anything illegal, okay?"

The Guidance Counselor looked relieved, glad to be almost finished with a meeting that she, like Ginny, had not been looking forward to. She even forced a smile. "Good, good, that's great. I am truly sorry if I offended you but I hope you understand, I'm just trying to do my job and watch out for my kids, that's all."

Ginny stood up, the short story still in her hands. "I get it. No worries. I'll have another chat with Emily, or should I say 'E.'" That was it, she was back to her old self and both women smiled. "May I take this copy?"

"Of course."

"Thanks."

Ms. Bodega stood, they shook hands politely and Ginny made her way down the corridors, past the quiet classrooms, past the trophy cases and student artwork, past the youths with their futures ahead of them, most filled with promise and possibility. She exited the high school and paused, staring once again at the papers in her hand. And while she knew she'd committed no crime, she could not escape the feeling that the essay, or short story as it were, was a warning of sorts, a signal to return to reality, to think things through, to reconsider. Maybe it wasn't just a lark, something different to do. Maybe there would be real repercussions, maybe it was serious business. Maybe, she thought, she had screwed up.

*

Max felt refreshed, well rested. Maybe naps were a good idea after all. Yes, he'd felt lethargic and disoriented upon waking, but that feeling passed quickly with a cool shower and small snack. Now, as he exited his apartment and began the familiar walk to work, he moved with a sense of purpose, relaxed, ready. It wasn't as though he usually hated going to his job. But neither was it something he looked forward to. For most of his life, Max had wrestled with opposing notions. Quite often, he felt pangs of jealousy, waves of envy, resentment towards all those with prettier girls, better jobs, more money. At other times, he was content, almost happy, grateful that he was better off than a great deal of the world's inhabitants. If he was feeling a bit down about his lot in life, all he had to do was turn on the news. That would help you appreciate your half empty glass pretty swiftly.

The morning, he decided, could have been worse. Nuggets, who may or may not have proven to be a problem down the line, was stuck in the hospital. Ribs and the boys were going to try and deal with Charles. Ginny still appeared to be on board with both he and the plan and though he knew that he had some tough explaining to do, he still felt good about himself and even better about her.

Perhaps, he hoped, things were going to work out. Maybe things would go smoothly from then on. Maybe the whole heist would go off without a hitch and soon he'd be, for the first time in his life, a fairly wealthy man. He entered 'Sully's through the rear, hung up his coat and clocked in, emerged into the dim light to relieve Millie. The lounge was busier than usual for that time of day, some faces in the crowd recognizable, others not so much. Tony was the only regular present at that hour. Plumbers got out earlier than their white collar counterparts, and he seemed slightly annoyed by the noisy strangers infringing on the solitude he usually enjoyed while nursing his first brew. Frannie was in earlier than usual and was engaged in conversation with a blonde woman who Max could not quite make out, her face turned toward the middle school teacher, her light tresses concealing her profile.

Millie gave Max a brief hug, a hasty rundown on the customers at the bar; who'd had what, who owed money, who was waiting on food. She pulled her cash drawer and headed for the office. Max walked down to say hello to Frannie but as he approached, the blonde woman turned her head, looked at him and smiled. Max stopped, shaken, all the positive thoughts from earlier rapidly draining away. Frannie's new friend was Candy, the beautiful wife of Cranky Sam, the angry midget, the violent groin kicker and very possibly pint-sized bank robber.

"Hello, Maxwell," said Frannie, smiling.

"Maxwell," said Candy, obviously amused. "Is that your real name, Maxie?"

"No," said Max, "but Frannie likes to call me that. How you doing, Fran?"

"Parent teacher conferences today so I got out early."

"Doesn't that mean you're supposed to be there?"

"Um, I suppose. Anyway, you know my new friend, Candace."

"Yup. From the other night. How's your husband, Sam?"

"That guy was your husband?" asked Frannie. "For real?"

Candy ignored her, looked at Max. "You didn't call."

"Yeah, Max, why didn't you call?" said Fran.

This was not how Max had envisioned the beginning of his shift. "Look," he said. "Candy just wanted me to let her know how Nuggets was doing, cause, you know, she felt bad. Isn't that right...Candace?"

"Yuh, sure." She turned to Frannie. "I was concerned."

"I'm sure you were," said Fran, though she sounded doubtful. "How about Sam? Is he concerned about our disfigured friend?"

Max was happy to notice Tony's empty mug as well as some other customers who required service. "Duty calls, ladies." He hastened down the bar, pausing at the taps to fill a chilled glass for the patient plumber.

Tony didn't bother with formalities when Max set the beer in front of him. "So," he said, glancing to the side, "that's who I think it is, right?" Max nodded. "I thought you threw her number away."

"I did," said Max. "You think I called her? I didn't call her. You think I have a death wish?"

"Well, what's she doing here?"

"I don't know. I'm afraid to ask."

"I thought Sully banned her."

"No, no, not her. She didn't do anything." Tony was about to speak but Max held up a finger. "Hold that thought." He needed to take care of the crowd, get his head in the game. A busy bartender had to be in a zone. Thirsts required quenching, hungers satisfied and customers entertained. A good barkeep had to keep a lot of balls in the air and appear to enjoy it all. There was no time for distractions and when it came to distractions Candy was hard to top. The only positive was that she'd come alone. There was, at least momentarily, no sign of Cranky Sam.

Max surveyed the lounge. A decent bartender took at least some pride in his or her work. They may not be satisfied with their career trajectory, they might feel that they would be happier in a more fulfilling occupation with better benefits and chance of advancement. But a decent bartender, no matter what, will hustle and move and pour and do their best to keep the customers content. And Max was, if nothing else, a decent bartender. And so, though he knew Tony was awaiting his return with more questions and Candy was waiting with questionable intentions and maybe Frannie was waiting, too, he still took time to fix a good drink and make a good impression.

Soon, convinced that his patrons were temporarily appeased, Max made his way back to Tony, carrying a cold mug and wearing a smile. "So," he said, "you probably have more questions."

"You bet your ass I do but they'll have to wait because right now Marilyn Monroe there is standing at the service station."

Max swiveled quickly and sure enough, Candy had excused herself from Frannie's probing and was, like a patient cocktail waitress, hoping for the bartender's attention. The blonde seductress gave Max a small wave. He looked at Tony. "Be right back."

Tony grinned. "Promises, promises."

Fortunately, Max thought, there were no real waitresses waiting for drinks; in fact he hadn't even seen Ginny yet. He reached the service area, looked at Candy, easily the most attractive woman in the joint, and tried to be stern. "What are you doing here?"

"You mean here?" She pointed to the trays. "In the waitress place?"

"No, no. Here in 'Sully's.'"

Candy looked at him as though he'd asked her why a thirsty man would ask for a drink. "I'm here for you, silly."

"Me? But you're a married woman."

"Sort of."

"Sort of. What does that mean?"

"It's a secret. Anyways, makes it more exciting, don't you think?"

"Not when your husband's a maniac."

"Sammy? He's a puppy dog...Usually. That man was crowding him."

Max turned and looked down the row of stools, hoping someone needed him. No dice. "Okay," he said, "let's say, for argument's sake, that your husband is not a sociopath with a bad temper and that you two have some sort of bizarre open marriage, that still doesn't explain why me?"

Candy licked her lips, thinking. "Because you're interesting."

"Oh, no," said Max. "I am not interesting. In fact, I'm a pretty dull guy."

"And you're funny."

"No, definitely not funny. Ask anyone. I don't know where you got that idea."

Candy laughed. "See?"

Max had had a lot of conversations with a lot of women in his days, but never one like this.

And, as much as he'd always dreamed that a drop dead gorgeous woman like Candy would talk to him in such a manner, regrettably, this was just not the time. "Look," he said, "you know what I think? I think you're either a scam artist or some kind of danger freak and either way I end up hurt."

"Wow," said Candy. "What an imagination. I like that, too." She stood up straighter, puffed out her chest, brushed back her golden locks. "Max, you're not dumb. You do realize that every man in here is dying to get with me."

"The important word in that sentence is dying." Candy laughed again. "Now why don't you go back and continue your nice chat with Ms. Francis. I'll fix you a drink...On me."

"Okay," said Candy, turning to go. "But we're not done."

Oh, yes we are, thought Max. In fact, he wished he was done with the whole thing. A week ago his life was a nice straight line; now it was a yo-yo, up and down with every passing hour. He took a deep breath, composed himself, looked around at the booths surrounding the bar and for the first time noticed Ginny seated in one of those booths across from a middle-aged gentleman in suit and tie. Could it be her ex? As far as Max understood, Emily's father was no longer involved in her or her mom's life and judging by previous descriptions was unlikely to show up in a suit. Plus, this guy was listening intently as Ginny spoke, and taking notes on a small pad of paper. Max realized Connie, another one of 'Sully's long time waitresses was waiting for her drinks.

"Earth to Max," said Connie. "Earth to Max."

"Sorry," said Max, grabbing her drink order from the ticker. "Daydreaming, I guess."

Connie glanced at the well occupied bar. "Kind of busy to be daydreaming."

"Yeah, true that. So, ah, who's that guy with Ginny in the booth. Looks serious."

"I guess he's some kind of detective. Remember that bank robbery with the trick-or-treaters that Ginny was kinda' near? He had more questions."

"Oh," said Max, for at this point what else could he say? He wanted to shout 'enough', 'uncle', 'I give up', 'I quit', but Connie would have probably assumed that his outburst was his declaration of a conclusion to his bartending career, and as such had been brought about by her rather uncomplicated order, that order being the proverbial last straw. He couldn't saddle Connie, a perfectly nice person, with that sort of guilt and so he calmly fixed her drinks. Just great, he thought, turning back to his patrons. First a maniac, then a sex bomb, and now a detective. Who was going to walk into 'Sully's next? Max shuffled back down the bar, avoiding Frannie and Candy but checking on everyone else.

"Well," said Tony.

"Well, what?" said Max.

"Are you gonna' do her?"

"Am I gonna' do her? No, I'm not gonna' do her."

"I would."

"You're a married man."

"I know." Tony looked glum.

Max stared at the front door. Biz and Joey were entering, obviously surprised by the crowd.

"Thank God," said Max, sighing.

Tony swiveled, saw his pals approaching, looked at Max curiously. "Do you say that when I walk in?"

Max smiled. "Of course I do."

Joey and Biz made their way to the bar, looking around at the unusually large crowd with a mixture of surprise and annoyance. Finding no open seats, they each staked out a small patch of floor directly behind Tony's broad shoulders.

"What the heck is going on?" asked Joey.

"Yeah," said Biz, "what is this, 'Cocktail? You juggling bottles back there, Max?"

"No such luck. Just one of those days, I guess."

"Hey, Max," said Tony, "tell these boys they're crowding me. Don't forget what happened to Nuggets."

Joey and Biz immediately wedged in closer to their plumber pal, each now resting his chin on one of those broad shoulders. Tony tried to look serious but couldn't keep a straight face and all three were soon laughing. Joey and Biz backed up a bit and Tony sipped his beer. "Hey, nitwits," he said. "Look who's hanging out with our Frannie."

Joey and Biz turned toward the two women. This time their faces registered no sign of annoyance; rather they appeared amazed as though they'd just seen a ghost or a gorgeous crossing guard.

"Is that who I think it is?" asked Joey.

"You bet," said Tony.

"I thought she was banned," said Biz.

"No. Just the midget."

"Why the Hell would she come back here?"

Tony stared at Max. "Why do you think?"

Joey and Biz turned back to Max who shrugged. "Beers?" he asked, not bothering to wait for an answer, plucking two frosty mugs from the chiller and pouring their drafts simultaneously, watching the glasses as though concentrating on the task at hand and not simply avoiding the glare of his envious friends. He placed the pints in front of the new arrivals and rushed away before he could be peppered with more questions from the curious trio.

Max waited on a couple at the far end of the bar but kept an eye on Ginny and the detective who was now extracting a thin, zip-locked freezer bag from a manila envelope. The bag contained a sheet of paper and was placed on the table in front of Ginny. The curious waitress was about to open the bag but the detective indicated not to, so instead she leaned forward and read through the clear plastic cover. Max had to shift his attention to constructing some cocktails and when he looked back, Ginny was recoiling from the paper, her hand covering her mouth, her eyes wide. The detective took back the plastic bag and carefully returned it to the envelope, then sipped slowly from his coffee, apparently giving Ginny a moment to regain her composure. By the time Max had gone to the kitchen and emerged carrying a couple BLTs for a pair of retirees watching the news, the detective was finishing up with Ginny, standing, shaking her hand, offering his card. Max felt like he was watching a television show; the detective just needed a trench coat and fedora.

*

Ginny was shaken. She'd seen a lot of stuff and heard a lot of crap in her time, but she had never, ever, read anything as vulgar, as vile, as deranged as the note Detective Popowski had produced from the manila envelope. It was, he'd said, the original given to the teller at the bank robbed by the trick-or-treaters, the same crime which she and Max had witnessed from afar and was, as yet, unsolved. No wonder the poor woman had fainted. The heinous acts of violence threatened within that note would have caused even the most hardened homicide cop tremors, never mind an innocent young bank clerk used to small talk and pleasantries. Not only was the investigation ongoing, said the detective, a long time veteran of the force and a man who took his job quite seriously, thus far they had no leads and no suspects. Though they surmised that at least one, if not all, of the perpetrators was a midget or dwarf, the current climate of political correctness would not allow those in charge to bring in every little person within the city limits for questioning. The ACLU would have had a field day with that kind of profiling, as would the small folks themselves, once again pointing out how they were being discriminated against. According to Popowski, the lawmen were retracing their steps, revisiting every witness and bystander, hoping that maybe someone somewhere might recall something they'd originally left out, any little clue, no matter how minuscule, that might point in some direction. The note, the detective said, was simply meant to jar a memory, to make clear just how dangerous these diminutive thieves were. And if Mr. Popowksi's intention had been to shock Ginny, then surely he'd succeeded, though that success was tempered somewhat by the lack of additional observations it had failed to produce. Once again, Ginny had not mentioned the presence of her current co-worker and possible crush, Max. Why? Was she concealing what she'd assumed at the time was an innocent coincidence? Was it because she'd not included him in her original statement and feared that now it would lead to more questions and complications? Or was she protecting Max from the consequences of some nefarious activities he'd been involved in? That would explain his hasty exit from the cafe that day and his subsequent reluctance to get drawn into the investigation. And what about that damn midget, the little bastard who'd almost castrated poor Nuggets? Was that another coincidence? Ginny headed for the service bar and waited for Max, though it wasn't a long wait. He seemed as anxious to talk to her as she'd been to speak with him.

"Hey," he said, glancing at the empty ticker, "you need drinks?"

"No. I haven't even got a table yet. That detective was here when I walked in. Sully said to talk to him first, not to worry about it."

"So what was it all about?"

"The trick-or-treat robbery we watched."

"We?"

"Yes, we, Max." Ginny seemed annoyed.

"Did you tell him that?"

"No, I didn't. But then I started to wonder. Why wasn't I telling him about that? What's going on? What are you hiding?"

Max looked around. He needed to escape this conversation. Thank goodness a couple patrons were attempting to get his attention, raising their empty glasses in the air. "Look," he said, "it's way too busy for this right now. We'll talk after work, on that recruiting mission I mentioned."

"Yeah," said Ginny. "We will talk. And we'll talk about that midget friend of yours, too." Max turned away but Ginny continued. "And the blonde floozy talking to Sully, too."

Max noted that his boss had joined Candy and Frannie in conversation. Candy was smiling and laughing, her hand resting on the big man's arm and Sully showing no sign of ending the visit anytime soon. Max turned back to Ginny, his hands raised in surrender. "Okay, okay, we'll talk later."

The day had gone South fast, Ginny was thinking. First the guidance counselor, then the detective, and now Max was, once again, less than forthcoming. She had a mind to skip out on the late night recruiting session but she wanted answers and didn't feel like waiting. No wonder she'd resisted dating guys from work all these years. She made her way to the hostess station. The best thing right now was to grab some tables, take care of some customers and make some cash. Fortunately, the place was busy and she could occupy her mind doing what she was best at. The other stuff could wait til later.

*

Max realized he'd have to come clean with Ginny sooner rather than later but right then duty called. He canvassed the bar, quickly mixing drinks and pouring drafts. Food orders were sent to the kitchen and dishes cleared. He was in such a state of overdrive that the entire bar was taken care of, no one, at least momentarily, in need of anything more. Max stepped back, took a breath, appraised his domain, then ambled back over to the girls.

"Hey, Maxie," said Sully, grinning broadly, "you're like a one-armed paperhanger back there. Glad to see you're your old self."

"Yeah, well, pretty busy in here. Figured you'd be in the kitchen by now."

"Well, I was on my way there but I had to say hello to Candy here." The Irishman placed his hand on the knockout's shoulder. She didn't flinch. "The poor girl was wondering how Nuggets was doing. Very concerned." Sully seemed to realize something, removed his hand and turned toward Frannie. "And, of course, I always have to say hello to my favorite educator."

"Oh, Sully," said Frannie, "you're full of shit, but you are a sweet talker. Maxwell, you should take a lesson."

"Yeah, Maxwell," said Candy, smiling, "you should take a lesson."

Max ignored them and turned to Sully. "Listen, Boss. Can you watch the bar for a second before you save the day in the kitchen. I need to hit the little boys room."

"Sure thing, buddy, but make it quick."

Max nodded and slipped under the service bar. The men's room was unoccupied and he was standing, already unzipped, at one of the two urinals when he heard the door open. He didn't turn at first; men don't turn to see who's about to join them in urination. It wasn't until he heard her voice that he looked.

"Hey, it's not so little," said Candy.

"Jesus Christ, Candy, you can't be in here." Max wanted to put his member away as soon as possible but a man couldn't zip up in midstream.

"Don't mind me, honey. You just finish up your business." She leaned against the tile wall next to the hand blower. Max finished, tucked himself in, turned to glare at the crazy blonde.

Candy grinned. "You didn't shake."

Max didn't smile, moved to the sink. Things were getting out of hand. Why couldn't this have happened to him when he was twenty-three, twenty-four years old, back when he was sure he'd live forever, danger be damned. Now he was a grown man with cautious tendencies and a clear awareness of his own mortality. True, hooking up with Candy would probably be as close to Heaven as he'd ever get, but being viciously murdered by a cuckolded little person was not high on his list of ways to go.

"This," he said, washing his hands vigorously, "is getting ridiculous. You're a beautiful woman..."

"Thank you."

"...and you'd probably be a lot of fun..."

"You have no idea."

"...but you're a married woman. I do have some principles."

"You do?"

"Yes, yes I do."

"Are you sure?" asked Candy, licking her lips and sensuously sliding her manicured nails down her voluptuous curves.

Max placed his hands under the blower and stared at his palms as the hot air gushed downward. He couldn't look at her; a man can only take so much temptation and Max was at his limit.

Candy looked down at the machine and smiled. "I'm better."

Max tried to brush by her but Candy put her arm out, grabbed his shirt with her other hand, pulled him against her chest and kissed him deeply. She smelled like vanilla and tasted even better. It was all Max could do to pull away. He looked at her seriously. "I gotta' go." And within seconds he was back behind the bar, happy to be safely ensconced in the one place where he always knew what to do and how to do it, surrounded by familiar faces with familiar problems, none of which he had to rectify. Merely lend an ear now and then and keep the liquid libations coming. What could be simpler?

*

Considering the size of the crowd and the amount of work required to clean and restock the bar, Max was surprised that by the time he'd finished and everyone had left, it was not yet midnight. Plenty of time, he thought, and went to find Ginny. She was nestled in one of the back booths, quietly counting her bank, and barely raised her gaze when he slid in across from her.

"Almost ready?" he asked.

Ginny stopped counting, looked at him seriously. "Yes, I'm almost ready. But I'll tell you what. If you don't come clean as soon as we're done, then this is it. You tell me the truth about everything, exactly what's going on or I'm out. Get it?"

"Got it," said Max. "Fair enough. You tell Sully goodnight when you bring your bank in and I'll call us a cab. Meet you out front." He quickly exited the booth as Ginny looked up.

"A cab?"

Max nodded and smiled, then turned away before she could ask another question. Outside on the sidewalk, standing under the moonlit sky, he weighed his options. If he lied to her again, she'd probably stick it out to the end, continue to help with the recruiting, maybe even sleep with him. But by the time he'd made his escape, left the city with his ill gotten gains, she'd realize the truth and hate him forever, a result that would be difficult to bear. If, on the other hand, he was honest with her, that he'd lied to her, misled her, involved her in an enterprise far more criminal than she was aware, she'd be angry, in fact probably very angry, but she might not hate him, perhaps even empathize with his having yielded to temptation and, after all, he'd never actually asked that she join him; it had been her idea. However, one thought was inescapable. No matter what, he was screwed, situated between the proverbial 'rock and a hard place', damned if he did and damned if he didn't. The woman he was falling for, a pretty woman, smart and funny, a woman he'd be lucky to have, would never look at him the same way again. That realization must have shone on his face when Ginny stepped outside and stood beside him.

"What's the matter?" she asked.

Max shifted back to the task at hand, shook his head and smiled. "Nothing. Just thinking."

"Don't hurt yourself."

"Very funny. You're a riot."

"Where are we going?"

"You'll see. I told you it's a surprise. Come on." The cab pulled up and he held open the door as she climbed in, then followed behind. Max leaned forward, spoke loudly so the dreadlocked driver could hear him over the booming reggae beats. "Three hundred Washington."

The cabbie hesitated, turned and looked at Ginny, then at Max. "Three hundred Washington?" Max nodded. The Jamaican grinned broadly. "Okay, mon, you got it."

Ginny looked at Max. "What was that about?" He shrugged.

The ride proved short which was, Max figured, a good thing since Ginny seemed in no mood for small talk. He'd tried inquiring about her night but her answers were brief, no jokes, no laughs, no warmth. When the taxi came to a stop, Ginny stared out the window. They were in a mostly industrial part of the city but the building they'd arrived at was lit up like a Christmas tree, giant neon letters announcing its name, 'Bottoms Up', the outline of a buxom dancer flashing on and off against the darkened buildings.

"Are you kidding me," said Ginny.

"Come on," said Max, "it's a recruiting mission. Think of the possibilities." He opened the door, jumped out and paid the grinning cabdriver through the open window.

"Have a good time, mon."

"Thanks." Ginny was still in the car. "You coming?" She hesitated, then slowly pushed herself out. "That's my girl."

Two husky behemoths in dark suits stood on either side of a blood red door, their hands folded in front of them, their expressions impassive.

"Good evening," said one.

"Welcome to 'Bottoms Up'" said the other, opening the door.

Tweedledum and Tweedledee, thought Max, as he ushered his reluctant date into the shadowy interior. Another offensive lineman sat on a stool a few feet from the door.

"Welcome to 'Bottoms Up,'" he said. "It's a ten dollar cover." Max handed him a twenty, the jumbo gentleman stamped their wrists and few steps later they were greeted again, this time by a scantily clad young woman leaning on a half-door, chewing gum and reading a college text book.

"Welcome to 'Bottoms Up,'" she said. "Check your coats?"

Well, Max decided, they certainly were a congenial staff. Some of the employees at 'Sully's could learn a few things, but they politely declined the coat check girl's offer and she returned to her studies.

"You gonna' try to enlist the bouncers?" asked Ginny as they headed for one of the small round tables circling the stage.

"No," said Max. "I've got a better idea."

Moments after Max had helped Ginny with her coat and seated himself in one of the plush red velvet chairs that filled the room, a curvy cocktail waitress carrying a tray was kneeling by his side.

"What can I get you?" she asked.

Ginny felt sure that 'Bottoms Up' was unlikely to have an extensive wine list and asked for a light beer. Max did the same and watched the server walk away, her shiny two piece barely containing her generous assets. He'd never been one to frequent strip joints, not for any particular principle or ethical reason, but more because of the inherent tease required by the nature of the business. It was as if someone was offering an expensive chocolate bar, then pulling it away when you went to grab it. But on those rare occasions when he'd found himself a guest in just such an establishment, he'd spent an inordinate amount of time wondering about the cocktail waitresses. Most times they were as lovely and voluptuous as the girls on stage, the only apparent difference being their amount of clothing or lack thereof. Why would a young woman choose to work in a business based on lust and populated for the most part by lecherous old-timers, drunken salesman, philandering husbands and lonely hearts, and yet resist performing the task that would reward them with the most cash? Was it some kind of moral code? Were they ex-dancers who had burned out on the pole? Or had they simply applied for a job at a night club with no knowledge of the entertainment and then decided, what the heck, might as well give it a try.

Max turned his attention back to Ginny who was watching the dark-haired dancer in front of them as though she'd encountered a new and exotic creature at the zoo. "Never been to a gentlemens' club before?" he shouted over the pounding music. Ginny panned the room, taking in the sparse crowd of voyeurs seated stage side and the quiet loners occupying the tables nearby.

"Gentlemen?" she said.

Max was laughing as the waitress returned with their bottles. He gave her a twenty, told her to keep it, then sheepishly realized a twenty would barely cover the tab in a place like this and swiftly proffered another five. He sipped his beer, slowly assessed the club's interior, careful not to remove his gaze for long from the girl twirling around on stage. He knew the dancers' pet peeve was patrons not paying attention. After all, they were working up there, they were entertainers. If you were at the movies, would you look away from the screen? If you were at the ballpark, would you not follow the game? So, moment by moment, Max took it all in. The all female bartending staff (no job for him here, he thought) whose over-inflated chests were encased in girls' junior tank tops, apparently an oversight when handed out by management. The over caffeinated DJ trying thanklessly to rev up the rather sedate audience. ("Let's hear it for Siren! That's not the only pole she knows how to handle!") The bored bouncer staring at his smartphone, having forfeited long ago the thrill of seeing a naked member of the opposite sex. For him, just another day at the office. The aforementioned customers donating singles to the strippers' college funds, but never before at least some piece of clothing had been discarded. And lastly, the women themselves, the reason he and Ginny were in attendance, wearing outfits that would have gotten them arrested anywhere else and heels so high they probably induced vertigo, canvassing the room, pausing to ask the suddenly shy patrons if they'd care for a drink or a dance, their plastic smiles glued on like false eyelashes. Max knew he and Ginny would soon be visited. Most strippers liked the novelty of interacting with a couple; at least it was different.

Sure enough, an impressive pair of breasts were soon dangling between Max and Ginny's chairs, a well manicured hand resting on each of their shoulders, the scent of cheap perfume in the air. Max turned to see those breasts and hands belonged to a pretty blonde with only a few tattoos and piercings. Maybe she was knew, he thought, and they were like flair buttons and metal clips at a TGIF; the longer you worked there, the more you got.

"Hey, guys," the blonde said, kneeling between them. "Having fun?"

"So far, so good," said Max.

The dancer turned to Ginny. "Have you been in here before? You don't look familiar."

Ginny glanced at Max. "Oh, no. No, we haven't...We're from out of town." Max gave Ginny a look. She shrugged.

"Well," said the blonde, looking at Ginny, "you're pretty enough to be a dancer." Then, turning to Max. "She could work here."

"I know," said Max, smiling. "That's what I told her." Now Ginny gave him a look and he mimicked her shrug.

The blonde dancer rested a hand on each of their arms. "I'm Vixen. Do you think you might be interested in a private dance in the V.I.P. Room?"

"Oh, I don't know," said Max. "How much is that?"

"It's twenty for three songs. Sixty for a half hour."

"Tell you what, Vixen. How about twenty for three questions?"

Vixen stood up, looked at Max, her smile quickly vanishing. "You a cop?"

"No, no, of course not. We just..."

"Let me guess. You're a writer doing a story on the poor, misbegotten, objectified dancing girls. Drug habits, childhood abuse, daddy issues, blah, blah, blah."

Ginny looked impressed, Max stunned. "Wow," he said. "No, not a writer. Actually, maybe you should be the writer. That was good." Vixen, kneeling back down, glanced at Ginny who nodded. "Anyway, um, we might have a proposition for you and a couple of the girls to make some good money..."

Vixen rose again, this time her hands on her hips, obviously annoyed. "No, no, no, we don't do that. We are entertainers, not hos. No sex, no threesome. None of that."

"No, no," said Max, "you're getting the wrong idea."

"We're making a film," said Ginny.

"Jesus," said Vixen. "You just said no sex and now you want girls for a porno movie."

"Not a porno," said Max. "A regular film, no sex, no nudity." He looked around the club. "Well, maybe a little nudity."

Vixen stared down at him. "No sex?"

"No sex. I swear no sex."

Vixen knelt down again. She was good at it, Max noticed, could have been a catcher. He took a twenty from his pocket, held it out. "Okay?" Vixen nodded, took the bill and stuck it in her garter. "So," continued Max, "just to make sure this would be worth your while, how much do the dancers make here, how much do they earn?"

"Depends on the girl, depends on the night."

"You know, on average."

"Well, after you pay the club, tip out the DJ and the bar, probably about three or four hundred a night."

Ginny thought she'd misheard. "What do you mean 'pay the club'?"

"We have to pay to dance here. They claim we're renting the stage."

"That's ridiculous."

"I know, right. But all the clubs do it."

"Unbelievable." Ginny leaned back in her chair, shaking her head.

"Anyway," said Max, "sounds like five thousand dollars would be a good amount of money for some of the girls."

"Depends on what they had to do for it."

"I said no sex. I promise. Okay, next question. Who do you think is the fastest girl in here?"

"What?" Vixen glanced at Ginny who tried a smaller shrug.

"Who do you think," asked Max, "is the fastest runner in here. If all the girls had a race, who would win?"

Vixen stood up. "This is weird."

Max stood. "No, please, Vixen. This is serious. The film's finale requires running, fast running. Here..." he said, reaching into his pocket and pressing another twenty into her hand. "Please stay."

Vixen paused, looked around. Max grabbed a chair from an adjoining table, gestured for her to sit. "All right," she said, "let me think. Probably somebody in good shape, right?"

"Like yourself."

"I was a cheerleader. We didn't run much."

"Me, too," said Ginny. "I was a cheerleader."

Vixen smiled at Ginny, turned to Max. "Is she in the movie?"

"No, she's the cameraman, ah, camerawoman."

"You got a girl looks like this and you're putting her behind the camera?"

Max paused, took a breath. He was having trouble concentrating. Between the inevitable conversation to come with Ginny, the close proximity of Vixen's bare flesh and the changing of guard on stage, one curvaceous temptress after another straining to steal his attention, his mission was at risk of going off course. Vixen sat, her arms crossed, staring at him with a quizzical expression, as though he'd just requested that she put on more clothing.

"Look," he said, "I think we're getting off topic here. I told you we need speed, not looks, but, ah, I mean looks, too. Both. We need pretty girls who can run fast and, ah, be elusive and, ah, bouncy." Max wiped his brow. Was he sweating, he wondered.

"What do you mean bouncy?"

"You know, bouncy, jiggly." He glanced at Ginny who seemed to be enjoying his discomfort. "Breasts, boobs, you know, for a distraction."

"So there is nudity?"

Well, I don't know about nudity, maybe a loose top, maybe see-through or like, what you're wearing."

"So you want real titties, ones that'll bounce?"

"Yes, yes, real titties, preferably large ones." Max felt disgusted with himself. "They have to be visible from a distance."

"Okay," said Vixen, "this is getting ridiculous and I gotta' go up pretty soon so why don't you tell me exactly what you're doing."

"May I?" asked Ginny.

Max was relieved. "Please."

Ginny gave Vixen her full attention, as though they'd been friends for years and were about to have a serious woman to woman chat. "Listen," she said, "I know it sounds crazy but there's good money in it. We're making a very low budget film and for the finale we need a bunch of interesting people to run onto the field at the game this Saturday...At the end of the third quarter...Just for a few minutes, then back into the stands."

"The game? At the stadium?" Ginny nodded. "You got tickets?"

Ginny was momentarily surprised by the question. "Yes, yes, you get a free ticket. And a lot of money."

Vixen addressed Max. "You do know it's illegal, right?"

"Well," said Max, "it's a misdemeanor. If they catch you. And we'll pay to bail you out. And your court costs."

Vixen turned back to Ginny. "How much money we talkin' here?"

Ginny was about to answer but Max interrupted. "Five thousand dollars. One thousand before the game. Four thousand after if you don't get caught. Three if you do."

Ginny looked at Max. He'd raised the stakes for strippers. Was there going to be anything left for the landscapers? Or for herself? Vixen was quiet, possibly doing some quick calculations. She craned her head, looking for a particular dancer, spotted her and called out. "Hey, Ebony, come here!"

Ebony stood up from the table she'd been visiting and excused herself from two well dressed businessmen. She was a big girl but by no means fat. Black as a pearl, immaculate hair and nails, sporting a small fortune in jewelry and an enormous bosom which, as far as Max could tell, was quite real. Ebony sashayed over, her considerable curves undulating hypnotically.

"Ebony loves football," said Vixen, before the plus size stripper arrived.

"Hey, sugar, what's up?" asked Ebony, checking out Max and Ginny. "Ooh, a couple. I love couples."

"I told them you love football."

"Yeah, that's true, too."

"They got tickets to the game."

"No shit," said Ebony, obviously impressed. "This Saturday? The big game?"

Max nodded, got up, grabbed another spare chair. "Please sit." Ebony wasn't exactly what he'd had in mind. She didn't look fast but she'd sure be bouncy. The big girl plopped her ample posterior into the seat, looked at Max seriously.

"What I gotta' do to get a ticket? We don't do no ho stuff in here. We're exotic entertainers."

"They want you to run on the field," said Vixen. "At the end of the third quarter."

"Say what? I'll miss the end of the game."

"Five thousand dollars," said Vixen.

Max chimed in. "You just jump on the field, run around for five minutes with a bunch of other people and if you can get back in the stands without getting caught, maybe you can see the end of the game."

"Honey," said Ebony, "I don't jump and I don't run."

"Well, you have to move around, you know, be elusive. You're part of a distraction."

"A distraction from what?"

"They're making a film with a big finale. Gotta' distract the security guys."

"Oh, I can distract all right. But I still don't run. You gonna' run?" Ebony asked Vixen.

"I'm thinking about it. That's a lot of cash."

The dark dancer turned to Max. "I could skip."

"What?"

"You know, skip. That's almost running."

Max was speechless. What do you reply to a half naked stripper who's just made a ridiculous proposal to the ridiculous stunt that's part of the ridiculous caper you're involved in? Thank God for Ginny.

"Can you show us," she asked.

Ebony paused, but only for a moment, then stood and, as though she'd had similar requests in the past, skipped nonchalantly to the front door and back again. Customers turned to watch, the bouncer looked up from his phone and the coat check girl from her studies. Had anyone ever skipped in a strip joint before? Vixen and Ginny were laughing but Max was silent, his mouth agape as he viewed Ebony's massive pair of breasts bounce up and down in her flimsy top like two cantaloupes in a sling. Where was slow motion when you needed it?

"That," said Max, "was amazing." Ginny shot him a look. "Well, it was. And you know, while I was watching you, I had another thought. You wear something that says 'Bottoms Up' on it and think of the publicity. Hundred thousand people in the stands, millions more watching on TV..."

Ginny interrupted. "They don't usually show that stuff on TV."

Max was undeterred. "We're filming it, and other people will be, too. This thing will go vital or virus or whatever the Hell they call it..."

"Viral," said Vixen.

"It'll be everywhere," Max concluded. "You girls will be famous. This place will be jammed!"

Vixen and Ebony looked at each other, the young women trying to determine the flaw in Max's sales pitch. Meanwhile, the skipping stripper had caught the eyes of the other girls who began circling Max's small group, wondering what all the fuss was about. The customers, too, were intrigued but they were wise enough to remain seated and concede at least most of their attention to the dancer onstage.

"What's going on?" asked a slender brunette.

"They need runners," said Vixen.

"Runners?" This from a petite blonde whose assortment of piercings would probably compromise a small airport's security gate.

"Yeah. For five thousand bucks."

"What? For running where?"

"At the game on Saturday. On the field."

"For real?"

"For real. But you could get arrested."

"You have to be fast," said Max.

"Why?"

"So you don't get arrested."

"Ebony's not fast," said the brunette. "She wasn't even running."

Max looked at Ebony, smiled. "Ebony's special."

Ebony puffed out her chest with pride, though in Max's opinion that particular portion of her anatomy needed no puffing. The mention of five thousand dollars had succeeded in attracting everyone's interest, motivating some of the girls to boast, likely for the first time in their lives, that they were, indeed, fast, though that adjective may have been used to describe some of these young ladies as far back as high school; in this case it indicated speed of another nature. The subsequent mixture of brags and bluffs was like some kind of athletic trash talk. Amusing but not very helpful.

That is until one dancer declared, "Bullshit! I'll race anybody here, anytime."

Finally, thought Max, a voice of reason. "Everybody, everybody, hold on a sec." Looking at the dancer who had laid down the challenge, Max had but one thought and it was an exciting and unfamiliar one. A week ago he would have deliberated long and hard about such a proposal, a footrace at a strip club. He would have calculated the pros and cons, imagined what could go wrong, pictured worst case scenarios. He seldom took risks or threw caution to the wind. He didn't gamble and he didn't invest in his patrons' hare-brained ideas, usually that is. But since accepting Chubster's proposition his mind seemed somehow altered, more open to novelty and instinct. So when the race gauntlet was thrown down Max, the new Max, was quick with his decision.

"Why not," he said, smiling. The women appeared genuinely intrigued, something to break the monotony, the customers curious and the bouncers amused. "What time does this place close?"

"Last call is one, forty-five. Out by two." This from the cocktail waitress who had quietly slipped between the dancers.

"Okay," said Max. "We'll do it when you get out. We'll figure a distance out on the street. But, until then, I guess we'll need another round." He grinned at Ginny and she couldn't help but smile back. This might very well be it for her and Max but the night had a good chance of being interesting and fun and exciting, so why not enjoy it? They could talk afterwards.

During the next hour or so, the tension was building, a different kind of expectation than 'Bottoms Up' was used to. For the first time ever, the girls were arguing not about who was the best dancer or who made the most tips or who was the skankiest ho spreading her legs on stage, but rather who was the speediest. The bouncers seemed to be spending an inordinate amount of time on their phones and speculation was that they were setting odds and taking bets. Max surveyed the scene, his expression inscrutable, the rosy glow of alcohol enveloping his aura. He turned to Ginny whose consumption had been matching his own. "America," he said, laughing. "What a country!"

*

Ginny was having a hard time pacing off the hundred yards. She felt like she was being given the longest sobriety test in the history of traffic stops and failing badly. Max was as tipsy as she and it was all he could do to organize the contestants and maintain some sense of order. He had handed out crisp one hundred dollar bills to all the girls as a sign of good faith and he'd tipped the bouncers for their help as well. But none of that was aiding Ginny in her struggles.

She knew there were three feet in a yard but was her foot really a foot long or shorter? Maybe four of her feet made a yard. She tried the toe to heel method but felt like she was walking a tightrope, a task most difficult in her inebriated state, so switched to simply counting off one hundred long steps. Not the most accurate method but this, she thought, wasn't exactly the Olympics. When she was done she dragged two large trash cans to either side of the finish line, one on each sidewalk, took a position to the side and signaled drunkenly to Max that she was ready. Max seemed confused by her gestures so she raised a hand in the air, her thumb thrust upwards, and yelled "ready!"

Now she watched from a distance as Max endeavored to line up the racers, apparently straining to convince them that their position at the start line would be no factor in the outcome. Ginny was impressed that one of the strippers even got down in a three point stance. A bouncer raised what appeared to be a real pistol to the sky but Max moved quickly and convinced him to put it away, choosing instead to go old school. Ginny heard him yell "go!" and they were off.

Of course a race in which the girls were forced to compete in the shoes they performed in, the five inch stilettos, the see-through platforms containing live fish, the modified Greek sandals laced to the knee, would likely have proved far more amusingly treacherous. But these women were no fools. After hours spent balancing in discomfort at work, they were not going to journey home in the same impractical footwear. They'd all brought sneakers and flip flops and now they were sprinting down the street toward Ginny with serious intent, the only thing treacherous being the possibility of slapping their own chin with an uppercut from a bouncing breast. Apparently strippers after work clothes did not include sport bras.

Those dancers who'd elected not to compete got caught up in the excitement, jumping up and down and loudly rooting on their friends. Ginny tried her best to delineate the order of finish but between her own alcoholically impaired powers of judgment and the surprisingly competitive nature of the last few yards, determining what place each contestant had come in was nearly impossible. She was fairly certain that a thin redhead with A cups had won but the little blonde and slender brunette from earlier were right there as well. A couple of girls were slowed by their over-sized bosoms and one beautiful dancer with stationary fake boobs lacked the bounciness that Max had declared he was seeking. Though both he and Ginny had expected some jostling or tripping, some elbows thrown or dirty tricks, no evidence of such behavior was observed. Just because these women made their living doffing their clothes didn't mean they'd lost their sense of fair play.

Fortunately, as far as Ginny could recall, Max had not actually promised a spot to the first few finishers but instead had said the race would be a test of velocity, a means of separating the braggarts and boasters from the true speedsters. Thus, the pressure was not on Ginny to produce accurate results or be an immediate arbiter of ability. Rather, she led the gasping group back to the start line where they gathered around Max as though awaiting word from a Roman orator.

"Wow," said Max, "that was amazing. Absolutely amazing. Anyway," he continued, "you all did great. Who knew you girls were so fast. And competitive! That was some finish, huh, Jeannie?"

"Spectacular," said Ginny, wondering if the booze had actually increased her vocabulary.

"Yeah, but who won?" asked the brunette.

"I won," said the redhead. "Ask the finish line chick."

"Doesn't matter," said Max before Ginny could reply. "The important thing is now we know you're all fast. I'm just glad," he went on, pausing to sip from the bottle he'd snuck out of the club, "that no one got hurt, you know, broke an ankle or something, 'cause then, you know, we'd have to put you down." No one laughed and Max turned to Ginny who shook her head; he wasn't funny when he was drunk. "Anyway, we're gonna' talk it over, figure how many of you we can hire, how much money we've got and so forth. Please don't talk about this with anyone or we might have to cancel the film and you'll ruin it for everybody. Ah, I think that's it..." He looked at Ginny.

"Don't forget," said Ginny. "Wear something that says 'Bottoms Up'. Big letters so it can be seen from a distance. Tight but not too tight. We want bouncy, right, ah, Jim?"

"Right. Bouncy. Bouncy's good." Max grinned like a halfwit. Oh, boy, thought Ginny, searching for a pen and paper in her purse as the girls lined up around her. Here we go.

*

In the cab ride back to Max's place, Ginny sat close. She rested her head on his shoulder, her hand on his thigh. "Jesus," he said, staring straight ahead, "what a day."

"Yeah," said Ginny. "No kidding."

"I haven't drunk that much in a long time."

"Me either. But we're still going to talk. You promised."

Max turned, stared at her face, put his arm around her and pulled her closer. Not only was she beautiful, he thought, but she was shrewd. It had been wise not to pay the girls that night, but make them wait. Just like the ballplayers. That way he didn't have to pick immediate winners. No sore losers to blab and blow the whole thing. And though the last thing he wanted was to sabotage a budding romance, he had promised. And he always kept his word. "You're right," he said. "We'll talk."

*

For Max, following Ginny up the stairs to his apartment was torture. This should have been the big night, the first time, the beginning. This was a woman he could grow to love; perhaps he already did. He was fairly sure she felt the same way. After all, this wasn't some sudden romance, some passing fling. They'd worked together a long time, become close, their flirtations only stifled by her workplace dating rules. And now, now that she'd chosen to bend those rules, now that they would be alone in his home, both intoxicated, their inhibitions shed, now, of course it was time to talk. Once again, he felt, he was to be punished for embarking on his new life of crime.

But Ginny surprised him. She threw off her coat, went straight to the kitchen and began opening cupboard doors. "What do you have around here for a night-cap?" she asked, rummaging through the shelves.

Max sat in the living room chair. The couch seemed presumptuous. "You're sure you need one?"

"Who are you, my dad?"

"No, I'm your bartender. Cabinet next to the microwave."

Ginny pulled down a bottle of Remy, took two glasses from the dish-rack, poured a couple generous shots and carried the glasses to the living room.

Max smiled. "What, no snifters?"

Ginny handed him a drink. "I'm not a snifter kind of girl." She sipped from hers, paused, appeared to examine Max for a moment, then sat herself in his lap, another cruel temptation. He tasted the cognac, felt the burn, waited, not wanting to make the first move, read things the wrong way. They were supposed to be talking. Ginny drank from her glass, then took Max's glass and placed both on the adjoining side table. She leaned in, kissed him softly, then harder. Max kissed back, following her lead, not quite sure where this was going. Ginny pulled away, picked up her glass and finished it, then set it back down. Max kept his mouth shut and was rewarded when Ginny began to slowly unbutton her blouse. Is this really happening, he thought, this shouldn't be happening, we're supposed to talk, I need to tell her the truth, this can't be happening, but his growing member disagreed. Ginny tossed her shirt on the floor, leaned in again, kissing him passionately, her well filled satin bra pressing against his chest, her flesh warm and smooth. Max reached around, grabbed her ass with both hands, that same ass he'd been admiring for so long. How could he not, what choice did he have, wasn't this what she wanted? He was a man, wasn't he? How much self control was he required to possess? And yet, he knew.

Even as he squirmed underneath her, Ginny's hips sliding back and forth across his throbbing erection, even then somehow he knew. And when she paused again, took a sip from Max's glass, smiled and began to unbuckle his belt, he realized his time was up. He may have turned into a criminal but he was not going to turn into an asshole. And though he was still inebriated and in such a state of arousal it was difficult to think, and though there was nothing in the world that he'd rather do at that moment then make love to the gorgeous woman on his lap, he knew, God help him, he knew it was time for the truth. She deserved the truth.

He clutched her wrists, held them softly. "What's wrong?" she asked.

"We're supposed to talk. Remember?"

She smiled. "We'll talk after."

"I can't, Ginny. We can't."

Her smile disappeared. "What the...Are you kidding me?"

He released her wrists, held her waist. "Listen to me. There is nothing I'd rather do right now, nothing in this world. I've wanted this from the day we met and if I could die right afterward, I'd die a happy man. But with my luck I wouldn't die and if I told you what I need to tell you after we did this you'd hate me even more than you're going to now. You'd never forgive me and I'm not taking that chance."

"Max," said Ginny, getting off his lap and backing toward the couch, "you're scaring me."

"I'm sorry. Please. Just sit down and listen. Please."

Ginny grabbed Max's glass from the table, downed the remaining liquor, plucked her blouse from the floor and quickly put it on. She seated herself on the couch, leaning forward, her knees clasped together, her hands on her thighs, her lust replaced by apprehension. "Okay," she said, "I'm listening."

"We're not shooting a film at the stadium," he began. "We're helping to create a diversion so Chubster's friends can rob it."

"What?"

"I never intended to involve you but you saw the film equipment and you seemed so excited to help out and it meant more time I could spend with you and obviously I didn't think it through and..."

"I told you to stay away from Chubster. I told you, I told you."

"I know, I know. I should have listened to you. God, I wished I'd listened to you."

"So now what? I'm a criminal?"

"No, no. You haven't done anything illegal. Even I haven't really done anything against the law yet."

"All these people we've been getting to run on the field are going to be helping a robbery. And you're paying them to do it."

"I know. You're right. And there will be repercussions. That's why you can't be in it anymore. That's why I had to tell you now. No one knows you had anything to do with this, not even Chubster."

"Except for all these people I've been helping you recruit."

"Yes, but they don't know who you are or where you work or anything. So hopefully this won't come back to bite you."

"Yeah," said Ginny, unconvinced, "hopefully."

"Ginny," said Max, standing up, "I can't even begin to tell you how sorry I am. I'm an idiot. If I'd just put that film equipment in the closet, none of this would have happened."

"All right, well, you didn't, and now you're going to tell me the whole story. You're going to tell me the truth, every detail. You owe me that."

"You're right. The truth. Okay." Max began to pace. He knew she was right. It was time to come clean, throw himself at the mercy of the court as they say. Chances were she'd hate him, never speak to him again. But maybe, just maybe she could eventually forgive him. Maybe when he came back to town in a year or so, they could start over. He hadn't taken advantage of her, hadn't slept with her. He'd stopped, done the right thing. Shouldn't that count for something?

So he did what he was told. He began at the beginning and left nothing out. The initial conversations with Chubster MaGee, the meeting with King, the visit to Cranky Sam's garage. He confessed to the real reason he'd been at Ginny's neighborhood cafe that morning, his suspicions as to who those pint-size crooks actually were, though Ginny seemed to have put two and two together before he suggested it. The subsequent assault of Nuggets, the arrival of the detective, the amount of money in Max's briefcase and the fake names and lack of phone numbers on his business card all were, judging from Ginny's expression, adding up. She listened silently, nodding occasionally, and when he was finished he plopped back down in the chair, mentally exhausted.

She addressed him seriously, her words hitting him like left hooks. "So you were just gonna' take the money and skip town, no explanation, no goodbye, no nothin'?"

"No, of course not, not now. I guess that was the original plan, but that was before, when you had your rules, when you said you couldn't go out with me."

"But we were still friends, Max, close friends. I thought we told each other everything."

"We did," Max protested.

"Well, obviously we didn't."

"I know, I'm sorry. I screwed up."

"Yeah," said Ginny, standing up and putting on her coat, "you screwed up." She headed for the door, paused and turned. "And you know what the worst part is? And your story has a shitload of worst parts. The worst part is you lied to me. After all this time, I trusted you completely and you lied to me. I guess I'm the idiot."

And before Max could reply, or beg forgiveness, or even shed a tear, something he hadn't done in years, she was gone, out the door and likely out of his life forever.

*

Ginny stood on the sidewalk outside Max's walk-up, hugging herself in the cool October air, waiting for the cab she'd called on the way down the stairs. She wished she had a cigarette. She hadn't smoked one in years, not since she was pregnant with Emily, but right then she would have paid a hundred dollars for one. Goddamn Max! How had things gone from great to shit so quickly? She should have stuck to her rules, not listened to her daughter, not gotten involved. Finally a guy she truly cared for and he decides to become a conniving crook.

But she knew that wasn't exactly true; she was being too simplistic. That was a Hell of a lot of money they'd promised him. What would she have done? Didn't really matter right then.

What did matter was what she should do. Call Detective Popowski, turn in Max and Chubster and that horrible midget, sink the whole enterprise. She'd never snitched before; in the neighborhood where she grew up, you just didn't do that. She wasn't thrilled with the thought of Max behind bars but she had to think of herself. She was a simple working mom with a life. Was it a great life? No, but it was better than going to jail and leaving a sixteen year old to fend for herself, or worse, go live with her dad. Maybe, she thought, the cabbie will have a cigarette.

Exiting the taxi, Ginny was surprised to see a light through her living room window. Emily should have been in bed hours ago and her daughter, unlike most teens, seldom failed to turn off the lights. This, she thought, better not be more bad news. She'd barely stepped through the front door, closing it as quietly as possible, when she noticed Emily staring at her. The youngster was dressed in a night shirt and slippers, a throw blanket over her shoulders, sitting slouched on the couch, one of Ginny's magazines laid across her lap.

"What are you doing up?" asked Ginny.

"Where were you?"

"I was at work," Ginny said, tossing her coat on a chair and sitting down heavily next to Emily.

"Work closed hours ago."

This was a switch, considered Ginny. Wasn't she the one to be waiting up, asking questions? "I had a drink. With Max. After work."

"A drink," said Emily, sitting up and sniffing her mother like a puppy. "You mean drinks."

"Okay, drinks."

"What else did you do with Max?"

"What? What is this. You're supposed to be in bed. What's with all the questions?"

"I was worried."

Well, that was a first. "You were?" asked Ginny, clumsily hugging her daughter. "Oh! You're drunk!"

"I'm sorry," said Ginny, not letting go, as close as she'd been to tears since Max's revelations.

"Did something happen? Did he do something to you?"

Ginny leaned back, regained her composure. "No, he didn't do something to me. The only thing he did is lie. What a surprise, huh?"

"What do you mean?"

"He's a man, isn't he?"

"And all men lie? Is that what you're saying?" Ginny nodded. "What did he lie about?"

"Doesn't matter. It's not important."

"Does it have to do with the movie you're making? The one you're so secretive about, the one you can't tell me about?"

Ginny stood up, went to the kitchen, opened a cupboard and looked up at the liquor bottles, then closed the door and poured herself a glass of water. "Speaking of which," she said, returning to the living room, "I met with Ms. Bodega today."

Emily looked anxious. "You did? Why?"

Good, thought Ginny. Let her be nervous. She needed to get this conversation turned around. She was the mom, she was the adult, not her precocious teenager. "She wanted to discuss the paper you wrote, the one about me."

"That was fiction," Emily protested, folding her arms across her chest.

"Was it?"

"Sort of. Mom, you have to admit you've been acting weird, working on something you can't even talk about. You always said we'd tell each other everything and now you're not."

Now it was Emily's turn to suppress tears. Ginny sat down next to her. "You're right. You're right. I'm sorry. I still can't talk about it and that's not fair. But I'm done. I'm done with the film and I'm done with Max. Back to normal, okay?" She put her arms around Emily's shoulders, pulled her close.

Emily snuggled for a moment, then lifted her head. "Just tell me one thing. It wasn't a porno movie, was it?"

Ginny was shocked by the question, though by this time she probably shouldn't have been. Seemed like every mention of film-making these days brought up the porno possibility. "No," she said. "God, no. It wasn't a porno movie. Besides, look at me. I'm almost forty. Who's going to want to see me in a porno movie?"

Emily considered the question. "You look great," she said. "You could be a milf."

"What?"

"You know, you could be in a milf movie. Lots of the boys at school watch them."

Ginny wasn't naive. She'd heard the term before, mostly muttered by some of the young drinkers at 'Sully's, and she surely wasn't going to make her young daughter go over the acronym or its connotations. The revelation that her sixteen year old was familiar with the term and that boys her age were watching that stuff at school shouldn't have been surprising but after the night she'd had, everything seemed surprising. She placed a hand on each of Emily's slender shoulders, looked at her youthful face and realized once again how beautiful and wise her little girl had become and what an amazing life awaited her.

"Listen," she said, "I didn't do anything to be ashamed of or that would cause you to think less of me. Except maybe to get fooled by another asshole. Now, I'm exhausted and you've got school so let's go to bed and tomorrow we start over, me and you, a new beginning, no more secrets." She kissed Emily on the forehead, rose from the couch and helped her daughter to her feet, the throw blanket still draped over the young girl's shoulders. Ginny watched her walk to the bedroom, wondered, like every other parent, where the years had gone.

In her own bedroom, Ginny undressed quickly, stared at herself in the bathroom mirror as she brushed her teeth. Yes, she thought, Max was a bastard, a liar, but one mitigating circumstance gnawed at her. Given the chance to sleep with her, to have what may have been, considering the lustful, drunken state they were both in, hot, unforgettable, passionate sex, he'd declined. He'd chosen instead to confess, to apologize and beg forgiveness. Most men, she felt, would have fornicated first, confessed later or maybe not at all. But so what, her other voice countered, he'd still lied to her, misled her, possibly involved her in illegal activity and a potential stint in prison. The whole thing, combined with the inevitable hangover that awaited, made her head throb. Jesus, she thought, I've got to go to sleep.

*

Max lay on the couch, stared at the ceiling. He wouldn't allow himself the comfort of his bed, didn't deserve it, needed instead to be punished for his recent spate of mistakes and wrong turns. Rufus sat on his stomach, languorously stretching, lifting one paw after another only to bring each small claw down through the folds of Max's shirt and into the sensitive skin of his belly. Normally Max would gently grasp the cat's legs, hold them for a moment as if to say 'that's enough'. But not this time. This time he would endure the tiny pricks, for the least he felt he merited was some feline flagellation. How could he have been so stupid? What did he think was going to happen when he told her the truth? He'd always prided himself for looking at things from the other person's point of view, and doing that now was no solace. He'd lied and misled Ginny, which was bad enough, but he'd also admitted the caper's coda involved leaving the bar, taking off to parts unknown, no warning, no forwarding address. Of course she was hurt and angry; who wouldn't be? But so much had happened in a week. He wanted to tell her his plan had changed, that somehow or other he would stay, stick around to see where this budding romance would take them, no matter the consequences.

But Ginny wouldn't hear it. She'd been betrayed by someone she trusted, someone she cared for, and was in no mood to accept apologies and pleas of forgiveness. The fact that he'd not taken advantage of her, that he'd ceased and desisted while his testosterone was peaking as was his manhood, appeared to earn him no points and things being what they were he was certainly not going to play that card. Maybe he should have just gone ahead anyway. Ginny was the second sexy woman he'd turned down in the last two days. And how had that worked out? Rufus eyed his owner curiously. "You wouldn't turn down a sexy cat, would you, Rufus?" asked Max. Cats are lucky, he thought. No conscience.

*

FRIDAY

Over the course of his bartending career, waiting on shy guys, lonelyhearts, bullshitters and desperados, Max had learned well what not to do with women. So, after finally rousing himself from the bed he had no memory of climbing into, and downing enough aspirin to put a slight dent in his massive headache, he did not call Ginny. Nor did he text her, send a card and flowers or, Heaven forbid, show up at her door. A woman scorned and all that, he figured. Besides, this was not your typical romantic dust-up. She could probably put him in the big house if so inclined. He was certainly not going to do anything that might provoke her further. He'd bide his time and hope that the passage of same does truly heal all wounds.

He took his time beginning the day. A long, hot shower, a toasted blueberry bagel, a large glass of juice and the midday news on the television occupied his attention. He was reluctant to descend the stairs, open the door and confront whatever or whoever might await him on the sidewalk. Charlie, the blackmailer, Cranky Sam, the irate midget, Detective Popowski, the curious cop, Candy, the perilous siren, take your pick. Surely nothing good to look forward to. Not the way things had been going lately.

Max was a big believer in streaks, both lucky ones and unlucky, and if this wasn't the latter, he didn't know what was. Ignited by a lamentable decision to join Chubster's criminal enterprise, followed by a series of strange happenings and questionable characters, this had all the earmarks of a long one. Though Max knew that all bad streaks eventually end and are quite often replaced by a sequence of fortunate events, there was no assurance that such a turnabout would take place by Saturday afternoon when it was most needed. He dared not contemplate the ramifications of this particular bad luck streak reaching its boil during the game.

Thankfully, there was no pressing issue pushing him down those stairs and toward the door, at least not until he needed to leave for work. He and Ginny had recruited what appeared to be an adequate number of individuals willing to charge the field, an amount he felt would please King, the nefarious ringleader of this felonious circus. So, for the time being he could remain in the apartment, unencumbered by chance encounters and shady figures, safe to read the paper, take a nap, watch TV, content to sit silently, Rufus curled up in his lap, and try mightily not to dwell on streaks, good and bad.

*

Ginny didn't want to get up either, didn't want to go anywhere, do anything. She must have slept soundly; she hadn't even heard Emily leave for school. But, unlike some people, she had a conscience, a conscience which was reminding her that she'd told the landscaping crew she would return in the morning. It was true that she'd quit, that she had no money for the boys or the older laborers, nothing to offer except an apology for misleading them and the decency to at least show up as promised. She hoped that was her true motivation as she showered and dressed, tried to rid herself of the thought that she simply wanted to see the handsome young collegian again. After all, he was much too young for her and hadn't she just sworn off men the night before? But he was polite and he seemed nice and sweet and funny and she would simply tell him the money had dried up and the opportunity had passed. The bottom line was she'd said she would be back and she always kept her word.

The crew was at the same residence as the day before but Ginny must have arrived earlier; they were still at work, raking and blowing leaves, covering shrubs with canvas, sweeping the long asphalt driveway. The sun was shining but it was cool. The boys wore bright orange hoodies, the older workers the same, only faded. Ginny kept her distance, not wanting to disrupt their efforts, waited patiently for the mid-morning break. She enjoyed watching them work. It reminded her of a busy night at the restaurant, everyone moving in sync, each busy with the task at hand, no time for slacking, no room for nonsense. The University students labored as strenuously as the older men; perhaps millennials were getting a bad rap.

It wasn't until the crew chief had looked at his wristwatch and declared it break time that Ginny approached. The more skeptical of the collegians saw her first, nudged his friend. The handsome young man shook his head. "You came back."

"I said I would."

"Yeah, well a lot of the girls we know don't always do what they say they're gonna."

"I'm old school," said Ginny. "I keep my word."

"Cool. We were hoping."

She glanced at the older men who were slowly unwrapping their snacks and eyeing her curiously, regarding her as they might a large squirrel intent on snatching their food. "Bad news, though. I'm leaving the project so I've got no money. I'm really sorry I misled you."

"What happened?"

"Um, creative differences, I guess."

"I knew it," said the skeptic. "Fucking knew it. Now what do we tell the guys?"

Ginny looked concerned. This was not part of the plan. "What guys?"

"It's not what you think," said the other young man. "We were drinking with our friends last night and asked them what they'd give us if we ran on the field Saturday, you know, increase the payoff. We never mentioned the film."

"Got the pot up to eight hundred dollars," the other collegian said, shaking his head. "Shit."

Ginny felt bad. "Well, I might still be able to get you the tickets but there's no way I can guarantee the money. It's possible but no promises."

"Tell you what," said the handsome one, casually biting into an apple, "I do this thing, I run onto that field for these ex-associates of yours, for this film that you promised we could be a part of..."

Ginny interrupted. "I don't remember promising."

The young man ignored her. "I do that and you agree to go out with me. How's that?"

"What?"

"Just a date. You and me. No pressure. Drinks and conversation."

Ginny may have been slightly flattered but she wasn't easy. "I'm old enough to be your mother."

"I doubt that. Come on, what's the big deal? You're not wearing a ring."

That's true, thought Ginny, glancing at her bare hand. It had been a long time since she'd worn a ring of any significance. Some of the other single waitresses wore fakes just to keep the leches at bay. Ginny saw no need; she could handle herself.

"What about me," said the whiner.

"Well, she's not going out with both of us."

Ginny shook her head, amazed and annoyed at the good looking kid's confidence. "I didn't say I'd go out with you either."

"You didn't say you wouldn't."

Trying to change the subject, Ginny looked at the older men. "What about them?"

"You want to date them?"

"Very funny."

"They weren't gonna' do it anyway. They can't risk getting arrested, you know, green cards and all that."

Ginny paused, stared up at the blue sky. Why was everything a decision now? A week ago there were no decisions, no stress. She woke up, got Emily off to school, went to the cafe for coffee, ran some errands, did some laundry, relaxed until it was time to go to work and there were no decisions there either. Sure, once in a while you had to decide whether to shut someone off or not but mostly just show up, do your job, keep smiling, make some money and go home. No muss, no fuss. Not exactly an exciting life but it wasn't going to give her an ulcer. She looked at the boys, the one nonchalantly eating his apple, the other anxious and irritable.

"Okay," she said, reaching into her purse for a paper and pen. "What are your names?"

"I'm Teddy," said the first boy. "This is Simon. What's your name?"

"Ah, Jeannie. Look, write down your numbers and I'll see what I can do. Be ready to go Saturday morning. If things work out, you'll get a call and be told where to meet, maybe get your grand. Same for after the game." She looked sternly at Teddy, handed him the pad and pen. "No promises."

"Hey," said Teddy, grinning, "you just asked for my number." Ginny didn't laugh.

Simon actually seemed appeased for the first time that morning. "So," he asked, "you think there's a decent chance of this happening?"

"Yes," said Ginny, taking back the paper. "There's a decent chance."

"What about us," asked Teddy, smiling. "Is there a decent chance for us?"

"Slimmer," said Ginny, turning to leave. The men all watched her go but she never looked back.

*

Max didn't leave the apartment until the last minute. If one of his new found nemesis or some other scoundrel awaited him on the sidewalk below, they would have been standing there for quite a while. He hadn't even left to get the newspaper. The way things were going, it would have contained all terrible news anyway. No, he and Rufus stayed indoors, content to watch 'SportsCenter' and read an old 'National Geographic' he'd been meaning to get to, all the while trying futilely not to think about Ginny and what could have been.

When Max did finally bid goodbye to Rufus, lock his door and alight the stairs, he pushed open the building door just enough to poke his head out and look both ways. He felt silly, like he was in an old 'Warner Brothers' cartoon, on the lookout for Wiley Coyote or the Tasmanian Devil. He had to resist looking upward, as though fearful an anvil might be plunging toward his head. This is ridiculous, he thought, get a hold of yourself. Just take the short walk to work, do your job, don't pester Ginny, go home and get a good night's sleep and maybe in thirty-six hours you'll be a wealthy man. Which reminded him, shouldn't he be making some kind of provisional plan? Getting his things in order, buying an airline ticket, maybe give Sully some kind of heads up. And what about Rufus? Was he taking a cat with him on the run? Who knew criminals needed a to do list?

Thankfully, no one was lurking outside, ready to ambush Max on the concrete so he began what seemed like the longest walk of his life. Head down, hands jammed in his pockets, he moved quickly, pausing only when he could no longer help but glance back, certain that being tailed was still a strong possibility. So preoccupied was he with completing his short trek and arriving at the safe confines of 'Sully's that he almost bumped into Miss Peabody standing near the tavern's front door. Max apologized quickly, noted that the older woman had been speaking with Detective Popowski who was now giving him the once over. Not waiting for an introduction, Max excused himself, claiming he needed to get behind the bar and relieve Millie.

Not until he'd clocked in and given Millie a hug did he finally relax. He stood back, took a deep breath, surveyed the lounge. A slow start, only a few customers, one being Mr. Vanderbilt, seated on the stool next to Miss P.'s vacant spot. Ginny was setting some tables and paying no attention to Max's presence. Sully was probably in his office and the rest of the day's wait staff was going about their business, another day in paradise as they liked to sarcastically proclaim. All was calm.

Max greeted a couple of salesmen at the end of the bar, fixed their dirty martinis and offered menus. When he walked back, Miss Peabody had joined Mr. Vanderbilt at the bar. Max greeted her a second time, began to fix her cocktail. "So what was that all about?" he asked.

"What's that, dear?"

"Outside," said Max, setting down her drink. "With the detective."

"Oh, he wants to talk to anyone that Ginny told about the bank robbery. He's hoping that maybe she forgot something that she originally observed and that we might recall what she had described."

"Really?" Max realized Ginny was now conversing with the detective and both were looking his way.

"Max," said Mr. Vanderbilt, "Are you okay?"

"What?"

"I don't mean to offend but you seem a little jumpy, a bit on edge."

"Me? No, what, I'm fine. Just got some stuff on my mind."

"If you need someone to talk to," said Miss Peabody, "you know, about your stuff, if I could help in any way. Lord knows you've listened to enough of my nonsense."

"That's nice, Miss P. Thanks." Max watched Ginny walk to the service station. "Be right back."

Ginny didn't smile when Max met her at the end of the bar. "Hey. Need drinks?" he asked.

"No. Detective Popowski wants to talk to you. Thought you might remember something I told you about the robbery."

"Did you tell him I was there, with you?"

Ginny glanced at the detective who appeared to be observing them seriously. "No."

"Thanks. You didn't tell him about anything else?"

"Not yet. I'm still deciding."

"Oh, um, okay, fair enough. Listen, Ginny, I am truly, truly sorry for lying to you."

"Yuh, whatever. Look, just go talk to him. I'll watch the bar."

"Oh, okay." Max raised the small, wooden drawbridge next to the service station, switched places with Ginny, Max careful not to touch her as they passed. All right, he thought, just be cool. Nothing to worry about. He approached the detective as calmly as possible. He'd watched enough police procedurals to know that nervous is not what you want to be.

"Max, right?" asked the detective.

"Yes, sir."

"I'm Detective Popowski. We're still working the Halloween bank job. Ginny's a witness and she said that you're a good friend and that she described the incident to you after the fact."

"She said I was a good friend?"

"That's right. Sometimes secondary sources can prove valuable, you know, recall things the witness originally mentioned but then left out, not intentionally of course, just skipped over or forgotten. You okay to answer a few questions?" Max nodded. "Good. Have a seat."

Max and the detective slid into opposite sides of a corner booth. Detective Popowski pulled a small notepad from his shirt pocket. Max folded his hands on the table, tried to breathe naturally, wished he'd taken those meditation classes an old girlfriend had suggested. A week earlier Max might have actually enjoyed this interview; he'd never been interrogated before. A week earlier he may have cracked a joke, made a wise remark, maybe asked the detective about his job. But not today.

Popowski placed his pen carefully on the notebook, looked at Max as though again assessing his character. "So," he said, "nothing to be nervous about. You're not a suspect or anything."

"Am I a person of interest?" Max wanted to take back the question as soon as it left his lips. Why couldn't he keep his mouth shut? Jesus.

"No, you're not a person of interest. Funny, that 'Biz' guy, one of your regulars at the bar, asked the same question. What's with you guys? I think you're watching too much TV."

"Did Ginny say he was a good friend?"

"What?"

"Never mind."

"All right. Why don't you tell me how Miss O'Riley related the incident to you. Whatever you can remember. Start at the beginning."

Max leaned back, looked up as though remembering was a strenuous activity. This was tricky, he supposed. He was a primary witness who had to describe events second hand. He looked across the booth at the detective and began.

"Well, Ginny, uh, Miss O'Riley, said she was at some cafe, I guess about a half block from the bank, opposite side of the street. Said she goes there almost every weekend, good coffee, I guess. Anyway it was Halloween, but you know that already," Max continued, trying to be vague but not evasive, detailed but not precise, the detective occasionally taking notes and asking questions. Upon concluding his narrative, Max felt he'd only screwed up once. When describing the arrival of the trick-or-treaters he had said "we thought it was a little odd".

Popowski jumped on that. "We?" he'd asked.

But Max was quick; at least he still had that. "When she told me about them showing up, we both agreed it was unusual." The detective had nodded and Max hoped he'd avoided that bullet.

When Max had finished his account of that day's occurrences, as allegedly relayed to him by Ginny, the detective seemed satisfied. The burly lawman carefully returned the pad and pen to his pocket, leaned back and addressed Max somberly.

"Did Miss O'Riley tell you about the note?"

"The note?"

"The paper the lead robber handed the young teller. Did she describe it to you?"

"Oh, yeah, of course, the note. Ginny said it was pretty bad."

The detective leaned forward. "That's an understatement. I've been doing this for twenty years and that was the most brutal, most foul, most disgusting thing I've ever read. This guy is a sick individual and he needs to be off the street. This is one dangerous little criminal." Popowski placed his card on the table, slid it to Max.

"You remember anything else, anything you or Miss O'Riley may have forgotten, you call me."

Max picked up the card. "So it's not a kid?"

"Don't think so. Not judging by that note. We think he's a midget or a dwarf, you know, little person, whatever."

"Well, that's a good lead."

"Yeah, but we need more. We can't just go hauling in every midget in the city. Profiling. The ACLU would have our heads".

Max tried not to sound relieved. "Yeah, I see what you mean."

"Anyway," said Popowski, getting up and extending his hand, "like I said, you recall anything that might help, you let me know."

Max nodded, shook hands, hustled back to the bar.

Ginny was waiting. "How'd it go?"

"Good, I think. Did you tell him about Nuggets and the little nut kicker?"

"No. Did you?"

Max shook his head. "No, not me."

"Should I have?"

"Um, I think it's better you didn't. For me anyway."

Ginny just nodded, exited the bar, changing places with Max. Max watched her talk to the detective for a moment before Popowski left 'Sully's. Ginny glanced back at Max, but only for a second. She had work to do.

Max noticed that Miss Peabody and Mr. Vanderbilt were still observing him and that Biz had arrived while he'd been away from the bar. The entertainment expert waved him over, motioned for Max to come closer, lowered his voice. "You talk to the law?"

"The law?"

"Yeah, you know, the detective."

"Jeez," said Max, "He was right. You do watch too much TV."

"What?"

"Nothing. Did you mention Nuggets and the midget?"

"Ginny told me not to."

"She did?"

"Yeah, she said it wasn't relevant. But" said Biz, his voice rising, "I don't see how it's not relevant. The robbers were probably midgets and a couple days later Nuggets gets assaulted by an angry one. How is that not relevant? Did you mention him?"

"No," said Max. "I didn't think it was relevant."

Biz was nonplussed. "What? But..."

Max held up a finger. "Hold that thought." He headed to the service station where Ginny was waiting for drinks. He smiled at Miss P. and her elderly flame as he passed them on the way, pulled the slip from the ticker. Ginny said nothing. Max glanced at her stern expression, put his head down and began the order.

"Thanks," he said, "for not mentioning Cranky Sam. I owe you again."

"Yeah," said Ginny, still serious as an IRS agent, "remember that when you're collecting your share."

"I will," said Max as she grabbed her tray and turned to go. "I promise." He swung back to the bar, assessed the clientele hoping for some newcomers or at least someone with an empty glass so he wouldn't have to return to Biz's questions or the older couple's concern. Unfortunately, the only new face belonged to Chubster MaGee and he didn't look happy. Now what, thought Max, making his way down the bar.

"Hey, Chub. Everything okay?"

"We got trouble. King wants to meet with us tonight."

"What? I thought we never had to meet with him again. He said that, he's the one who said it."

"I know, I know. I guess something's come up. You didn't do anything stupid, did you?"

"Me?"

"Yeah, you. He specifically said to bring you. So I ask again. Did you do anything stupid, you know, while you were recruiting? Anything I should know before this meeting?"

Max stepped back, thought about the question. It had been an eventful week, full of all manner of strange happenings and memorable characters, but as far as he was concerned the only stupid thing he'd done, beside signing up for this caper in the first place, was lying to Ginny.

"Well," he said, "I have found us some pretty odd ducks for Saturday, but what did he expect, doctors and lawyers?"

"No," said Chubster, shaking his head. "I don't think he cares who runs on that field. Must be something else. I don't know...May as well give me a short one while I'm here."

Max poured a small draft, set it down in front of Chubster. "What time is this meeting, anyway? You see I'm working."

"Button this place up as fast as you can. King said twelve-thirty but I'll get there first and stall him if you're late. But don't be late." Chubster sipped his beer. "You're sure there isn't something you're not telling me?"

"Can't think of any. Guess we'll find out."

*

Tim Griffin prided himself in not fitting the image of a typical male nurse. He'd been in the Army, been to Iraq and been shot at more than once. When he'd gotten out, he'd gone to nursing school on the G.I. Bill and now he was gainfully employed at Saint Elizabeth's, working in a profession that had been considered for years to be the domain of women and gay men. But times change and Tim was as masculine as any other man in any other line of work, probably more so, and so were many of the other male nurses. He still worked out, still drank beer with his friends, still went to the firing range. He stayed in touch with his Army buddies, saw them when he could and he pursued some of the hot, young nurses at the hospital, hooking up with them when the opportunity arose. He was a grown man and like most men, he watched porn. Maybe a bit more than most but he didn't consider it a problem. It wasn't as though it was dominating his life; he was still getting the real deal. It wasn't his fault he had a good memory and could identify a lot of the adult actors and actresses in the business. So when he noticed the name on the room chart for 3C belonged to Louis Papasian, he had to find out if it was the Louis Papasian, aka 'Nuggets', the big balled adult entertainer he'd watched many times. Tim had wondered why Nuggets no longer appeared in new releases and now he could ask the man himself. It was like finding out the ballplayer you'd watched on TV for years was in your ward having rotator cuff surgery.

Tim used his break to head for 3C. He arrived at the door as Laverne was coming out. Laverne was a large woman with an even larger personality, an institution in the nursing department, a veteran LPN who had encountered so many characters and seen so many medical oddities that it seemed as though nothing could surprise her anymore. Tim liked Laverne as much as everyone else and took any opportunity to flirt with the older nurse, knowing full well she was married and would chew him up and spit him out even if she wasn't.

"Hey, Laverne. Looking good. Great smock."

Laverne looked down at her ancient, stained scrubs, then at Tim who was grinning broadly. "What you want, Romeo?"

Tim was undeterred. "When we gonna' hook up? I can't wait much longer."

"Soon as you win the lotto. What you really want?"

"That patient in there. You know who he is?"

"What you think, fool," said Laverne, glancing at her clipboard. "Name of Louis Papasian."

"You don't know what he's famous for though?"

"Famous? That boy's got no money. He'll be lucky he pays his hospital bills in twenty years. I had to loan the dude change for the vending machine. Said he was down on his luck. What kind of famous is that?"

Tim mulled this over for a moment. He wasn't stupid; he knew the porno girls made more money than their costars but he assumed the male performers, at least the ones with name recognition, did well.

"What's he here for?" he asked. "Anything serious?"

"You could say that. He got kicked in the balls by a midget. Broke his damn testicle and leaked out a bunch of testicle fluid. I didn't even know there was such a thing."

"What? Come on."

"Turns out they were implants. Can you believe that? This guy got saline implants so he could have giant balls. What is the world coming to?" Laverne turned to go, paused. "What you say he was famous for?"

Tim saw no need to tell Laverne the truth. She was a known gossip and he didn't want his coworkers aware that he knew who the male porn stars were; seemed a little creepy. "Oh," he said, "my mistake. Thought he was a football player, used to play for the Browns but must just be a similar name."

Laverne glanced at the door to 3C. "Dude in there ain't no football player. He's a skinny white boy. Those balls probably fifty percent of his body weight. At least they were."

She laughed and headed down the corridor, shaking her head. Tim waited until she turned the corner, then entered the room. The patient in the bed was indeed Nuggets and Tim was pleased that he'd recognized the injured entertainer by his face and not something else.

Nuggets looked annoyed. "The other nurse was just here. She checked everything."

"I'm on my break," said Tim. "Just wanted to meet you. Big fan."

This was obviously not what Nuggets was expecting. "You know who I am?"

"Sure, man. I've watched your movies. You're a star."

Nuggets wasn't thrilled to be recognized by a male fan. He would have preferred a woman. "Was," he said. "Was a star. No more."

"I was wondering what happened to you. Haven't seen you in anything lately."

"I was a novelty, man. The girls didn't want to deal with me anymore and my DVDs stopped selling."

Tim hated to see one of his favorites so sad. "You could make a comeback."

"Not after this I couldn't."

"Yeah, I heard. That's harsh. They lock the little bastard up?"

"No. I didn't press charges. My family's already disappointed in me. This publicity would kill 'em."

"Well," said Tim, "you had a great run. Look at the girls you were with. Unbelievable. Lot of guys were probably jealous, including me."

Nuggets almost smiled. "Yeah, it was pretty sweet for a while." He paused, surveyed his surroundings, the tray holding a half eaten assortment of bland food, the bed pan resting nearby, the dull beige walls of his nondescript hospital room. "Don't think anybody would be jealous of me now."

"Maybe not. But you got your memories. Lot more than most of us."

"I guess."

"So," said Tim, attempting to be a casual as possible, "you still have any connections in the business? You probably get asked a lot but, you know, I always thought I might be good at it."

Nuggets had heard this before. Seemed like every red blooded guy he ran into felt he could perform on camera. "It's not easy," he said.

"Oh, I know," said Tim. "I'm sure it's not. People watching and everything. But I think I could do it. I mean I'm pretty young, I work out, I'm in pretty good shape and, uh, I got a decent sized dick. You want to see it?"

Nuggets had no desire to see Tim's penis and let him know so as diplomatically as he could. But the wheels in Nuggets' head had started turning again. He was still dying to know what Max and Chubster were up to.

"Listen, uh, what did you say your name was again?"

"Tim. Tim Griffin."

"Listen, Tim, maybe we can work something out. You know, I introduce you to somebody in the industry and you do me a favor."

"Absolutely. Anything. Name it."

"Well, I'm not suppose to get out of here 'til Sunday. But I've got some important stuff happening and I'd like to leave tonight. You think you could make that happen?"

This was not the request Tim was expecting but neither was it a deal breaker. He could simply switch the discharge date on the clipboard and no one would know he'd done it. The shit might hit the fan later but by then Nuggets would be gone, he'd have his introduction and it would be very tough to prove he was the one who'd changed the paperwork. Besides, it wasn't like the patient was in intensive care. He seemed to be doing well so what difference would a day or two make?

"Nuggets," he said, "I think we've got a deal."

*

Ginny couldn't concentrate. Her entire career in the service industry she'd been taught that you don't bring your troubles to work. You suck it up. You get your mind right and put a smile on your face before you walk in the door. And through parenting and heartbreak and divorce and a myriad of other everyday annoyances she'd followed that restaurant golden rule. But tonight was different. The friend she'd cared for, the guy she was ready to give herself to, possibly even make a commitment to, had betrayed her trust, had placed her and her daughter in jeopardy, had dashed whatever future she and Max may have had together. Maybe not intentionally, maybe he was just another dumb man, but he'd done it nonetheless. Then why couldn't she hate him, why didn't she turn him and his confederates in to the detective? Why was she so confused?

He'd messed up and he knew it and she knew that he knew it. He was contrite, apologetic, sad, maybe even heartbroken. At least he was smart enough to keep his mouth shut instead of constantly begging for forgiveness, asking for another chance. That was the thing, she thought, Max was smart, at least she'd always considered him as such, so why in the world did he get involved with Chubster MaGee in the first place, and more importantly, how could he have been stupid enough to think he could mislead and involve her in his illegal activities and then somehow make it all right down the line?

So now he was a criminal, a liar and apparently a fool and yet she must still care for him because she didn't want to see him behind bars. She could easily punish the man who'd done her wrong but was unwilling to do so. She'd always considered herself a logical person, street smart, a woman of common sense. But she was wise enough to understand the power of attraction often had little to do with logic.

Ginny tried her best to keep it together that night, keep her distance from Max, not let on to the regulars the state of her emotions, just continue working and smiling. What was that saying she'd been seeing everywhere, on t-shirts and coffee mugs – 'stay calm and carry on'. Easier said than done, she decided. She was desperate for a distraction and that distraction arrived in the form of Tony and Joe coming through the front door, the 'Norm and Cliff' of 'Sully's, who could always be counted on to debate some mundane subject of little or no consequence. Ginny hustled over to greet them as they made their way to the bar, and was pleased to find that today would prove no exception.

"Hey, boys," she said, "what's the good word?"

"Eggs," said Tony, without hesitation.

"Eggs?" asked Ginny, trailing them to the bar.

"Yeah," said Joey, placing his jacket on a stool back. "We're arguing about the first person to eat an egg."

Tony plopped his large frame onto the stool next to Joe's. "We're not arguing," he said. "We're discussing."

Ginny played along. "You mean the old argument about which came first, the chicken or the egg?"

Max placed two frosties in front of the boys. He kept his head down, didn't even look at Ginny. "Hey, guys," he said.

Tony and Joe greeted Max, swiveled their stools to face Ginny. "No," said Joey. "Not that. We're talking about who ate the first egg."

"What?"

"Let me ask you," said Tony, "say you were one of the first cave women. And, you know, your cave guy is out hunting and gathering and, you know, you're cleaning the cave or whatever..."

"Why am I cleaning the cave? 'Cause I'm the woman?"

"That's not the point."

"Who's cleaning what cave?" asked Frannie, climbing onto the next stool over.

"No one is cleaning the cave, okay. Forget that. Anyway, you go outside and you see this fat, feathery bird sitting around and you notice it poops this round, solid thing out of its little chicken butt, would your first inclination be to go over and eat it?"

"Wow," said Ginny, "never really thought about that." Man, she thought, these guys are just what I needed.

"Now remember," said Joe, "you're used to eating some strange stuff, animals the cave guys bring home, or let me re-phrase that, the cave guys or girls bring home, maybe some weird looking plants and berries, too. Plus, you're probably really super hungry all the time."

"I'm out," said Max, wanting no part of this conversation and scurrying off to wait on other customers.

"So," said Ginny, "Tony, you're saying you would not have been the first person to eat an egg that came out of a chicken butt, and Joey, you're saying you probably would. That about sum it up?"

"Gotta' eat," said Joey. "Gotta' survive."

"Don't have to eat what might be a big, smooth bird poop," said Tony.

"Gross," said Frannie.

"Exactly," said Tony.

"Jeez," said Ginny, "good thing I just got sat 'cause I'm gonna' need some time to think about this. Plus I don't think I'll be having an omelet anytime soon." The boys chuckled, turned back to the bar as their favorite waitress strode away.

*

Max, too, had been pleased to see his two regulars. He knew how fond Ginny was of the pair, Frannie, too, and anything that might cheer her up, take her mind off the prior night, maybe make the shift go a little faster, was fine with him. He returned to their section only after he was sure Ginny had moved on. "Hey," he said, "still discussing chicken butts?"

"No," said Joey, "we've agreed to disagree."

Max nodded. "Hey, ah, did any of you talk to the detective yet?"

"The detective? No. Why would he want to talk to us?"

"He's going over Ginny's account of the bank robbery with anyone she might have described it to."

"Really. He hasn't asked us anything."

"I'd talk to him," said Fran. "Never been with a detective before."

Max placed his hands on the bar, leaned forward and lowered his voice. "Well, if he does ask, do me a favor and don't mention the midget."

"What midget?" asked Tony. "The one that kicked Nuggets?"

Joey gave him a look. "What other midget would he be talking about?"

"I don't know. But it's a strange thing to ask."

"I know it sounds strange," said Max. "But just trust me on this. It's better for the bar if we don't mention him."

Tony and Joe looked at each other, paused. "You know, Max," said Joe, "you been acting kinda' funny lately."

"Yeah," said Tony, "you're not your usual self. You're not cracking jokes, you're not flirtin' with the girls, you're not even staring at Ginny's ass when she walks away."

"You noticed that?"

"C'mon, man, you're not exactly subtle."

"Damn," said Max.

"Never mind that," said Tony. "What's the matter with you? You can tell us."

Oh, boy, thought Max. Okay, think fast. He leaned back from the bar, looked around, hesitated. "It's my cat," he said. "My cat's sick."

Tony and Joey looked as though Max had just revealed a third arm. "You have a cat," they said simultaneously. "You never mentioned a cat."

"Yeah, well, it's not the most manly thing for a single guy to talk about."

Tony shook his head. "Never figured you for a cat guy."

"Your sick cat's making you that upset," said Joey. "You must really care about that cat."

"Well, he's been with me a long time."

"Glad to hear it's a he," Tony said.

"What difference does that make?" asked Joey.

"I don't know. Might just seem a little weirder if it was a girl cat."

"Look, guys," said Max. "It's not like I'm an old cat lady takin' in strays. I got one cat. He's in rough shape and I feel bad about it. Probably distracted, too, not myself, but you know, he'll be okay. I'll take him to the vet and..."

"You didn't take him to the vet yet?"

"Um, no. Thought he'd get better. But, ah, I will. No worries, though. I'll get back to normal."

"Okay, okay, take it easy, Max. We were just concerned about you, that's all."

"I know, I know. Sorry. He's like family, you know."

Tony and Joe felt a hand on their shoulders, turned to see Biz.

"Hey, boys. What's up?"

"Max has a cat. Did you know that?"

"No, I didn't. Cat, huh? Cool."

"Cool?" asked Tony.

"Yeah, I've got three."

Joey shook his head. "Why does that not surprise me?"

"What's that supposed to mean?" asked Biz.

"I don't know. You just seem more like a cat guy, I guess."

"But you were surprised that Max had one. So he doesn't seem like a cat guy?"

"All right, all right," said Tony. "Take it easy. The point is that Max's cat is sick, Max is our friend and he's a little down about it."

"Oh," said Biz. "Sorry to hear that. Anything serious?"

"No," said Max. "He'll be fine. Let me get you a beer." And as he walked to the tap, hopefully having avoided suspicion, he was thankful for his three not-so-wise men, a trio of regulars who could be counted on to jump start any conversation and lighten any mood.

*

When Max entered the 'Fremont' a few minutes past midnight, everything was the same. The bartender was the same, the waitress was the same, King, his bodyguard and Chubster MaGee were seated in the same booth, same seats. As far as deja'vus went, it was pretty depressing. Max made his way to the table, stood, waiting, not sure why. The bodyguard rose, began to frisk him.

"I told you I would never carry a gun," said Max.

King was calm as ever. "He's not looking for a gun." He motioned for Max to sit. There was no sign of Duffy and Chubster didn't seem thrilled to be there. The bodyguard paused, sat back down only after Max had slid in.

"Max," said King, "you appear apprehensive."

"You said we'd never have to meet again."

"True. But occasionally circumstances, such as they are, require alterations."

"Circumstances?" asked Max.

King sensed the presence of Tracey beside their booth without ever looking in her direction. "Drink?"

Max glanced at the waitress. "Just coffee," he said. "Thanks."

"Max, as I'm sure you'll recall, Chubster here vouched for you most vociferously. He said you were a straight shooter, a man of integrity, someone who could complete a task efficiently and without distraction. That I could, in essence, count on you."

Max glanced at Chubster. "I did complete the task. And I think you'll be happy. Got a lot of interesting runners. You wanted a diversion. I got you a diversion."

Tracey delivered the coffee, waited for a nod from King, then backed away. "In fact," Max continued, "I think I came up with a pretty good angle. Everyone jumping out of those stands on Saturday thinks they're being filmed, that they're making a movie."

"I'm aware of your con, Max. Quite impressive. But, as I'm sure you're aware, discretion is of the utmost importance in our endeavor." Max opened his mouth to protest but King held up a fat finger. "Max, you are, I assume, familiar with the internet and its social media offspring – 'Facebook', 'Instagram', etc."

"I know about it but I don't really keep up. Not on any of that stuff."

"So then I guess it's safe to say you haven't seen this video from last evening." King nodded to the bodyguard who pushed a laptop across the booth. Max looked to Chubster but his friend only shrugged. The bodyguard leaned over, pressed the 'play' button. The video that appeared was of the previous night's stripper race. Damn, thought Max. Must have been one of the bouncers filming, the same guys he had generously bribed to keep their mouths shut. You couldn't trust anyone these days. Max watched the race, heard the cheers, even made out snippets of his own voice. The neon lights outside the nightclub had lit up the action pretty well and there she was, Ginny, blurry but visible standing at the finish line. It was dark and she was a small figure, a good distance from the camera but he could tell it was her. Which meant that other people – family, friends, regulars from the bar, might be able to tell as well.

"Max, do you know what hits are when applied to online videos?"

"That's how many people have watched it."

"Yes, that's basically true, though one person could of course watch it more than once. This video, as you could imagine, is apparently quite popular. In the last twenty-four hours it has been viewed two hundred and ten thousand times."

"Jesus," said Max.

"So you can see how this might prove a problem."

Max surveyed the restaurant; he needed time to think. He glanced over his shoulder at the few remaining customers as if making sure no one could overhear what he had to say. Chubster MaGee, who could usually be counted on to interject himself into any conversation had nothing to offer, no help, no excuse, no plea.

"Listen," said Max, "I know it seems like I screwed up. I thought strippers would be a great idea. I mean, what a distraction, right? And I didn't front them any money, told them to keep their mouths shut or they'd get nothing, which I assume they did, keep their mouths shut that is since they're looking at a pretty good payday Saturday. But I guess I didn't give the bouncers enough. Looks like one of them decided he shoulda' got more and filmed the race. And put it out there for a laugh because, you know, it is kinda' funny."

So far, Max was scrambling and King seemed unimpressed. "I'm afraid in this case humor is quite beside the point," he said.

"Anyway," Max continued, "The good thing is that you can't see me in that video and no one knows who I am, no one has my real name or number and all the people watching this thing don't know what it's about, why it happened. You can't even see the club's name. To them it's just another funny video. Plus I convinced the girls to wear the club's name on their outfits when they run on the field, make it look like a big publicity stunt."

"We don't like publicity."

"Publicity for the club, not for us. The strippers will have to convince the cops it wasn't the club's idea, that it was all organized by some mystery man. And, like you said, by the time they actually start trying to figure out who I am, I'll be gone. Right?"

"Will you be gone, Max? Have you even bought an airline ticket yet?"

Max was spent, nothing left. "Not yet," he said quietly.

King sipped his drink, turned to Chubster. "Do you have anything to say in your friend's defense? You did, after all, vouch for him originally."

Max didn't have much hope but Chubster surprised him, apparently inspired by Max's attempts at justification. "First of all," he said, "I think the strippers are a great idea. I think it's gonna' take two or three security guys for each girl because if it's just one he might put his hands in the wrong place, you know, inappropriate, me too and all that and they don't want lawsuits and shit. Second, you can't see Max, like he said, no name or number so they can't trace him to me or me to you. It's just another stupid video that won't mean anything until after the fact. And by then it'll be too late." Chubster leaned back, satisfied, as if he'd presented a strong argument for the defense in a courtroom melodrama. King looked at the bodyguard for the first time, perhaps finally asking for his opinion though he received no overt gesture from the big man either way.

Max and Chubster sat quietly, as though awaiting a verdict. King emptied his glass, raised it in the air, requesting another without even looking in Tracey's direction. The brief lull allowed Max time to consider tendering his resignation, knowing full well it was not really an option, probably never was. King could likely fire him but what that act would actually consist of was too unpleasant to think about.

King set his glass down, delivered moments before and addressed Max and Chubster. "All right, gentlemen, we are going to continue as before. I, too, believe the dancers are a good idea and the movie as well. The race was obviously not. You need to think ahead, be aware of surroundings and repercussions." He paused, glanced at the bodyguard who stared straight ahead, serious as a statue. "Especially repercussions. We can't have any more shenanigans distracting us from the task at hand. Agreed?"

Max and Chubster looked like two students in the principal's office. It was all Max could do not to sigh and wipe his forehead. He began to slide out of the booth but King was not finished.

"Now then, moving on."

Moving on, thought Max. Now what?

"Max, what exactly is going on with you and Samuel's wife?"

"Samuel?" Max asked.

"I believe you know him as Cranky Sam."

Chubster almost spit his drink. "You're banging Cranky Sam's wife?"

"No, I'm not banging his wife. I'm not banging anybody. She came on to me."

Chubster smiled. "She came on to you. Right."

King looked pained. "I do hope that's not true."

"I swear."

"Max, you're not even supposed to be in contact with him at this point in the operation."

"He showed up at my work. With the wife. I think that was just a coincidence but she won't leave me alone."

"She could have any man she wants," said Chubster.

"I know," said Max. "That's what I told her. Why me?"

"So," said King," you are not having relations with that woman? Because, believe me, I know her quite well and it would behoove you to keep your distance."

"I know. Look, I don't mess around with married women and besides, that little bastard's crazy. And dangerous."

Chubster mumbled. "Wish she came on to me."

"What was that?" asked King.

"Nothin'"

King looked directly at Max. "You're to have no further contact with that woman. Or Sam. Is that clear?"

"Absolutely."

"And we will have no further contact as well. Tomorrow morning you'll receive the tickets from Duffy. Chubster will have the pre-game money and the post-game money. I advise both of you to make arrangements to leave town as quickly as possible after the payoffs. Remember, we never met and these meetings never took place. And please, don't forget what I said about repercussions."

"Yes, sir," said Chubster, practically pushing Max out of the booth. "We don't want any."

King nodded. "Good boys."

*

Ginny was glad to have that night's shift over with. Her feelings toward Max were still somewhat jumbled. Maybe him leaving town was for the best. She didn't think she could work with him any more and she didn't want to leave 'Sully's. Never seeing him again, angry as she was, probably made the most sense. Wasn't that the rational desire to have? Wasn't it the most logical? Turning him in would also remove him from her life but she couldn't take the chance of his arrest coming back to haunt her and Emily. Detective Popowski would love to hear what Ginny had to say but, for now at least, she would keep her mouth shut, let things play out and hope for the best. All she could do was try not to drive herself crazy with worry.

So, arriving home late that night, she was happy to see most of the house lights turned off and Emily's bedroom door closed. She was far too tired for another heart to heart with her precocious teen. A small glass of wine, she decided, and then off to the cozy comfort of her bed.

Sleep meant no more thinking and that was the goal. Taking down a glass from a kitchen cupboard, Ginny noticed Emily's Ipad open on the small breakfast table they shared. That was odd, she thought. Emily never went anywhere without the Ipad, including her own bedroom. A note rested beside the device, large block letters spelling out 'Play Me'. Ginny recalled 'Alice in Wonderland', a book she'd read out loud to Emily years before. She had a feeling this wasn't going to be as pleasant an experience. She poured the wine and took a generous sip before pushing 'play'. She listened to the strippers' voices from the previous night yelling encouragement, watched as they raced down the darkened street, the glow from the club's neon sign offering just enough light to illuminate the participants. And there she was at the finish line, small and distant yes, but still recognizable to those she was close to. Like, for instance, her daughter.

*

SATURDAY

Max was up early; it was almost getting to be a habit. He'd been bartending nights for twenty years and a morning person he was not. But on this particular day, sleeping in was not an option. He had lots to do and not much time to do it. First, a rendezvous with Duffy to get the tickets, then numerous phone calls arranging meetings with the recruits awaiting their seat assignments and pre-game cash. Max made coffee, sat at his kitchen table, the briefcase open before him. He had names and cellphone numbers to put in order, a map of the city to help scratch out a distribution route and the rest of the seed money to sort out. He still hadn't purchased an airline ticket or even a bus pass out of town, wanting to first see if things played out as planned, feeling that if they did, it would take the authorities a day or two to connect the dots, time enough to get out of Dodge. With all that on his to do list, it was a bit easier not to think about Ginny, though she was never far from his mind.

Max was again relieved to find no one waiting for him on the sidewalk outside his building. He recalled it wasn't so long ago he could exit his apartment without a care in the world. Now, who knew what trouble might be there to greet him. No time to dwell on that though. He had places to go, people to see.

First stop was a coffee shop not far away. Duffy, who he'd been told was on a tight schedule of his own, would be there to hand over the tickets. That should be easy, Max thought, entering the crowded cafe, nothing illegal about it. He spotted the colorful stadium employee at a small table near the window. Duffy was using both hands to drink from his mug, a task made far more difficult by the two tiny white casts encasing each thumb. He looked up as Max arrived.

"Don't ask," he said.

"What do you mean don't ask," said Max. "We're both working for the same big shot and you show up with two broken thumbs and I'm not supposed to ask how you got 'em."

"Keep your voice down."

"Sorry," said Max, sitting down.

"Repercussions," said Duffy.

"Repercussions. That's all you're gonna' say?"

Duffy nodded. "Look, I don't have much time." He pushed a manila envelope toward Max. "There's over thirty tickets in there, all different sections of the stadium, all close to the field. Not easy to get. You got enough runners?" Max nodded. "Good." Duffy took another two handed sip, stood up. "You got your plane ticket?"

"No. Not yet. You got yours?"

"Damn right. These guys are no joke. Finish your job, get your money and get the Hell out of here. Or don't, whatever. But you stick around, get caught, start yapping, your repercussions gonna' be a lot worse than these." Duffy held up his injured thumbs. "Don't screw this up." And with that he was gone.

Max opened the briefcase, removed the game tickets from the manila envelope and, as quickly as possible, put one ticket in each of the white business envelopes he'd brought with him. This was real, he thought, locking the briefcase and standing up, this was actually happening.

He made his way to the diner where he'd previously eaten with Chubster, though this time there'd be no time for breakfast. Chubster was standing outside the door when Max showed up. Apparently everyone was in a hurry today. The idea man was holding a small gym bag, rocking back and forth on his heels as if he'd finally realized just what he'd gotten them involved in and had come down with a late case of the jitters.

"Hey," he said.

"Hey," Max said. "Have you seen Duffy?"

"No. Duffy? Why, was I 'sposed to?"

"He's got two broken thumbs."

"What?"

"I kid you not. Both thumbs. Like in the movies."

"Jesus."

"I know. Right."

Chubster looked around, shook his head. "Okay. All right. Just take this bag. It's got all the money."

"Pre-game money."

"Right. Just the rest of the pre-game. No post game 'til he sees those runners on the field."

"My money in there, too? You know, so I could just take off right now?"

Chubster looked like his friend had lost his mind. "What?"

"Never mind. Just kidding." Chubster handed over the bag. "Meet up at six o'clock, right?"

"That's the plan."

"Listen," said Max, "how long have you known this King guy anyway? You ever see him mad or violent or anything?"

"Well, nobody really knows him. You see him once or twice, do a job, some legit, some not so much, then you get paid by the bodyguard, you know, Mr. Personality, and then you wait for the next time he gets in touch."

"So that's why you were flush sometimes. We thought you'd gotten an advance on some of your ideas."

"Matter of fact, King listened to some of my ideas. Almost invested in the 'Knock-Abouts.'"

Max remembered the 'Knock-Abouts'. The old kids' toy, a plastic inflatable, about three feet tall, sand at the bottom and a clown's face on the surface, the ones with the superimposed facial photos. Chubster's idea was that you could work out your anger while pummeling those personal punching bags. Frannie had said she'd buy twenty-four of them, which just happened to be the number of students in her home room that year. One of Chubster's better than average get-rich-quick schemes, Max had thought.

"Oh, yeah," he said. "I remember those. What happened with 'em?"

"King figured we'd have too many lawsuits. Libel or slander or copyright or something. His lawyers scared him off."

"Too bad. I'm sure Ginny would have bought one."

"What?"

"Nothin'. What about the violence? Seen any?"

"No, not me. You know, you hear some things but who knows what's true or not? I figured just do what I'm supposed to do and no worries."

"Well," Max said, "I didn't just hear about Duffy's thumbs. I saw 'em."

"Okay, okay, I get it. But like I said, just do your job. That's what I'm doing. Then we both need to take a long vacation. Right now I gotta' go. See you at six."

Max watched his co-conspirator slip away. Well, he thought, consensus of opinion seemed to be pointing to a fast getaway after the deed was done. Even though Max knew that to be the rational course, something was holding him back. Or, rather, things. He'd be leaving Sully in the lurch, no doubt about that. He'd made no arrangements for Rufus and certainly wasn't going to take a cat on the lam. The boys at the bar who were, let's face it, his friends, would be clueless, left to wonder, maybe to worry. And then there was Ginny. Likely the real reason he was hesitating. Yes, she was mad at him, actually mad was surely an understatement, but maybe she wouldn't stay that way forever. Maybe there was hope.

Max pulled out one of the burner phones, checked the time and dialed Tulip's number. One thing was for sure. He had to get moving.

*

Max met Tulip and Gooch not far from the copy shop where she worked. Tulip appeared ready for a marathon and Gooch appeared ready for a nap. Decked out like an entrant in the psychedelic Olympics, she wore neon orange running shoes, paisley stretch pants, two-toned purple windbreaker and, curiously enough, a bright white baseball cap, no logo. Gooch had on gray high top 'Converse Allstars' that may or may not have been white at one time, brown corduroy pants that Max seriously doubted would be conducive to running, and a fraying black hoodie which the big fellow had apparently purchased at an 'Insane Clown Posse' concert. A white headband holding back shambles of long red curls completed the ensemble and just below, at the center of his generous forehead was what looked like a small camera lens. Tulip interrupted her stretching long enough to give Max a hug. Gooch shook hand, noticed Max staring at his face.

"It's a 'GoPro,'" he said. "Figured I could film the stuff on the field, you know closeups, action shots. Maybe the producers can use the footage, maybe good for a few more bucks. What do you think?"

Once again, Max was surprised. "Yeah, maybe. How's it work anyway?"

Gooch held out his palm, revealing a small silver disc with a red button in the center. "I just press this button. It's wireless. Cool, huh?"

"Yeah," Max said, "cool."

"Here," said Gooch. "I'll show you. Walk toward me."

"No, no, not me." Tulip and Gooch were not expecting Max's tone.

"What's the matter?" Tulip asked.

"No, nothing. I just hate to see myself on film. I'm not very photogenic." Tulip and Gooch glanced at each other, shrugged. "No time anyway. Lots to do. Got to give out the tickets, money, you know."

"Speaking of which," said Tulip, now doing a vigorous set of jumping jacks.

"Right," said Max, "let's start walking."

He opened the briefcase as they moved along, extracted two envelopes he had earlier prepared and casually handed them to the pair. "As promised," he said. "The rest after the game. I'll let you know when and where."

Tulip paused, bent down and tucked her envelope in her athletic sock. Gooch watched her, intrigued, as though he'd made no plan for concealment, then followed suit, though the worn, floppy sock he inserted his envelope in was, Max feared, cause for concern.

Crazy Ed was standing in front of his pawn shop when the trio arrived. A 'Closed' sign hanging on the door, a cigarette dangling from his lips, an extra large sweatshirt barely hiding his gut, he looked more like a race-fixer than a racer. Gooch seemed almost svelte in comparison. Max had to remind himself that they were merely two of the heavier recruits and that though they might not last the five minutes on the field that King desired, they would at least be difficult to remove and would occupy more security personnel than some of the other more athletically inclined participants.

Max made the appropriate introductions, handed Ed his white envelope which the big man slid through the slot in his shop's front door. "What's that," he asked, eyeing Gooch's forehead.

"GoPro," said Gooch. "Newest version. Wireless."

"Really," said Ed. "you want to pawn it after the game."

"No way." Gooch glanced at Tulip as though Crazy Ed had just asked him if he'd like to sell his children.

"So," said Max, "how you feelin', Ed?"

"Good," said Ed, stomping out his cigarette on the filthy sidewalk. "Did I mention that I was on my High School track team?"

Tulip looked doubtful. "Really?"

"Yeah. Shot put, discus, you know."

"How does that help?"

Ed was defensive. "I don't know. I'm just saying."

"That's fine, Ed," said Max. "You never know. Those skills might come in handy. Anyway, we need to get going. Athletic fields for some head shots, hand out more tickets, then we'll split up. Let's go."

Gooch hesitated. "Ah, Max, just a quick question before we go. We were wondering, ah, that is Tulip and I, when we run on the field for the film, um, what is our motivation?"

Max looked at Tulip, then at Crazy Ed. Slight smile, slight shrug. "Your motivation?"

"Yeah," Gooch continued. "You know, why are we running around on a football field. How is that part of the story?"

Tulip tried to help. "He reads a lot of trade magazines, you know, from the entertainment industry."

"I know you're not the director but it might help our performance if we had, you know, motive."

Max didn't have time for this. "Your performance?"

"We're making a movie, right," said Tulip. "So we're performing."

Max kept his cool. "Yes, right, of course. You're actors, you're performing. So why would your, ah, characters being doing this scene?"

Gooch seemed relieved. "Exactly."

"Well," said Max, "to be completely honest, I have not seen the finished script, especially the end. The producers are being very hush, hush, don't want anything getting out, you know, spoil the surprise. But I can tell you that the main character, the, ah..."

"Protagonist?" ventured Tulip.

"Yes, yes. The protagonist has been hiding from a number of different bad guys and now he's been spotted at the stadium and chaos ensues." Gooch didn't look too thrilled with this answer. "But for now," Max continued, "why don't you just use the money for motivation. That's what I would do."

Gooch glanced at Tulip who gave him a slight nod. "Okay," he said. "Good enough."

*

The small band made their way to the fields where Max had enlisted his first group of volunteers. They'd left the business district behind and it being early on a chilly Saturday morning, other pedestrians were few and far between, some hardy joggers and the occasional dog walker being the exceptions. The basketball courts were just a short distance away when Max heard a familiar voice.

"Hey, Max," said Nuggets, stepping out from behind a tree.

Max was beginning to hate surprises. "Nuggets, you're out already?"

"Sure am."

"What are you doing here?"

"I could ask you the same thing."

"What?"

"I was waiting for you."

"Really?" Max turned to his entourage. "You guys go ahead to the park. Just hang at the bench. I'll be right down."

"You sure?" asked Tulip.

"Yup. I'll be fine." The threesome headed off and when they were out of ear-shot, Max addressed his old friend. "So what's up, Nuggets? What do you want?"

"Well," said Nuggets, "originally I just wanted in on the deal. Supposed to be my job anyway."

"We discussed this at the hospital."

Nuggets ignored him. "But now I want that briefcase you're holding."

"This?"

"You heard me," Nuggets said, revealing a pistol from behind his back.

"Are you kidding me? You're robbing me? We're friends. I visited you in the hospital. We talked about this."

"Sorry, Max. Guess I'm just one of those desperate guys you hear about."

"You're crazy, Louis. I'll report you. You'll go to jail."

"I doubt that. I believe the cops are looking for the bills in that briefcase. I go to jail, you're coming with me."

Well, thought Max, he had a good point there. Was this it then? After the week he'd had, after all the hard work, the close calls, the heartbreak with Ginny, was it all for not because of a frustrated ex-porn star turned mugger? How would he explain this to King? He doubted the man in charge of repercussions was a fan of excuses.

"Nuggets, come on, you can't be serious."

"Afraid so. Hand it over."

Max stared down at the briefcase in his hand and heard another voice, this one unfamiliar. "Hey, asshole!" Max looked up and was happy to see the newcomer was not addressing him. No, Tim Griffin, the nurse from Saint Elizabeth's was speaking to Nuggets and when the novice stickup man turned to face his accuser, the angry vet was quick to use his army issued combat boot to kick him in the one over-sized testicle he still possessed. Again, Nuggets was down in a heap, screaming in great pain and writhing in agony, none of which appeared to have any affect on the ex-soldier's ire. Nuggets pistol had dropped from his hand and the saline fluid from his ruptured ball spread slowly over the brown Autumn grass as Griffin's own motivation was revealed.

"You fucking liar," he yelled. "I get you out early, risk my job, get my hopes up and you sneak off, no contact, no introductions, not even a number. You son-of-a-bitch!" Griffin was ready to strike again with his shod foot but seemed to think better of it. "Jesus," he said, "what a mess."

"Yeah," said Max, "you might want to get out of here."

Griffin nodded, looked down at the gun, then bent and picked it up. "Well, this has to be worth something."

"Try Crazy Ed's Pawn Shop," said Max. "Corner of Main and Lexington."

Griffin nodded, stood over Nuggets. "From now on, keep your fucking word."

Nuggets made a slight attempt to nod, then went back to suffering as the angry nurse made his getaway. Max almost yelled thank you, decided against. He stared at his physically deflated ex-friend, still laying prone, twitching silently on the cold ground, and weighed his options. Normally he'd be on his phone calling for an ambulance but nothing was normal about this week. He was tempted to bend down, try to comfort the poor bastard but that twinge of pity was swiftly overcome by a feeling of betrayal. Nuggets was not only going to rob him, he was going to ruin everyone's payday and maybe even get Max killed or at least disfigured. So no then, the Hell with the prick. He could lay there until some do-gooder found him. He hurried down the hill to the courts, somewhat relieved that Nuggets didn't know exactly what the money was to be used for.

Ed, Tulip and Gooch were resting on a bench, the ballers Max had selected were chatting in a semi-circle and a few of the unchosen were practicing their jump shots.

"What was that all about?" asked Tulip.

"Yeah," said Gooch. "Sounded like someone screaming."

"Oh, yeah, we had an argument. I didn't pick him for the film and he was yelling."

"Is he going to tell the cops?" asked Ed.

"Tell the cops," said Max. "About what?"

"About the film."

"Oh." Max looked back up the hill. "I don't think so."

Ribs walked over, shadowed by the others. "What's shakin', cousin? We doin' this thing?"

"Yup. We're still on. Everybody here?"

"Yes, sir. But Malcolm brought his twin. Said they'd split the money. That cool?"

Max noticed the duplicate brothers. Why not, he figured, he had extra tickets and maybe it would help with the confusion. "Sure," he said, "that's cool."

Rufus stepped to the front, pointed at Max's companions. "Who these folks?"

"More runners."

"What's that on his head?"

"A GoPro. Action shots on the field," said Max. "Maybe make you famous."

Rufus was unimpressed. "They don't look like no runners."

"Hey," said Tulip. "Race you anytime."

"Not you, home girl. But these two..."

"Have you taken a look at Ribs?" Max glanced at the big fellow. "No offense, Ribs."

Ribs just laughed. "He's got you there, Rufus."

"All right," said Max, "we're on a tight schedule." He opened the briefcase, took out the first envelope, was about to read a name but paused, looked around. "Where's Charles? Did you talk to him?"

"Oh, yeah," said Ribs. "We talked to him. Took some convincing."

"He was not too happy," said Rufus.

"But," said Max.

"But he come around," said Ribs. "I don't think he'll cause no trouble."

Some of the others looked unconvinced. But what was Max to do? The snowball was rolling. He looked at the envelope again. "Benny B.", he said. A skinny sprinter stepped forward and Max handed him the envelope. "The rest after the game. I'll let you know where and when. Malcolm..."

*

Saturday morning and again, Ginny didn't want to get out of bed. She lay awake, staring at the clock on the nightstand, dreading a knock on the door which would mean Emily wanted to talk. Between Emily, Max, the Detective and Ms. Bodega, the Guidance Counselor, Ginny was about talked out. She simply wanted to lie on her back, the warm comforter tucked to her chin, and carefully examine the ceiling as she slowly drifted back to sleep.

So why then, as she tried to unclutter her mind from the previous days' litany of incidents and characters, was she focused on the young landscapers, the vision of the two boys dressed and ready to go, waiting impatiently for the phone call that was not to come? Why did she care if she broke her promise? She barely knew them. She was likely saving them from embarrassment, both legal and personal. Oh, she admitted to herself, who was she kidding? She was thinking of the young men and the promise she'd made because, unlike Max, she never lied and she always kept her word. She cursed her own decency and threw off the covers.

Ginny could tell that Max, though he tried his best not to show it, was surprised when she called. It was her intent that he call the landscapers and meet them with tickets and cash. But Max, while assuring her that he would do most anything she asked if only time allowed, explained that his route had required precise planning and that he'd not set aside time for the college kids seeing as he had no information on the boys and no expectation that Ginny would be forthcoming with any since she was probably never speaking to him again.

"Fine," Ginny said, which Max and every other man knows is the worst word a woman can utter, especially if you hoped to win her back one day. Just tell her, she said, the best place to meet him. She'd take the money and tickets to them herself. When that was settled, she determined the amount of time it would require to travel from the appointment with Max to the landscapers and texted Teddy. She didn't wish to actually talk to him on the phone. Texting was, she felt, contrary to what her daughter and a million other teenagers thought, more impersonal, less likely to get his hopes up. This was a business deal, plain and simple; they do the job, they make some money. It was not going to be, as Biz would have dubbed it, a 'Mrs. Robinson' thing.

Max directed her, oddly enough, to meet him in Chinatown. As far as Ginny knew, they'd enlisted no Asians in the pursuit of speedsters, not out of any prejudice or stereotype. They just hadn't been presented with the opportunity. She dressed quickly, didn't bother with makeup and tucked her crimson locks under a baseball cap. She had no interest in increasing Teddy's desire and no longer cared about impressing Max. She wanted to get it over with and go back to bed, maybe watch the news later, see if anything actually happened. At least that's what she told herself.

Max was standing in front of 'Chow Lee's Noodle Shop', as promised. He was staring at his phone as Ginny arrived, tried to act casual, just a nod and a half smile.

"Only you," said Ginny.

"Yeah. I already saw Crazy Ed, Tulip, Gooch and the basketball guys. They're all on their way to the stadium."

"What about Charles?"

"They said they convinced him to stand down. We'll see."

Ginny nodded. "So you're really doing this?"

"Don't think I have much choice."

"Really?"

"Really."

"Why Chinatown?"

"Remember the Babushkas?" Max asked. "The Romanian acrobats I told you about. They live in that building over there." He pointed to a nondescript brick structure across the street, apartments on the upper floors, Chinese markets with plucked chickens hanging in picture windows at street level.

"Why would Romanians live in Chinatown?"

"Beats me. Maybe they like the food."

"Anyway," said Ginny.

"Right," said Max, taking two envelopes from his jacket and handing them to Ginny.

"What about after the game?" The last thing Ginny wanted was to come back out and meet the handsome young landscaper again. She was a strong, independent woman but she had her limits.

"I'll take care of them. I'm sorry you even had to do this. You could have just stayed home. It's not like they signed a contract or anything."

"I gave my word," said Ginny, handing Max a scrap of paper with Teddy's number on it. "And I don't lie."

Max, to his credit, said nothing, merely nodded. He looked like a dog watching his owner leave him at the kennel but that, Ginny knew, was not her fault. She tucked the envelopes in her purse and walked away.

⋆

The Babushkas were eating breakfast in an Oriental mini-mart. Who does that, thought Max. They were taking up one of three small tables that sat among the shelves of Chinese delicacies, the dining area apparently an afterthought, another way to increase sales. The acrobatic brothers were sipping tiny cups of tea and slurping something from the plain white bowls set in front of them. Max realized, probably for the first time in his life that though, like most Americans, he had eaten his fair share of Chinese foods, he had no idea what Chinese people ate for breakfast. He knew Hispanics might have 'quevos rancheros' and the French crepes and croissants, the Canadians bacon, but what the heck were all those Chinese people eating? Oh well, he figured he could google it later, maybe bring it up for debate at the bar. Right now he had more important things to think about.

The Romanians seemed happy to see Max, smiling and inviting him to sit. Max declined, set the briefcase on the table, looked all around the small shop. "Still good?" he asked while giving a 'thumbs up' sign.

"Yes, yes," said Bishku. "Very good. And we bring extra. Is good?"

Before Max could consider the question, he felt someone's warm breath on his shoulder, turned and was face to face with a young Oriental man in a long white apron.

"This Hung Hong," said Bishku. "Is very fast. Very fast."

Max was not happy. "You told him what we're doing?"

"Is okay. No worry. Hong is good man, tells no one." Hung Hong, grinning like a madman, extended his hand which Max felt it best to shake. "He come with us to game. Is okay?"

"No, not okay," said Max. He knew he had extra tickets but also that there was no spare cash, not with all the money already promised. "No more money," he said.

"No," said Bishku. "Hong not run for money. He run for fame."

"You make film," said Hong. "Movie...Hollywood...Bruce Lee!" With this last he quickly assumed a striking martial arts pose which Max could only surmise must have been one of Lee's more well known fight stances.

Max was entering a 'why not' phase in the day's caper, maybe in his whole life. "No money?" he asked.

Hong shook his head vigorously. "No money." Still grinning.

Well, thought Max, if this crazy kid wants to run on the field for no money, who am I to stop him? By the time it made the news, maybe he would be famous. "Okay," he said, "but no fighting, no Bruce Lee." He didn't want the poor sap arrested for assault. The week might be heavily taxing his mind but he hadn't yet lost all concept of action and consequence.

Hong's smile faded but only for a moment. "Okay," he said, "no fight." He turned to the Babushkas and the smile returned. "But I run!" High fives all around. Max was aware once again of being the only participant in this venture who seemed cognizant of the gravity involved, the serious nature of the acts they were about to embark on. Was the possibility of film and fame really that intoxicating? It couldn't be just about the payoff. After all, it wasn't life changing money like the reward he was expecting. Nevertheless, back to work. He opened the briefcase, handed each acrobat an envelope, then fished around in the lining until he found a spare ticket for Hung Hong.

"Money and tickets," he said. "More money after game."

Bishku translated and the men looked pleased. "The tickets," Bishku said, "we watch game together?"

"No, not together," said Max. "Apart. Better for movie." Bishku translated again, this time with less enthusiasm. Max closed the briefcase. "Okay, you run on field at end of third quarter. Five minutes, then out. You understand? American football. Third quarter done, then run, run, run. Five minutes, yes?"

The brothers nodded and Max could only hope they truly understood. He felt a a finger poking his shoulder, turned to face Hong again, the young man's smile big as ever. "I run first," he said. "Yes?"

"No," said Max. "No first. Together. Same time. Together." He looked to Bishku, pleading for help.

"No worry, my friend. We explain him."

Why, thought Max, am I not reassured? "Okay," he said, "we meet here after the game. I'll text you the time. Yes?"

"Yes. No problem. Everything good. You go now?"

"Yes, I go now." Max took a step, turned back before departing. "Good luck," he said.

*

The young landscapers were waiting in front of the house where Ginny had first approached them. They were leaning against a rusty Dodge truck, staring at their cellphones.

No sign of the older Hispanic workers. The boys looked up when Ginny arrived, happy to see her.

"We were a little worried," said Simon. "Game's in a couple hours."

"I told you before. I always keep my word."

"That's true. You did say that."

Ginny paused, looked at the two collegians. They were so young, their whole lives ahead of them. They were about to break the law, probably get arrested, maybe get kicked out of school, all for a few thousand dollars and yet they acted like they were heading to a kegger, smiling, relaxed as though this was just another cool thing to do on their day off, to make a memory, another story to tell their pals.

"So," said Teddy, "we still on?"

Ginny nodded. "We are. But you don't have to be. You guys understand this is serious business. You could get arrested. You can still back out if you want."

Teddy smiled. "Sounds like you're concerned. That you care about us."

That was not the response Ginny was expecting. She tried to think of a snappy comeback but Simon spoke first. "Did you bring the tickets?...And the money?"

"You know," said Teddy, "this was your idea. You came to us."

"I know, I know. Just hope you know what you're getting yourselves into." She took two white envelopes from her pocketbook, handed them over. "The seats are not together. Everyone is sitting in different sections."

"Everyone?"

"Yes, you and the others. You'll all jump out of the stands at the end of the third quarter, run around for five minutes, then get the Hell out of there."

"And after the game?"

"After the game, you'll meet up with my partner, Jim. He'll have the rest of your money." Ginny paused again. "Either that or someone will come down and bail you out. I'm not sure who."

"Your partner?" asked Teddy. "Boyfriend?"

"No. He's another producer on the film."

"So, when will we see you again?"

"You won't. This is it."

Teddy was disappointed. "You sure?"

"Yes," said Ginny, "I'm sure. Now you better get going. Jim will contact you after the game, arrange a meeting. Good luck."

"Thanks," Teddy said, stepping toward her. "Can I get a hug? For good luck."

"Jesus," said Simon.

What the heck, she figured. She could probably use a hug right about now. "Why not," she said, extending her arms. The handsome collegian hugged her close, then looked her in the eye, his hands still on her shoulders.

"Until we meet again," he said.

Ginny gently removed his hands. "Don't wait underwater," she said, smiling. There, she thought, that was more like it, that was the old Ginny.

Teddy laughed. "Beautiful and funny," he said, emphasis on the 'and'. "Come on, Simon, let's go make a movie."

The young men jumped in the Dodge and rode off, their arms extended from the windows as they waved goodbye. Ginny stood, her hands on her hips as she watched them drive away. She'd kept her word but perhaps she shouldn't have. Was it possible that sometimes, in extreme cases, it was better to break a promise than to keep it? What about all those romantic comedies where someone who's vowed to wed leaves their betrothed standing alone at the alter, heartbroken, in shock, and yet everything seems to work out for everyone in the end? But these boys were not starring in a Hollywood fairy tale and if everything worked out at the end of this crazy plan, well, Ginny would be pretty damn surprised. Nothing she could do now though. May as well go home and watch the news.

*

Max wasn't sure how many dancers would show up at the appointed site. He doubted strippers were known for their reliability. But when he exited his cab at the prearranged diner, he was pleased to see almost all the girls standing outside, shivering in the cool November air, coffee cups and cigarettes all around. Ebony, snug in a faux fur wrap, a king-size mochachinno in her hand, was holding court as Max approached the group.

"That dude obviously did not know who he was dealing with but he sure does now." The girls laughed, saw Max who was trying to maintain an appearance of relaxed confidence.

"Hey, girls, you look chilly," he said, noting most were wearing short shorts or skin tight leggings.

"That's your fault," said Vixen, opening her leather jacket to reveal a thin white t-shirt with the club's logo printed on it and no bra underneath. "This how you said to dress, right?"

Max's assessment of the ladies' frigidity was verified by Vixen's bullet-like nipples struggling to poke through the thin cotton fabric. Wisely, he chose not to comment. "Yes, that's right. It's better for the film and, ah, the fans and, um, the club, too."

The redhead was unconvinced. "You gonna' pay our medical bills when we all catch pneumonia?"

Max laughed. "Oh, ah, don't think that's in the budget."

The redhead was not laughing. "I'm not kidding. I'm freezing my ass off."

"Come on, Stormy," said Ebony, "you don't got no ass to freeze off anyway."

Everyone but Stormy laughed. "Yeah," she said, "well I'm sure your giant booty will keep you nice and warm."

"Okay, girls," said Max, "let's not forget we're a team, all in this together. Now, a few quick things before we get going. You girls know the race last night ended up on the internet. Somebody filmed it."

"Yeah, we saw it. We think Fat Matt did it on his phone. But he ain't sayin'"

"Fat Matt?"

"The bouncer. The bald one."

"Fat Matt. That's what you call him?"

"Yeah, he don't mind."

Nicknames, thought Max.

"Thing got a shitload of likes," said the short, busty blonde.

"But did you tell anyone why you were racing?" asked Max.

"We didn't," said Ebony, "but some of the girls not running did."

"They did?"

The slender brunette spoke up. "Yeah, but nobody believed 'em. The customers all just thought it was a big joke. Like we were trying to get on the news or get publicity for the club or something. But not one of 'em thinks we're really gonna' run on that field."

"Okay," said Max, "but you're gonna' run, right?"

Ebony laughed. "Show us the money!"

Max smiled, opened the briefcase, began handing out envelopes. "Tickets and half the money now. The rest after. You have my word." He pulled some spare cash from his coat pocket. "Look, there's no sense being cold the whole time. Take this..." He peeled off a couple twenties for each girl. "When you get to the stadium, buy some cheap sweatshirts outside, not at the concessions. But take them off before you run, all right?" The strippers nodded. "I suggest you take out the ticket, keep it somewhere safe, and stash the envelopes with cash somewhere in route."

"In route?" The blonde looked confused.

"On the way," said Max. "Somewhere or with someone for safekeeping. You don't want to lose them on the field."

"That's good thinking," said Ebony. "Hey, Lucy. Your place on the way, isn't it?"

A young strawberry blonde in a ponytail nodded. "Yeah, but I live at home. With my parents."

"You live at home," said Vixen.

"That's perfect," said Ebony. "These parents of yours. They trustworthy?"

"Yes, they're trustworthy. But they don't even know what I do. They think I'm a waitress."

"That's okay. We tell 'em we all waitresses and we leave all the cash at Lucy's."

"Oh, jeez," said Lucy.

"Okay," said Max. "You girls figure it out. Just get yourself to the game and when that whistle blows at the end of the third quarter, go, go, go. You're gonna' make money, you're gonna' be in a movie..." This wasn't a total lie, Max told himself. The game would be televised. "And you might even get famous."

"Might get arrested, too," said Stormy.

"Man, Stormy," said Ebony, "you a real downer sometimes, you know."

"All right," said Max, hailing another cab. "Good luck. See you after the game."

*

That's it, he thought, as he sat in the back of the taxi, that's everyone. He'd handed out all the tickets but one. He looked down at the cabbie's hack license. Bismack Bojibo. "You like football?" Max asked him.

"American football?"

"Yes, American football."

"No. I do not like. Many rules, little action."

"Don't tell me. You like soccer."

"Yes. Real football. Much action. No timeouts. Why you ask? You go to game? We are going wrong way."

Max considered the question. Obviously he should be going home, making plans for Rufus and a quick getaway. But he did have that extra ticket and to say he was curious as to how King's grand plan would go down was one one heck of an understatement. Sure, he could use the time to pack some stuff, find Rufus a home, maybe leave Sully a note, but...

"Yes, I'm going to the game. Please turn around."

"Okay, boss," said Bismack. "Hope game is good for you."

"Yeah," said Max, "me, too."

It wasn't a long ride to the stadium. But as Max stared out the window at the familiar sites of the city, his city, the place he'd spent most of his life, his mind wandered. Was this really the last time he'd see some of these spots, was he actually moving on, after years of procrastination, to the next phase of his life. Memories were flashing by like a cinematic montage, some chronological, others random. The teams he'd played for in High School, the girls he'd longed for. His marriage at an age and level of maturity that never had a chance, the college degree not completed, the jobs not pursued, the risks never taken. They were passing streets he'd been up and down, streets where he'd seen bars for sale, businesses that could have been his. He was going to open his own place, wasn't that the plan? He recalled the old Sinatra line, 'Regrets, I've had a few, but then again...' Yeah, a few. At least. He'd always been annoyed when overhearing one of his patrons avowing that he, and it was usually a he, that he had no regrets. How is that possible, Max wondered. How do you live a whole life without regret? Every turn taken has been the right one, every decision correct, every choice perfect? Max wanted to beat those people bodily about the head and shoulders. Sure, maybe it was more a philosophy, a means to rid oneself of the doubts, but still. If that's what it is, then say so. Don't make everyone who admits to regret, whether large or small, feel inferior.

And now he'd made one of those big choices, one which he was hoping and praying he would not come to regret. Though he certainly had his reservations after signing on to King's caper, at that moment he was feeling good. He'd survived every curve ball the week's events and characters had thrown at him. He'd completed his leg of the race and appeared close to securing an amount of money he couldn't have saved in ten years of bartending. He was curious, excited, alive. Nervous, too, but wasn't that part of the deal? At that moment, on that day, heading to the scene of the crime, he did not regret that first conversation with Chubster Magee. Would he still feel that way in a few hours? That, he told himself, was a very good question.

His ruminations were interrupted by an unfamiliar and unusual sight. On the corner of Fourth and Babcock, maybe a quarter mile from the enormous parking lot which encircled the stadium, and not far from 'The Birch Street Inn', one of the city's oldest shelters, was a cadre of homeless men, each standing next to a shopping cart. Instead of overflowing with the usual cargo – blankets, trash bags filled with cans and bottles, cardboard boxes and other miscellaneous claptrap, items cast aside by the area's more solvent citizens, each cart contained a solitary white cloth sack. A disheveled, hirsute member of this community was speaking to the others, handing out bills, pint bottles and small rectangular cans. This particular vagrant did look familiar. It was the same bum that Max and Ginny had watched that day near the bank.

"Stop the car," said Max.

"We not there yet," said Bismack.

"That's okay. I'd like to walk the rest."

"Okay. You the boss."

Max handed the young driver a fifty, told him to keep the change and jumped out of the cab. He quickly approached the group of men and addressed the one who appeared to be in charge. "Chubster?" he said. Disguise or not, there was no denying Max's hunch.

"Max," said the startled idea man, "what the fuck. What are you doing here?"

"I could ask you the same." Max noted the small cans contained lighter fluid. "What's in the sacks?" he asked.

"Kindling. King wants more diversions. Now would you get the Hell out of here."

Max didn't recall burning down the stadium as part of the plan. Chubster read his thoughts. "Don't worry. It's just special effects..." He glanced at the curious expressions surrounding them. "For the movie."

Max nodded slowly. "Oh, right, the movie." Jesus, he thought. Why was he even surprised at this point? What was next? Was King going to parachute in some storm troopers, maybe sneak in some lions and tigers?

"It'll be outside the stadium, you know. Just smoke, you know, another distraction."

"Okay," said Max, resigned, no fight left in him. "I'll see you after the game, right?"

"Absolutely," said Chubster. Max turned to walk away. "Where you going, anyway?"

"I ended up with an extra ticket. Hate to see it go to waste."

Chubster shook his head. "You should be home packing."

"You're probably right. But I have to see this for myself."

"Suit yourself. But..." And here Chubster lowered his voice. "...you get caught later 'cause you stayed too long, and you start talking, Duffy's broken thumbs gonna' look like a walk in the park."

Max nodded. "Understood."

Chubster nodded. "All right. I'll be in touch after. Enjoy the show."

They parted company, Chub coaching up the homeless team he'd assembled and Max walking briskly toward the stadium, the throngs of pedestrians growing larger the closer he got. The smell of cooked sausage and roasted peanuts filled the air, sidewalk barkers hawked their pennants and souvenirs, frat boys chugged their pregame beers. Everyone from the oldest alumni to the youngest fan was excited and yet, thought Max, not one of them knew what they were about to see.

*

Teddy and Simon were not happy about sitting apart, Simon more so than his handsome friend. They wanted to run on the field together; that way neither could back out. They'd seen enough aborted pranks and abandoned 'Truth or Dare' games to know that young adults did not always do what they claimed they would. Neither collegian wanted to discover he'd been played by the other, cash reward or not. Simon was somewhat reassured by his buddy's infatuation with Ginny. Though the age difference made a future tryst problematic, he'd witnessed Ted talk a lot of young women into a lot of situations in a lot of places, and knew the charmer would not want to spoil whatever chance he may have by not completing the agreed upon task. And, of course, there was the money. Winter was coming and their landscaping dollars would be drying up. Nevertheless, Simon knew, there could be consequences. The two students were, arguably, the participants with the most to lose. Certainly, if things went awry, they could claim it had all been just a juvenile prank, a dare gone too far. But still, what would their school think, what would their parents think?

The Babushka brothers were excited and had no doubts concerning each man's resolve to run. Naturally, they would have enjoyed sitting together but Max had at least situated them in neighboring sections, hoping they'd reconvene once out on the field, flipping and tumbling for all they were worth. But right now they were content, happy with everything, the festive atmosphere, the concession treats they'd never seen back in the old country, the ripe young coeds prepared to cheer their team on. The Romanians smiled broadly, waved to each other, took it all in. Perhaps American football wasn't so bad.

As for Hung Hong, he was chomping at the bit, ready to be the first, the fastest, the most entertaining. Somehow he'd convinced himself that this was his fate, his road to American fame, the day he would achieve his destiny. It would be difficult to sit still for three quarters but soon he would be a movie star. Consumed by nervous energy, the only way to stay calm, he decided, was to drink as many of the foamy, overpriced beers as he could afford, surely not the best plan for a young man who was by no means an experienced drinker.

The ballplayers were the most serious. They had a job to do, decent money to make, and whether or not they were really participating in the making of a film was not high on their list of concerns. Jump down from the stands, sprint around for five minutes, avoid security, then get out of there. And if you saw your buddy getting caught and hauled away, well, that was not your problem. This was not going to be a team sport. Today it was every man for himself.

If Max had expected the strippers, by keeping a low profile, behaving themselves in their generic hoodies and sensible shoes until it was go time, would not draw attention to themselves, he was sadly mistaken. Difficult for an attractive woman sitting alone among various frat boys, louts and blowhards in any alcohol soaked section of any sporting venue in today's America to go unnoticed. Not that the girls were unused to being surrounded by inebriated fools; they were. But to put up with rude behavior with no tips offered in return was not going to play with these ladies. You might receive a smile for a free brew or a pat on the arm for a slice of pizza but that was it. There would be no lap dances in the stands. And Heaven forbid one of the local loudmouths said something unbecoming. After years of entertaining lowlifes and losers, the dancers had learned to give as good as they got. And their zingers were, more often than not, better than yours, especially if, as they often did, make reference to the size of your manhood or your inability to use it.

A nondescript Ebony was never a possibility no matter how she was dressed. Bouffant hairdo, long lacquered nails, yards of bling and bright red lipstick were hard not to notice even if your sweatshirt was gray and your shoes were flats. By the time she shimmied and shaked into her seat, she'd earned most everyone's attention. And Ebony, pleasant and outgoing most days anyway, was particularly happy that day. A free ticket to the game, a lucrative payday and the chance to be in a movie. What else could a girl ask for? She introduced herself to her seatmates, an old buck in a 'Members Only' jacket and V.F.W. Cap on her left and a young wide-eyed lad attending with his father on her right, the later quickly asking his son if he'd like to trade seats, the former even more rapidly declining the offer. Ebony shook hands with them and settled in, her impressive booty gathering looks with every wiggle.

While Ebony could likely draw attention to herself in a burka and veil, the other girls were receiving their fair share of scrutiny as well. Vixen, the well spoken dancer Max and Ginny had first encountered, may as well have been running for mayor, handing out 'Bottoms Up' business cards, taking group selfies and teasing her section's denizens with promises of spectacles to come.

Bambi, the short, buxom blonde, had somehow managed to squeeze herself into a form fitting hoodie and was constantly standing up to get a better view, her bosom jutting out and causing the men around her to lose track of downs and distance.

The only stripper showing signs of discomfort was Stormy, the aptly named redhead whose lovely face seemed etched into a permanent scowl. Disinterested in the game at hand or the sport of football in general, she spent her time complaining about being cold, about the flat beer and bland snacks, about her uncomfortable aluminum seat, about, basically, anything and everything. The only thing she showed the slightest enthusiasm for was the handsome gentleman seated directly in front of her, and whose girlfriend was not taking kindly to Stormy's flirtatious behavior. On most any other day Stormy would have stomped the poor girl and taken her man but this day was all business. No time for cat fights when there was money to be made.

Gooch and Tulip were separated as well but these two seemed quite content with their decision to participate. They were more excited than nervous, more zealous than anxious. For a couple of minimum wage earners this was big. Money, excitement, maybe fifteen minutes of fame. They both were on their way to useless degrees, Tulip in Eastern Philosophy, Gooch in Medieval Folklore, so school was not a factor. Their families had resigned themselves to neither of them ever making anything of themselves, so who knew, maybe the stunt might even impress them. Besides, they weren't exactly preparing to climb the corporate ladder. Nothing they did, no matter how stupid, was going to curtail a career of any significance. Moreover, their small group of like minded friends, anarchists all, would be nothing but proud. For Tulip and Gooch, it was all good.

Unfortunately, Gooch had forgotten to remove the 'GoPro' from his forehead and was being peppered with questions. Not so much what the tiny camera was but why would someone merely watching an athletic event be wearing a device that was generally used to share video of exciting physical endeavors with the world. Nothing very exciting about sitting on your ass and watching a college football contest. Or, as one suspicious coed wondered out loud, was he being creepy and filming the other young women in his section without their permission. Gooch denied and protested, claimed he'd simply forgotten to remove it following his strenuous morning jog. But this, too, seemed doubtful to those fans in close proximity to the flabby slacker. His physique, they surmised, was not that of someone who regularly goes on a Saturday morning run. No matter, they had beers to drink, crap to eat and a game to watch. So when Gooch tucked the 'GoPro' into his hoodie's front pouch, slumped down in his seat and kept his mouth shut, he was quickly forgotten. It was not, he felt, the time to stand out, not yet, not until the third quarter whistle blew. Then it would be his time, then he'd show them. He couldn't wait.

As for Crazy Ed, this would be another chapter in the memoir he was penning, 'Confessions of a Pawnbroker'. Far as he knew, no one had yet written a tell all about the business, so why not him. He'd certainly met his fair share of characters over the years and heard a lot of interesting stories concerning the origins of items to be pawned, some that sounded true, others not so much. Ed had realized early on that one did not meet a lot of upstanding citizens in a pawn shop.Besides, Crazy Ed had encountered a number of detectives over the years, flatfoots looking for fenced jewelry and stolen goods. If he got nabbed, he figured, maybe one of them would give him a break.

*

Max arrived at his seat well before kickoff, surveyed the stadium, wished he'd thought to bring binoculars. Try as he might, there was small chance of spotting a particular person in a crowd of that magnitude, at least not until they were on the playing field. He had thirty some runners among a hundred thousand fans, not even enough to put one in every section. What was going through their minds, he wondered, how were they behaving? For years, he'd watched games on TV, heard announcers brake for commercial because, as they said, some drunken clown had run on the field, or the court, or, Heaven forbid, the ice. But the broadcast director would not deem to show them; they would not be rewarded for such moronic behavior with televised notoriety.

Morganna, the Kissing Bandit, she of the long, blonde hair and over inflated breasts, was probably the last interloper to make it on camera, but she was a novelty, a sexy one at that, and the ballplayers appeared to mind her interruptions not one bit. Not anymore though. Sure, you might be able to find some clips on the internet, perhaps an inebriated hooligan being blindsided by an irate lineman, or perhaps a skinny streaker revealing more than any viewer hoped to see. So why did they do it, why risk public embarrassment and possible arrest? Was it spur of the moment, was it on a dare, was it temporary insanity? At least his crew had proper motivation and if apprehended and questioned by the authorities, that motive would not be determined to be their involvement in a robbery they knew nothing about, but rather to take part in the production of an independent film. Perfect.

Max noticed a young boy a few rows away, surrounded by what he surmised was the youngster's family – mother, father, sister, all decked out in the home team's colors. The brother had taken out a spy glass, the kind you saw in pirate movies when they were about to spot land.

It didn't look like a toy from where Max sat so he made his way over to the family.

"Excuse me," he said, "could I look through that for just a quick second? Please."

The boy looked to his father for approval and the gentleman nodded. Max took the instrument, aimed it at the field. It was indeed a toy but a well made one and allowed a nice close shot of the pregame warm-up. Max lowered it, addressed the young man.

"I'll give you one hundred dollars for it."

The boy's eyes bugged out, the father glanced at the mother and the daughter appeared apoplectic.

"Can I?" asked the young lad.

The father shrugged. "It's your toy."

The girl turned to her mother. "That was a gift!"

"Now, Kasey," said the mom, "this is Jack's decision. Nothing to do with you."

"Deal," said Jack, proffering the instrument.

Max took the roll of cash from his pocket, peeled off a crisp bill and handed it over. The kid looked like he'd won the lottery, the girl like she'd lost her kitten. "This isn't fair," she protested.

"Hey," said Jack, "I got a spy glass, you got an anklet. How is that not fair?"

"All right," said the dad. "That's enough, you two."

Kasey stared down at her feet, then up at Max. "Do you want to buy my anklet?" She knew immediately it was a stupid question, hung her head in shame.

"Uh, no thanks," said Max, examining the spy glass, "but I appreciate this. Trying to spot a friend." He returned to his seat, aware he could now add disrupting a pleasant family outing to the week's list of regrettable behavior. However, at that point, guilt and remorse seemed to have vanished. He was focused on his surroundings, his minions, the enterprise at hand. There would be plenty of time for guilt and remorse when the deed was done. He put the scope to his eye, panned as many sections as he could clearly see. Only one of his recruits was easy to make out – Ebony. And she appeared to be causing a ruckus.

*

'Big' Bob Spokane was, indeed, a big man. No irony this time. Six feet, four, three hundred pounds on a good day and loud as he was large, Bob had been coming to the game since his own days at the University, back when, unrecruited, he'd managed to make the team as a walk-on through sheer enthusiasm and attitude. Never as strong as he looked nor as athletic as he hoped, he'd still lasted all four years, riding the bench without complaint and cheering his teammates on as best he could. He'd gotten his letters, he'd gotten his varsity jacket and he'd gotten invited to the same parties as the High School All Americans and inner city studs he practiced with. Everyone liked Big Bob. And now, twenty years later, married with twin tween girls who alternately adored and ignored him, holding down a boring but well paying middle management position, these games had come to be, for better or worse, the highlights of his rather ordinary existence. There, in that stadium, still wearing the same varsity jacket, now somewhat frayed and faded, there, surrounded by friends both old and new, Big Bob was in his element.

But in all his years in Section 128, he'd never seen anything like Ebony. Dressed in skin tight booty shorts and the gray hoodie failing to hide her curves, decked out in more jewelry and nail polish than a wannabe rap star, she was by no means your typical female football fan. And, it seemed, her personality was as impressive as her figure. Ebony appeared to be flirting with the entire section at once, all wisecracks and innuendo, everyone laughing, enjoying the show. The game had yet to start and no one, especially the men, was minding the diversion, so when Ebony spotted Big Bob a couple rows away, she had to take note.

"Oooh," she cooed, "you a big one, aren't you? Everything big?"

Bob's buddies almost spit out their beer and the husky fellow, usually quick with a comeback, hesitated for a moment before recovering. "Bet you'd like to find out, wouldn't you?" Now the boys were laughing, high-fiving like their team had just scored. This was entertainment they hadn't bargained for.

"Big talker, too," said Ebony.

"Only one way to find out," said Bob, and now his friends were grinning like kids in the schoolyard. What was happening, they wondered. Big Bob was a happily married man. Who was this crazy chick?

"Maybe later," said Ebony. "Right now I gotta' make a plan."

"A plan?" asked Dewey, one of Bob's long time sidekicks. "A plan for what?"

"A plan to get on that field, sugar. I gotta' run around down on that field later."

"Yeah, right."

"For real, fool. And your big friend there is gonna' help me."

"I am?" Bob said.

"You a gentleman, ain't you? You help a lady in need, right?"

"Well, I'm not going on that field."

By now everyone was listening to this exchange and only the player introductions managed to refocus their attention. "You don't have to," yelled Ebony over the roar of the crowd. "Just gotta' help me down."

Bob nodded, turned back to the game about to begin but, naturally, found it hard to concentrate. Who was this plus-sized temptress? Was she really going to run on that field? And if so, why? Bob and his mates had talked about doing just that for years, especially after the requisite number of brews had been consumed. They'd discussed the consequences, regarded the thrill, debated and dared. But nothing had ever come of it. Was this sexy mama going to actually show them all how it was done?

*

Max was straining to watch Ebony through the spyglass but his inability to wink had come back to haunt him. Either he kept both eyes open and viewed two things at once which proved disconcerting, or he held the uncovered eye shut with his free hand looking, he felt, like an uncoordinated dufus. Add to this the focus of his observations, which was seldom the game itself, an event whose ticket price had probably cost the neighboring spectators a pretty penny, and the frequency with which he was poking the heads of fans seated nearby with the tip of the instrument, a minor mishap perhaps, but one that was obviously causing escalating irritation and, well, this was not how Max had envisioned his afternoon.

However, as far as he could tell, things in Ebony's section had settled a bit and the brazen dancer was no longer the center of attention. Though she'd been visibly having a rather spirited conversation with a big man to her right, things had apparently quieted down. Max set the spy glass down for a moment, turned back to the game.

*

Ginny didn't bother to try and resist turning on the television. She'd lived long enough to know which urges she could resist and which she couldn't. Besides, it wasn't as if she never watched football. She'd attended a few of the University's games over the years, spent a few Sunday afternoons on the couch with ex-boyfriends watching NFL contests and when 'Sully's was packed with local sports nuts cheering on their teams, she knew what was going on and could hold her own when everyone was loudly debating why the idiot ref had made such a stupid call.

So it wasn't totally out of character to find her slumped on the sofa, her feet on the coffee table, a cold bottle in her hand, her eyes on the screen.

That was the sight greeting Emily's sleepy eyes as she emerged from her bedroom, still in pajamas, her hair uncombed, her face unwashed. Ginny watched her pad toward the kitchen and, hoping for things between her and her daughter to return to normal, acknowledged Em with the same dumb exclamation she'd used a hundred times before, the same silly line a thousand other parents had used to address their late-rising teenagers, a phrase the adults found hilarious, their kids not quite as much.

"She's alive!"

Emily didn't pause, didn't turn, didn't reply. Rather, she proceeded directly to the cupboards, took down a bowl, poured herself some cereal, then over to the refrigerator for milk and juice, not once glancing at her mother. Satisfied, the bowl in one hand, a glass of OJ in the other and a spoon in her pocket, she headed back to the bedroom.

"Come on, Em. Eat out here. Watch a little football with me."

Emily paused, looked at her mom as though she'd just suggested the teen take up crochet. "Yuh, right. Since I've always been so interested in football."

"Come on, honey. Just sit and talk to me a minute."

"Why you watching football anyway? No stripper races on?"

"That's funny."

"Not really."

"Look," Ginny said, I made another mistake with another man in what probably seems like a pretty endless series of mistakes with men."

Emily set the bowl and glass down on the coffee table, folded her arms across her chest. "You think?"

"And I'm sorry. I'm so sorry. I'm sorry I'm such a lousy judge of men. I'm sorry I have a heart and I'm sorry it's so easily manipulated. But most of all, I'm sorry for you. My poor judgment has nothing to do with you. I love you unconditionally and it breaks this stupid heart of mine that my actions affect you."

Ginny looked like she might cry, something her daughter had not often seen. The young girl sat down next to her mother. Ginny wiped her eyes, tried to smile.

"Mom, you're supposed to be tough," said Emily. "You're a single mom raising a teenage girl. You're a waitress dealing with dumb men all the time. And you're Irish, for Christ's sake."

"I know, I know." Ginny shook her head, almost laughed between sniffles. Emily took a napkin from her other pocket, handed it to her mom. Ginny wiped her face, blew her nose. "I thought Max was different," she said. "So did you."

"Yeah, maybe I inherited your crappy judgment."

"Oh, God, I hope not."

Emily put her hand on Ginny's shoulder, looked her in the eyes. "You want some cereal?"

*

'Sully's was generally slow on Saturday afternoons. Max, after years of working weekends, had earned the Monday to Friday night shift, Millie had the days and Ginny could handle the bar in a pinch. Sully's twin nieces, Shannon and Shelly, were behind the taps on Saturday and Sunday nights, and though they weren't the quickest with a draft and had a tendency to gab rather than get, their fresh faces and sunny dispositions made up for any professional shortcomings. Sully himself manned the bar on weekend days, reliving his youth pouring suds at his father's pub. Usually he had time to putter, do some inventory, maybe tell a few jokes to the few customers that wandered in, but not on this Saturday. Not when every TV in the lounge was tuned to the big game and every stool occupied an hour before kickoff. Tony, Biz, Joey, Frannie, all the regulars, Miss Peabody and Mr. Vanderbilt, too. The tables and booths were full as well, most of the patrons outfitted in University sweatshirts and ball caps. Sully had been in the business long enough to know he would need help and had scheduled the girls early. If he could make it to halftime by himself, Shannon and Shelly would arrive like the cavalry.

Max had, in previous years, shown up for a few of these games, seating himself on the social side of the bar and immediately complaining about the service to anyone who'd listen. Sully would ignore him, then threaten to give him a beating and finally serve him a brew. Any stranger overhearing this exchange would probably wonder what sort of establishment they'd entered but the regulars loved it.

Sully was already sweating, racing back and forth with drinks, taking orders, trying to keep up but the boys did manage to get his attention for a quick minute.

"Max coming in, Sully?" asked Joey.

"He didn't say but I doubt it. The lad's been acting a bit off lately."

"What do you mean off?"

"I dunno'. You haven't noticed."

"No, no, we have," said Tony. "Ginny, too."

"Maybe they're finally together," said Biz.

"Oh," said Sully, "I don't think so. "Max has had a hard-on for that girl forever..."

"I beg your pardon," said Miss Peabody.

"Sorry, Miss P. I mean he's had a crush on Ginny. But she don't date co-workers," said Sully, before rushing off.

"Or customers," said Biz, sighing.

"That," said Miss Peabody, "is nonsense. You can't put boundaries on the human heart. The heart wants what the heart wants."

"That's right," said Frannie, "and so does the rest of the body."

"I'm not referring to lust, my dear. I'm speaking of love. Lust is fleeting, love is forever."

"Well put," said Mr. Vanderbilt.

Frannie was not convinced. "Well, forever can get a little old. Am I right, boys?"

The gang glanced at Miss P. before answering, the stern expression on the older woman's face obviously influencing their replies.

"I plead the fifth," said Tony.

"I fold," said Joey.

"Check, please," said Biz.

"Pussies," said Frannie, shaking her head.

"You know," said Biz, "it's funny. The women at my job have that same no dating co-workers rule."

"Well, of course the women where you work have that rule," Joey said. He glanced at Tony for the big man's approval.

Biz looked chagrined. "What is that supposed to mean?"

"No worries, Biz," said Tony. "All the female plumbers I work with have that same rule." Joey laughed out loud and Biz had to smile.

"Speaking of busting balls," he said, "wasn't Nuggets getting out of the hospital pretty soon?"

"Yuh, I thought it was this weekend, but maybe Monday. He'd be here if he was out."

"Chubster usually comes in, too. Usually has money on the game."

Miss P. sipped her drink. "That Chubster fellow has been acting rather strange lately. What do you suppose he's up to?"

"I have no idea," said Tony, "but you can bet whatever it is..."

Joey finished his sentence. "It's not good."

That, everyone felt, was deserving of a toast. They all knocked glasses and returned their attention to the screen.

✳

Big Bob had spent the first two quarters of the game sneaking peaks at Ebony and considering just what he'd do if she did, indeed, follow through on her proposal to storm the field. Would he help her? Should he help her? There was a decent chance he'd be escorted from the stadium and miss the fourth quarter. There was also the chance that assisting the crazy bombshell would be one of the most memorable things he'd ever done. Think of the stories, he told himself. Bob loved a good story, especially if he was doing the telling.

On the few occasions when Ebony caught Bob looking at her, she stared right back, smiling, licking her lips, batting her eyes, anything she could think of to encourage the big galoot. She was going to need help in a little while and she didn't want him to forget.

Big Bob's crew knew something was up. He wasn't pounding brews, wasn't hollering at the refs, wasn't even ogling the cheerleaders. Dewey elbowed him in the ribs. "Hey," he said, "are you even watching the game?"

"What?"

"The game. You're not paying attention. Are you actually considering helping that crazy chick?"

Bob glanced at Ebony who gave him a little wave. "What? No. Maybe. I don't know. She's not gonna' really do it anyway, right?"

Dewey was unconvinced. "That's not the point."

Feldman, an otherwise mild mannered CPA whose inner hooligan sometimes emerged at these sporting events, had apparently slipped a few nip bottles past the gate. He leaned across Dewey, his booze soaked breath a few inches from Bob's face.

"We should all run on the field," he said.

Dewey pushed him away. "You're drunk."

"We been talking about it for years. We should all do it." Feldman took another pull from the tiny bottle, offered it to Bob and Dewey. Dewey shook his head, drank his beer but Big Bob grabbed the bottle.

"What the Hell," he said, and finished the nip.

*

Hung Hong had never attended an American football game, never even watched one on TV. As the game went on, both his excitement and alcohol intake increased dramatically. By the time the second quarter came to an end, he was more than ready for his big moment, but was disappointed and confused when the players began to run off the field.

"What happening?" he asked of no one in particular.

"It's halftime," said a skinny young boy sitting nearby.

"Halftime?"

"Yuh. They play two quarters, then halftime, then two more quarters."

"Oh, I see. Thank you. How long halftime, please."

The boy turned to his father. "Dad?"

"Probably twelve, fifteen minutes. Plenty of time to go to the men's room, get a snack, whatever."

"Time for more beer?" said Hong.

The older man looked at his son, then at Hong. "Sure. Time for more beer. If you really think you need more beer."

"Yes, more beer very good. Almost time."

"Almost time for what?" asked the boy.

Hong stared out at the field. "You see."

*

Max had put down the spyglass, leaned back, tried to relax. Attempting to check up on his recruits in a crowd that size was pretty hopeless anyway, spyglass or no spyglass. And if he was focused on the stands, the fans around him would likely think he was some kind of loser, looking for hot chicks among the throngs. They may even remember him later and that was the last thing he wanted. He turned his attention to the marching band performing on the field below and then to the local youths in their over-sized shoulder pads and helmets, competing in the 'Punt, Pass & Kick' contest. But, as usual, his thoughts returned to Ginny. He took out his cellphone, hesitated, then sent her a quick text, 'Hey'. She texted back fairly quickly, 'Hey'. The fact that she texted back at all, Max felt, was somewhat surprising.

He typed: 'You're still mad, right?'

Another rapid response: 'Right.'

'Are you watching the game?'

'Yes. Where are you?'

'At the stadium.'

'What? Shouldn't you be home packing?'

'Yes. Probably should be.'

'???'

'Just couldn't miss this.'

'Doubt they'll show it on TV.'

'True. Ginny, I'm still sorry. I'll be sorry forever.'

Max stared at the phone as the seconds ticked by, surveyed the crowd, glanced at the field, then back at his cell. No reply.

*

Jim Eastman and Scooter Mackie had been broadcasting the University games for as long as anyone could remember. They'd outlasted coaches, athletic directors and a few TV stations as well. They'd called the games when the team was good and they'd called them when the team was bad. As Jim was fond of saying, they'd seen it all. There was, on occasion, a year when the team had jelled and was playing at a high level, winning often enough to bring National attention and causing Jim and Scooter to be replaced in the booth for a game by a couple of big guns from the network. This was not one of those years. The team was decent, as was their opponent, but no matter the year, and no matter the records, the rivalry with State was always huge. The fans were involved, the band was rocking, the play on the field intense, and as the first half concluded, Eastman and Scooter could not have been more pleased.

"Hell of a first half, Scooter," Jim told his sidekick and the listening audience. "Just as we expected. Every yard hotly contested. Looks like we've got an old fashioned barn burner on our hands. This one should go down to the wire."

"That's right, Jim. Games like this are what college football is all about and I feel privileged to be up here in the booth on this beautiful Fall day watching these kids play their hearts out. It just doesn't get any better than this."

"Couldn't have said it better myself, Scoot, and for an old tailback like yourself, this must be bringing back memories of your own gridiron glory."

"Well, the key word there being old, partner. These young men are bigger, faster, stronger than we ever were. And I'll tell you one thing, we never played in front of a crowd like this. These folks are into it."

"Yes sir, they are loud and proud and probably will be even more so in the second half. This is usually when I tell everyone to stay tuned and not go away but I don't think anyone watching this game is even considering that. So we'll be back in a few, ready for what should be a terrific second half."

Eastman and Scooter turned off their mics, noticed Georgie, their young spotter, staring through his binoculars at the stands below.

"What's up, Georgie," said Eastman. "Whataya' got there?"

Georgie spoke without lowering the specs. "There's a big, black lady in section twenty-eight and she just took off her sweatshirt and she's got the biggest melons I've ever seen and she's shaking them to the music and everybody's goin' crazy."

"Gimme' those," said Eastman, taking the binoculars from Georgie and focusing on Ebony's section. "Mother of mercy, George, you weren't lyin'. Bless her soul, that young gal is packin'!"

Scooter looked at his colleague, waited his turn. It could be, he felt, a while.

✻

Ginny was off the couch and into the kitchen as soon as the first half ended. Sitting still was proving difficult, anxious as she was for the third quarter to come and go and she certainly had no intention of listening to the blowhard Eastman and his sycophantic sidekick Scooter's inane patter. What kind of name for a grown man was Scooter anyway? She busied herself at the stove; perhaps something to eat would alleviate her restlessness, her state of agitation. Emily had kept her company for a quarter but Ginny took pity on the bored teen and let her go back to her bed and her phone. A nice grill cheese should fit the bill she figured. Why had Max texted her? What did he think, that they'd have a pleasant back and forth about his impending criminal enterprise and subsequent flight out of town? Was he stupid? Of course he was sorry. They're always sorry. Here's an idea, she thought, how about just not doing anything that you're going to be sorry for later.She plated the sandwich, grabbed another beer from the frig and, what the heck, a bag of chips, too. Why not? Maybe she'd let herself go, gain a few pounds. All her figure ever did was attract losers and liars anyway. By the time she returned to her seat the marching band had left the field, the 'Punt, Pass & Kick' kids were being ushered out, the trophies they now held nearly the size of the youths themselves. Ginny considered muting the sound on the television but thought better of it. When the third quarter ended and the shit really did hit the fan, the two nitwits in the booth wouldn't have a clue. Who knows, she figured, they might even be entertaining for a change.

✻

Eastman and Scooter had spent part of the break watching Ebony but still had time to grab a dog and a smoke before returning for the second half kickoff. The broadcasters were looking forward to the exciting conclusion of the game as was the rabid crowd. Some of those in the stands, however, were more concerned with the conclusion of the third quarter.

"All right, Scooter," said Eastman, "we're ready for the second half and it should be a doozy. So buckle up, folks, it could be a bumpy ride."

"Sweet Virginia pie!" said Scooter, a declaration that had somehow become his catchphrase though no one seemed to remember why. The two men called the action, the crowd roared its approval and the clock counted down the minutes. When the whistle blew to end the third quarter, Eastman and his color man prepared to go to commercial.

"That's the end of the third quarter and with the score tied seventeen to seventeen we, ah, hold on...Oh, some nutjob has run onto the field but, you know, we never give these bozos the satisfaction of being on the air so we'll be right back after this."

*

Max was not surprised that Hung Hong was the first one out of the stands. He was surprised, however, to see Hong hold out his palm to the group of security guards rushing toward him, then bend over and throw up on the sideline. The burly men in uniform, obviously not used to such a delaying tactic, hesitated just long enough for Hong to finish his alcoholic purge, straighten himself and take off like a jackrabbit. Max was surprised, as well, to look up and see thin gray plumes of smoke rising from outside every part of the stadium. And when, moments later, his gaze returned to the playing field, he was actually thrilled to watch as the rest of his troops were racing across the gridiron. The basketball players, the acrobats, the strippers, Tulip, Gooch, even Crazy Ed, they were all doing their best to evade the mounting forces in pursuit.

Nor had the landscapers chickened out. Teddy and Simon had jumped down, run toward each other, high-fived and taken off in different directions as fast as they could go. Vixen, Stormy and the rest of the dancers had left their sweatshirts behind and were brazenly waving to the crowd, their 'Bottoms Up' t-shirts and the bountiful racks within jiggling for all the world to see. Had he actually told the girls not to wear bras, Max wondered. He couldn't recall. The Babushkas were proving as elusive as Max had hoped, leaping and flipping over the guards like they were part of the act. The ballers were as quick on the field as they were on the court and Tulip was right there with them, step for step. Gooch, on the other hand, was as slow as he'd appeared and was soon surrounded, but he kept spinning like a top, getting all the 'GoPro' footage he could. Ribs had chosen an unusual maneuver, making his way to the fifty yard line, sitting down on the home team's logo and basically daring the staff to pick him up and carry him off.

Dozens more police and security personnel were pouring out of the stands and emerging from the tunnels. The smoke was growing thicker and the fans had begun to take notice. Ebony had worked her charms and Big Bob, Dewey and Feldman were gently lowering her onto the field. Once there, unnoticed for the moment, she began to skip and Big Bob, perhaps mesmerized by the sight of her incredible bouncing curves, made a decision that he might or might not live to regret. He turned to Dewey, Feldman, the rest of his crew and, in fact, anyone within hollering distance, and bellowed, "Let's go!" The big man went over the wall, followed swiftly by Dewey, Feldman, a few others and then, to Max's utter astonishment, almost the entire section. Like lemmings over a cliff, they flooded the field en mass, and once sections one twenty-seven and one twenty-nine realized what was happening, they, too, were storming the turf.

Jim Eastman had called a lot of games, seen a lot of amazing things both on and off the field in his time. After all, wasn't that one of the great appeals of sporting events, that every game was different. But in all his years announcing athletic contests, he'd never witnessed anything like this.

"We're back, folks," he said, "but man, oh, man, we may not be for long. We have numerous individuals out of the stands and onto the field. Whole sections are following suit. We've got smoke outside the stadium, maybe in the stadium, I don't know. It's like a riot here, friends. It's pandemonium!"

Scooter stared down from the booth as if in a trance. "Holy shit," he said. "Holy fucking shit!"

"Ah, yes," said Eastman. "Sorry about that, folks. He looked around the booth, noticed Georgie and the statisticians had jumped ship, came to the swift conclusion that he and Scooter should do the same. "Okay, that's it. We're out of here. Come on, Scooter." He took off his headphones, removed his shell shocked partner's as well, then pushed him out the door.

Max was in shock as well. Never in his wildest dreams had he imagined the scene he was now viewing. So many thrill seekers and drunken hooligans from all parts of the stadium had crashed the game that they now easily outnumbered the security guards and police details. Max had determined that the smoke rising all around was emanating from Chubster's troop of homeless pyromaniacs and their kindling filled shopping carts and that the stadium was not actually on fire. But the crowd didn't know that. If things got too crazy, he thought, people could get hurt. Thank God for the P.A. Announcer.

Primarily used for calling downs and distance, the booming sound overhead was the voice of reason. "Please stay calm. There is no fire. We repeat, there is no fire. Return to your seats or exit the stadium. You must vacate the field. If you leave the field, you will not be arrested. We repeat, leave the field immediately and you will not be arrested. Failure to do so in a timely manner will result in fines and possible jail time."

What a break, Max was thinking. He remembered reading something about herd mentality but King couldn't have planned this, could he? The sound of a text alert interrupted his thoughts. It was Ginny.

'What's happening? The network went off the air. Screen is black.'

Max typed quickly. 'They did it. They ran on the field. And lots more.'

'Lots more what?'

'Lots more people.'

'Are you kidding?'

'No. It worked. It's unbelievable!'

'Wish I could see it.'

Max was about to type a reply but heard a voice behind him. "Hey, asshole!"

He turned and there was Charles. Damn, he thought, just when things were going so well, though he was likely the only person amid the chaos all around who saw it that way. "Charles," he said. "What the...How'd you find me?"

"I told you. I find people. That's what I do. Besides, you ain't exactly James Bond. You met the guys on the same court we made the deal. You're pretty easy to follow."

Max considered that for a moment, shook his head, but why would he have suspected he was being tailed? Nuggets was down and out, Cranky Sam was undoubtedly involved in the robbery and Charles, well, Charles he'd been told, was standing down. "But Ribs said they spoke to you."

"That they did."

"And that you were cool. No more blackmail."

"They said that."

Max was almost yelling now. Conversing over the sound of the mob was becoming more difficult. "Yes, that was my understanding!"

Charles shook his head. "Miscommunication!"

"Mis...How did you get in here anyway?"

"Shit, man, they ain't exactly checking folks at the gate right now." He held open his jacket so Max could see the pistol tucked in his belt. "As you can plainly see."

"What do you want?"

"You know what I want. Let's go."

Max glanced at the craziness below. "We'll miss the end of the game."

"You're funny," said Charles without cracking a smile. "Come on."

Max took a last look. People were running in every direction, most climbing back into the stands, fleeing for the exits. He caught glimpses of his recruits making their escapes. Ribs had been abandoned by the guards and, after struggling to his feet, was casually walking off the field. Big Bob was clearing a lane for Ebony, a gentleman to the end. Maybe most members of the operation wouldn't need to be bailed out after all, though that, Max decided, would be small consolation if he was dead. He looked at Charles, nodded. Time to go.

No one paid attention to Max and Charles as they slowly made their way down from the mezzanine and toward the gates. Most in the ever fleeing crowd appeared solely concerned with exiting a stadium which they now believed to be either the center of a riot, the target of an unorthodox terrorist attack or the heart of a dawning inferno. Possibly all three. The crowd was so thick, Max considered making a run for it. It would be difficult for Charles to keep track of him in the chaotic scene surrounding them. But, Max felt, Charles, by all indications, was something of a loose cannon and the vision of him firing into the horde of innocents as Max fled, possibly hitting someone, perhaps fatally, would have been more than Max's overburdened conscience could bear.

They had passed through the turnstiles and onto the concourse, the streets outside a sea of ambulances, fire trucks and police cars, when Max heard another familiar voice, one that he'd truly hoped he'd never have the misfortune to hear again.

"Hey, asshole!"

No, he thought, this can't possibly be happening, as he turned to face his pint-sized nemesis, Cranky Sam, now for some reason outfitted in a football uniform – shirt, shoulder pads, cleats, everything but the helmet.

Max couldn't hide his displeasure. "Oh, Jesus."

"What," said Sam. "You're not happy to see me?"

Charles had no time for delays. "Who's this little fucker?"

Cranky Sam, surprisingly, did not immediately jump on the disrespectful blackmailer and pummel him, nor did he even take time to assault the gunman's testicles. Rather, he ignored Charles, his gaze never leaving Max.

"I was hoping I'd run into this asshole again."

"Well, sorry, junior, but he's my asshole right now."

Cranky Sam turned to Charles, his eyes blazing with rage. "This bastard fucked my wife!"

Charles looked at Max, incredulous. "You fucked a midget?"

"She's not a midget," shouted Max, "and no I didn't. I haven't done anything with her."

"Bullshit!" This from Sam.

"Well," said Charles, "I don't have time to deal with some angry half-pint."

"Don't call him that," said Max.

"Look, you two can figure out your shit some other time. Right now, we gotta' go. Sorry, little fucker."

Charles gave Max a push and they turned to go. He was probably quite surprised to suddenly feel a weight on his back and then two small but powerful arms wrapped around his neck. The crowd was probably surprised to see an infuriated little person taking a much larger man to the ground, the pistol spilling out of Charles hand and skidding across the concrete. Those who'd spotted the gun seemed to panic even more as Charles and Sam grappled on the pavement and Max, probably by now the most surprised of all, watched as Charles, face down on the filthy asphalt, bucked like a rodeo bronco, trying in vain to dislodge Cranky Sam from his back. Soda cups, empty popcorn boxes and hot dog wrappers flew all around as Charles struggled to his feet and spun around, the obstinate midget hanging on to his neck, the two now appearing like one of those cartoon clouds of action, the details of their struggles barely visible.

Max, having quickly weighed the alternatives, seized on that moment to make his escape. Hustling along with the other fans, he felt confident that the fight between the two stubborn sociopaths would be no rapid knockout. No, it had all the markings of an epic bout, a battle of blood and guts, a contest with Max's own head as the prize. Charles had been right; it was time to go.

Reaching the parking lot, he glanced back but was relieved to spot neither of his tormentors in pursuit. Curious as to who the fight's victor would be, but not curious enough to stick around and find out, he continued in his quest to remove himself from the vicinity of the stadium. There was no time to wonder why he'd chosen to ignore Chubster's advice and place himself at the scene of the crime. He had a getaway to make.

There was no chance he or anyone else would be hailing a cab. Emergency vehicles of every kind clogged the lot and surrounding roads, sirens blaring, lights flashing. The first responders paid no mind to Max as he maneuvered through police cars and fire engines, past ambulances and EMTs. And why would they? He was merely one of thousands fleeing alongside all the other terrorized fans, families trying desperately to stay together, older, slower folks struggling to remain upright and not knocked to the ground where it was questionable whether they would be helped up or stepped over. If King had planned and envisioned this scenario, Max felt, then he truly was a criminal mastermind, perhaps even a genius. And if they did indeed come away with all the concession cash and credit card receipts, and no one besides Sam and Charles sustained significant injuries, well then, he had to acknowledge at least a modicum of respect.

*

Normally at 'Sully's, if a big game's broadcast is interrupted by some bit of breaking news which the regulars deem unworthy of interest, then that unwanted break in the action would be greeted by a disapproving uproar throughout the bar. The current interruption, however, caused no such lamentations. The networks, apparently deciding that the chaos on the field was newsworthy and outweighed their policy of not televising athletic interlopers, were now showing as much of the bedlam as possible, and all eyes were turned to the scenes of mass confusion on every screen. Moreover, no one was loudly demanding that the damn network return to the game if, in fact, there was still a game, and judging by the evidence right in front of them, there probably was not.

"This is unfucking believable," said Joe.

Tony stared at the TV. "You think?"

Sully and his nieces were watching, too. Nobody was demanding a cocktail. Apparently there was a break in the drinking action as well.

"This is worse than back in the old country," said the big Irishman. "We've got plenty of soccer hooligans but usually just a dozen or so at a time. This is, this is…"

"Nuts," said Shannon.

"Yeah, that's right. Nuts."

"So this," said Miss Peabody, "is what they've been up to."

Mr. Vanderbilt gave her a look.

"What who's been up to?" asked Joe.

Mr. Vanderbilt spoke before Miss P. could answer. "This is what our American hooligans have been up to."

"We don't have American hooligans," said Tony.

Biz piped in. "We do now."

"Try another channel," said Frannie. "See if it's everywhere."

Sully used the remote to switch networks and sure enough, there was a different feed focused on a reporter standing just outside the parking lot, a young man who'd likely been in the vicinity and was now getting his big break. He was speaking into a microphone, gesturing to his surroundings.

"...As you can see behind me, the crowd is still pouring out and more and more first responders are arriving. It is obviously a chaotic scene here at the stadium but as far as we can tell this is not an act of terrorism. The small brush fires which caused the enormous amount of smoke have been extinguished, there is no evidence of gunfire or bombs and, miraculously, no serious injuries to report."

A voice-over from the anchor back at the news desk: "James, any word yet on what precipitated this mass exodus? We're receiving reports of fans invading the playing field."

"That's right, Chet, multiple sources have confirmed that a large group of fans, individuals scattered throughout the stadium made their way out of the stands and onto the field at the exact same time in some type of organized flash mob or something. And this was quickly followed by dozens of other ticket holders joining them, in some cases entire sections, virtually taking over the field and halting the game."

"Which would usually only occur at the end of a huge win. Anyone reporting a motive?"

"Not as of yet. Right now it's anyone's guess. Should be interesting as more information comes in."

"And no injuries you said. No one trampled? No one hurt resisting arrest?"

"Yes, Chet, that's true. Pretty amazing when you consider the size of this crowd but so far..."

The young reporter hesitated, distracted by a commotion behind him where a black man, Charles, had been leapt upon by a midget, the permanently irate Cranky Sam, and had been taken to the pavement once again. The reporter watched for a moment as Sam attempted to strangle Charles, then turned back to the camera.

"Ah, we may have to revise the injury report. Back to you, Chet."

The network shifted to the anchor desk where the well groomed and unflappable Chet Collins addressed the viewers. "Indeed we may. We will stay with this story as more updates come in. Back after this."

"Did you see that?" asked Joey.

"The fight?" said Tony.

"Yeah. You see the little guy?"

"The midget?"

"Yeah. I think that was the same guy."

"Same guy as what?"

"Same midget that kicked Nuggets."

"With the bombshell wife," stated Frannie.

"How could you tell? He was dressed in a football uniform."

"I know. That was weird. But I'm pretty sure."

"That guy has anger issues," said Biz.

"Well," said Sully, "he is a midget, isn't he?"

"What's that supposed to mean?"

"He's probably mad at the world. Figures he got a bum deal. Always gettin' stared at, made fun of."

Biz disagreed. "I would think bein' a midget and all, he'd be extra nice."

"How so?" asked Joey.

"It's like with fat people and ugly people. If you're not attractive, you usually try to be popular by being pleasant and courteous. If you're good looking, you don't have to be nice. You just get by on your appearance. You could be a total asshole, long as you look like George Clooney, you'll do just fine."

"What about Ginny," said Tony. "She's super good looking and she's super nice."

"I didn't say pretty people can't be nice. Just that it's more important for the rest of us."

Biz sipped his beer, contemplating the ramifications of his own argument.

Frannie spoke up. "You know, he's got a good point there. I've slept with a couple of threes just cause they were nice guys."

"Yah," said Joey, "but are all midgets necessarily unattractive? That seems kind of discriminatory."

Frannie again. "Well, I've never done one."

"Oh, boy," Sully said, turning to fetch more drinks.

"Hold on a sec," said Joey. "What if you're an ugly asshole but you're rich?"

"Exception to the rule," said Biz. "If you're rich, you don't have to be nice to anyone and you'll still be popular."

"I must say," said Mr. Vanderbilt, "this is a rather depressing conversation."

Tony ignored him. "I'll tell you another thing. If I had a wife like that little bastard has, I'd never be angry."

"You mean," said Frannie, "the same wife that wants Max to give her the high, hard one?"

Tony shook his head. "Oh, yeah, forgot about that."

"Speaking of Max," said Miss Peabody, doesn't he usually come in and watch the big games with you?"

"Yeah, usually. But who knows, maybe he got a ticket. Hope he didn't run into the midget."

"Or his wife."

Everyone laughed, turned back to the television, an act so synchronized they could have been liquored up 'Rockettes'.

*

Ginny, too, had switched channels. Every network was, naturally, on the scene or as close as they could get. Ginny was amazed by what she was watching, transfixed, the half eaten grilled cheese growing cold on the table before her. And if she was amazed, she thought, someone who was in on the plot, who had an idea of what was coming, what then was every other viewer thinking? It looked like something out of a 'Marvel' movie – chaos, panic, sirens sounding, emergency vehicles hurrying every which way. All that was missing was an outlandish super villain claiming responsibility and demanding a ransom to spare the city. Ginny turned up the sound.

A young reporter on screen was trying to maintain her composure as people rushed by all around her. She gripped the microphone tightly; she'd been pushed and jostled throughout the remote. She would have liked to grab an interview or two but no one was stopping to talk. She paused, held her earpiece for a moment, then began.

"This just in. Not only is this no longer considered an act of terrorism or some kind of spontaneous riot, it now appears to be all part of a well planned heist. We've learned that the stadium's counting rooms were compromised during the chaos and a significant amount of money has been stolen. Details are sketchy right now..."

She was interrupted by a voice-over, no doubt emanating from the station's newsroom. "Gina, do yet have any idea what sort of amount we're talking here? And who, or how many robbers were involved?"

"Well, it's my understanding that all the day's proceeds are funneled to what was thought to be very secure areas inside the stadium. So, a hundred thousand fans spending money on concessions and souvenirs, not to mention all the credit card receipts that have now been breached, well, you do the math. As far as suspects, no word yet but my guess is at least some kind of inside job. But Ken, this whole thing is still a mystery. How the storming of the field, the brush fires outside, the robbery itself, whether they were all connected and how and by who, obviously a lot of questions and not many answers."

"Thanks, Gina. Stay with us for more on this developing story."

The network went to commercial, giving Ginny moment to pause. A lot had happened in one short week. First she was an old school waitress taking orders and clearing tables. Then she was part of the underground film industry, or at least she thought she was. Next, one half of a budding romance that proved short lived. And finally, accessory to the biggest crime the city had seen in years. She took a long pull from her beer bottle, looked at the sandwich, picked up the remote instead and tried another channel. She'd never been one for speaking to herself out loud but the image on the screen seemed to call for just that.

"Oh, my God," Ginny said to absolutely no one. "Are you fucking kidding me!"

The network's on site reporter had found someone to interview and that someone was familiar to Ginny. Ebony appeared quite content to participate in the remote, smiling and preening for the camera, plumping her hair, adjusting her curves and occasionally glancing over at a large man wearing a University jacket and giving her a 'thumbs up'.

"I'm here with Ebony, uh, Miss Ebony, ah..."

"Just Ebony, honey."

"Okay, I'm here with Ebony and she claims to have been one of the first fans on the field. Is that right?"

"That's right. Me and the girls were out there soon as that third period whistle blew."

"You mean the third quarter?"

"Yup. We were all over that field."

"And the girls are?"

"The girls from 'Bottoms Up.'" Ebony pointed to the letters spelled out across her chest. "You know, the dancers from the club. Corner of Sixth Street and Industrial Way. Open every day from noon to two A.M."

"Okay, I'm guessing that's a gentlemen's club."

"No guessing needed, sugar."

"And can you tell our viewers why you and the, ah, girls, ran on the field?"

"For the movie."

Ginny, out loud again. "Oh, Jesus."

"For the movie. What movie?"

"The picture we was making for Last Nickel Productions. It's what you call an underground film. Low budget."

The reporter was momentarily taken aback but recovered quickly. "And were all the people on the field part of the film?"

"Oh, I don't think so. I know I was the only one from my section, least the only one getting paid."

More surprise. "You were getting paid?"

"Ooops," said Ebony, grinning. "Not really. I was kidding."

The reporter paused, cocked her head, adjusted her earpiece. "Ah, Miss Ebony, I'm being told to ask if you and the girls were the same strippers, ah, I mean dancers, seen on the internet recently racing down a city street at night, in some kind of competition?"

"Well, I didn't have to race. They put me in the movie with no tryout, 'cause, you know, I have, you know, star quality." Ebony glanced over at Big Bob, who was nodding like a bobblehead.

"Right," Ginny said to the TV.

"But," continued Ebony, "those were my bitches you saw racing. Oh, can I say bitches?" She waved to the camera. "Hi, girls. And we got some pretty fast ladies, I'll tell you what. Come down the club and see for yourself."

"And you weren't aware of, or involved in, the robbery that took place inside the stadium?"

Ebony's smile disappeared for the first time, "What? Robbery? I don't know nothin' about that. Less it was part of the film."

"Well, Miss Ebony," said the reporter, "thank you. Thank you very much. That was, ah, enlightening."

Ebony's smile returned. "Thank you."

Ginny was shaken. She was at that strip club. She'd helped recruit Ebony and the others and now here was the plus-sized dancer telling all the world. What was next? She was afraid to change channels, fearful she might encounter the basketball players signing autographs or, Heaven forbid, Teddy the college boy giving her a shout out on national TV. She got up, walked to the kitchen, then back again; she needed time to think. She badly wanted to text Max. But why? What was the point? She'd gotten all the information she wanted from the reporters. Besides, for all she knew, he could be in custody right now, handcuffed in some small interrogation room, being questioned unmercifully until he gave the bulldog cops a name, any name, her name. No, she decided, he would never do that. Or would he? She'd been wrong before. What then? Was she actually hoping he'd met with Chubster, received his share of the loot and was on his way to the airport, never to be seen again?

Ginny was pacing and cursing when Emily reemerged, the young girl bewildered not just by her mother's profane words but by the fact they were being uttered out loud. "Jesus, Mom," she said.

"Oh, sorry, honey. I, uh..."

"What happened?"

"Oh, I don't know. Just, you know, having a bad day."

Mothers and daughters generally can tell when one or the other is lying, Emily being no exception to the rule, but the teen determined to play along this time. "You think you're having a bad day. Did you see the news?"

"Um, yeah. You mean the stadium?"

"Yuh, the stadium. It's like a riot down there."

Ginny tried to busy herself, brushing crumbs from the table onto her plate and carrying it to the kitchen. "Yeah, awful. Terrible. It's all over the TV."

Emily had heard enough. "Mom, you know some of those girls who ran on the field were the strippers from your race the other night."

"Really?" Ginny was cornered, almost ready to give up. Who was she kidding? Emily was a smart young lady.

"Yeah. One of them even claimed they were making a movie. How about that?" Emily folded her arms, stared at her mother, waited for her to crack. "Mom, didn't we just talk about this? Honesty, remember?"

"You're right," said Ginny. "You're right. "But, ah, you should probably sit down."

✳

Max, too, was watching TV. Seated at a dingy men's bar a couple miles from the stadium, a cold beer and an ice water in front of him, he awaited Chubster's arrival. It had been a long walk, no cabs available, no public transportation running, and had been especially taxing since Max had maintained a brisk pace and constant lookout for his two unhinged stalkers.

He had not yet seen Ebony's interview but was aware that the slow-footed

271

Gooch had been one of the only participants taken into custody. The authorities confiscated the big oaf's 'GoPro' and the footage within and were now showing it on the newscasts, asking for help in identifying suspects. Thankfully, thought Max, Gooch was no expert and his inexperience and manic attempts to elude the guards by zigging and zagging had succeeded in making the majority of the video an indistinct blur.

Max was trying to piece together the particulars of the robbery, using bits of information gleaned from the competing networks when he was joined at the bar by the ever excitable Chubster McGee. The talkative idea man had changed out of his hobo attire and back into his everyday clothes though, Max noted, in their current surroundings it was hardly necessary.

"You watching this?" asked Chub.

Max gave him a look, beckoned the bartender and bought his friend a cold one.

Chubster stared up at the screen. "I can't believe this worked."

"What?" Max tried to keep his voice low though none of the other patrons seemed interested in what he had to say; they were all mesmerized by the continuous updates. "You said this was a great plan, easy, a sure thing."

"I never said sure thing."

"Well, you inferred it." Now it was Chubster's turn to give Max a look. "So," Max continued, "how'd they do it?"

"How'd who do what?"

"You know, how'd they get the money?"

"I can't tell you that."

"Why not?"

"Because. We went over this at the meeting. No one knows anything they don't need to know. That way no one can tell everything even if they are, let's say, under duress."

Max nodded, sipped his water, then his beer. Various law enforcement big shots were beginning to hold their briefings, offering the usual vague details and asking for the usual help in identifying and apprehending the bad guys. Damn, thought Max, I'm one of the bad guys. He turned to Chubster.

"I got a theory."

"I don't care."

"I think it was Cranky Sam and his boys. And I think Duffy got 'em into the counting rooms. What I can't figure out is how."

Chubster eyed Max seriously. "You getting out of Dodge after this?"

"That's the idea."

"Ah, what the Hell. They'll have it on the news eventually anyways. But you didn't hear it from me. You understand?" Max nodded like a dog waiting for his next treat. "You remember the 'Punt, Pass & Kick' kids?"

"No way," said Max.

"You were right about Sam. Duffy dressed 'em up in pads and helmets, uniforms, the whole deal, convinced the counting guards it was the only safe place for 'em, what with the riot and everything."

"Unbelievable. I was wondering why the little bastard was dressed like that."

"What little bastard?"

"Sam. He found me in the stands."

"He didn't go up?"

Max was confused. "Up? Up where?"

"Never mind. What happened? You get in a fight?"

"No. But if I didn't have another maniac after me, I wouldn't be sitting here right now."

"Another maniac?"

"Forget it. Long story. You have the money?"

"Not in this dump I don't. But it's close."

Max didn't like the sound of that. He'd watched far too many movies and TV shows where, friends or no friends, the criminals always seemed to be double-crossing each other for extra shares of the loot. Chubster must have read his mind.

"Don't worry," he said. "Nobody's setting you up. King's a man of his word, honor among thieves and all that. You'll get your money. Everybody gets their money."

Max looked hurt. "I didn't say anything."

"You didn't have to. I'd be thinking the same thing." Chubster glanced at his watch. "Soon as I get the word, we go."

Max nodded and both men resumed drinking and watched as another newscaster broke in with new footage. "This just in, folks. As you can see, a variety of helicopters flew over the stadium during the melee, most of them, like ours, belonging to local news stations. However, if you look at the copter on the far right, you'll see it has no logo. Now watch." The helicopter flew low, dangled a long rope ladder to the ground and hovered.

"What the..." said Max.

The 'Punt, Pass & Kick' kids, actually Cranky Sam's minions, still in uniforms and helmets, each of them with three large gym bags strapped to their bodies, began clambering up the ladder.

The reporter continued. "What was originally thought to be a daring rescue of the young 'Punt, Pass & Kick' contestants is now considered to be all part of the robbery, a way to get the stolen money out of the stadium."

"Genius," said Chubster, a look of outright admiration on his face.

"That's what you meant by up," said Max.

The broadcaster seemed impressed as well. "These crooks apparently thought of everything. Of course if you have any information concerning the location of that helicopter or the pint-sized thieves, please contact the police. We'll have more news as it comes in."

Max shook his head. "Unbelievable."

Chubster smiled. "Pretty cool, huh?"

"Well, that wasn't the word I was thinking, but yeah, I guess, pretty cool."

Max and Chubster took a drink as Gooch's indistinguishable footage returned to the screen.

"Can you believe this," said Chubster. "One of these nitwits was wearing a 'GoPro."

"Yeah, what a moron."

"He was your moron, wasn't he?"

Max nodded. "Yup."

Chubster laughed, patted Max on the back. The successful heist had put him in a good mood. "Don't worry. You did great. The movie idea was brilliant. It's all good."

Max was unconvinced. No one had their money yet and no one was out of town. This thing, he felt, was far from over. He was still considering all the things that could go wrong when Chubster again looked at his watch.

"Okay. Time to go. Drink up."

Max downed his beer, threw a twenty on the bar and the two were out the door, greeted by likely the first stretch limo to ever pull up in front of that dilapidated dive. Mr. Doe, King's bodyguard, was holding the door to the car open, silent as ever, serious as a cigar store Indian.

Climbing in, Max was only slightly surprised to see King, the big man dapper as always, a gold plated walking stick in one hand, a glass of champagne in the other. "Gentlemen," he said, motioning for the two to sit. "Champagne?"

"Oh," said Chubster, "we just had beers. Probably shouldn't mix."

Max glanced at his friend. What was this, Chubster finally showing some restraint? King set his own glass down, picked up two others and the bottle as Mr. Doe, who'd seated himself at the steering wheel, pulled away from the curb. "I insist," said the genteel crime boss. Neither Max nor Chubster were prepared to argue; instead they simply shrugged and accepted the glasses, each filled to the brim.

"A toast," said King, "to a job well done."

"Pardon me for saying," said Max, sipping the bubbly, "and don't take this the wrong way, but this is the second time I've seen you since the meeting where you said we'd never see each other again, that that would be for the best."

"Very true, Max, very true. However, I felt compelled to congratulate you in person. I must admit I was a bit concerned following the rather indiscreet video featuring your erotic dancing friends, but in the end you came through just as Mr. McGee said you would. I'm proud of you both."

All right, thought Max. This was weird. Getting a pat on the back from the person responsible for Duffy's broken thumbs was not what he'd expected. It was as if King fancied himself the CEO of some crime corporation and was about to bestow bonuses, or perhaps promotions on his employees. All well and good, but the only thing Max wanted at this point was his money and his freedom. He was done.

"Now then," said King, "may I inquire as to your plans?"

"Plans?"

"Yes, plans, intentions. What is next?"

Chubster spoke first. "I intend to get the Hell out of town, a long way out of town, as soon as you give me my money."

"Very good. And you, Max."

"Same. But I have to pay my runners so, you know, could take a little time."

"Well, don't take too long. Many people are going to be asking many questions and I fear that some of your, shall we say, amateur associates, are not used to being interviewed in the manner they might encounter."

"Understood."

"Wonderful." King pulled two thin briefcases from under his seat and handed them to Max and Chubster. Chubster opened his, peered in, Max did not.

Chubster looked annoyed. "There's nothing in here."

"Au contraire. You'll notice a small pouch in the bottom. In it you'll find a key to a locker at the bus terminal. Your share is in that locker. The briefcase is merely a means for safekeeping, a receptacle for the large amount of cash you'll be traveling with."

Max couldn't tell whether Chubster was satisfied with King's explanation or not. He opened his own briefcase, was surprised to see that it did contain some money.

"Max, yours has a bus locker key as well but we've also enclosed the necessary funds to pay your recruits as promised. Now, I suspect you are thinking, how do I know my shares will actually be in those bus lockers. Here is where a bit of trust comes into play, and wouldn't it be a sad, sad world if we were unable to trust our co-workers."

Did he really just call us co-workers, Max asked himself.

King continued. "So, gentlemen, you have my word. And in this life, all a man truly has is his health and his word. Your reward awaits you, fair and square as they say." They could feel the limo slowing down and pulling over, coming to a stop. "Thus ends our pleasant and lucrative relationship. I wish you both a marvelous future, one in which you will never have cause to utter my name."

Max had one last question. "What about Cranky Sam?"

"Ah, yes," said King. "No need to worry about him for the time being. I'm afraid he's in the hands of the authorities. Appears he was involved in a totally unrelated scuffle with some other hothead upon whom he inflicted a great deal of bodily harm. Both men are locked up and Sam's prior incidents and lengthy record being what they are, his bail is quite high. I don't think he'll be getting out anytime soon."

"I thought," said Chubster, "you were bailing out anyone who got caught."

"Anyone who got caught as part of our project. Cranky Sam's arrest had nothing to do with the task he was hired for."

"He's gonna' be pissed," said Chubster.

"Oh, he usually is."

"But," Max said, "then he might talk."

King found that amusing. "Oh, my, no. Samuel is old school and though he certainly possesses his fair share of character flaws and distasteful personality traits, he is efficient and loyal to a fault."

"He had a few choice words to describe you."

"I'm sure he did. Moreover, he is not a fan of law enforcement and would never deem to assist them in any way possible..."

"Well, that's a relief."

"Even," King continued, "if it meant bringing down the man he suspects of having relations with his wife."

"Oh," said Max. He wondered if the big man had smiled slightly or was it his imagination? No matter, it was time to go. Mr. Doe opened the door from the outside and stood like a sentry.

"Gentlemen," said King, "good luck."

Max and Chubster clambered out, stood straightening themselves without so much as a nod from the stoic bodyguard. As usual, Max couldn't resist, addressed the mute henchman.

"Okay then, I gotta' say it's been great working with you. I've especially enjoyed our little chats. We should stay in touch, really. Are you on 'FaceBook'?"

Chubster grabbed Max's arm, tugged him away as Mr. Doe closed the door, then went around to the front and resumed his position in the driver's seat, unamused as ever.

Chubster was unamused as well. "Come on. What the Hell is wrong with you? You think this is a joke?"

"I don't know. King was in a good mood, very pleasant."

"For now."

"What do you mean for now?"

"He just made a bundle and everything went well so of course he's in a good mood. But things can go wrong in a hurry. So just do your thing, hand out the dough and then scoot. That fucking midget is going to get out eventually and I doubt you want to be around for that. He's going to have a lot of pent up anger to release."

"Okay, okay, fine. Calm down, I'm going. Will I see you again?"

"Not unless I fuck up." Chubster took a breath, settled down. "Look, Max, it worked. It all worked. Now go enjoy your reward, you know, find a girl, raise a family, whatever, have a great life. Just don't do it here."

The quick talking idea man stuck out his hand and Max shook it. But as Chubster McGee hurried away and out of Max's life, the only bit of advice he'd really taken to heart was to find a girl. Wasn't that what he'd already done?

*

Max got busy. He felt sure handing out the money would be the best part of his stressful week. He mostly walked the streets, only occasionally catching a short cab ride. Everyone he passed seemed to be in a hurry and police cars still raced by in all directions. Though he was on a schedule of sorts, he could take his time, unnoticed, just another middle-aged, blue collar guy in a city full of them. No one, least of all the law, knew that without his efforts, none of the days events would have taken place. No one would have charged the field, no riot would have broken out, no robbery would have occurred. Or would it? Was he giving himself too much credit? Wouldn't they simply have chosen some other smooth talking orchestrator? Nuggets most certainly would have taken the gig. And besides, he asked himself, was he actually taking pride in what he'd done? He'd been trying for years to convince himself that bartending wasn't only a profession that helped people spend their time and money on booze, a job that enabled alcoholics and wastrels alike, but rather was a boon to mankind, a career in which entertaining patrons, taking confessions and supplying free therapy sessions was surely of some service. And now, there he was, congratulating himself on his first foray into criminal conspiracy. That was not the direction he'd expected his life to take.

First stop on the payoff trail was Lucy's house, where Max was greeted by most of the girls with great salutations and an extraordinary amount of hugs and kisses. The dancers led him to the dining room where they had obviously been celebrating their cinematic debuts with numerous bottles of champagne and a hastily laid out buffet of snacks. Lucy's mom, a short energetic woman, was bustling about, clearing plates and filling glasses, apparently under the impression her daughter and friends were budding actresses. Max was enjoying some bubbly himself when the doorbell rang. He surveyed the room. How had he not noticed Ebony's absence? He wondered if she'd been arrested but only for a moment, putting that thought to rest when the big girl and Stormy walked in. The other dancers were glad to see them, but Ebony was more concerned with Max.

"How come you didn't tell us about no robbery?"

"What?" said Max, finally short on words.

Stormy looked even angrier than usual. "You said we were making a movie."

Max looked around, the other dancers puzzled, not quite as thrilled with him as before, Lucy's mom suddenly motionless. "We were. We did."

Ebony shook her head. "Haven't you people been watchin' the news?"

"We were," said Vixen. "We turned it off."

"Somebody robbed that stadium. They got a shitload of money."

"Must have been the rioters," said Max. "That was not part of the film."

Stormy folded her arms, looked straight at him. "I don't believe there was any damn movie. I think this was all a setup to steal that money. We were nothing but a goddamn distraction."

"But," said Lucy's mom, an expression of parental disappointment on her face, "I thought you were all actresses."

Stormy again. "What? Who's this crazy lady?"

"Don't you call my mom a crazy lady," said Lucy.

"Be quiet, Stormy," Ebony said, turning to Max. "Now, Mr. Johnson, if that's even your real name, why don't you tell us the truth."

This was supposed to be the fun part, wasn't it, thought Max. Champagne, money, snacks. "Look," he said, "there was filming. They even showed some of the footage on TV."

"That blurry shit?"

"The bottom line is none of you had anything to do with that robbery."

"We know that," said Ebony. "The police don't."

"Yeah," Stormy added, "they may think we're some kind of accessory."

Lucy's mom was still in a state of shock. She looked at her daughter, shook her head. "You're not an actress? You're a robber?"

"No, mom. I'm not a robber. I'm a stripper." Lucy regretted the words as soon as they left her mouth. Her poor mother put her hand to her forehead, slumped into a chair, grabbed a glass.

"All right, all right," said Max, "let's just everybody take a breath and settle down. Everything went well, nobody got hurt, nobody got arrested, so why don't I just hand out the money. How's that?"

That appeared to have a calming affect on the group so Max set the briefcase on the table. Thank God, he thought, that he'd stopped in a bank and sorted the cash into envelopes, each runner's name imprinted in the corner. He imagined that the sight of that many bills may have inflamed the ladies further. Momentarily distracted from Ebony's robbery revelation, the girls busied themselves opening their envelopes, counting their shares. Max had been around tipped workers long enough to know people liked cash. They liked to look at it, they liked to count it, they liked to put it in order, fold it up. Most of all, they liked to have it. But he was smart enough to realize the air of satisfaction he'd created was fleeting, another diversion.

He began to go over various scenarios in his head. In the first, the dancers demand the rest of the money and Max acquiesces. Screw all the other runners, he says, it's all for us. Why not; he'd already misplaced his moral compass. He and the girls proceed to party hard and soon they're all hammered and he's the only man in a house full of horny strippers and...

In the second scenario, he's tied to a chair as they discuss what to do with him, all options seemingly on the table. Someone suggests turning him in to the authorities to collect the reward. Someone else says what reward, no one said anything about a reward. And the first person says there's always a reward. But Stormy and a couple others just want to keep all the money and get rid of him. How do we do it, asks someone and that discussion begins...

In the third scenario, the one Max decides to make happen, he slowly edges his way to the dining room's doorway, locked briefcase in hand, the girls preoccupied with their loot and then boom, he turns and takes off, down the hallway and out the front door. The way Max had envisioned the escape, he's on the run for precious minutes before his absence is noticed. In reality, the pursuit was almost immediate. Stormy, her skeptical nature developed over countless hours dealing with big talkers, liars and creeps, had kept an eye on Max even as she made sure she'd been paid what she was promised.

"Hey!" she yelled. "Come back here!"

Max, only seconds away, heard her but didn't stop. He'd seen hundreds of movies where somebody runs away and their captor yells 'come back here!' but the escapee never stops and never goes back there. Max had no intention of being the first to do so.

"Motherfucker!" said Ebony as Stormy and the others sprinted out of the house. They quickly spotted Max and the chase was on, like some sort of R rated 'Keystone Cops' short, scantily clad young women, bouncing and jiggling, hot on the heels of a middle-aged man carrying a briefcase. Cars slowed and pedestrians gawked. Max hadn't run like that since High School football and now he was carrying a satchel instead of a pigskin. Why, he wondered, did he have to recruit such speedy strippers but, of course, he knew the answer. The dancers were younger and in better shape than he was; evasive tactics were called for. He ducked behind a triple-decker and charged down a long driveway, ignoring the sounds of barking dogs, and leaped over a hedge like it was a linebacker coming in low. He rolled under a tier of rose bushes, laid still, silent as possible, enduring the cuts of a dozen thorns while contemplating his current circumstance. Wasn't it only a short time ago that he had been the man, the recipient of warmth and affection, the toast of the town? And there he was, sprawled among dog poop and anthills like some fugitive from a chain gang who hadn't yet made his way to the river. Was it all worth it? Could he have a do-over? His ruminations were cut short by the girls' voices growing near.

He tried not to breathe, focused on the rivulets of blood trickling down his forearms.

"Where the Hell is he?" said Stormy. "He couldn't have got far."

"I don't understand," said Lucy. "What difference does it make? We got our money."

"We got chump change! That stadium was packed. They probably got a million bucks at least. That motherfucker used us!"

Max heard Ebony breathing hard, just then catching up. "Any sign of him?"

"Not yet," said Stormy. "But we're gonna' find him. And when we do, I'm gonna' tear his balls right off. You wait and see."

Max winced, tried not to move. What was with all the focus on balls of late? He liked his balls, always had, was not keen on the idea of losing them.

"Come on," said Stormy. "Let's spread out. He's around here somewhere."

Max watched the girls fan out but Ebony stayed behind. "I'm just gonna' rest a minute. I'll catch up." She sat herself on a large rock, mere yards from Max, and called out. "Oh, Jimmie! Mr. Johnson! I know you're out here. Come out, give us the money and I won't let Stormy rip your balls off."

Max considered the offer but he wasn't sure about Ebony and he certainly didn't trust Stormy. No, he decided, he'd take his chances, wait them out, then make his move. Sure enough, after a brief rest, Ebony sighed, pushed herself up and wandered off down the driveway. Max waited just the same; a few extra minutes weren't going to make a difference at that point.

Trusting the coast was clear, Max raised himself up, careful not to place his palms in poop. Bad enough he was dirty and bloody, no need to smell shitty, too. Unsure which way to go, he elected to avoid the main streets, stealthily making his way through backyards, passing swing-sets, old sheds and above ground pools, praying he'd not encounter any large, loud dogs.

Emerging onto a quiet cul-de-sac, he took note of the address, called a cab, leaned against a tree and waited. One oblivious old-timer washing his car, a couple kids on bicycles but no sign of the stripper posse. The wait seemed interminable and the last thing Max wanted at that point was more time to dwell on what he'd done or what he was going to do. He wished he could take a long nap, maybe wake up and realize the whole week had been a bad dream and he could return to his perfectly ordinary life at the bar. But real life wasn't like a lousy TV show. The week had been no dream. The cab pulled up. He brushed himself off and got in.

*

Max had arranged to meet the basketball players at a different location, an inner city playground where a white person like himself might stand out some but, considering all that had gone on at the school court, he'd decided to take his chances.

The ballers were all there, even Ribs, though a pair of handcuffs dangled from one wrist. Some of the men were shooting hoops while others sat on benches, possibly discussing the day's events but one thing was certain; they were excited to see Max.

"There's the man with the plan," said Ribs, pausing as Max drew closer. "Shit, man, what happened to you?"

"Long story," said Max.

"You get beat up, too?" asked Rufus.

"What?"

"Charles in the hospital. Got beat up by a munchkin."

"Don't call him that."

"Don't call who what?"

"The munchkin, I mean midget. He's a midget."

"What's the difference?"

"Never mind," said Max. "You guys told me you spoke to Charles, said he wouldn't be a problem."

"Well, apparently he wasn't no problem for that dwarf."

Everyone but Max laughed. "Midget."

"What?"

"Forget it." Max looked at Rib's handcuffs. "What's that all about?"

Ribs fiddled with the cuffs. "Them security dudes had a hold of me, putting the cuffs on and everything but then the shit hit the fan. They saw the smoke and they saw all them fans runnin' at 'em, they took off like poodles from a pitbull. You didn't mention no fires being in the movie. You get some good footage?"

Jesus, Max thought, they still believed they were making a movie. Was it possible they hadn't seen a TV yet or heard a radio. If that was the case, he needed to move quickly.

"Oh, yeah," he said, "the film's gonna' be great. Great finale. Who knew that many fans would follow you guys onto the field. And none of them are even getting paid."

"Speaking of which," said Ribs.

Max sat down on a bench, the briefcase on his lap, and opened it so its contents were somewhat shielded from the players. No need for enticement, he'd figured, everything seeming fairly civil at that point. He pulled out an envelope, read the name inscribed. "Rufus." Rufus stepped up and Max handed him his reward like he was giving out diplomas, looked the young man in the eye and said "good work." Soon, everyone had received their cash and were happily deciding how to spend it. Max shut the briefcase, locked it and stood.

"Okay, gentlemen," he said. "Great job today. I'll stop by the school court when I know the release date for the film. And when Charles gets out of the hospital, can someone try and talk some sense into him?"

"We already tried that. Maybe you should get yourself an itty-bitty body guard."

Max ignored the laughter. "All right. Talk later."

"Hey, Johnson," said Ribs, "there's more money in that briefcase, ain't there?"

Oh, boy, thought Max, here we go. He should have known; this distribution had gone way too smoothly. "It's for the other runners."

"Really," Ribs said.

"Yeah, really," said Max.

Ribs smiled. "Take it easy, man. I'm just playin' with you. Now get outa' here before somebody less honorable than us notices your lily white ass. And let us know if you need us for another movie."

Max was relieved, tried not to show it. "Will do," he said, and quickly took his leave.

✶

Ginny couldn't sit still. She tried to eat, tried to read, tried to relax. She needed a joint, a valium, a quaalude, anything to calm her nerves. But it had been so long since she'd done any of those things, she wouldn't know where to begin. She wasn't going down to the corner, that was for sure. She was an adult now, an adult with a daughter. No, it would have to be three fingers of Irish whiskey and if that didn't work, well, maybe another three. She kept returning to the couch, turning on the TV, changing channels with the remote, her arm thrust forward like she was firing bullets. The heist was still all over the news and that's what it was now, a heist. No more shenanigans, no more spontaneous riot, no more accidental brush fires. This, the commentators said, had been a well thought out robbery, aided by some remarkable diversionary tactics. Rumors of the amount stolen were all over the map. Some said hundreds of thousands, others claimed millions, and everyone who'd been there and used a credit card was concerned as well.

Ginny wanted desperately to go to the bar, talk to Sully and the gang, see what everyone thought, or even suspected. But she wasn't due in until Monday and she'd not made a habit of hanging out at her place of employment on her day off. Young cooks and waitresses did that, not seasoned veterans like herself. Too many ways to get into trouble, which is fine when you're twenty-two but not so much when you're thirty-eight. She could, of course, claim that she'd gone in for her check but that would likely appear strange, too. Again, she wasn't a fresh-faced party girl blowing her tips on clubs and drugs. She didn't live paycheck to paycheck and everyone knew it. No, she'd just have to wait it out, show up for work on Monday. Would Max show up, she wondered. That was the question.

*

The Babushkas were waiting for Max in the Chinese grocery where they'd previously met, but there was no sign of Hung Hong. The young man, Max theorized, was likely still basking in his fifteen minutes of fame. The acrobats appeared anxious, nervously sipping from small cups of tea, and burst into simultaneous chatter upon Max's arrival. Unlike the basketball players, they took no note of Max's disheveled clothing or scraped skin. Max, as usual, attempted to stay calm.

"Hold on, boys, take it easy," he said.

"How we take it easy?" asked Bishku, obviously agitated. "Look at this." He held out his cellphone, the small screen facing Max as video began of the Babushkas doing their thing on the field, running, jumping, flipping and tumbling as the crowd roared in the background. "You see, we are everywhere, everyone see us. We are virus!"

"Viral," said Max, trying to keep his cool.

"Yes, we are on world of web. And now we are thieves!"

With this, the others started haranguing Max in Romanian. At least he assumed he was being harangued. It certainly sounded that way. "Okay," he said, "Listen, you're not thieves. You didn't steal anything. Somebody else did that. Not you. You just made a movie."

"You say we just make a movie. But now everyone say we part of steal. They put us in jail or kick us out of USA!"

"Look, there were thousands of people on that field. They're not just gonna' focus on you. You're not in Romania now, they're not gonna' throw you in jail for something you didn't do."

Bishku was unconvinced. "They have Hong."

"What do you mean they have Hong?"

"The Chinaman. From this store. Hung Hong. He run, too."

Max was exhausted, physically and mentally. "I know who he is. What do you mean they have him?"

"Arrested. Talking on TV."

"He was smiling. Did you watch it? Smiling. He wanted to be arrested. He thinks he's gonna' be famous."

Bishku shook his head. "He talks, he gives names." The others seemed to understand this, nodding solemnly in agreement. "In old country, you are arrested, you give names, very bad."

Max placed the briefcase on one of the small round tables, opened it and swiftly extracted a handful of envelopes from one of its pockets. "This should cheer you up." He distributed the envelopes, watched the acrobats tear into them like hungry shylocks at a cash buffet. "There," he said, "feel better?"

No one answered though some managed a snort. They sat back down, put the money away and whispered among themselves, occasionally raising their heads to eye Max suspiciously. No matter what was being said, Max felt sure he was not being praised. His gut told him to bolt but he was too tired to elude another posse and besides, he much preferred to leave on good terms this time. He had realized he didn't like being the bad guy.

The chatter ended, Bishku said something and two of the Babushkas raised their hands, then the other raised his. Max's heartbeat sped up. "What's happening?" he asked.

Bishku looked at him seriously. "You may go."

"Did you guys just vote? Was that a vote?"

"Go now!"

Okay, thought Max. So what if it was a vote? He won. Accept the reprieve and scoot. Keeping your end of the bargain and being thanked for it didn't matter. Staying alive and out of jail did. Plus, he had lied to them so there was that. Just nod, smile and take your leave. "Okay, great," he said. "Good doing business with you. I'll let you know when the movie comes out."

Bishka glared at him and spoke the first English words Max had heard him utter.

"Movie!" he spat. "Fuck movie!"

Well then, decided Max, that's it. Time to go. It was all he could do to maintain his composure, turn and quietly leave the grocery store when what he really wanted was to run out of there like the 'Cowardly Lion' fleeing the 'Wizard'.

Outside and a block from the store's entrance, Max glanced back over his shoulder to see if he was being followed, a nervous tic which had rapidly become a habit over the previous few days. Between Charles, Cranky Sam, Nuggets and the strippers, he was beginning to feel like one of America's most wanted. How did those culprits do it, he wondered. How did they live a life on the run, always fearful they were being watched, the possibility of capture a constant sword hanging over their heads, being free but never at ease? Max had been at it for only a few days but was ready to throw in the towel, give himself up. Apparently, he decided, he hadn't the constitution necessary for a career criminal and promised himself that if he did indeed survive the week, he would never, ever break the law again.

Next he was supposed to meet Teddy and Simon, the college landscapers but, the possibility of pursuit weighing heavily, he chose a circuitous route, pivoting this way and that, ducking down alleys, pausing at street corners. He probably looked like a crazy person, more suspicious than ever. Perhaps, he thought, he was being overly cautious, paranoid even. After all, Charles was in the hospital, Cranky Sam was under lock and key, Nuggets was down and out.

The girls were unlikely to leave their comfort zone and the basketball players appeared to be men of honor. That left the Babushkas and that worrisome vote. Had there been a recount? He'd read things over the years, watched documentaries. Angry Eastern Europeans were, it seemed, not men to be trifled with. Confronted by them, broken thumbs would probably be the least of his worries. He turned a corner, leaned against a wall and waited. No sign of Babushkas. Max took a deep breath, got a hold of himself. He felt that things had gone pretty well so far, all things considered. He'd done his job, everyone was getting paid and, if King had kept his word, which thus far he'd done, then all that was left was for Max to pay off the college kids, give Tulip money for herself and Gooch, leave an envelope for Crazy Ed, find a home for Rufus, then get his ass to the bus station and skip town. Easy enough, he figured. Or was it?

*

Back at 'Sully's the network broadcasts were still dominated by news of the robbery and the regulars were paying as much attention as their various stages of inebriation would allow.

The latest visual was focused on a storefront – 'Cranky Sam's Auto Body', where Eva now stood doing a remote.

"Authorities now feel certain that the 'Punt, Pass & Kick' competitors seen in earlier footage being air-lifted from the stadium were in fact involved in the heist. The auto body shop you see behind me is owned by Samuel Woznichick, a little person who was arrested in an unrelated altercation outside the stadium. He is known for only hiring other little people to man the bays at his well known business and was once featured in a human interest story on a competing network. Following his arrest, the police arrived here to find the gate locked and no employees inside. These men are now considered persons of interest and conjecture is they may have been involved in last week's Halloween holdup as well. If you see any of them, please call the number on the screen".

A slide show began of faces, Cranky Sam's crew, a tough looking bunch, not a smile among them. The pictures were more mug shot than selfie, stern characters evidently unhappy to have their photos taken.

"Man," said Tony, "not exactly a cute and cuddly group."

"The third one looked familiar," said Frannie. "I think he dated my sister."

Joe gave her a look. "You don't remember?"

Frannie shrugged. Everyone considered the question as a newcomer squeezed onto the stool next to Biz. A husky, middle-aged man in sports coat and tie, he looked vaguely familiar, but an afternoon spent drinking can lessen powers of recognition. Sully's niece, Shelly, greeted him.

"What can I get you?"

"Johnny Black. Neat."

The gentleman sensed the others struggling to remember. "Detective Popowski. We met the other day."

"Oh, yeah."

"Of course."

"Yuh, sorry."

Shelly delivered his drink.

Joey hesitated. "Um, shouldn't you be out, you know, ah, looking for the robbers?"

"I am. I needed a drink."

Biz's alcohol content was too high for tact. "The detectives on TV don't stop for a drink."

"Well," said Popowsk, "I'm not a TV detective." They nodded in unison. The lawman drained half his glass. "You know the midget who kicked your friend is in jail?" Another nod. "Did you know that same friend got kicked in the nuts again? He's back in the hospital."

"What?"

"Come on."

"Another midget?"

"We don't know. Your pal's not talking."

"Poor Nuggets," said Frannie. "Those big balls were all he had going for him."

"Listen," said the detective, "any other little people been in here? Any of those guys they showed on the TV?"

"No, I don't think so."

"Haven't seen any. But we're not here all the time."

Popowski looked skeptical. "Really?...Okay, how about that waitress, the redhead?"

"Ginny?"

"Yes, Ginny. She around?"

"She doesn't work weekends," said Frannie. "She doesn't drink with us either. Not like Max."

"Max?"

"The bartender."

"Oh, right."

"He'll have a pop with us once in a while," said Tony.

Popowski looked around. "But not today?"

"No," said Joey, "not today."

The detective finished his drink, stood and threw a twenty on the bar, followed by a handful of business cards. "Any more midgets," he said, "anything funny, anything unusual, you gimme' a call."

Biz watched him exit the bar. "What's up with Colombo?"

"Whataya' mean," said Joe.

"I mean," said Biz, "he comes in here a couple of times, he's interested in all of us, he's interested in Max, he's interested in Ginny and the midget but he never asks about Chubster."

"So," said Tony.

"Well," continued Biz, "of all the regulars that come in here, or the people who work here, who should be the most interesting to a detective?"

"I think Miss P.'s pretty interesting," said Frannie.

"No," said Biz, "not that kind of interesting. I mean sketchy, you know, secretive. Chubster's always up to something."

"Well, I don't know," said Tony. "Haven't seen Chubster in here as much lately. At least I haven't seen him."

"Exactly," said Biz.

"Exactly," said Tony. "Exactly what? What are you saying, Biz? Chubster might be sketchy but he's our friend. What do you think, that he masterminded this whole stadium thing?"

"No, I'm not saying that. But if I was a detective on the case, I'd be focusing more of my time on shaky characters."

"You're a shaky character," said Tony.

Joey smiled. "I'm gonna' tell Chub you called him shaky."

"All right, all right," said Biz, putting his head down. "Never mind. Sorry I mentioned it."

"Look, look," said Joey, staring at the TV. "There's Chubster in a white Bronco going down the freeway!"

Biz raised his head quickly. No Bronco on the television. "You're a riot," he said to Joe. And judging by the laughter, maybe he was.

*

The college kids were waiting for Max at 'T.s Pub', a popular dive bar not far from the University. He probably should have gone there first but wanted to let some time pass before returning to the area. 'T.s' smelled like beer, looked like a frat house and was packed with all manner of scholastic underachievers.

Max stood by the door, surveyed the scene. The young adults, if they could be called that, were doing shots, chugging beers, playing pool and throwing darts. Though a few of the numerous televisions were tuned to the news, none of the hard partying undergrads appeared to be paying them much notice. Apparently, thought Max, the future leaders of America had better things to do than concern themselves with current events.

Ginny had given him an abbreviated description of Teddy and Simon and when Max's gaze fell upon a small crowd gathered around the foosball table, he suspected he'd found his marks. The two young men engaged in an enthusiastically contended contest seemed to fit the bill but, Max felt, getting their envelopes to them might not be as simple as he'd hoped. He'd caught a glimpse of himself in the mirror behind the bar and knew that between his age and attire, the briefcase he still carried and his various scrapes and scratches, he stood out like the proverbial sore thumb in a sea of t-shirts and hoodies. Moreover, a decent amount of the well lubricated patrons looked to be treating Teddy and Simon like minor celebrities, cheering them on, buying them beers. Obviously, the boys exploits that afternoon, their dash from the stands to the field, and back again, had been duly noted and tribute was now being paid by their pie-eyed peers. For the first time in years Max felt no guilt for having not finished college.

Before he could reflect further on that thought, three coeds approached. Dressed in as little clothing as early November would allow and pretty enough, they were younger than the women Max was used to flirting with at 'Sully's and at that moment the last thing he needed was to be noticed.

"Hey, mister, you lost or something?"

Max went into bar banter mode. "No, I don't think so. Why, do I look lost?"

The second girl looked him up and down, gulped her 'White Russian'. "You look like you got beat up."

"You should see the other guy," Max said and the girls giggled at that old line.

The third girl peered at him over the rim of her glass. "You know," she said, "he's kind of a DILF."

"What's a DILF?" asked Max.

The girls laughed and the second one stood on her tiptoes to whisper in Max's ear, though as far as whispers went, it was the loudest he'd ever heard. "It means," she said, "a dad I'd like to fuck."

"Oh," said Max, "um, ah, but I'm not a dad."

"That's not the point," said the first coed. "What's with the briefcase anyway?"

Max ignored the question. "You see those boys playing foosball, the two closest to us, you think you can get their attention for me?"

"You mean Teddy and Simon? You know they ran on the field today?"

"So I've heard." Max pulled a fifty from his pocket. "Get them to meet me outside for a minute and the next round's on me."

The third girl grabbed the bill. "Huh. Thought you'd want to meet us outside."

"Maybe next time. Thanks."

Max watched the girls reach the foosball table, wait for a break in the action, then make their move. One of them must have been better at whispering because Teddy soon looked his way, then tapped Simon on the shoulder and retired from the game, much to the group's dismay. Max decked outside quickly before the rest of the students could spot the cause of the interruption. Soon the three were looking each other over, standing on the sidewalk a few steps from the front door.

"Teddy and Simon, I presume."

"That's right."

"Which is which?"

"Does it matter?"

"No, not really."

Teddy looked up and down the pavement. "Is Ginny coming?"

"No, afraid not."

"She with you? You know, you a couple?"

Ginny hadn't mentioned Teddy's crush to Max. "No, not a couple. Anyway..."

Teddy interrupted. "Can you tell her to call me?"

"What? Why?"

"He wants to ask her out," said Simon.

Max smiled, looked at Ted. "What? You're just a kid."

Teddy was undeterred. "Maybe she doesn't feel that way."

"Then why don't you call her?"

"When she texted, said she was changing her number."

Max nodded. "Oh, that makes sense. Anyway this is rhetorical since she's a big girl and I can't tell her what to do. I assume you'd still like your money."

Simon nodded. "Absolutely."

"Speaking of money," said Teddy, "you know somebody robbed that stadium while we were on the field."

Max remained calm. "I heard something about that. Got a little crazy out there I guess."

"Yeah," said Simon. "You get your footage?"

"Footage?"

"Yeah, you know, for the movie."

"Of course, right, for the movie. Yup, got some great footage."

Max rested the case on his knee, paused, waited for the inquisition to continue but no more questions were forthcoming. The booze soaked young men hadn't put two and two together. God help us, he thought, the best and the brightest. He extracted two envelopes and handed them over.

"Thanks," said Simon. "You want to come back in, have a beer?"

Max was surprised by the offer. "Oh, thanks, but I'm on a pretty tight schedule."

He glanced down the sidewalk and was further surprised to see the Babushkas turning the corner. "Shit!" he said. "Change of plans."

He re-entered 'T.s', followed by the confused collegians. "Look," he said, "is there a back entrance to this place?"

"I don't know. I guess so. Has to be, right?"

Max pulled more bills from his pocket. "A hundred bucks for each of you if you can get me out the back."

Teddy hesitated. "And Ginny's new number."

Max shook his head. "I'm sorry. I can't do that."

"Then you tell her to call me."

"What? I'm not her boss."

"You want out or not?"

"Yes, okay, fine. I'll tell her."

"Promise!"

Max glanced at the door as the first Babushka appeared. "Yes. Promise."

Teddy said something to the bartender who raised the hinged section of the bar. All three slid behind it, then through the swinging doors to the kitchen. Teddy, in the lead, was confused, trying to remember the bartender's directions. Come on, thought Max, this kitchen is not that big. It wasn't like they were in the 'Copacabana' scene in 'Goodfellas'. Thankfully, an older cook took pity on them and pointed down an aisle to their right. They hurried past fryolators, prep tables, ice machines and out a screen door into an alley.

"Thanks. Thanks, guys."

"Hey," said Teddy. "Don't forget your promise."

Max didn't have time for any more nonsense. "Okay, okay. I gotta' go." He turned to bolt, then back to the boys. "Watch out for the Romanians." And he was off.

Simon watched him go. "Romanians?"

✳

Tony and Joe had reached their limits. Enough beers, enough stadium coverage, enough of Biz, Frannie and the rest of the gang. They were almost out the door, nearly collided with Miss Peabody and Mr. Vanderbilt, apparently returning after a brief respite.

"Oh, hey, Miss P. Thought you guys were still inside," said Joey.

"Oh, boys. We took a break over an hour ago. Went for a walk."

"Oh," said Tony. "Sorry. I guess we should have noticed."

"Perhaps a few too many today, gentlemen," said Mr. Vanderbilt.

"Perhaps," Joey said, smiling. "Anyway we gotta' get home. The wives have been texting us for hours."

Tony, doing his best Ricky Ricardo impression. "We gotta' lot'a 'splainin' to do."

"Oh, boys," said Miss Peabody, "before you go, did Chubster ever show up? We were hoping to run into him."

"No, no Chubster. But funny you should ask. Biz was just talking about him. But we haven't seen him in days."

"Oh, my."

"Why, what's up?"

"Oh, nothing important."

Mr. Vanderbilt spoke up. "Miss Peabody needs some floors refinished and Chubster had said he knew someone."

"Yeah, sounds like Chub," said Joey. He always knows somebody who knows somebody."

"Don't worry," said Tony. "He'll show up sooner or later. He always does."

"I'm sure he will. Now you two run along home. You're probably already in the dog house and you don't want to make things worse."

Tony barked and they all laughed, the two booze hounds heading out into the daylight, shocked by the sight of the sun like a pair of startled vampires.

*

Max's paranoia was growing exponentially. He moved in jerks and half steps; he sensed shadowy figures lurking everywhere. How many pursuers could he elude in one afternoon? Why wasn't everyone just happy with their money? Why were they all so greedy? And angry? He pictured himself in an old silent film, chased down the road by an ever increasing mob. But those films were funny. There was nothing even remotely humorous, he felt, about his current situation.

He simply had to reach Tulip, run by Crazy Ed's, then the bus station and he was done. At least that's what he told himself. Tulip, he figured would be fine. She'd be perfectly pleased with her payoff and if she was mad at anyone it would be that big galoot, Gooch, and his stupid 'GoPro', both of which were now in the hands of the authorities. But Tulip was a good girl and if he left Gooch's share with her, he was confident she'd see that he got it.

Max turned a corner, ducked into a dry-cleaners and stood with his back against the plate glass window, waiting. He was anxious to see if the Babushkas would go by. The tiny Asian woman behind the counter eyed him suspiciously.

"You here for pick-up?" she asked him.

"No. No, just waiting."

Her gaze intensified, as if a cockroach had invaded the premises. "You no wait here."

"What?"

"Too busy. You go."

Max examined the empty interior. "Too busy?" he asked.

"Yes, yes, very busy. Customers come. Not for waiting. You go now."

Max had always prided himself on his civility, his ability to remain calm, no matter the circumstances. Years spent dealing with demanding drunks, obstreperous fools and fussy matrons left him with two choices, serenity or rage. Max had chosen the former. He seldom raised his voice, he didn't scream at telemarketers and never flipped off bad drivers. But on that day, his patience had run thin.

"Unbelievable," he began. "I just need to rest a minute."

"You rest outside. Not here."

Max didn't have the energy to protest. He felt he'd entered an alternate universe, somehow fallen down a rabbit hole of absurdity, his reward for a week's worth of bad decisions.

The woman called out without lifting her gaze from Max, and two chunky men in filthy aprons emerged from a door behind the counter. Three sets of hostile eyes were now boring holes in him and finally, whether through sheer exhaustion or perhaps even simple common sense, he was able to bite his tongue.

"Okay, okay, I'm going." He opened the front door, about to exit, looked both ways. No sign of the Babushkas as he emerged from the store. Maybe they were having beers with Teddy and Simon, impressing tipsy coeds with their swarthy complexions and exotic accents. One could only hope.

*

Tulip's copy center was a few blocks away. The fact she'd played her part at the stadium and still made it back for her late shift at the store was impressive. That,

Max felt, was true dedication. He needed one easy stop on what had become the delivery route from Hell, and when he saw Tulip's smile, he dared hope for relief. Could it be, was it possible, that she was truly happy to see him, and not just for the money?

"Great finale, huh?" she beamed.

"What?"

"You know, for the movie."

"Yes, yes. Great finale. You guys were awesome."

Tulip still believed they were simply making an underground film. Had she not heard the news, was she unaware of the robbery? Max listened to the alternative music station being broadcast by satellite radio on the overhead speakers. No commercials, no interruptions. And he doubted Tulip was the type of girl whose earbuds had been tuned to news stations on her walk back to the shop. He may have finally gotten lucky.

"Did you know Gooch got arrested?"

"Yeah," she said, shaking her head. "I knew he was too slow. He texted me though. Someone bailed him out."

"Really," said Max. That King was a man of his word continued to surprise. "Did he say anything else?"

"No. He said he'd talk to me when he gets here. I guess they kept his 'GoPro.'"

"When he gets here?"

"Yeah, he's on his way. Man, running on that field was so cool. It was like a giant mosh pit, insane." Max made no reply, lost in thought. "What's the matter with you? You should be psyched. Today was fucking lit!"

Max snapped out of it. "Yeah...lit. Totally. Sorry, just have some things on my mind." He forced a smile. "How'd you like some money?"

Tulip grinned. "Yes, please."

Max set the briefcase on the counter, glanced over his shoulder at the shop's entrance, wary of other customers arriving or worse, Babushkas. He opened the case, removed two of the remaining envelopes and handed them to Tulip.

"Can you make sure Gooch gets his. I'm in a hurry and I don't have time to wait."

"Really? You gotta' go? Okay, no problem. But we want to know what's going on with the film. Can you keep us posted?"

"Oh, absolutely," said Max, closing the case and preparing to depart. "And please tell Gooch I'm sorry I missed him. And Tulip, thanks for all your help.

You're the best." He gave a little wave, turned toward the door but stopped short. "Damn it!"

One of the Babushkas, he wasn't sure which, had found him and barged in, furious. "You!"

Max backed up, holding the briefcase to his chest. "It's all over. There's no more money! Plus, you guys voted."

The Babushka brother delivered what was, judging from his tone and inflection, a storm of Romanian curses and, even more alarming, pulled a knife from his pocket. This can't be happening, thought Max. He was done, the job was over, he'd kept his word. True, he hadn't mentioned the heist but everyone had received their share and hardly anyone was in jail so what was the problem?

The angry acrobat advanced toward Max, switching the blade from one hand to the other in a menacing manner, a sight which Max would most likely have been concentrating on if he hadn't noticed the remaining Babushka brothers crowding through the copy shop door. This is it, he figured, this is what you get for a life of crime, well, actually a week of crime, maybe even just one day. But that interior monologue, that personal lament, was cut short by the sound of a gunshot and the image of the first Babushka, now injured, hopping on one foot and screaming in pain, his boot gushing blood onto the tile floor. Max turned, saw Tulip holding a pistol with two hands, still aimed at the wounded intruder and his comrades.

"Get out!" she yelled. "Get out of my fucking store!"

Bishku, the English speaking brother, tried to protest. "No," he said, "you no understand." He pointed at Max. "He bad, very bad man!"

Tulip fired a warning shot at his feet. "Now!"

The Romanians scrambled out the door, one of them lending a shoulder for their damaged brother to lean on. Max was, to say the least, relieved. Impressed, too. "Wow," he said.

Tulip lowered the gun. "You'd be surprised how many times people have tried to rob this store."

"Well, you're a damn good shot."

"I was aiming for his dick."

"What?"

Tulip smiled. "Just kidding. What were they so pissed off about anyway?"

"Um, you know, a misunderstanding."

"Must have been a big misunderstanding. You want to go out the back?"

Now Max smiled. "Yes, please. And thanks again. You saved me. I owe you."
"No worries. Follow me."
Tulip opened the back door; another alley. She went out first, holding the pistol, checking to make sure the coast was clear. Max gave her a hug. He couldn't help himself. Perhaps she'd be mad later when she found out about the robbery, maybe she'd be irritated she hadn't let the Babushkas slice him up, but at that moment they were friends and a nice, warm hug at the end of that extraordinary day was just what he needed.

*

Ginny was in the kitchen pouring herself another drink when Emily walked in. Though not thrilled to be found drinking before the sun had set by her disapproving daughter, Ginny was nonetheless grateful for the company.

Emily set her jacket on a chair back, placed her hands on her hips. "You're drinking before supper? You never drink before supper."

Ginny set the bottle down. It was true, at least generally. Once in a while at a cookout she'd have a couple beers but mostly Em was right. "You're right, but, you know, this was not your average week."

Emily sat down. "Yeah. Looks like your buddy, Max, and his gang made their film while the stadium got robbed. What a coincidence, huh?"

"Em, come on."

"One of my friends saw some big, goofy guy on TV who was on the field and he didn't even know he was involved in a robbery. He thinks he's in a film."

"I know, I know. They all do. But I told you what was going to happen."

"Unbelievable. So you helped them rob that stadium."

"Not really."

"Yes, really."

"I got out as soon as I found out the truth. I told you that."

"I know, Mom. But you were in on it. What if they catch Max? What if he talks about you?"

"He won't. Max wouldn't do that."

"Oh, my God. Do you hear yourself? You don't know what Max will do. Apparently, you never did."

Good point, thought Ginny. Was Max capable of such a betrayal? Who knew. She wasn't sure of anything any more. "Look" she said, "I didn't do anything. I wasn't there. I helped early on but I was duped and stopped as soon as I found out. I'll take a lie detector test if I have to."

Emily almost laughed. "A lie detector test. Jesus, Mom."

Ginny's phone, set next to the bottle on the counters, went off, a text alert. Both women raised their heads but Emily was quicker, grabbed the cell, stared at the text on the screen. "It's Max. Can you believe that? He wants to know how you're doing."

Before Ginny could wrestle the phone away or raise her voice in protest, Emily was angrily punching in a message. Ginny slumped down into a chair. "What did you say?"

"I told him he's an asshole and to leave you alone."

"He'll think it's from me."

"So what. Why do you care?"

Ginny shook her head. "I don't know why. I really don't."

*

Max proceeded cautiously and who could blame him. He'd paused to text Ginny but her response was not exactly warm and fuzzy. The question dominating his mind, and rightfully so, was just what exactly was next? A pleasant or at least indifferent answer from the woman he still prayed might forgive him would have helped him decide. He knew, of course, what should be next – the bus station. But should isn't always the course of action taken; he'd certainly learned that over the past few days. Try and make it to the bus depot, unscathed, Babushkas or no Babushkas, get the money, catch a ride to anywhere and start over. He'd watched enough films, read enough books to know that's what you're supposed to do when you get away with something. But what about Rufus? And Sully? And his land-lord? Did those other criminals tie up loose ends? Or did they lack a conscience? And if having a conscience was important, and he apparently had one, then why had he gotten involved in a criminal enterprise in the first place? Okay, he thought, this was futile. He was giving himself a headache. He would go home, take care of a few things, pack a bag, be on his way. No one, he felt, would be looking for him yet, no one could have connected him to the day's events. If he could just avoid any more encounters with the bloodthirsty Romanians and the ungrateful strippers, he might be all right. The setting sun, he hoped, would aid in his trek. A couple more alleys, a quick appearance on the street, hail a cab and home free.

Slow down, he told himself. Think. Was he forgetting anything? Or anyone? Over the years, working at a variety of bars, 'Sully's included, he'd often been given the responsibility of closing up alone. Not a difficult task, but one which required a checklist of sorts. Doors, ovens, freezers and grills, everything had to be scanned. Were the doors locked, the burners on, the restroom lights switched off? Max would always do a final walkabout, ask himself if he was forgetting anything. And there on that unfamiliar sidewalk, at the end of that highly irregular day, he did the same. What was he forgetting? It took a moment but thank goodness he was a man of routine. Crazy Ed. Of course. He'd forgotten about the big pawnbroker, a businessman who was likely not fond of deadbeats who didn't keep their word.

But what about Ed's money? Max quickly opened the now empty briefcase, was about to panic but reached in his back pocket and pulled out Ed's envelope. He recalled thinking that of all the recruits, Ed would probably be the most agitated if he'd run on that field for nothing. Max, hunted by various adversaries intent on claiming a larger share of the proceeds must have earlier stuffed the big guy's payment in his pants. He wiped his brow theatrically, let out a sigh. Okay, he thought, the pawn shop, then home.

Usually, upon entering a taxi, Max would examine the interior, check the driver's hack license, the name displayed on the back of the front passenger seat. If the radio wasn't too loud, he'd engage the man, or occasionally woman, in conversation, maybe comment on the day's news, maybe inquire about the driver's background. But not today. Max took no notice of the license. He simply gave the pawn shop's address, then leaned back in his seat and rested his eyes. He relaxed as best he could until he felt the vehicle come to a stop.

"Okay, buddy, we here."

'Crazy Ed's Pawn Shop' sat empty, a 'Closed' sign in the window. No sign of the owner. Max tried to remember if he'd seen Ed on any of the news broadcasts. He didn't think so. Ed certainly wouldn't have been hard to apprehend but then again, neither would Ribs or Ebony and they'd made it out. Well, he figured, he would just slide the envelope under the door. "Wait here," he said to the cabbie.

It turned out the door had a slot for just such envelopes. Apparently Ed's patrons dropped off money at all hours of the day. Max pushed Ed's through, then paused, wondering if he was finally done. Was that everybody? Yes, he said to himself, that was it. Done. He returned to the cab, gave his home address and closed his eyes. He must have dozed off because he woke to the driver's voice.

"Hey, man, you home. We here."

Max cleared his head, looked out the passenger window. Standing next to his building's doorway was Candy. Dressed provocatively, one leg bent, her high heel resting against the brick wall behind her, slowly taking drags off a cigarette, she could have been the city's loveliest streetwalker which, for all Max knew, she may have once been. For some reason, he was not surprised. There must be, he felt, a limit to how many times a man can be amazed in one day. He was beginning to feel like Ulysses on his Odyssey, one calamity after another and there she was, his own personal siren, temptation incarnate. Damn, he thought, why hadn't he gone to the bus station. Sure, the cat, Sully, blah, blah, blah. He knew the real reason – Ginny.

He pulled out his phone, addressed the driver. "Circle the block, would you."

"What you mean circle the block?"

"Just drive around the block. I need a minute. Please."

"So we are here. And now we go where?"

"We go here."

"But we are here."

This, Max decided, never happened in the movies. You asked the guy to circle the block, he circled the block. What happened to civility, what happened to dealing with the public, what happened to 'the customer is always right?'

"Please, I'm asking nicely. Just drive around for a couple minutes, then back here."

"All right," the driver said, "but meter is running."

"That's fine. Thank you." Max glanced at Candy again as they pulled away from the curb. He texted Ginny one more time, held the phone and waited as they navigated the traffic. He realized there might be no response but he wanted a sign, an indication that he should resist Candy, that he should continue to show restraint and pray for forgiveness. He knew the odds were against him; her last text had made that quite clear. Still...He heard the alert, stared at the screen. 'Fuck off! I said leave us alone.' Us? What did that mean? The 'Fuck off' part was pretty clear.

The taxi pulled over again. Candy hadn't moved. She was still puffing a butt, ignoring the stream of men who made no effort to conceal their leers. The driver waited. Max sighed, paid him, got out of the car.

"Hi, Maxi," said Candy.

"Hello, Candy. What are you doing here?"

"Waiting for you."

"Why?"

"Oh, Max," she said, taking a long drag, "you know why."

"How'd you get my address?"

"Your boss, the big guy, Sully. He didn't want to but I can be pretty convincing. Plus, he said you'd been acting weird lately and might like some company."

"Sully said that?"

Candy nodded. "Well, in so many words."

"What about Sam?"

"Oh, Sammy's in jail again. Probably will be for a while. He's got a record."

"What a surprise."

Candy laughed. "See, that's why I like you. You're funny."

Max didn't feel funny. "So your husband gets arrested and a few hours later you're ready to hook up with me?"

"Well, you know, sometimes a girl just gets an itch."

What was the use, Max thought. A beautiful woman wanted to have sex with him on what was likely his last night in town. Ginny wanted nothing to do with him, justifiably so, why then was he resisting?

Candy read his mind. "You know, Max," she said, stamping out the cigarette, "I heard someone say that the best way to rid yourself of temptation is to yield to it."

"Oscar Wilde," said Max.

Candy shook her head. "No, wasn't him. I don't know him."

What was that, thought Max. Another coincidence? He quickly decided he didn't care. He was tired. "Okay," he said, "come on up."

Candy showed little reaction to the interior of Max's apartment. He had no idea what kind of home Sam had supplied her with and wasn't about to ask. Besides, with her obvious disregard for monogamy, she' probably seen her fair share of bachelor pads.

"How about a drink?" he asked. "I know I can use one."

"Rough day?"

"You have no idea."

"You do look a little worse for wear."

"Thanks."

"Oh, Maxi, you're still adorable."

Max went to the kitchen, poured a couple brandies, returned to find Candy sitting on the couch. He handed her a glass and she motioned for him to sit beside her but he deferred.

"Actually," he said, "think I'm going to take a hot shower. It has been a very long day. Make yourself comfortable."

Candy smiled, her idea of comfortable most likely different from most. "Okay," she said.

Max loved showers, always had, the hotter the better. The soap felt good and the brandy was helping calm his nerves, making it easier to concentrate on the money, the new life he would soon embark on, about the blonde sex bomb waiting for him in the living room, anything but Ginny. He stepped out, dried off and wrapped the towel around his waist, downed the remaining brandy.

Candy had, indeed, made herself comfortable. She'd shed her outer garments and now sat in brilliant white lingerie – peekaboo bra, thigh high stockings, garter belt and pencil thin thong.

She was a vision, every teenage boy's dream and, Max had to admit, pushing aside whatever guilt he'd been grappling with, the woman was an absolute knockout. How she'd ever ended up with a miserable bastard like Cranky Sam was still a mystery, but a question for another day.

Rufus had arrived on the scene and was now seated in Candy's lap, purring contentedly as the voluptuous visitor stroked his fur. Max refilled his glass, sat down next to them.

"I see you've met Rufus."

"He's almost as cute as you."

"You like cats?"

"Um, humn."

"Well, he seems to like you."

"Is he a boy cat?"

"Yup, he's a male."

Candy smiled again. "Well, there you go."

Max laughed. The brandy was having the desired effect, relaxing his resolve, his mind drifting, his apprehension eased. Watching Candy gently pet Rufus gave Max an idea. Actually two as the rise in his towel proved, but one thing at a time.

"So you think Sam might be away for a while?"

"I'm afraid so. But let's not talk about him right now." Candy adjusted her position, one bra strap slipping down her creamy white shoulder.

Max tried to concentrate. "No, it's just that you and Rufus seem to be getting along so well and I, um, I have to go away for a while."

"Really?"

"Yeah, and, uh, Rufus is going to need a place to stay and, uh..."

"Hold on," said Candy, "This is a first. Are you trying to trade your pussy for my pussy?" She grinned. "Is that about it?"

"Well, ah..." Max was unsure if he'd screwed up. Seemed like a good idea when he'd thought of it.

"Oh, relax, Max. I'm just teasing. Of course I'll watch Rufus for you."

Max leaned back. "Oh, that's great. That's a relief."

Candy addressed the cat. "All right, Rufus, that's enough for you." She carefully lowered her new furry friend to the floor. "Right now your owner needs a different kind of relief."

She pulled open Max's towel, drew closer, placed her hands on his thighs and for the first time in a week, as Candy slid the towel from his waist, all Max's troubles seemed to slide away as well.

*

SUNDAY

Max slept better than he had in days and wasn't disappointed when, upon waking, he discovered Candy had risen before him and made her departure. He felt guilty enough about sleeping with another man's wife and, after a full week of various transgressions, he needed no reminder of one more. He did note Rufus's absence and the possibility that Candy had kept her word. Though her morals were, at best, questionable, she did seem sincerely fond of the cat and Max took comfort in that regard. He would have liked to say goodbye to his little friend but the decampment from town would be that much easier, both physically and emotionally.

He made the bed, a habit he'd had for as long as he could remember, started a pot of coffee, then headed for the bathroom, grabbing his phone along the way. The chances Ginny had texted were slim but he had to check. No luck. Max sat on the toilet and stared at the blank screen. No message from Ginny, no message from Candy, no message from anybody. Why, he felt, shouldn't he grab the money and go? What, or for that matter, who was keeping him around? He stood at the sink, splashed cold water on his face, clearing his mind. He had to think, there was a decision to be made and the time had come to make it.

*

Ginny barely slept. Yes, she'd undressed, brushed her teeth, washed her face and slid under the covers as she'd done a thousand nights before. But there would be no rest that night, no pleasant dreams, no tranquil thoughts concerning the day's events. No, that night she could have used a sleeping pill, maybe three. She tried not to think about Max, tried not to think about the lie, the fake film, the actual robbery but, as everyone knows, trying not to think about something never works. She couldn't turn to her phone for distraction. Emily had confiscated it, not trusting her mother's tendency to forgive rotten men. So Ginny stared at the ceiling, watched the numbers on the bedside clock gradually change, and worried. She was, fairly or not, connected to the biggest crime the city had seen in ages. She'd spoken with people involved, helped recruit accomplices, even appeared on film. How could Max have done this to her? And more importantly, why wasn't she more enraged, more furious with him? She should have been ready to do to Max's balls what the midget had done to Nuggets. Or, at least turn him in, go to the authorities, tell them what she knew, plead her case. Thank goodness, she thought, that Emily had her phone. Who knew what she would do. Instead, she would wait, not say anything, see what happens. But if Max got caught, tough luck. He deserved whatever he got. Max was an asshole, wasn't he? That's what Emily had called him and lately her daughter had seemed a lot tougher than her mom.

*

Max had dressed, he'd packed a small suitcase, he'd written out a check for the next month's rent and left it in an envelope on the kitchen table along with his keys and a short note. He would, he thought, call the landlord later, apologize for his abrupt departure. He'd retrieved the fifty grand from the bottom of the cat food sack in the closet, still safely stashed in one of the 'Crown Royal' blue cloth bags that bartenders often collected. He wedged the plump pouch into his coat pocket. Thank God Candy hadn't fed the cat, hadn't asked him where his food was. It had never occurred to him the night before to move it to a different spot.

He sat, one last time, at the kitchen table, sipping his black coffee, staring at the mug, deciding. But what was there to decide? Just get up, grab the coat and suitcase, hail a cab and on to the bus station to start a new life. He could call Sully later, explain his absence. But no, Sully deserved better, a face to face meeting. The big man had been his boss, his drinking buddy, his friend. Besides, Max felt, he had time. The authorities couldn't have possibly connected all the dots yet. A quick trip to the bar, in and out, then on his way.

But hold on, where was the key to the bus station locker, he wondered. He was fairly certain he'd left it in his pants pocket the night before. He went to the bedroom. The pants were right where he'd left them, draped over the back of a chair in the corner, his belt still dangling from the loops. He reached in the pockets. His wallet was there, a small amount of cash as well but no key. He held the pants by the legs, shook them. Nothing. He got down on his hands and knees, looked under the chair, then crawled around the floor, peering under the bed, under the bureau. He stood up, looked around, some frustration, a hint of panic. He pulled the covers from the bed, searched every inch. Think, he told himself. But he knew, he was sure he'd put the key in those pants. He was not a guy who lost things, never was, even at the bar. He always knew where he'd left things, an opener, a pen, a corkscrew. No, the key was not where he'd left it, the key to a hundred thousand dollars, the key, as it were, to his new life. And then it hit him, hit him hard, the realization that yes, for probably the hundredth time in his under achieving life, he'd been a fool. Candy, of course. Candy had the key!

But how? How did she know about the key? Was the whole thing a set-up?

Was everyone's payoff at the bus station and was Sam actually clever enough to determine how to obtain Max's share? Maybe the original plan was merely to beat the key out of him but Charles had intervened and once the little bastard was behind bars a new scheme was necessary. But what kind of degenerate tells their wife to sleep with a stranger, even for a hundred large?

Max knew he'd been played, taken advantage of, that he was, for want of a better word, a chump. There weren't a lot of phases to go through. No denial, no grieving, no acceptance. Mostly just shame and anger. How could he have been so stupid. He'd flirted with hundreds of women at the bar over the years and not one had ever come on to him as strongly as Candy had. Sure, he knew most men would have done the same, would have given in, likely with less resistance than he'd shown; the woman was, after all, a stone cold fox, but that made him feel no better.

Damn it, he thought, why couldn't Ginny have forgiven him, at least been willing to talk or even text? Any word of encouragement, any sign of hope and he wouldn't have slept with that seductress. But no, that wasn't fair to Ginny. This wasn't her fault, this was all Max. There was no one else to blame, not Chubster, not Cranky Sam, not King, not even Candy. He had, indeed, yielded to temptation and look where it had gotten him. God works in mysterious ways, that's what Sully was always telling him, and maybe he was right.

He returned to the living room, gave it a cursory once-over but his heart wasn't in it. He would never have taken the key from his pocket and placed it on the coffee table. And small keys didn't just fall out of deep pants pockets. Was Candy a pick-pocket? Was that another of her wicked skills? She was certainly good with her hands, that he knew.

He tried the bathroom as well but he'd undressed in the bedroom so that proved as futile as the rest of his search. Finally, resigned to his fate, he returned to the kitchen where he sat, dejected, humiliated but mainly just mad, really mad, mad at himself. He pounded the table, swore out loud, watched the coffee breach the edge of his cup but didn't care. "Son-of-a-bitch! Damn it! Fuck!" He thought letting it out might make him feel better but instead realized he'd broken his rule about not swearing and just felt worse.

Now what, he asked himself. Fifty thousand wasn't enough to start a new life but it could buy him some time, enable him to lay low for a while, watch from a distance as the investigation played out. He would still visit Sully, tell him he needed some time off, maybe quite a bit of time, that he should, in fact, hire a new bartender. Max knew he couldn't stay in his apartment. Cranky Sam and Charles wouldn't be locked up forever and who knew if the strippers or Romanians would track him down. No, it was time to go. A fast trip to the bar, then out of town, at least for a while. He put on his coat, picked up his suitcase, looked around one last time but hesitated. One more text to Ginny, he decided. Why not? 'Meet me at 'Sully's' he typed, 'Please', then headed out the door.

*

Sunday mornings, Emily, like any good teenager, slept in so Ginny was able to quietly regain her cellphone. She stood in the kitchen, staring at Max's request. Why was he going to the bar on a Sunday? Max would never work on a Sunday, hadn't in years. Said he'd worked enough of them starting out and though he'd fill in on the occasional Saturday, Sully knew better than to ask him for a Sunday. Plus, shouldn't he be leaving town as planned? Was he in trouble? Was she in trouble?

Ginny turned on the TV. If Max or Chubster had become suspects, surely their images would be all over the news. The investigation was ongoing, the reporters said, no arrests had been made, nor anything concerning persons of interest. The usual plea from the authorities asking for any information that might assist in the capture of these violent criminals. Jeez, she thought, was Max a violent criminal? Apparently a couple of the security guards in the counting rooms had been pistol-whipped by Cranky Sam and his miniature thugs. But Max couldn't have been involved in that, could he?

Her curiosity was off the chart, so overwhelming it was making her dizzy. She could think of nothing else. Any chance of taking her usual Sunday walk to the cafe and having a leisurely cup of coffee while perusing the newspaper was, she knew, out of the question. The juxtaposition of intending to never speak to Max again and the desire to ask him what was going on were, she feared, driving her mad. There was only one course of action that might provide relief. She turned off the television, grabbed her jacket and left for the bar.

*

'Sully's Brew & Chew' didn't open until 11:30 on Sundays so an 11:00 visit would, Max felt, give him enough time to speak to the big Irishman, apologize and be on his way. He had little hope of Ginny actually responding to his text so when he spotted her entering the bar from a block away, his pace quickened, as did his heart.

Approaching 'Sully's front door, Max stopped, felt the 'Royal Crown' bag in his pocket. Strange things had happened the past week, unexpected events, unwelcome encounters. Though the heist itself had gone well, he wasn't exactly riding a lucky streak. And he was about to enter the bar with fifty grand on him. He simply had a feeling and it wasn't a good one. What was it Chubster had told him? 'You got a hunch, bet a bunch'. Chub had plenty of sayings but maybe, just maybe...

He turned down an alley which led to the tavern's rear entrance, a door used only by employees or for deliveries, paused, surveyed the scene. Cases stacked with empty beer bottles, kegs ready to be returned to the distributors, a pair of dumpsters, one for trash, the other for cardboard and, sitting in the corner of the small paved area, a wooden pallet piled high with discarded refuse. Dented kegs, broken tap handles, worn out brooms and dusty stepladders. Max had seen the heap a thousand times before but this time he examined it more closely. Sully had intended to do something about the mess for as long as Max could remember but somehow never got around to doing so. Max took out the bag of money, now the entire reward for all the week's labors, and placed it inside the bottom drawer of a rusty, battered file cabinet. Better safe than sorry, he thought, as he left the alley.

Ginny was sitting at the bar, her back to the door when Max walked in, and though he intended to join her, explain things, do some more apologizing, Jamison, the large Dominican cook stood between the two of them. That was odd, thought Max. Jamison should have been in the kitchen, prepping for the day's orders. Not only that, his co-worker appeared not the least surprised to see him on a Sunday.

"Hey, Jamison," said Max, "what's up?"

"Boss want to see you in the office."

"He knew I was coming in?"

"I don't know nothing about that, Max."

Ginny glanced over her shoulder at the two men but said nothing.

"Okay, okay," said Max. "But I just want to talk to Ginny for a minute first." He took a step to pass Jamison but the cook grabbed his arm, held it firmly.

"Boss said now."

Now? Max was curious. He supposed he could speak with Ginny afterwards. Shouldn't be a big deal. He gently removed Jamison's grip. "Okay, fine. I'll speak with Sully now. Aren't you supposed to be chopping onions or something?" Jamison, usually quick with a smile, made no reply, watched somberly as Max turned toward the office, paused for a moment to look at Ginny and shrug. She didn't smile either.

Sully's small, windowless office was, Max observed, filled to maximum capacity. The Big man himself stood leaning against a wall, his large arms folded across his barrel chest, his expression as stern as a disappointed parent. At the desk, seated in Sully's old leather chair, was Miss Peabody, her hands folded in front of her like an elderly school teacher about to call class to order. Across from her, on the other side of the desk, were two folding chairs, one empty, the other occupied by Mr. Vanderbilt, and completing the tableau was Detective Popowski, standing next to an ancient filing cabinet, a manila folder in his hands. Max, as always, tried valiantly to keep his cool.

"Wow," he said. "Full house. Hey Miss P., Mr. V." No one spoke, no one greeted him warmly. No one greeted him at all.

"Take a seat, Max," said Miss Peabody, but she didn't sound like the Miss Peabody Max had come to know.

Max looked around the tiny room, wondered how they knew he was coming in. Had they guessed? Had they assumed? If they were surprised to see him, they weren't showing it. He sat down in the chair next to Vanderbilt.

"What's going on?" he asked.

The woman across from him, the woman he'd been serving old-fashioneds to for the last year, the same woman who'd treated him like a favorite nephew, took a badge from her pocket, placed it on the desk.

"Max, my name is not Miss Peabody. I am Agent Elizabeth Walker, F.B.I. The gentleman next to you is Agent Al Romero, ATF, and I believe you've met Detective Popowski."

Max shook his head. "Is this a joke?"

"No joke," said Romero, unzipping his jacket to reveal a badge hanging from his neck.

Max stared at the badge; he felt sick. What, no joke? No one was laughing. And Sully, who never could keep a straight face when they were pranking a new waitress, well, he looked serious as a mortician. But Miss Peabody an F.B.I. Agent? Come on. She had often requested Max put the news on when she enjoyed her cocktails but so had lots of other patrons. Mr. Vanderbilt was more believable. He was new to 'Sully's and his claim to being a retired gigolo should have been a red flag. A retired gigolo! What the heck were they thinking? That there was a union for gigolos? That he was collecting a pension? Jesus! He was suddenly aware of someone shaking him, realized it was Vanderbilt.

"Max, are you all right?"

Max cleared his head. "Well, I'm kinda' shocked, you know. Miss Peabody is an F.B.I. Agent. You're with the...ah, what did you say you were?"

"The A.T.F. The Bureau of Alcohol, Tobacco and Firearms."

"Well, we do serve alcohol."

Miss Peabody didn't crack a smile. "Look, Max, this is serious. We know what you've been doing this week. We've been watching Mr. MaGee for over a year and we know both he and you were involved in the stadium heist."

Max was bewildered, his head dizzy. "You've been sitting at that bar for a year, drinking, talking like 'Oh, Max, my good man, could you be kind enough to mix me a fresh cocktail? Jesus."

"That was an act, Max. We do whatever we need to do. What's important now is that we know you helped commit a crime."

Max tried his best to feign innocence, plead ignorance like all the suspects he'd seen questioned on all the television shows he'd watched. "I don't know what you mean."

She continued. "Listen, Max. I like you, always have. I have no idea why you got mixed up with Chubster but you and I both know you did. There's still time to fix this. You help us, your life might not be ruined."

Max looked around the room, the solemn faces staring at him. He was used to being the center of attention behind the bar but not like this. "How'd you know I was coming in anyways? I never come in on Sundays."

"Because, Max, you're a good guy. You have a conscience. We knew you wouldn't skip town without letting Sully know. But you got involved with bad people, Max. You can deny it all you want, but you know it's true."

"I think," said Max, "this is about the time where I ask for a lawyer."

The detective approached the desk, laid down the manila folder in front of Max. "Look, asshole," he said, "you're in the shit. Deep. We know you paid people to run on that field. We know you were there. We've got you on tape."

"What are you talking about?"

"Norman Guccini," said Romero. "Believe you know him as Gooch. He must have had the 'GoPro' on when you were going to the stadium. Big mistake, Max."

Damn, thought Max. Gooch and his stupid 'GoPro'. Now he was straining. "Big deal," he said. "Gooch filmed me walking to the stadium. That's not a crime."

"He's cooperating."

"His word against mine."

The detective opened the file. "Receipts from 'Crazy Ed's," he said, pointing at the stubs. "For film equipment. You're a pretty careless crook, Max." Max opened his mouth but Popowski cut him off. "And we've got Crazy Ed." Satisfied, he closed the folder. The detective bent over, his face now inches away from Max's own. "So, we got you for instigating a riot. That's ten years even if we can't connect you to the robbery. If I was you, I'd do everything possible to cooperate with the agents."

Walker gave the detective a quick nod and he backed away. The sweet old woman Max had known as Miss Peabody now slid a large photo across the desk. "Max," she said, "do you know this man?"

He picked up the 8 by 10, stared at the portrait. King. "Can't say as I do." He laid the photo down, leaned back in his chair.

"Really," said Walker. "His name is Alphonse Spanopolos. You probably know him as King. We've been after him for some time and with your help we can put him away. He's a very violent individual."

Max picked up the photo again. Just behind King, a bit to the side, was a familiar blonde. Candy. "Who's the blonde?" he asked, sliding the photo back to Walker.

"That's his wife, Mrs. Spanopolos. Why?"

What! How many gut punches could one man take? Candy was actually King's wife, not Cranky Sam's? That did make a little more sense. But why the ruse, Max wondered. So the visit to the bar, the night Nuggets lost a testicle, that was no coincidence? That was King checking up on Max, maybe checking up on Sam as well. Candy was some kind of spy, the operation's mole. What else? Was she looking in on Chubster? Flirting with Duffy? And why was Cranky Sam so mad about his fake wife being attracted to Max? That anger certainly didn't seem fake. Jeez, thought Max, so many questions. What about the seduction? King was already making plenty. He didn't need his wife to sleep with Max and steal the key. No, that must have been her idea, some money of her own, a little secret marital stash, one more reason not to acknowledge the man in the photo.

"No reason," he eventually answered. "She looks familiar. Maybe she's been to the bar."

Everyone in the room was convinced Max was lying. A long pause before Romero spoke.

"Max, you've got a big choice to make. You can walk out of this room in cuffs or you can walk out in protective custody. We're prepared to offer you a deal. Testify against King and we'll put you in the witness protection program. No jail time. You help us get him off the street and we'll set you up far away with a new life. Maybe even a new bartending job. You were going to leave town anyway. Not much difference."

Walker returned to her matronly voice, the one he'd grown so fond of over the preceding months. "Max, you don't want to go to prison. You're not a criminal, never have been. You just made a mistake, gave in to temptation. They'll eat you up in jail. This is your chance for redemption. You can make up for what you've done."

Max looked up at the ceiling. "Witness protection. That means I can never come back, right?"

"So what," said Romero. "You have no family here. No wife, no kids. The best friend you've got is Sully and you were going to leave him in the lurch, no notice."

"That's not true. That's why I came in."

"Another mistake," said Popowski.

The detective was getting on Max's nerves. He turned back to Walker. "Why me? Why not Chubster? Or somebody else?"

"Chubster's gone. He drove, no flight, no bus, no train. There's an A.P.B. But he's clever. We grabbed Duffy at the airport but the broken thumbs seem to have muzzled him. And Sam, well you've met Sam. He's not fond of the authorities. No, Max, it's you, you're the key. You help us, we help you and you get to live happily ever after. What do you say?"

Max glanced at Sully who nodded, hopeful Max might take the deal. The closed circuit screens on the office television were blank but Max could imagine Ginny, still seated at the bar, waiting. He looked at Romero. "Lawyer, please."

"That's it," said Popowski, irritated as ever. "Stand up, hands behind your back. You are under arrest. You have the right to remain silent. You have the right..."

How many shows had Max watched where some punk got read his Miranda Rights? But he would never hear the whole thing. The first line or two, then they would cut away. This was his chance to listen to the entire speech but, understandably, he didn't care.

Ginny kept her head down when the detective perp walked Max out of the bar. She'd seen enough to know he was in trouble, his hands cuffed, arms behind his back, expression grim. She wondered if she was next. After all, if Max was the jerk Emily had proclaimed him to be, he'd give her up and everyone else, too, to get a reduced sentence. But that thought passed quickly. She'd known him far too long. That Max would throw her under the bus, no matter what the reward, seemed inconceivable, and though the past few days had been chock full of the unexpected, in this instance she felt secure. What she was unsure of was the reason Miss Peabody and Mr. Vanderbilt were trailing Max and the detective out of the building. Was that some kind of badge hanging from Mr. V.s neck? She had a lot of questions and while Sully was nowhere to be seen, Ginny knew he couldn't stay in his office forever.

*

As was the custom during every Autumn Sunday at 'Sully's Brew & Chew', all the televisions in the establishment were tuned to the National Football League games. That was how it always had been and, according to the owner's instructions, how it always would be. Though no fan of the American sport himself, Sully was savvy enough to know the NFL was what the majority of his customers wanted and the NFL was what they would get. Customers, particularly newer ones, would occasionally request a golf match or college basketball contest but the answer was invariably no. No nastiness, just a firm denial and a suggestion that if the patron truly wanted to watch something besides America's game, there were plenty of other watering holes in the area. When it came to music and television, Sully was not known for being flexible.

But on this November afternoon, an exception had been made. Tony, Joey, Biz, and the other regulars, seated comfortably at the long wooden bar and normally involved in vociferous debate concerning pigskin prognostications were instead staring at a large flat screen turned to the news, mesmerized by images of men the authorities now claimed had taken part in the stadium heist. Chubster MaGee wasn't really a huge surprise, his activities over the years always seeming vaguely suspicious, and the angry midget made sense, but Max, their Max, their bartender, their friend, what was he doing up there on the TV screen?

"I can't believe Max was involved in this," said Joey.

"I can't believe Chubster got away," said Tony.

"Forget that," said Biz. "Miss Peabody's a frigging F.B.I. Agent! Come on, it's like a bad TV show."

"Mr. V. too," added Tony.

"I know but we should have figured something was up with him. A retired gigolo? What the Hell were we thinking?"

"Because we wanted to," said Joey. "Because it was cool, because old people don't usually lie. If it had been a young guy claiming to be an escort, we would have called bullshit."

Biz looked doubtful. "What? Old people don't lie?"

"Well," said Joey "as a general rule, no, no they don't. They don't need to. They're old, they're tired, they're not trying to pick up chicks, they're not trying to get hired, they're not trying to hide something from their wife..."

"Or husband," said Tony, nodding.

"Exactly," said Joey, drinking his beer.

"What are you knuckleheads talking about?" asked Frannie, climbing onto a stool.

"Joey says old people don't lie."

"Nonsense," said Frannie, flagging down Shelly for a drink, or was it Shannon. "I'm going to lie like crazy when I'm an old bag. You think I'm gonna' tell my grandkids the stuff I've done?"

Biz was surprised. "You've got grandkids?"

"No, but I might some day." The others took a moment to digest that, turned back to the newscast. "What's the latest? They catch Chubster?"

"No, still looking. Max is in jail. The midget's in jail. They got some inside guy named Duffy. The whole thing is crazy."

"Checked on Nuggets," said Frannie, "He's still in the hospital."

"Did you visit him?"

"No, but I know a couple nurses over there. The other testicle is a goner."

"You gotta' be kidding."

"Can't make this stuff up."

"Was he in on the stadium?"

"They don't think so. Found him over at the athletic fields near the High School. Laying in a puddle of saline."

"Oh, my God," said Biz.

Frannie glanced down at her chest. "Glad I never got a boob job. That stuff is dangerous."

"Probably," said Tony, "your students would have been distracted anyway."

Frannie shook her head. "Maybe the little bastards would have paid attention. At least the boys."

"Never mind that," said Biz. "Why are Sully and Ginny having such a long powwow? What's up with that?"

The group turned toward the booth where the big man and his favorite waitress appeared to be in deep conversation, a serious discussion that had been going on for some time.

"Whataya' think they're talking about?" asked Joey. "Sully loved Max, maybe Ginny did, too. They're probably more surprised than we are. Probably more concerned."

"Hey," said Tony, "I'm concerned."

"I know you are, buddy," said Joey, patting his friend on the back. "We all are."

"Max is probably gonna' go to prison," said Biz. "I've never had a friend go to prison."

Frannie shook her head. "Half the boys in Mr. Peterman's shop class ended up behind bars, at least Juvi."

Before the prison pal discussion could go further, Tony interrupted. "Look, they're getting up. Think they're done."

All eyes turned to Sully and Ginny who were now involved in a lengthy embrace.

"Man," said Biz, "that is one long hug."

"Quiet," said Joey. "It's over."

Everyone quickly returned to the TV screen as Ginny made her exit and Sully headed for his office, walking by the regulars without a word, not even a nod.

"You see that," said Tony, "I think Sully was crying."

*

MONDAY

(Four Months Later)

Jail wasn't so bad, at least that's what Max told himself. A minimum security facility, populated mostly by white collar criminals who got caught because they were either too dumb, too greedy or both, and an assortment of drug traffickers, from low level street dealers to kingpins. Mixed in as well were a smattering of informants who wouldn't have been safe at a hardcore institution, and the occasional odd duck like Max who'd been given two to five years for instigating a riot, accessory after the fact and withholding evidence. His cellmate was an embezzler with countless excuses for why he'd stolen money from his company and why he actually deserved it. But he was tidy and well spoken and never once threatened to make Max his bitch which was, judging from all the prison movies Max had seen, a win.

No, Max figured, the place was no Shawshank. No rapists and murderers, nobody getting assaulted in the shower, no one getting shived in the yard. The guards weren't all sadists and the warden wasn't a Nazi. All things considered, it could have been worse. Sully had hooked him up with a decent defense attorney. Why the big guy knew a defense attorney, Max never asked. The fees for the lawyer's services were likely hefty but Max felt sure he could pay back his friend following his release, as long as no one at the restaurant suddenly decided to do some Spring cleaning out back. From the little Max heard, Cranky Sam and Duffy hadn't been so lucky. They were said to be doing hard time up state in a joint full of thugs and gang bangers. Max wasn't worried about Sam. He knew the tiny terror could hold his own but Duffy might need protection and who knew what that incurred. As for Chubster, he was out there somewhere, no doubt living large off his share of the loot. No one ever did locate a wife. Or kids for that matter.

Max did have visitors now and then. Sully, God bless him, came religiously every two weeks. He knew Max had screwed up but figured everyone makes mistakes and that he had almost fallen for some of Chubster's schemes himself. He would sit with Max for an hour, catch his old friend up on all the comings and goings at the bar and listen intently to Max's desriptions of prison life. Sully even went so far as to assure Max that his old job would be waiting for him when he got out.

Some of the regulars would visit, not nearly as frequently as Sully but why would they? Visiting a prisoner wasn't exactly like popping over your pal's house. There were forms to fill out, searches to be subjected to, grouchy guards to deal with. Max was surprised anyone came at all. Naturally Biz was the most curious. He wanted to know how realistic all the crime shows he'd wasted time watching were. He seemed anxious for Max to start a riot or attempt an escape.

Max received letters as well, not a slew of them, but they did trickle in. Some of the other patrons from 'Sully's who'd always appreciated both Max's service and personality but weren't quite willing to spend their free time visiting a convicted felon would at least take a moment to send a card inquiring as to his condition, his state of mind, his release date and any other questions they could think to ask. A few distant relatives who'd somehow heard the news sent mail, too. The letters were usually very short. Max took no offense from this. He knew determining what to say in a letter to a jailbird was likely almost as hard as visiting said criminal. Max would, of course, like any decent human being, which is what he had considered himself prior to his incarceration, reply to each and every piece of mail he received. He certainly had plenty of time to do so. Prison life was so structured, so routine that even the slightest deviation was more than welcome.

He did write the occasional letter to Ginny but resisted sending more than one a month. He knew better than to beg and grovel for forgiveness. Rather, he stuck to small talk, describing his days behind bars and inquiring about her and Emily's lives outside. He expected no reply so was only slightly disappointed when none arrived. He'd heard time heals all wounds and this, Max felt, was a true test of that proverb.

A few months into his sentence Max had been handed an interesting envelope by the guard in charge of mail call. It was pink, had no return address and emitted a scent of strawberries or perhaps a more exotic fruit. Max tucked it quickly into his prison issue trousers, not wanting his fellow inmates to spot the fancy letter and give him a hard time. Only later, momentarily alone in his cell, would he open and read it.

Dear Max,

You're probably surprised to hear from me. In fact, you probably have pretty harsh feelings toward me. I wouldn't blame you. But I thought you might be concerned about Rufus. You'll be happy to know he's doing fine. He's well fed, he got his shots at the vet and we make a great team. And no, I'm not out every night stealing money and having sex with random men. I suppose I am kind of a thief and a pretty big flirt but nobody's perfect, right? Stealing that key and getting that money was the only way I could get away from King. Yes, I have left him and hopefully he has no idea where I am. You might take pleasure in knowing that if he finds me, my punishment will be far worse than yours.

A few things you should know. It's true I was sent to check up on you and did deceive you with Sam and I stole your money, too. But I really was attracted to you and enjoyed our night together. Besides, you and I both know I probably could have finagled that key from you without the sex. As you must know by now, I am smarter than I look.

Finally, I happen to know that King is real pleased with you and you have nothing to worry about when you get out. You kept your mouth shut and he has no clue about us. I'm not sure why Sam was so angry. King had me play the little guy's wife a few other times. The bastard thought it was funny but I guess Sam got carried away. Really crazy when you consider he could have been sitting pretty right now.

Anyway, I promise to take care of Rufus and I am sorry your share was the one I had to steal. Perhaps one day you can forgive me.

xoxoxo, Candy

Max folded the letter, put it back in the envelope, tucked it between the pages of a book he was reading and laid down on his bunk. Forgiveness, he said to himself, forgiveness.

*

It was on a Monday, some weeks later, when Max, notified by a guard that he had a visitor, knew it would be Sully. Mondays were easiest for the owner to get away, Mondays being the slowest day of the week in the restaurant business. What Max was unprepared for was the sight of Ginny sitting next to the big Irishman at a table in the visiting room. Max's ability to remain calm was called upon once again. He would have liked to jump up and down, shout to the ceiling but knew that type of behavior would be unacceptable to both prison policy and the pretty redhead herself. So he simply walked over and smiled.

"Hey, Sully," he said. "Hi, Ginny. This is a pleasant surprise."

Sully rose quickly, gave Max one of his legendary bear hugs, glanced at Ginny. "I'm gonna' get a coffee from the machine, maybe a snack, too. Anyone want anything?"

"Um, no, I'm good," said Max.

"No, thanks," said Ginny.

Max took a seat as Sully lumbered off. "So, uh, it's nice to see you. How have you been? How's Emily?" He felt he had to be careful not to babble, not to over-react, careful not to say the wrong thing.

"Pretty good," Ginny replied. "Em is applying to colleges. I'm still working for your pal, slinging beers and fending off creeps. You know, same old. How's life in the big house?"

"Basically boring," he said, looking around. "Not as exciting as on TV, much to the disappointment of Biz."

"So I heard." She hadn't smiled or laughed yet but hadn't seemed angry either. Hard to read, he decided "I can't believe you came. Does Emily know?"

"Oh, yeah. She's not too happy about it." Max stared at the table. "I know you've been asking Sully about me."

Max looked up at her. "I tried not to pester him but, you know, I was worried about you. Thought they might accuse you of something. I wouldn't have been able to live with that."

"Really?"

"Yes, really. Have you been getting my letters? You know how sorry I am." Ginny nodded. "I know."

"So they never tried to pin anything on you?"

"Well, a few people mentioned a red haired woman but whether they didn't have enough evidence or whether Miss Peabody, I mean Walker, stepped in for me, I don't know. Pretty lucky though."

"Thank God. So, uh, did you ever call that kid?"

"What?"

"The landscaper. I promised him you'd call."

"Oh. And you always keep your promises?" Max was speechless. "Anyway, it's none of your business, is it?"

"Right, yes, absolutely, you're right. None of my business."

"Max, take it easy." Was that a slight smile, he wondered.

"Sorry, I'm a little nervous."

"You're nervous? Since when do you get nervous?"

"Well, you may have noticed I've been full of surprises the past year."

Sully returned, set his coffee cup on the table and a candy bar beside it, took one look at the serious expressions on his friends' faces. "I gotta' hit the head," he said, and wandered away again.

"So," said Ginny, "I hear you're coming back to work. When you get out that is."

"Oh, that's just Sully talking. I would never do anything to make you uncomfortable. I owe you that at least."

Ginny paused, surveyed the barren surroundings, the gray walls, the plastic chairs, the guard standing a short distance from them, his arms folded, his expression stern. "You must have a lot of time to think in this place."

"Oh, yeah, you have no idea. Everybody in here, especially me, has plenty of time to reflect on how badly we screwed up, like, how could we have been so stupid, what the heck were we thinking?"

"Greed," she said.

"Yeah, that's part of it, a big part. But I think there's more to it. Maybe wanting a change, something unusual, something exciting, I don't know."

"Easier ways to make a change," she said. "Safer, too."

"I know, you're right. But I do think we get in a rut sometimes, a routine, you know. And what I realize now is that we don't appreciate that rut, that comfort, that familiarity. We think we need different, we need new, we need unexpected."

"Jesus," said Ginny, finally smiling. "You sound like Dorothy in 'The Wizard of Oz'. What are you trying to say, that there's no place like home?"

Max laughed, stared at Ginny. She was still funny and as beautiful as he remembered. "Look," he said, "I've told you how sorry I am a hundred times. I'll probably tell you a hundred more. But Ginny, you know me, you've known me for a long time. This is not the real me, Max the criminal. I should be behind the taps, laughing, flirting with you, busting balls with the boys." He put his head down. "I made a mistake. A big one."

Max heard Sully's voice. "I miss anything?" The Irishman carefully lowered his large frame into the frail chair. The conversation turned to more mundane topics, business at the bar, gossip among the regulars. No word from Chubster McGee, whereabouts unknown. Nuggets had gotten out of the hospital and headed back to California, hoping to use his contacts and get a job behind the camera. Besides, he had said, it was safer there. No sign of the hotheaded midget or the busty blonde either.

When the guard let them know their time was up, Sully rose first. He gave Max another hug, said he'd go warm up the car and took his leave. Max expected no hug from Ginny and made no move to initiate one.

"I'm glad you came," he said to the woman who could have, should have, been his girl. "I can't even tell you. Do you think you might visit again, I mean, you know, not right away, not next week but, you know, maybe some day?"

Ginny shrugged. "Maybe."

Max knew he should say no more, leave it at that. But like so many other times throughout his bumpy life, he couldn't help himself. "Ginny, again. I'm sorry. I hope some how, some way you can forgive me, that we can be friends again, good friends, you know, maybe even more."

The tiniest of smiles appeared to cross Ginny's face. "We'll see," she said. "We'll see." And she turned to go.

We'll see, Max thought, as he watched her walk away, watched her as he'd done so many times before. We'll see. Nothing definite there, that was for sure. But at that place, at that moment, we'll see was enough.

The End

About the Author

Greg Tarlin is a retired bartender. A graduate of the University of Massachusetts with a degree in Journalism, his writing career was interrupted some years ago by the arrival of triplets. He splits his time between New Hampshire and South Carolina and resides with his wife, children, a good natured dog and ill mannered cat. This is his first novel.

Don't Listen To Chubster MaGee

Made in the USA
Middletown, DE
26 March 2021